ON THE RAVINE

Also by Vincent Lam

FICTION
Bloodletting & Miraculous Cures
The Headmaster's Wager

NON-FICTION
The Flu Pandemic and You (co-written with Colin Lee)
Extraordinary Canadians: Tommy Douglas

ON THE RAVINE

a novel

VINCENT LAM

ALFRED A. KNOPF CANADA

PUBLISHED BY ALFRED A. KNOPF CANADA

LIBRARY AND ARCHIVES CANADA CATALOGUING IN PUBLICATION

Title: On the ravine : a novel / Vincent Lam.
Names: Lam, Vincent, author.
Identifiers: Canadiana (print) 20220149526 | Canadiana (ebook) 20220149542 |
    ISBN 9780735277717 (hardcover) | ISBN 9780735277724 (EPUB)
Classification: LCC PS8623.A467 O5 2023 | DDC C813/.6—dc23

Book design by Jennifer Griffiths
Image credits: (shadows) mesamong / Adobe Stock Images

Printed in the United States of America

10 9 8 7 6 5 4 3 2 1

Penguin
Random House
KNOPF CANADA

For those who are gone,
and those who carry on.

"We shall find peace.
We shall hear angels, we shall see
the sky sparkling with diamonds."

ANTON CHEKHOV

AUTHOR'S NOTE

In my first work of fiction, *Bloodletting & Miraculous Cures*, I explored the lives of four medical students who were immersed in the challenges and transformations that unfolded as they became young doctors. *On the Ravine* revisits two of these characters. Now, several years on, Chen and Fitzgerald have remained close friends, and have devoted themselves to the treatment of opioid addiction, each in a very different way.

For the last decade, my own real-life medical work has focused on the treatment of opioid addiction, amidst an ever-growing opioid crisis in North America that has left thousands dead within a still-growing gulf of human loss. As much as this is a medical emergency and a scientific challenge, the opioid crisis is a deeply human tragedy.

The characters in *On the Ravine* yearn to be whole, and to be their best selves. They navigate a world of unpredictable drugs, rule-bound medical treatments, scientific ambitions that are tainted with commerce. They hope that someone will be true—someone will stand by the side of those whom they care about.

Like so much of our lives, the plot of this book is driven by desire—the desire to feel a certain way, the desire for things to happen as we hope they will, the desire to help those around us. The book is also driven by the question—what does it mean to help someone, when the things they desire are consuming them?

On the Ravine seeks to honour patients, families, and caregivers who grapple with addictions, while in it I explore truths that can only be told through fiction.

—VL

1

CHEN OPENED HIS EYES into a taut, buzzing awareness. It was early, still dark out. Below his window, the barrel-roll rumble of the King Street streetcar. More distant but howling, the air brakes of a large truck, then the engine noise climbing an octave as it geared down into the left-hand overpass where the expressway turned north. Away from the lake and up through the city. There was a particular aloneness that came to him from being awake while others slept. Chen knew the differential diagnosis of early morning waking—depression, hyperthyroidism, anxiety. His overall picture did not fit any of these conditions. The doctor would have asked his patient, *Is something bothering you?* He sat up in bed, took his phone, squinted against the bright icons, and opened a folder of photos, swiped methodically through a few faces.

Junior's baby-face scowl for the camera, teardrop tattoo beneath the left eye, shaved head razor-nicked. He had promised to pull himself together when his mother made his bail. *The last time I'm paying,* she had told him. *Almost off the meth juice,* Junior pouted whenever he saw Chen and insisted, against Chen's advice, on dropping the dose again. *Coming down fast, doc, see? I can tough it out.* One morning, Junior's mother called the clinic saying he had locked his bedroom door and was ignoring her. How important was it to get him to the pharmacy for his methadone? Would it be alright if he missed a day—maybe he needed the sleep? *What should I do, doctor, if he's not answering? Haven't heard a sound since yesterday.* Later, she wept in Chen's office. *I didn't mean it . . . about the last time.* Who had been the Senior to Junior? Chen now wondered.

Siobhan, whose mascara was smudged in her photo, as it often was in the mornings after work. The smeared halos made her eyes appear brighter, but oddly sunken, and her face more sad when she sat alone in the waiting room, until Dr. Chen called her and then, reflexively, she propped up her usual smile. One of the early in-and-out crowd, Siobhan shrugged off the results of her urine tests while locking eyes with Chen, a teasing, inside-joke grin, *Let me guess doc, Everything-cocktail? Molecule-mud-pie? Got my script?* Then to the pharmacy, because her dose helped her sleep. Until she missed a week, then two. *It wasn't the first time she'd partied with those guys, so when I warned her she was like—Whatever,* her friend Nan told Chen. *Can you tell the cops she was with them? She saw something she shouldn't have. But you know Siobhan, thought I was being dramatic. Oh no, doc, I can't say what she saw. I'd be next. Just tell the pigs who she was with.*

Chen swiped the screen, found Ahmed, hard-faced. No one would guess he knew how to knit, or how much his appearance could soften with concentration, counting the stitches. In his file photo, a yellow-and-purple cap pulled to the eyebrows—an uneven, lumpy thing. *Got the yarn from the women's drop-in. And look here, doc . . .* The little flap within for his stash. *Who's gonna look in there? My grandma once made me one like it—told me that's where you hide a coin. For emergencies.* The cap was what Chen recognized, one afternoon when he was riding through a park and passed the pile where city workers heaped snow scraped from the ice rink. Shaded by spruce trees, late to melt, a yellow-and-purple diagonal stripe protruding.

Had Ahmed missed the shelter bed cut-off, and dug himself into the snow pile? The way kids made forts? Did he get beat up? Or had he just fallen down and been covered?

Faces he would never again see in person looked out to Chen from the screen. Photos taken for the clinic record now lived in his pocket, on his desk, on his bedside table. A banner popped up—in his news feed—*Surging Deaths in Shelters: Coroner's Report*. Over the previous week the words "Fentanyl Crisis" had appeared on his phone's home screen again and again. Upcoming investigative reporting on the "Toxic Drug Supply" was promised on the six o'clock national news. Chen had started in this area of medicine when the call to *do something, fix this problem,* was fresh. However, for a few years now, rather than suggesting to him that urgency would soon lead to solutions, Chen had come to understand upticks in media coverage as signs of slow news cycles, lulls in other rhythms of public outrage, or a transient absence of political scandal. When massive wildfires were doused to coals, when protesters were on intermission, when deadly epidemics retreated, and following the climax of sports playoffs, journalists could turn reliably to the opioid overdose statistics in order to summon shock, pity, unspoken disdain, and clicks. *A Record-Setting Number of Deaths.* Chen's phone still glowed, the faces of the what-ifs.

When he was new to addictions work, Chen spent sleepless nights turning over the possibilities, long after nothing could be changed. Was there something he could have said to keep Junior on methadone, to cool the defiance with which he wanted off *the liquid handcuffs*? Siobhan had once asked Chen to provide an employment reference, rushing to thank him in the same sentence for convincing her to *turn it all around and go straight*. She had never actually worked as his receptionist—but what if he had found a more truthful way to vouch for her? Or if he had written a tiny lie? Would that have cost him so much? *It's about my integrity,* he had explained to her.

Which I wouldn't know about? she retorted, then let him off the hook by laughing, *that's not in my current job description anyways.* He had refused Ahmed the sleeping pills for years, finally agreed to *one prescription only* when Ahmed learned of his grandmother's death, back home. The empty bottle was in his hat, said the coroner.

Chen still woke unpredictably, alert like a page turned, unsure whether he had been startled by a dream or yanked from slumber by ropes that had been knotted in daylight. But now he had an approach. Chen taught this broad principle to the young doctors who trained with him: they couldn't expect to have a perfect solution in every scenario. They needed an approach, he told them. *In every field, the treatments change, but in addictions the pathophysiology changes. Is diabetes new this year? Is cancer suddenly different? But in addictions, it's all oxycodone until one day everyone is injecting heroin. Which vanishes, and voila! Fentanyl! Crack is king until crystal is dirt cheap. Pot is pot, until someone invents shatter. You still have your approach.* For himself, he had his approach to late night awakening. He took a good look at the photos, unrushed, but also trying not to linger beyond a certain point. The what-ifs jumbled and swirled—the recriminations against his own judgments; the frustration at his patients' actions despite intentions; how pleased—and yes, proud— he had been of a particular patient's streak of clean urine tests, of their new job, all of which later made the final news a gut-punch. *It's the change that the body experiences,* he taught both patients and the young doctors in explaining one of the medications, *if it goes from a full agonist opioid to a partial agonist; the sudden change from wonderfully warm to room temperature feels freezing cold—and painful.*

For those who had carried Chen's hopes, and something else, what was the right word—fondness? (that much you could say; it was permitted)—it was not a salve to think he had tried his best to help. Instead, this itself was cold, aching pain. Was that his best? And the outcome? He had learned not to fight those thoughts, but to allow them to drift and settle of their own accord. In one photo, he noticed the bright hazel of a patient's eyes, the fatigue in the creases of her mouth. He thought of what it had been like to be in the same room as each patient, recalled their moments of hope, accusation, sometimes gratitude. Some nights, Chen would stare for a long time at the face of one patient. Other nights, he was compelled to look through all the faces, and although their number grew, he couldn't rush it. Sometimes, after a while, he fell back to sleep. Other times he worried that he had not been paying sufficient attention, began again, and was up until morning. Had he let them down? Or the other way around? But they had not offered to carry anything of Chen's.

He went to the window—saw two dark shapes come together on the sidewalk. They came close enough to touch, and then parted. Who was buying and who was selling? Chen wondered. And what was it? What molecules skittered through the city like marbles tonight? Or maybe someone had just bummed a smoke. Or asked the time. Sleep was gone. Was there something else he should do? He had promised someone that he would write, and it had been a little while. He got up, found some paper and a pen.

To a student of medicine,

You asked me to teach you how to care for patients who have this problem. Did I seem pedantic, when I listed textbooks, mentioned recent protocol updates, noted the delay between trials and guidelines? But how to care, you asked? I have memorized risk criteria and titration schedules; I need to learn to care beyond the formulas. How you do it. But those are the tools, I said.

You insisted, Does following a cookbook make a chef? Meta-analyses, consensus statements—even the best recipe is not a meal. I have seen that moment when something shifts between you and a patient, and you convince them to taste a different dish. That's as important as your scientific papers. I want to learn the art of actually doing it. I can see it's about connection, about hope, and how is that done?

You continued to flatter me, and I deflected your praise. But I remember how that felt, and that I sought to hide it.

My reply—Ask questions with curiosity. And listen with imagination . . .

You said I was good at caring for my patients, that I should write down how it is done. You were too kind. More than ever, they slip through my fingers. What would you say now? I promised you I would write, and so I will.

Yours as always,
Dr. Chen

2

CHEN PEDALLED INTO THE steady resistance of the uphill, and the bicycle traced the rising arc of the Queen Street bridge. Spokes rotated, and the bridge's metal expansion plates clanked under the wheels. Beneath him the swollen Don River rippled towards the lake, swirling with leaves, twigs, and autumn rain. A crinkly whisper as skinny tires met first frost, night's dampness crystallized. Interrupted sleep left an aching residue, but the strain of Chen's legs against the incline produced in him a kind of alertness. Bent at the waist over the handlebars, he kept his weight low, his elbows supple. This, and smoothness of motion, a centre of gravity poised directly over the bicycle, were required on the slippery surface. At the crest of the bridge, the block known as the Factory Pit came into view. Its buildings had bricked-up doors, the lots fringed by crumbling curbs—placeholders for the land value that increased as the city grew upwards and more dense around the vacant industrial buildings. There was a parkette, perhaps a concession to a municipal councillor. Meanwhile, bright new portions of fences protected boarded-up windows, replaced when people who sought the shelter of the buildings sliced crude holes or careful flaps into the chain link. It was a lot of work, Chen thought, to forever replace fences.

The easy speed of gravity pulled Chen and his heavy panniers down the other side. He feathered the rear brake, controlled his descent, the freewheel clicking. Twice a week, this was his extra-early bicycle route, lugging bags he had packed the night before. A police cruiser rolled alongside—had it slowed? His heart pounded. Not that there was anything to hide. He was a doctor. There was no law against having two bicycle bags full of syringes, needles, works. If stopped, he could already hear himself outlining the public health evidence for safe injection equipment to a cop, expounding upon reduced infection rates while the cruiser lights flashed. *That's fine, doctor,* he could hear them saying. *So where are you taking the stuff?* Giving the cops an address was not an option.

Just beyond the bridge, the cruiser accelerated carelessly, suspension crashing over streetcar tracks. Perhaps an Asian guy on a bicycle did not fit a profile. Or maybe the police, like him, had simply slowed with caution on the downward side of the icy bridge. The lights and sirens came alive—and the cruiser sped away. Chen was relieved when the next car that passed him was a taxi, and he rolled slowly into the parkette.

Around the Factory Pit, condominium towers germinated like shiny mushrooms, glass-and-cream smoothness rising from recently decontaminated soil. A few sleep-bleary inhabitants of these structures were at the parkette with apartment-sized canines, squinting at phones while waiting for the dogs to sniff and squat, pod-like dispensers of compostable shit bags dangling from the owners' ends of the leashes. Chen was looking for more devoted users of the city greenspace: those who sorted and rearranged the contents of their bags on the benches, tucked them under shrubs if they had to go somewhere. Some he knew from the clinic, and others he had only met on the street. A woman looked up from the trash bin, holding a grocery bag of empty beer cans and bottles—each worth ten cents' deposit. She yelled at a man in a puffy down hoodie who had just picked up after a pug—*Hey, you didn't get it all. Ha! Made you look!*

A bundled figure lay wrapped in a blue tarpaulin on one of the benches. Still breathing hard from the effort of the hill, Chen stopped his bicycle. A gust flapped the edge of the tarp. Did a cloud of warm breath escape from it? He regarded the stillness of the form. If he shook the figure, would it be stiff? Perhaps that slight haze . . . an exhalation? He turned on the flashlight of his cellphone and lifted the corner of the tarp.

"TOUCH me I'll fuckin gut you!"

Chen glimpsed a quavering blade, which the man in the tarp clung to more than brandished. Did the hand shake from fear, cold, or withdrawal? The doctor took a step back, now embarrassed for having intruded. But now he had already disturbed the man's sleep, so he said, "Is that you, Rick? Dr. Chen here. You okay?"

"Issat the doc? Fuck off."

"You weren't moving."

"Got a hearing problem? Fuck off!"

"I was worried."

"That I was dead? I wish." Rick flung the tarp away from his face, rubbed it with a filthy hand. "Hope you fuckin worry, that's what you get paid for isn't it?"

"Have you been getting your medication?"

"You got anything to eat?"

Chen found a granola bar in the bag, handed it over. "You want a kit?" He retrieved one of the zip-lock bags which contained alcohol swabs, dry swabs, syringes, needles, filters, cookers, sterile water ampoules, a tourniquet, and a dose of naloxone.

"You got a half ball to go with it?" He shook as he tore open the bar wrapper.

"Just the works." Chen prescribed antipsychotics to Rick as well as methadone, and knew that fear compounded withdrawal when he missed both of his medications. "You know, the injectable anti-psychotic options would be—"

"Rick's the only fucker who fuckin sticks needles in Rick." He tossed the kit to the ground. "What's the fuckin works good for without the dope?"

"Did you get your medication yesterday?" Chen placed the kit on the bench next to Rick.

"Always fuckin asking me that."

Chen thought of all the obvious and useless things he could say: *You need your medications. You know how dangerous the junk is now? You would be safer inside a shelter. Have you spoken to a housing worker?*

"You waiting for a big thank-you? Didn't I say fuck off?"

Chen clipped his pannier shut. "You shouldn't be using out here, alone. There's places you could do shots. With staff. Or buddy up with someone."

"Yeah, fuck, someone to rob me if I go on the nod."

"They can give you the naloxone," said Chen, "if you go down."

"Been to the naloxone hell-hole! Fuck you very much!" Rick said through a mouthful, granola crumbs spraying. "I'm not some punk kid. I know what I can take."

One foot on a pedal, the other dabbing the ground each time the rear tire slipped, Chen rolled slowly down the steeper part of the trail from the parkette, onto the flat path in the valley of the Don River. His headlight traced the thin asphalt curvature that meandered now closer, and now farther from the water as he rode. A drift of woodsmoke, a whiff of marijuana, the fragrance of piss and shit. The camps were all around him, folded into thickets, tucked into angles of the riverbank. They were easy to miss but plain to see if

you looked. At each one, he rang his bell. At a couple of tents, someone came out, took a kit.

Chen rode north under the outstretched steel wings of the viaduct,
where subway cars hurtled on the lower level and cars drove up top.
Here the valley was too open for anyone to camp inconspicuously,
and the bridge too high to offer much protection from snow and
rain. Now and then, a runner in spandex or another cyclist. In the
place where the valley widened out there had been a brick factory
a century ago, and the digging for clay that built a city had hollowed
out a now-grassy amphitheatre. Then a stretch of open flats, folding
into dense, scrubby forest. A person whose bearing seemed familiar
to him trundled along where the path threaded into a narrower
ravine. Not a morning runner—instead, dirty clothing and fatigue
worn like a cape. As he drew closer to his destination, Chen saw a few
more people who he was certain had come from where he was going.
At a familiar birch, a pair of sneakers hung from a high branch. Up the
hill, there was now sufficient light for him to pick out the silhouette
of a particular house's roof.

Chen pushed his bicycle a little way into the woods, then locked
it to a tree. He tucked a pannier bag under each arm. He climbed the
thin switchbacks up the rocky incline—not planned paths, just a jumble
of lines traced by feet. Halfway up the slope, he could make out slate
roofs, freshly painted dormers. Atop the ridge, Rosedale's best houses
backed onto the valley, their flower beds and tasteful landscaping folding into forest, blurring the demarcation of property lines. A person
could find Fitzgerald's house if they had been told—*spot the old birch
with the sneakers tied up high, follow the red T-shirt in the upstairs window,
knock on the back door of the modern thing that's falling apart.* Chen crossed
the yard, matted with the red-yellow of wet, unraked leaves, their
perfume of fresh decay. Broken tree branches snapped by an autumn
windstorm lay where they had tumbled, amongst crushed aluminum
tallboys, plastic mickeys. Chen walked up onto the handsomely

proportioned stone patio, which was black with tree sap, littered with cigarette butts. As he approached the glass double doors framed in tropical wood, one opened, and a young man floated out. "Dr. Chen?"

"Hi, Brandon." A patient of Chen's, he wore a thin trainer jacket but spoke in a luxurious way. "Stunning—it's cold but so beautiful."

Brandon seemed calm, at peace. In the clinic, Chen knew him to jitter and pace, eyes always darting. This morning, his gaze was steady on the horizon, pupils pinpricks despite the early half-light.

"Are you here for . . ." said Brandon, conveying amusement, and a warm welcome.

"I'm here to see someone . . ." said Chen. What was Fitzgerald? Would Chen still say a colleague? "The guy who lives here."

"The other doctor? Fitz? So you appreciate the good stuff," Brandon winked, went down the stairs, turned to say, "Never saw you here. All cool."

"I bring the kits. Fitzgerald is an old friend," Chen said, putting his bags down to rap on the glass. He felt obliged to say to Brandon's back, "From when he used to be a doctor." Above them, three squirrels squabbled in the swaying branches of an oak. Chen rattled the door, which had locked when Brandon closed it, and peered through the glass. He stepped back, and could see Brandon's reflection disappear down the slope, into the woods. Chen went closer, looked inside for movement.

When Fitzgerald and Chen had still been working Emergency at the South General—a few years ago, but it felt like a different life— it was Chen who had first wanted to survey the prevalence of infectious diseases amongst the intravenous drug users who turned up needing to be resuscitated. *You think studying gomers is a career move?* Fitzgerald had laughed at first. "Gomer": *Get out of my emergency room.* But the goals of that study—to expedite antivirals and antibiotics for these patients, and to have the two junior doctors promoted from the rank of lecturer to assistant professor—were both achieved when Chen made a compelling cost-effectiveness case for the medications, and Fitz helped the chief of medicine to see that she could dislike infections without liking junkies. *We might as well give them clean needles and condoms,* Fitzgerald then pointed out to his co-author. This led to another publication, their study on reinfection rates when injection supplies were provided along with the antibiotics.

At a conference, a rep for HIV and hepatitis C medications asked Chen whether there might be some way to improve treatment adherence. When people didn't take their pills consistently, it made the medications look bad—because they didn't work as well. Unfilled prescriptions were also lost sales. Not that this was the main concern, the rep added, it was about patient care, keeping people alive. Fitzgerald suggested they start treating addicts with methadone, and link that drug to the antivirals: you had to show up every day for your methadone or else get sick, so if the pharmacist just said *and here's your antiviral pills too* . . . If it worked, that would be publishable. Chen liked the idea of progressing from assistant to associate professor, and Fitzgerald liked the idea of getting pharma to fund them, rather than doing trials for nothing more than an upgraded title.

As these trials ended, there were patients who would have been stranded without ongoing care, so the doctors decided to start a clinic. A little side thing, was the initial idea. Fitz saw the thick white paint on crumbling brick walls of the squat address in Kensington Market and chose the name "the Swan." The clinic became known as a place where you could get methadone and buprenorphine while earning a buck as a guinea pig, because the Swan was also becoming known by pharma people, who wanted the doctors to test their developing treatments for addicts. Chen grumbled, *Pharma got paid to light the fire, and now they want to get paid to put it out.* Fitzgerald replied, *Which is why we have to invoice them.*

They got so busy that they always seemed to be asking colleagues to cover their Emergency shifts in order to see patients at the Swan, or take another meeting with a pharma project manager. Fitzgerald suggested hiring some staff, and they soon formed a company separate from the clinic just to run pharma trials. Fitz questioned Chen's suggested company name, *Varitas*.

"The truth?" said Fitzgerald, "I think it's with an 'e'."

"But in research, the truth is variable." If they were short a few subjects, Fitzgerald went to nearby shooting galleries, disintegrating houses rented cheap to dealers—tenants who rarely complained—to find potential recruits. Now, standing in the backyard of Fitzgerald's house, Chen was reminded of those galleries: a broken window covered with plywood; others shielded by bedsheets and T-shirts where drapes had been damaged, the trim faded and peeling. This was Rosedale, though, not Kensington.

One rule of Fitzgerald's house was that customers climbed the hill and entered from the back. Less chance of pissing off neighbours. No one couch-surfed at Fitz's house. You got fixed, and then left. Cash and carry was fine. A rope was strung across the stairs leading upstairs. No turning tricks, no boosting, no dealing unless you were Fitzgerald. Fitz did not correct a rumour that he was renting the place from some rich foreign sucker who was unaware that people raging from withdrawal or jib occasionally punched fist-holes into the walls.

A familiar profile appeared in a silk housecoat. Dangling from his neck, a bulging pouch that had previously contained Crown Royal. He kept his stash on him. Fitzgerald waved, rubbed his eyes, opened the French doors and squinted. "Espresso?" he asked.

"Sure," said Chen, following Fitzgerald into the kitchen, which was dark except for the early morning glow from thin, high transom windows and the dancing flames of a few candles, whose ends were melted directly onto a granite countertop. "No ride today?"

"Flat tire."

The standing arrangement, at least in theory, was for Fitzgerald to meet Chen at the Factory Pit. Chen could pass him the injection kits and overdose rescue supplies, and then they could ride up the valley together for a bit, passing out kits. Depending on when Chen needed to get to work, he would peel off. In practice, Fitzgerald rarely got up early enough to be waiting for Chen. When Chen did not see his friend at the parkette, he rode up the path.

Fitzgerald fussed with the espresso maker, a little brass contraption that he heated over a camping burner. The house was sleek, with carefully placed built-ins and slate kitchen floor tiles that had once been warm underfoot with radiant heating. When it was first built, it had been featured in a glossy architecture magazine. Fitzgerald had mocked the article and Chen asked him how the magazine had known about the house. Fitzgerald rolled his eyes that his father and stepmother knew the publisher from their club, where else? They mentioned they'd built the house for their son when he'd graduated from medical school. Chen had wondered if he would ever be able to afford a home like this one. If so, he wondered, would he alert a magazine, or plant high cedar hedges, hide it away? Maybe you were more comfortable with wealth if you had been around it for a while. Though even rich white people were proud of their son becoming a doctor, Chen noted. Now, almost a decade later, the house looked as if it had been used as a refugee camp. There was the acrid smell of a sooty fire, from someone burning wood that was not yet dry. Chen had a little envy of Fitzgerald's lack of embarrassment, though none for his state of affairs.

Fitzgerald produced an espresso, delicate crema wafting on its surface. "Your drug of choice, sir."

Chen sipped it. "Good stuff. Busy here?"

"A little quiet. Strong batch of purple out there. Everyone chasing after it." He poured himself a whisky from a cut-crystal decanter.

"Lots of people dropping."

A young woman shuffled into the kitchen, bleary-eyed, shivering. She handed Fitzgerald a ten-dollar bill, and he reached into the pouch around his neck and handed her a pill.

"Get a fresh rig!" he called after her, as she shuffled towards the living room. "Lots of kits here."

"Thanks, Mom," she called without looking back.

"No! Re! Use! Sharps go in the yellow boxes!"

Fitz always had pills, real hydros and oxys. Accepted forms of payment included cash; whisky, if not peaty; wine might be taken in trade if boosted from Vintages. No credit was extended. This was standard dealer modus operandi, although everyone who came here knew that calling Fitzgerald a dealer would get you chucked out. *Trusted source* was preferred, though Fitzgerald used this term with a wink. *Wholesaler* was acceptable. Many called him "doc," but would have been surprised to learn that he possessed a medical degree. It's not like what he did was unique. Any drug user knew when someone's breathing was too noisy, and could roll them into the recovery position—on their side, one leg up so they wouldn't choke on their own vomit. It didn't take a doctor to watch over a junkie on the nod and occasionally nudge them to make sure they were alright. If someone was turning blue, either Fitzgerald or whoever was on "watch duty" would squirt naloxone up their nose or jab it into a butt cheek, ruining their nod, flinging them into agony, and restarting their breathing. "Doc" had been known to give a pill on the house to someone who was retching sick after naloxone. However, if, upon opening your eyes, you immediately tried to cook up another shot of purple fentanyl, Fitzgerald would take your stash from you.

The main house rule, which Fitzgerald yelled into the crowd when the music was thumping, was that dying in his house was forbidden. *If you do, I'll wake you up and kill you!* But mostly, it was more chill than other shooting galleries, though people only referred to Fitz's house this way when he was out of earshot. There weren't sketched-out wannabe hoodlums doling out a stepped-on eight-ball, man-spreading on the couch, pawing the girls, hogging a PlayStation, at any remark barking, *You know who you're talking to?* Instead, there was Fitz, balancing charm and benevolent authority with commerce, rattling a cocktail shaker, leaving the hard and the soft to his customers, handing over shiny, brightly coloured pills below the street price. Maybe it didn't hit like the fentanyl, but sometimes that did nothing. And you would still have your shoes when you woke up from the nod. One of his customers had once remarked to Fitzgerald that most dealers were low-lifes pretending to be rich, and Fitzgerald was a rich dude pretending to be a low-life.

"I didn't know Brandon came here."

"One of yours?"

"Yep," said Chen.

"Should have known. His cousin brought him."

"I'm trying to stabilize them both."

"In school?"

"Barely."

Brandon and his cousin belonged to a group of patients who were still deciding. They teetered on an edge, swore "never again"—but heard the whisper of "just once more," and dove deeper each time.

"Better that it's hydromorphone. Keeps them off the fenny."

"Does it?"

"So they tell me. Or using less, anyways."

"His term papers are due next week."

"Oh, well, I'm sure he won't use what I gave him until he's finished his essays," Fitz snorted. "Nice kid, anyways."

"Working on his carries now. Clear samples for three months," said Chen, who did not argue with Fitz's observation that a single dose of pharmaceutical-grade hydromorphone might be less dangerous than a shot of street fentanyl. If only single doses were the issue. "Family's really proud of his recovery. Mother calls to check on his pee tests."

"Three months clean, huh? Let me guess, he saw you in clinic yesterday. Funny, he comes in here every two weeks on the dot. Must be right after the piss test? Organizational skills—points for that. You give him two weeks?"

"Because of school. Maybe I'll have to see him weekly."

"Give him some credit. I mean, it takes consistency and self-control, to get away with it for three months. Big bottle of water every time he's in the office?" Fitzgerald chuckled. "Was he upset to see you?"

"No, because he was high."

"You want me to cut him off?"

"I'll talk to him," said Chen, finishing his espresso, "about what he thinks is really best for his future." He began taking the injection and overdose kits from his bicycle pannier and stacking them in the kitchen cabinet where they were kept. The cabinet was almost empty. Only a few kits remained from his last visit.

"Oh, yes. Vision of the future. Help them think of what's best. That's your speciality." Fitzgerald drained his flat-bottomed whisky glass. "Another espresso?"

"Sure. It's freezing in here."

Fitzgerald poured amber liquid for himself, held up the decanter.

"Maybe I need to adjust his medication. Or maybe he doesn't really want to quit." Chen shook his head. "Is your gas out?"

"I told the bank I'm not going anywhere, and they're trying to freeze me out. Cut off the gas. It will get turned on before the freeze really sets in."

"Because your lawyers are on it?"

"Because I'm going to remind them about burst pipes. The lawyers don't care. They bill their hours. Bank still thinks they'll get me out soon and sell it. But no one wants the pipes freezing and damaging the *modern mansion* we're fighting over."

Chen looked around. He remembered when the house was new. Sapele floors, soft wool carpet, programmable sun shades. It wasn't just that the stuff was expensive; it was that someone had known how to put it together, just so. Now, the gouged floors were tarnished like the family name, and the ceiling dark with soot. Of course, the land had probably tripled, so none of that money was really lost. That's how money got old, Chen thought. He'd bought his own condo pre-construction to secure a small discount. He'd haggled with the developer to throw in slightly upgraded finishes. The fixtures were still perfect. They had looked cheap when new, and still did. The condo had not tripled, but it had appreciated a bit. His was the kind of money necessary for wheels to turn, Chen thought, meanwhile the old families in this city turned a parking lot into a skyscraper, and maybe even made a profit on a wrecked house.

"Sure it's got patina. Could get a bidding war going anytime. It's all about staging," said Fitzgerald. "Meanwhile, the fridge works fine in the cold."

"You're happy with your new lawyer?"

"It's like being happy with a colonoscopy. Except these Bay Street assholes stick the scope right into your bank account."

"Hardly any naloxone left? Thought you said it had been quiet?"

"Nowadays it takes a few shots. One guy needed three doses to start breathing on his own." The whole point of what Fitzgerald was doing, or at least what he had told the newspaper and magazine reporters during their brief interest in the "dealing doctor," was to save lives by supplying a predictable form of opioids. But Fitzgerald did not forbid people from using whatever junk they brought to his house.

"It's all a crapshoot now," said Chen. "Carfentanil in the last stuff you gave me to run in the gas chromatograph. They make that for elephants."

"Really? The elephants must be jonesing."

"Anything you want me to send in?"

Fitzgerald stepped out of the kitchen and came back with a number of dime-bag-sized zip-locks. On them he had written locations where they had supposedly been bought, and the dates when he had exchanged a pill for each sample. Chen took the bags and tucked them into a small side pocket of his bicycle bag. Now he had something for the cops to find. Early on, Chen had asked Fitz why he let people use their own shit in his place, since he only sold pharmaceutical-grade stuff. *I am a gracious host. Also, it's a long walk for me to go down the hill and give them naloxone in the woods.*

Fitzgerald fiddled with matches, a lighter, but couldn't get his camp burner relit.

"I've got some coffee that's already made." Fitzgerald poured himself some from a Thermos—Chen could smell a slight fragrance of oranges.

"Well, if it's already made."

Chen sat at the kitchen table, a handsome live-edge piece that had been wrecked by cigarettes and cookers. Fitzgerald poured another coffee and Chen sipped it. He could taste the sweetener already in it. The table was littered with tourniquets, lighters, and a pill crusher. Chen heard chatter from the direction of the living room, the occasional laugh.

The dealing doctor did not use opiates, but when he was drunk he enjoyed the conversation of people who were high. That was part of the reason it was invite-only. *One of the great things about serious opioid users,* Fitz would say, *is that they don't drink much when they're using down. Why bother? They leave my stuff alone.* When he had been a doctor, Fitzgerald said that he drank to cope with being a doctor. Now, he said he needed booze to cope with the loss of his license. That, and he liked the taste. At just the right blood alcohol level, Fitzgerald was sensitive and empathetic, and would listen patiently to someone recounting their life's trials, while sixteen milligrams of hydromorphone seeped into their brain. Fitz offered advice and consolation drawn from his own life's missteps as he sipped a Burgundy.

The coffee warmed Chen. "If you're giving people multiple rounds of naloxone, you really should call an ambulance. It's short-acting. They go down again."

"I wasn't taking notes in medical school," said Fitzgerald. "You have a paper you can quote? Or is that just anecdotal, doctor—*expert opinion*? Anyways, I don't think my neighbours would like all the lights and sirens. Or my customers. When you say 'overdose,' dispatch sends police."

"Also if someone dies."

"Which is not allowed here, as you know." Fitzgerald sipped his coffee. "So, how's the exciting world of science for hire? Is the collective wisdom of the human species expanding?"

"We're tight for a few cohorts." From one pannier, Chen removed some documents—trial protocols, and some recruitment posters, the right size for a push-pin board or a telephone pole. Fitzgerald unfolded them. Each one said, in large font, *Are you interested in participating in a scientific study? Compensation provided*, and then detailed further parameters—specified age range, experience with certain drugs, abstinence from others. Each said something about the trial's purpose:

... *to reduce withdrawal symptoms* ...
... *potential treatment for cravings* ...
... *to test a new pain medication* ...

"If you happen to know anyone."

Fitzgerald whistled. "Eight grand for this one."

"There's a qualifier, and a few long stays for that." Chen indicated some of the smaller text. "And you need experience with heroin. But nothing in your system on check-in. First-in-human." That was always worth more.

"Right, the bona fide clean junkie."

"Someone that will stick it out."

"Not flake out."

Chen pointed to another pamphlet. "This one, we're short on female subjects."

"Always."

"Priority is this one," said Chen, indicating the third poster. "Way behind schedule—we need fifteen subjects ASAP."

"*Novel stimulant.* Cool! I'm more about the opium-den vibe, but disco lights rock . . ."

"I don't think you qualify. None of these trials are for serious alcoholics who are making no attempt at recovery."

"Seems unfair. Besides, recovery is overrated."

"Good coffee, thanks. Really warms you up."

"That's the Cointreau," said Fitzgerald. "My mom used to put it in hers. Thought no one noticed."

"Perfect." Chen regarded the remaining half cup. "I'm going into clinic now."

"As if any of your patients are going to notice a bit of booze breath!" Fitzgerald offered him the Thermos, turning towards the living room where a few voices were growing louder, tense.

"It's more a question of principle," said Chen, and poured a little more from the Thermos before gulping it down.

At some shouts, Fitzgerald rose to check it out.

Chen let himself out. Fitzgerald's bike was leaned against a Japanese maple. Chen paused, glanced back at the empty windows, and squeezed the tires—taut with air. As he picked his way down the slope from the house, he nodded to a woman who was climbing up the side of the valley. She was in running gear, wireless earbuds, her hair pushed back with a sporty headband, sweating despite the chill. She looked away from Chen. He guessed that she was on a detour from a morning run. Probably had to get back to sort out the kids' lunches. Most likely she would swallow one pill, pocket a few to get through the day, and jog home.

Chen rode down the valley, back towards the city. Now that the sun skimmed over treetops to warm the path, the grip of his tires was a bit more consistent. Chen knew that within a few days, the phones in the recruitment department of Varitas would ring more steadily. Subjects for three lagging trials would qualify, cohorts would be filled, and little cups with randomized doses of investigational product or placebo would be placed in front of those who would be paid to swallow them. Within weeks, data would be collected. Within months, papers would be written. Those who read the papers would call Varitas, new contracts would be signed, and they would look for subjects again.

At the clinic, patients would be waiting outside the door for him, appealing to him even before he dismounted his bicycle. *Just a quick question, doctor, I'm in a rush.* He would reply, *Some quick questions have slow answers*, and insist on delaying any reply until he could take off his jacket, turn on his computer, see each patient in his office. Over the course of the day, some patients would gush that he was saving their lives. And, predictably, someone who had said that same thing last week would exclaim today that he was ruining their life. Many patients would tell him lies. Except those who told the truth. Quite a few would pretend to have done what he'd urged them to do. Others would have actually followed his advice. He could not always distinguish between these, and the uncertainty was tiring. He wondered, *How often do I choose to believe what I want to believe? When does the truth not really matter so much?* As Chen rode, he thought about taking the other turn on the path. It led through the Port Lands. The morning wind had likely picked up the edges of the lake, furled it into shimmering peaks. Chen could pick his way along the lake, out of the city, to a quiet spot. Maybe a food truck would be idling near a beach, and Chen could line up at its window, order a bacon and egg sandwich with mayonnaise and hot sauce wrapped in foil paper, and a real coffee, take his breakfast down to the water.

But Chen's receptionist, Pamela, was surely already at the clinic. The patients would be lined up, complaining, *Where's the doc?* The local pharmacies were anticipating the prescriptions he would start writing, were perhaps already dispensing some predictable, steady doses. Pamela would be making coffee in the gigantic stainless-steel urn in the waiting room, checking the mail, the voice mail, the messages from the website, and the fax machine. Would things be better or worse, Chen wondered, if he put Cointreau in the clinic's coffee urn?

3

POUNDING, AND THE rattle of the locked door latch.

"Claire? Are you okay? Are you in there?"

Aching neck. The sea-green tiles a blur, and then they resolved into squares as grout lines wobbled into focus. Her nose and the side of her face were pressed into the grab bar. She must have slipped off the toilet, and now found herself half-wedged between the bowl and the wall, her arms folded in front of her like a closed book or a prayer. She tried to get up, and at first her legs would not push her up out of their tangle. She sank forward onto her knees, thinking, *I missed the best part . . .*

From outside, the voices of children from the beginner violin class she was supposed to be teaching: *Where is Miss Claire? Is she alright?* Another declared with excitement, *I saw her go in there, Miss Frances, it looked like she was going to barf!* Had she told her class that she was going to the bathroom, or did she just slip away while they were doing an exercise? The horsehair screeching over strings had grated more than usual, pulled her skin up through itself. It wasn't only the sound—and it would just take a minute to fix herself. She had been trying to teach the fluid bow arm, how to glide across the bridge rather than grinding down into the strings. But the morning shot hadn't lasted like it should, and her own sore arm had been shaky, then an unexpected burst of the sweats. Now she recalled stopping, turning to the children, *Show me, your turn.* Then a blank, now she was in the bathroom. *Is this one already fading?* she thought with sorrow, as she had hoped that the warmth would float her back to class, turn the noise into melodies.

"I'm here!" Claire said, pulling herself up with the grab bar, light-headed. "Give me a minute . . ." She steadied herself at the sink. The grab bar had left a red mark, a diagonal slash across her otherwise pale face. She splashed water over her eyes, her cheeks, and then felt a jab in her arm. She jumped, and the syringe sprang free, clattered under the sink. *Shit . . .* The tourniquet was still tightly wound over her bicep.

"Are you in there, Claire?"

"One second." With the pills, it had once been possible to get it just right. She could swallow a twenty-milligram oxy at the start of an afternoon and still be coasting cheerily at the end of two beginner group lessons. If she felt her energy waning, she might pop five more milligrams. Ten at the most, as a treat, but she had never ended up on the floor in the bathroom. "Coming!" Of course, by the time she switched to heroin—the down—she no longer even felt a twenty. And now everyone said it was different, that a lot of the junk wasn't even heroin anymore, but her connect assured her about his connect. *Get yourself together, Claire.* Trying to rub away the red mark just seemed to make it worse.

The Little Orchestra School promoted a modern method of violin teaching. At the beginner level there were no scores, and no theory. The children were supposedly playing music as soon as they picked up a violin, to harness their creative spirit. Most teachers allowed the free flow of clutched fists, jabbed fingers, and high-pitched wails from the instruments. The location of the school director's office at the far end of the building, where Frances listened to recordings of Yehudi Menuhin when she was not waxing lyrically to parents of prospective students about the child-centred spontaneity of the school's pedagogy, seemed like a deliberate choice. Claire felt this educational method was too close to her own present life, unhinged from any guidelines, improvising daily, stumbling into cacophony.

Instead, Claire tried to impart some fundamentals in teaching. She still drew from her first lessons with Josef, when she was four. She recalled hours spent learning how to hold the bow—that the soft part of her thumb should nestle into the dark wooden curve within the bow's heel, the three middle fingers of her right hand both supple and steady. Josef's hand over hers to adjust her finger position. The pinky was for balance. Behind him, the pendulum of a grandfather clock moved back and forth, and on the minute there was the faintest click. He had her swing the bow gently up and down using only the little finger, and Claire still used this as a game for her students: *raise the drawbridge, lower the drawbridge . . .* Josef had praised her focus, and she remembered the discovery; of the relief of paying singular attention, the exclusion of the whole world for the sake of getting this right—the feeling, the balance of the bow, wand-like. Josef, who always smelled pleasantly of soap and pipe tobacco, had been too reserved, too old-world to ever call Claire or her sister, Molly, his star pupils or prodigies, whatever others might have said. Even so, she knew that his ambitions for her had exceeded Teacher of the Year at the Little Orchestra School. What would he think of Claire now?

Claire heard Frances tell the children to go back to the studio, to sing the song they had been working on. The bathroom lock jiggled. The voices rang out: *Twinkle, twinkle, little star . . .*

"Everything okay, Claire?"

"Just give me a minute," Claire told the director, heard the non-chalance of her own voice, and constructed a truth to match its even, reasonable tone. After all, it was a tiny miscalculation. She had dissolved a speck too much powder, no big deal. Pressing the puncture in her arm, she tossed her hair back. She cupped cold water in her hands, drank.

"Do you need some help? Why don't you open the door? I'm worried about you, Claire. Please?"

"Just one . . . second." Claire told herself to stay calm, everything would be okay. Despite having missed the melted-butter moment, the warm-opioid blanket was still tucked around her body, and she was no longer sick. Annoyance at having to teach the class was quickly replaced by guilt, this wasn't the children's fault. Teacher of the Year. She would smile, and give useful pointers if a child was discouraged. If someone was very frustrated, she would give them a little hug. Her class was waiting. She could do this.

"Claire, I have the master key, I'm going to open the door."

As if watching urgency from afar, Claire reached under the sink to pluck the syringe and needle, slipped it into her purse. Then, she remembered the tourniquet, and pulled that off her arm, slipped it into her pocket as the door opened. Claire stood up from under the sink, smiled.

"Low blood sugar or something. I fainted."

"Why is there blood?" Frances was looking at the wall, where a few drops had flicked from the tip of the needle. "And your arm."

"Oh that? I got a nosebleed, I think, then I just—wow—out. I was trying to hold my nose, you know, by squeezing it in my arm . . . Crazy. Then . . . but I'm good now," nodding quickly. "Better get back to my class." Claire dabbed away the blood on the wall, pressed the toilet paper into her arm.

"And you cleaned up your face."

"Sorry?"

"From the nosebleed."

"Of course."

"Oka-ay," said Frances, drawing out the second syllable so that it became almost two. "Claire, you left your kids all alone in their class."

"I'm going to get right back to them." She would focus on the correct handgrip of their bows. *Raise the drawbridge . . . lower the drawbridge . . .*

Another long "Oka-ay."

"You're being kind of weird?" said Claire, and slipped past Frances. She followed the high, happy voices to the studio and swooped into the room, beaming, "What animals are we? Let's see everyone's happy birds, lifting our arms!" She took out her violin and stuffed her purse with the needles and filters into the instrument case, locked it. She clapped her hands to call the class to attention, and picked up her own bow. "Who wants to raise the drawbridge?" She smiled when the screeching began, the reassurance of the blanket enveloping her. She went from child to child, relaxing a grip, straightening a wrist, and the blanket stayed in place throughout the exercise, but felt a little light. Near the end of the class, as the children played—*Frè-re-Jac-ques, Frè-re-Jac-ques*—Claire felt a sneeze coming. No, that couldn't be right. Not so soon. *Must be in my head,* Claire told herself. And so she sneezed, just a sneeze? but the blanket fluttered. A few minutes later, her bad shoulder ached. She stopped playing, held the instrument under her sore arm, and conducted with her left hand. Then her back tightened, and her eyes began to water. She had them start "Twinkle, Twinkle, Little Star" again. Claire wished she had a nice, predictable oxy right now. Although it took at least eighty milligrams now to barely touch her—a green monster, which no one had anymore. How would that compare to a point of heroin? That was the thing with down, the quantity was almost fictional. Twenty bucks a point, whatever that meant. It usually had more staying power. Could it be this batch?—the colour had been slightly different, lighter. It had hit hard for sure, but it was wearing off—so soon? From Scooter, her usual connection. Had he winked when he told her how good it was?

At the end of class, when she handed the children off to their parents, one of the dads asked if Claire was okay. As soon as she was alone, Claire rifled through the rosin box in her violin case. Amber rosin, spare strings, wooden mutes, the sticky dust cloth for her instrument, needles, syringes, and alcohol swabs. No down. She texted Scooter, hoping he was around. Had she lost a flap? Had she been greedy in the bathroom? She couldn't remember which, but it didn't matter, her skin now prickling with dread.

"Lose something?" said Frances, behind her.

Claire slammed the case shut. "My phone."

"There in your back pocket?"

"Silly me."

"We need to have a conversation . . ."

"Late for my dinner gig," said Claire, as she rushed out.

On the streetcar, she checked her phone. No reply. She thought of ditching her dinner gig at the Dorado. She could find someone— another guy—but how? And without the tips she didn't have money for even another point. A week previous, she'd had five hundred dollars, and an opportunity. She still had the opportunity, Claire reminded herself, if she didn't flake out.

Two weeks ago, at the Dorado, a familiar-looking guy had approached Claire, saying, *Do you remember me? Jaroslav? Second-year composition workshop? Now I go by Jake.* He told her that she sounded better than ever, recalled her playful rendition of Samantha Parton's "Lonesome Blues" at a student jazz improv session that she had forgotten. She was the one everyone knew was going to be a star. *You mean Molly*, Claire thought. *I was pegged for an orchestra, mid-section.* He asked, *What are you doing here?* Claire shrugged. *Dinner music?* He told her that he had written a piece and had a grant, needed an ensemble. Could he hum her a tune, to riff off, as they used to do in class? Was it alright to record with his phone? Claire laughed, which was a safe reply when a guy was trying to pick her up. She had just done a point in the bathroom, so everything was cool. Improvise a tune? No big deal. She took his melody and twirled it, drew it out at the inflection points, and let it drift away. The dinner crowd applauded. Jake stopped the recording, made a silent *wow* with his mouth, and asked for her phone number, which she assumed was the whole point.

A week later, Claire had an offer to play in the world premiere of Jake's Punk Fugue Trio—modern music, intensely melodic, with demanding technical sections. Sure, he had to find two more musicians, his big talk about a tour seemed like just talk, and the rehearsal space was his parents' investment condo when it wasn't booked for short-term rental. Even so—it was the violin part in a modern trio. She looked up Jake's achievements since music school. Almost a Polaris Prize—well, longlisted, more than she could say. And he e-transferred the five-hundred-dollar signing advance without asking if he could come over to her place. That night Claire texted Scooter, promised herself she would only spend a hundred. *No Afghan brown*, he announced once at her place, helmet still on. After all his promises, that he was the guy with a solid connect, *My bro in Kandahar.* But it was definitely heroin, he assured Claire. He had the real deal even though everyone else was pushing that *China shit*, as he called fentanyl. So what, if the colour was a little different? A better deal if she had two hundred bucks on her. It hit hard and came off fast, left her craving without the slow, soft linger. Relief, but not much warm feather cloud. So that although she had vowed to make it last, Claire found herself texting Scooter again soon after, needing more to get through the following days of teaching, the highs faster and not better but sharp—and the lows a plunge—until she woke up with her face against the grab bar in the bathroom of the Little Orchestra School.

Claire hurried through the central plaza ringed by cafés, an Italian shoe shop, a Swiss watch store, and down the narrow lane towards a clutch of restaurants in former warehouses. The distilleries, abandoned for decades, were now revived into an aspirational chic of old brick buildings with LED lighting. Boutique chocolates, tourists on Segways, and a few condominiums. Each week when she came for her gig Claire felt that she, too, was pretending for the sake of possibility. Thursday was not the best night. It was an office dinner, or a budget first date. Friday was bebop, or reggae, or ska, a rotation of in-your-face acts. Saturday was locked in by a dark-eyed Spanish guitarist who sometimes left in the owner's car. The maître d' winking to Claire that—*if you play your cards right*—one of the prime tip nights might be hers. As if her artistic ambition was to go from Thursday to Friday.

Stopping outside the restaurant to check her phone. Hoping there would be a message from Scooter, that he was just around the corner, and would front her a point or two. She longed to hear him humming down the lane, one foot in front of the other on his little platform. *Come on, come on.* The last text on the screen was her own.

In the service galley of the Dorado, Claire forced down some of the staff meal. Refused the meat, the pasta. Just bread, cheese, fruit. There was nothing to eat in her apartment, so she had counted on this meal. But halfway through, she ran to the bathroom, threw it up. She sighed and did her makeup. Another bathroom episode, she thought, second in a day.

Checked the phone, *Come on, please.* No reply from Scooter. Texted him again. Probably on the nod somewhere. The shoulder of her bow arm throbbed.

That night, Claire didn't get too close to the tables, hoped that in a black dress at a distance no one would notice her sweating. One table made ridiculous requests—"Like a Virgin," "Yellow Submarine"— but with each tune she saw someone go from the table to her violin case and put some money in it. Claire wandered around the restaurant, wishing she could stamp her restless feet, wanting to kick something. When she went past her case, she saw it was mostly coins, a few stingy bills—cheapskates. The drunk table asked for "Twinkle, Twinkle, Little Star." *Sounds better than my kid,* Claire heard a man laugh. There was only so low she would go—she played "Stairway to Heaven," which was actually decent on the violin.

A man on a date—she could tell from the effort in his smile—asked Claire to play her favourite piece. She interpreted this as *Play something that will help me get laid.* Claire picked "Ave Maria," which was not her favourite, but was the right length and level of sentimentality for what he wanted. As she played, she swayed her body in a way that opened his wallet and caused his date's expression to tighten. He went up to the bar and when Claire wandered past her violin case, she was gratified to see a ten-dollar bill, *a half of a point.*

The night was quiet, and the maître d' asked Claire if she would go outside, try to draw some people in. She checked her phone as she went out—nothing. Claire stood next to the glass case that contained the menu, looking up and down the alley, playing Saint-Saëns. Claire knew that nearby, in a restaurant bathroom, or a rusty econobox with tinted windows, or the pocket of someone who was ambling down this alley, was what she needed. She noticed a man with a backpack who walked fast but dragged his heels and glanced from side to side, a woman in a butt-high skirt who slouched into her phone and tapped as she walked, wanted to ask them. One junkie could pick out others, but she couldn't just stop playing and yell over, *Hey, can you spare a point?* A few couples paused to listen, one went into the restaurant.

From down the alley, Claire saw a familiar Asian man wheeling a bicycle. He was a regular, always took the same table if it was free. Tonight he looked tired, not like he was headed out for dinner. Did he live nearby, in one of the shiny condos? Seeing her, he slowed and stopped to listen. This was the asymmetric etiquette of performance—that people watched her intently, and she looked past them. The man used to come to the restaurant late at night with a woman who was younger than him. Not as young as the cliché daughter, but young enough. Entering the restaurant at their particular distance, hands to themselves. An Asian guy, a white girl with shoulder-length chestnut hair and glasses a little too large, keeping the distance of two people who had just met, but speaking with intent and familiarity. At their usual table they would sit at an angle, not quite facing one another. They always pulled papers from folios, and Claire glimpsed the graphs and charts of their discussions over water and focaccia. Only when their main courses began to crowd out their files might each order a small glass of wine. But it had been quite a while since Claire had seen the woman. Still, the man preferred the same table.

The Asian guy half sat on the top tube of the bicycle, listening. These days, he mostly ate alone. He had settled into a few routine orders—seared tuna on braised greens, a striploin. Once, he had asked Claire if she knew the Moeran Violin Concerto. She lied and said she didn't. It wasn't the sort of thing you pulled out at the Dorado. Whatever she played, he always placed a banknote in her violin case. Sometimes he ate with a loud white guy who started with two cocktails and ordered oysters, steak tartare, and any extravagant special. Now Claire caught an eye, for just long enough, and smiled before looking away. He didn't want her number, Claire felt sure. He would have asked for it long before this. She watched him check his phone, put it away, lock up his bicycle and go into the restaurant. Felt her withdrawal chill settle for now.

Having drawn a few diners into the restaurant, Claire went back inside. She fastened herself to the stately pace of the Adagio from Bach's first sonata in G minor. Coins and bills fell into her case. She wished they would come faster. She tried to pass off the shaking of her hands as vibrato, but when there was laughter at a full table she was sure they were laughing at her. The Asian guy had ordered soup as a starter. *Soup!* He never ordered soup—that would slow him down.

Claire had counted on him eating quickly, slipping a bill into her case as he left.

The evening at the restaurant was quiet and slow, but the pace and intensity of Claire's withdrawal grew steadily. She was pushing the tempo of the B minor partita, playing it like an anxious recital contestant. *But who cared?* The Asian guy ate his main, a seafood pasta. The bartender shook his drink mixer, the clatter of ice cubes like castanets on her skull.

Later, Claire remembered switching back to Saint-Saëns, channelling her need to crawl out of her own skin, for passion was close to frustration. After her reliable tipper left, she went hopefully to her violin case—*Only ten bucks from him tonight? But the money in the case would be enough. And it was never enough . . .* Scooter had not texted back but she could not continue playing. She apologized to the maître d'. Said she was sick, and fled via the kitchen door. There was no clear memory of leaving—but a recollection of being outside, of a light drizzle, heels clattering on wet brick paths, *don't slip don't fall,* of the panhandler whose hurried desperation to put together a few bucks looked like her own. Sure enough, when she asked him if he could hook her up, he demanded she buy him a point. All the way there, he whined for cash. She said, *No, hook me up first.* A tiny, crooked house. Smashed toaster oven on the lawn. Porch light out. *Who the fuck?* was the greeting. The door opening, not much brighter inside.

Now, here she was.

Hovering above her, peering down from a couch, a girl with a torn earlobe, legs crossed in ripped jeans, held Claire's violin under her arm, plunked it like a guitar. *She's so beautiful, kind, sweet,* thought Claire. And everything was fine now, in her good place, the blanket tucked tight. Claire turned her face to the corduroy couch, thought of how nice it would be to snuggle with this person she had never met, but who felt like a sister. *The whole world will be fine, everyone is kind.*

"You should be more careful," the violin-plunking girl remarked. "Told you that stuff was strong."

"Can you be gentle with that? It's very—" and despite being high it occurred to Claire that she should not say what the instrument was worth—"important to me."

"They were going to steal your fiddle. Pawn it. I said I wanted to play with it."

"Okay. Thanks."

"First they were going to do it to you."

"Oh," Claire heard herself say.

"I told them to lay off being their usual assholes. So they went to get pizza."

Then Claire remembered something, laughter directed at her— not laughter *with* her—remembered pushing hands away, and said again, "Thanks." Not knowing what else to say: "Are *you* okay?"

A snort.

"Really, thank you."

Claire pushed herself up on her elbow, rolled onto the couch, which was fetid—a reek of bodily fluids, spilled food, whatever else had smeared into the fabric—saw where her arm had bled after her shot. Breathing quickly, fear not entirely dampened by the down, told herself she would still be okay, really it was okay. Forced her inhalations to slow. The girl tapped at the fine-grained wood with a dirty fingernail.

"I play bass guitar, but this thing sucks. Where's the frets?"

The girl took a long drag from the cigarette that clung to her lips. Tobacco glowed to snowy ash, and Claire wanted to ask the girl to take care not to drop any ashes on the violin, but now it seemed ungrateful to ask. The girl thwacked all four strings and sang tunelessly, "I did another hit / Get yo' hand off my tit / Nodding really sucks / Wakin' up an' getting fucked," and began to giggle, doubled over, spastic laughter that drew on more than the immediate joke and was private, not contagious. Claire's head throbbed, and she looked around the room—on the side table, the corners. A chill shot through her. This stuff wore off so quickly—was there any more? Sweat at her brow.

The girl answered before Claire asked, "Nah, you think they leave their stash here? You gave half to Bin Bob—he brought you here. You smashed the rest." The girl handed Claire the violin, which Claire took delicately, gratefully. An appraising look: "Boy, you don't look like a mad fiend, but you're jonesing bad already . . ."

There was no more money in the violin case. Flashes of memory came to Claire—following the panhandler up the porch, a bored-looking girl cracking the door, inside two wiry guys wide-eyed, bouncing and spazzing. She had seen Scooter like that when he did crystal meth, jib. Asking them, did they have heroin? Which they found hilarious. Yelling over the bass beat that she wanted down, not up. A reply. *No, I want soft! not hard!* she yelled. *What, you want it hard?* Laughter as if they were hilarious. Claire had repeated her plan to herself like a mantra, *pick up one flap for the night and get home, one flap for the night.* What had happened? The girl had passed Claire a joint. She recalled one guy offering her a beer, leering. She hesitated—because he had already opened it. And then? Had she decided to do a shot here? Whatever. The money from the Dorado was all gone, and the clock was ticking once again—here it was so soon—the twitch in her back, the flush.

"Thanks," said Claire, the violin case under her arm.

The girl unbolted the door for her, and smiled like they had shared a good joke. "I'm Julia," she said. "See you around?" She gave Claire a hug, and Claire wondered if the girl had tossed the case and taken the money.

Outside, the grey sky before morning. The lights and steel of

a GO train hurtled just above the line of houses. The raised embank-
ment cut the street diagonally, its dead end fenced. It was cold, and
she had lost her light jacket—was it at the restaurant? The house?
Sweating into the black dress, shivering, it took her a few turns down
shadowy, porch-lit streets before she was able to orient herself and
begin her walk home.

To a student of medicine,

On the transcript you sent, in asking to train with me, I saw that you scored highly on many exams. These tested your knowledge of neuroanatomy, pathophysiology, and diagnostic assessment. Like all medical students, you were taught in the tradition of assembling a jigsaw puzzle, to snatch and brandish shiny bits of information, gleaned from both live patients and dead scientific papers. Arrange them into an image, you were told. Line up the puzzle pieces in the correct order, your textbooks promised, and it will look just like the picture in the book.

I sent you to assess a new patient, and you returned to review the case together. You wondered, Does he meet the criteria if some items in this list are missing? You showed me which boxes were checked.

I replied that this diagnosis is one to approach by feel, confirming with criteria. Some of the shiny bits will be missing. You reddened—as medical trainees do when they believe they have fallen short. I reassured you that I was simply explaining that different diagnoses require differing ways of perceiving. Subtlety plucks an early appendicitis from the array of indigestions.

Suspicion lays triumphant claim to sarcoidosis. Cautious regard
nabs the subarachnoid hemorrhage masquerading as migraine.
The diagnosis of a substance use disorder is made by measuring
displacement, loss. Have enough stones dropped into the bucket of
water that it has begun to run over, soak the carpet, wet the feet?
But what if the water evaporates? Then what to look for?

And then you checked the urine tests, saw that the patient
had told you at least one mistruth. What should I do about that?
you asked. Within the picture of addiction, I told you, figures are
hidden in the shadows. What has pushed the patient to this point,
but is at first unseen? Perhaps the drugs were used to hide it away
safely? It's not that you must see it now—simply feel whether
something is missing. If the patient lies, close your eyes in formu-
lating the case. Not to ignore facts, but to sense the hidden shapes.
Doctors who believe that facts are the only truth conclude that lies
are deception. Resentment comes next, which impairs perception.
Believe, judiciously, in the truth of intent.

When exactly, Dr. Chen, to believe the truth of stated intent?
Everyone says they want to stop. But then . . .

Gradations and nuances will give you clues. The stones in the
bucket may have caused a slight overflow, or a spillage of nearly
all the water. Did the drug of choice feel like something that had
always been missing, or was it the delicious other? Is it about
deserving something? Or needing it? Was it not a big deal at first,
or such a big deal that they could not turn away? And what of the
weight of the bucket? Stones are heavier than water, but it's hard
to say by exactly how much.

Does the bucket cast a shadow? Shadows do not matter to
the surgeon, as she deftly inserts the laparoscope, careful not to
puncture bowel. She does not consider the pre-human evolutionary
heritage of the appendix as she bags, clips, cuts, and pulls it through
a tiny hole. But since your interest is in treating addictions, you

may consider the ancient role of desire, of escape. Also, young doctor, note the space between you and your patient—its density, its tension, the opportunity. The next words spoken might change the appearance of the picture.

After a pause, you asked, Addictions is the specialty of hiding?

You were a keen student, a quick learner.

You asked, Is the treatment, then, a kind of seeking?

Yours as always,
Dr. Chen

4

CLAIRE DID NOT sleep, but tossed through the growing light of morning.

Ding! A message on her phone: *Special if u can take a half ball.*

Can you do two points? she asked. That should get her through a day, figure out what to do.

I'm uptown. Three minimum.

Claire tapped a reply with a cute smiley hands-open emoticon, asked, where should they meet? He wouldn't refuse once they met. She would do the smile, in person, the pleading eyes if necessary.

Ding! CASH & carry babe! U got it?

He wasn't going to front her. Better chance if Scooter were straight. Her mattress was cold with sweat, her sheets balled up beside the bed. She opened a browser on the phone, the search results from late night tapping and scrolling on Whitelight—searching "detox" and "addiction recovery":

. . . Russian sleeper to detox from junk—like a pam but not a pam, doesn't show on piss test . . .

. . . if you do hotel detox, make sure you have no money, no phone, give your friends your shoes . . .

. . . recovery is another scam of the capitalist patriarchy, just another way of invalidating my needs, retraumatizing . . .

. . . just bought the House In the Valley, so fuck recovery—ditched my methadone script. LOL. Sick as hell . . .

What would she do, Claire wondered, if she got HIV? Now she added "methadone" to the search terms.

. . . the bupe was good, my lily pad until I fucked it up, so now the methadone handcuffs . . .

. . . do U even know what U are drinking? methadone = most evil opiate ever . . .

Jake had called recently. He had released snippets from the first rehearsal on a few social media platforms. No big deal. Just getting the ear of a few select influencers. *People who understand that classical music cannot be static, or it will die,* Jake pronounced. He admitted, *Not quite viral, but a start.* She could hear the pulse in the clips, though, of the violin, santouri, and the tabla, and it was good. For the sake of that session, she had used the last of a stash. Jake said that some key festival programmers had followed his channel. If the premiere went well, he enthused, they could absolutely, probably put a tour together. Would Claire be available for that? *For sure,* she replied, doubting it would happen.

Addictions doctors were reviewed on Whitelight, too.

. . . my doctor saved my life when no one else cared . . .

. . . another asshole getting rich off junkies . . .

. . . says I need to face my trauma if I want recovery, the cat on my back. What does she know about my fucking sabre-tooth tiger . . .

. . . my doc calls me on my bullshit . . .

One Whitelight user gave tips for navigating a particular clinic . . . to note the angle of the camera in the bathroom, block it with your shoulder. *Ha! Bottle comes out of my jacket pocket—clean pee every time!* Others had specific requests—*Anyone have a doctor who will do sleepers?*

There was a thread about a place around the corner from Claire's Kensington Market shoebox. She had seen the sign. It just said "Swan Clinic," but she knew what it was. A meth clinic. Where you went if you couldn't get a handle on things, which was what made you a junkie, not just a person who used drugs. The reviews in one of the Whitelight local forums mentioned two doctors, Chen and Fitzgerald:

. . . *Chen is the best meth doctor ever . . .*

. . . *Fitz will give you what you really need . . .*

. . . *Chen is the lamest meth doctor ever . . . other day he asked like some kind of deep meaningful question and sat there like a fucking Buddha. Pretended I didn't hear him . . . just write the script man! You're a meth doctor!*

Whitelight users described the treatments, using methadone and buprenorphine, as *waiting for bail with someone who used to beat you up in high school; the dinner table of an annoying aunt—who served all the dishes you loved as a kid but made them wrong; a flight stopover in a city where you once escaped an abusive partner—all flights grounded by heavy fog.* You arrived there through loss—losing your job, home, family, the last of your credit, or your dealer. Or, if you were luckier, you got there hoping to avoid a first—the first jail sentence, or trick, or descent below some line that you had previously drawn, however low to the ground. Someone wrote, *The thing about rock bottom is that it's only the bottom until you go lower . . . so the meth juice allows you to cling onto whatever hell you already made for yourself . . .* As for departure from this place? "Liquid handcuffs" is what everyone said. The stuff the doctors prescribed held you tighter, was harder to get off. It imprisoned you. Which the doctors loved, by the way, *ka-ching!* There was a sub-thread to a clinic review, in which someone mentioned that the doctors at the Swan, Chen and Fitzgerald, sometimes offered experimental treatments. Or at least it used to be both of them, Claire read further down, now it was just one doctor—"the

Chink." Apparently, there was a notice board at the Swan showing trials you could sign up for—*Be a human guinea pig . . . we're all buying shit anyways, why not get paid to take it?*

Chen sprinted out of the saddle through glass canyons, across lanes between honking cabs, then caught a yellow and swooped into an illegal left. He got stuck at a red, where a patient of his slopped soapy-dirty water from his bucket across the windshield of a large black SUV. Nomad waved his squeegee at the doctor. Up University Avenue, west on Dundas, Chen chased the shadow of his bicycle across town. Through Chinatown, a dogleg north, dodging the sparkling brown and green crystals of shattered beer bottles, to the west edge of Kensington and his clinic.

There was the usual morning huddle in front of the Swan. Pamela had already folded back the steel gates from the windows, turned on the lights, booted up the computers, filled the coffee maker, set the air purifiers to high, and begun to collect and process urine samples for the patients who had been lined up when she opened. Chen rolled his bike through to the back and locked it to a drainpipe. He checked that the back door was locked. Not that there was much to steal; from experience, Chen knew that if the caretaker had not closed it properly, he should check if anyone was slumped over in the basement stairs.

Pamela had her tall cup of matcha green tea poured over ice, straw at the ready, next to her mouse pad. Chen grabbed his morning stack of papers—labs to sign, pharmacy authorizations, messages on yellow Post-it Notes. She said, "Coroner called, cops stopped by, check your email—conference invite, Children's Aid Society wants to drop in later, new patient asking if she can come today—sounded super-sick. I told her yes. The rest you can just wade through . . ."

There were no appointments at the Swan. Patients were seen in the order they arrived, sometimes with small adjustments by Pamela,

who was immune to flattery and intimidation, but could be susceptible to sympathy for a patient's particular situation and might bump
them ahead. The start was mostly regulars, some of whom had been
smoking outside the doors for an hour before they opened, claiming their spots in line, eager to get in and out. The doctor checked
in quickly with people who were doing well, who had stopped
using drugs but needed what he prescribed. He saw these patients
less often and didn't say much about their medications—asked them
about their work, their pets, much like neighbours encountered on
the sidewalk. Other patients whose urine tests lit up with a cocktail
of substances said week after week that it was almost the right time
to make a change . . . *very soon, doctor, because this time, truly, I've had
enough* . . . or that the world was conspiring against them . . . *but
she knows that when she says that, I get triggered* . . . or that he shouldn't
bother . . . *I'm a junkie, so what do you expect* . . . Week after week,
he discussed possible dose changes, ways of handling feelings, the
doctor trying to establish realistic goals while fishing for hope,
casting the same as bait. Chen watched for drowsiness, was alert for
psychosis, navigated desperation. He was glad when they still had
an apartment, was curious about their hustles, inquired about the
inevitably painful presence of the people in their lives. Some spoke
at length, saying exactly what they'd said the week previous. Others
allowed only a few words to escape, a colour, a shape. Mosaic-like,
sometimes a few utterances each week became a conversation.
When each patient walked out, Chen made a few notes and called
the next. Until the murmur of the waiting room settled, and Pamela
knocked to say the new patient was ready, handed him the assessment package.

"Sure. Give me a couple minutes, then send her in."

The assessment package had been diligently completed. Every
page contained detailed answers to the questions asked: when the
patient had first used which drugs, dates of medical procedures,

ticked checkboxes in the symptom lists. The handwriting had a forceful angularity, ballpoint pressed hard on paper. Chen had learned that the degree to which an assessment package was completed often told him as much as the words written on the pages. A knock at the door, which the doctor stood to open. Her blonde hair was tucked into a fisherman's cap. She was bundled into a green hooded jacket, wearing sunglasses. The new patient was dressed like an actress hiding from paparazzi, or how a child might dress up as a spy. Chen extended his hand, which she seemed not to notice as she hurried to the chair and sat on its edge.

"I can't believe I'm here, a methadone clinic."

"An addictions clinic," he said.

"I've never been in a place like this before." She eyed her surroundings, as if the room itself would interrogate her. It took Chen a moment to recognize the familiar face of Claire, the violinist, out of context. At the Dorado, she was billed as *Clair de Lune*, and somehow it jarred him that part of this stage name was real, and was written on the top of the assessment package.

"You're taking a courageous step."

"Is that a thing you say? When people walk in and they're ashamed of themselves? You use that line hoping to change the way this feels?"

That was one way of looking at it, and not incorrect. "Am I wrong? Doesn't it take courage to be here?"

"Yes," and she swallowed a sob, made herself hard again. "Look, I really don't want to go on methadone." Claire gave no indication that she knew him from the restaurant. She looked around hesitantly, as if expecting something beyond what was visible in the room: a desk with a computer, chairs, a coffee table, art posters. She stared at the package in front of the doctor, the papers she had completed, as if it were a signed confession.

"First we have to assess what—"

"Or that other stuff, that pill-under-your-tongue thing. Basically methadone in a pill, right?"

"Buprenorphine?"

"Both handcuffs. Everyone says so," she said.

"Who is everyone?"

"Lots of people. Plenty. Did my research."

Chen saw her effort to summon confidence. He had watched on many evenings as she simply raised her instrument, enjoyed a pause of her own choosing, and played, the melody unfurling. But expertise in one area does not provide solid footing on unfamiliar ground. "First I need to assess your situation. And then we can look at treatment options—"

"I have a situation for sure: heroin. First thing is admitting you have a problem. So there—done. I've said it—heroin. Or whatever the junk is now. And I need something fast, something that will just deal with my problem, get rid of it. Not just get me hooked on something else. Everyone says you get stuck on the methadone and the buprenorphine."

"They maintain dependence. If that's what you mean. And provide stability."

"I read that you run experiments, try new treatments, on 'human guinea pigs.' That's what I want."

"*Trying* is why they're called trials. We don't know what will happen."

"I need something fast. And what have I got to lose?"

"Or whether they turn out to be useful at all. We wish for a magic bullet, but we're careful, slow in moving things forward."

"Like the doctors were slow to get me hooked on oxy?"

Chen looked to the assessment package. "I see that's what you used first."

"For pain."

"I am involved in trials. But to participate in the ones that are running right now, you have to be on one of the standard treatments. And stable." A first visit was not the time to tell a patient that most things that happened in pharmaceutical development, the science he practised, were tweaks of existing medications that worked; that game-changing innovations were rare, that there were more dead ends and disappointments than new solutions.

"So it's like the secret menu? Regular customers only?"

"Not exactly," said Chen. "It's more that first we offer you what works."

"'Offer,'" she scoffed.

"Opioids are an issue for you?" said Chen, scanning over the assessment package.

"Did I fill it in correctly?" She sat up straight, glanced down at it.

"You did. Very helpful, thank you." Find reasons to thank patients, he always taught his trainees—anything at all.

"I don't know what I expected. This looks just like any . . . doctor's office."

"That's what it is," he said. He could hear her violin playing in his head. He wanted to tell her he enjoyed her music, to say, *You are a wonderful musician—and the determination and ability that allowed you to learn that art is what will get you through.*

"Not that I was imagining straitjackets, or locked cells or anything." She forced a laugh. "Maybe a little."

"Tell me, what brought you here today?"

His student had first pointed out the Dorado to him. She was surprised to learn that he lived so near her favourite restaurant and had not been there on a Thursday, or at all. *All work and no play*, she had teased. *Let's set a date.* For days afterwards, he wondered with both trepidation and embarrassment if she would mention the spontaneous suggestion again. Chen did not bring it up—he was, after all, her academic supervisor, and wondered at her exact choice of words. A date, he told himself, was simply a square on a calendar. When she did bring it up again, she too seemed uncertain, but suggested they review data together over dinner. The food was decent, the music exceptional, and their conversation had the rare quality of being both genuine and comfortable. As they left, Chen's student said, *That was the best time I've ever had reviewing data.* Soon, fresh trial results mid-week were a pretext for an evening with Claire's violin at the Dorado. He saw how captivated his student was by the music and soon a phrase, a wisp, would play itself to him at the end of a difficult day, or during a bicycle ride. Once, as they listened to Claire play and he watched his student, he wondered, *Is there an answer in it? To a question you're asking?*

Claire put her head in her hands. "What brought me here? That implies a journey. Or a crisis. Both? What about the slow sliding descent? What if I say, I don't know how this happened? Bet you've heard that one. Ha! But of course I do. I did it to myself. Every step. Though I felt like I didn't have any choice. At this point, I really don't . . . Or maybe that's just an excuse to keep on doing it . . . At first I just wanted to feel the way I wanted to feel . . . Is that so bad? Isn't that what everyone wants? And now I need it just to feel normal. Am I saying what everyone says?"

"You're telling me what it's like for you."

"But is this the same sad song of one more junkie?"

"You want your words to be unique?"

"Doesn't everyone?"

"That's something people have in common," he said kindly.

"You've done this before, I can see," she said.

"Medicine relies upon what we share as human beings, to know what works. But you are one unique person, trying to get some help. From this one doctor."

"You seem like an okay doctor," Claire said, "But I wish I weren't here. If a friend of mine had this problem, I would tell them *Stop,*

stop, stop. Simple as that. So why can't I do it? It's what I have to do. I know."

"A paradox."

"So you're the expert. Talk to me."

"You're taking an important step now, by asking for help." In her profile, the usual progression—pills prescribed, pills bought, pills snorted, heroin snorted, heroin in needles—but there was a glaring blank, where the form inquired about overdoses. He asked, "Have you ever felt you used too much at once?"

"It's always too much and never enough."

He had a little spiel to introduce the Swan, and himself, and to put people at ease—"Substances may have caused problems in your life . . ."—words that could be grasped lightly, if not comfortably, physiological concepts and non-threatening phrases—"as with any other clinic . . ." It was hard to tell if Claire really heard any of it, or if she was simply listening to his tone. She looked into her hands, rubbed each with the other. The introduction slid into the clinical history. "When would you say you began to use on more days than not?" Chen asked Claire about dates, dosages of what were at first prescription painkillers, and later more approximate amounts of powdered heroin. "When did you first begin to feel sick when you didn't have it?" The violinist from the Dorado told him about her injured shoulder, then needing more painkillers in order to practise her violin, discovering that people crushed them. He asked, "And the way it made you feel at first, does that still happen when you use?" *You play so well despite the pain, despite the drugs. Imagine if we can help you,* he wanted to say, *the music you would make.*

Did she recognize him? There was a difference between being the performer and the audience, he knew. When he had worked in the emergency department, people in grocery stores, on the sidewalk, would recognize him as the doctor who had fixed their arm or sewn their cut a year previously, but he did not remember them amongst the thousands of patients he had cared for in the hospital. Now when Chen ran into one of his patients at the supermarket, or a wedding, or in a park, an agreed-upon fiction of mutual non-recognition was assumed. Chen guessed that this might be different for a foot doctor, or endocrinologist, but he didn't mind. It was easy for him to feign anonymity.

"I'm at this point where everything could fall apart. I need my life back, otherwise I'm going to lose everything." She looked as if she might cry, but pushed it down. "And probably end up dead."

"The stuff out there is worse than ever."

"When it was pills, I knew what I could handle. For the most part. Then heroin was more tricky, but I was careful. Not greedy— or at least not too greedy. . . . All the things I said I would never do, like needles. . . Then it was that I would never use fentanyl. Then I opened my eyes, and I was this close to being gone forever."

"Close calls?"

She nodded.

"When did you start fentanyl? It's in your sample today."

"Recently. I don't know, exactly. My dealer said he had heroin. But something was different. I'd wake up thinking, *crap, I slept through the good part.* In the movies they make overdosing look sexy. But it isn't. I went down twice yesterday. Then only later I realized how messed up it is, how close I was to being dead. Or was I dead? And I want to live. Really, doctor, I do. I have an opportunity, so I don't want to die and miss it."

"I'm sure it means a lot—what is it?"

"A music thing. I'm a violinist . . . I feel so silly even talking about it. It's so small," said Claire. And then, "I'm going to perform a composition by—you've never heard of him, a premiere, anyways, and okay, for you it's the same whether your patient is digging ditches or writing poetry. Digging ditches is more useful."

"Both matter."

"How diplomatic. Sorry. I'm here to see a doctor—you're the doctor. What should I do?"

"Having something you care about. That matters."

"Forget I mentioned it, okay?" said Claire, "Let's just talk about . . . you know, what I'm here for."

"Right, your situation," he said, mirroring her sudden matter-of-fact tone.

"I'm a junkie. How do you fix junkies? But not *that* fix."

"Is this your first time reaching out for help?"

"Honestly, I think it's all in my head. Mind over matter. Tell me, *yes or no?* Could hypnosis fix me?"

"No."

"Acupuncture?"

"Nope."

"I read that pot can fix it?"

"Not true."

"Could I go somewhere that they lock me up, straighten me out?"

"There's places like that. You'll probably lose tolerance, relapse, overdose, and die."

"It's not like I wanted to be a junkie. You keep on walking deeper into the forest following the wolf who's dressed in grandma's shawl . . . always saying *just a little further.*" As if Claire were playing music, the tone expressed as much as her words. "But I was trying, you know? I had reasons for using, not just to get high, at first. And now, I have an opportunity—at last, but I get so sick when I don't have down! It's just not fair. I have to salvage what's left of my life, grab this chance. I need to be free to play music. That's my dream. So I need to change everything. Stop this craziness. Right away. Just deal with it and get it done! Dr. Chen, can you help me?"

Now he could hear it. From the night before. The urgency in Claire's playing, flashes of hesitation, her bow held in the air between phrases, as if she were deciding which direction the piece would go.

Had that been pain? He had heard it as art. Suspending the audience in the music. And then when she played again it was beautiful and he had wished that his friend, his student, could hear the arresting transparency of Claire's expression. Her playing had captivated him, and he had been alone with it rather than lonely.

Claire considered her hands, and then looked directly at the doctor for the first time, he realized, since she had come into his office.

"I know you. Wait. From the Dorado . . . I saw you there last night? I didn't recognize you at first." She reddened.

"It's fine."

She stood, darted halfway to the door, "I just didn't expect . . ."

From the waiting room came shouts, two voices in argument. Then a stern word from Pamela, and after a few more terse exchanges it was quiet again. The walls in the Swan were thin, Fitzgerald having handled the renovation and shrugged, *There's construction that's worth spending money on, but this place?*

"Everything is confidential. But if you're not comfortable . . ."

She started to take deep, fast breaths, shifted from one foot to the other. "What am I doing? I don't actually know you. You don't know me. But here I am spilling my guts. It's like a dream where you strip naked thinking you're alone, but then there's a crowd. I'm trying to explain, and making it worse. But you're a doctor, so it's not like you're going to come into the restaurant and say *There's the crazy junkie* . . . Are you? Because this is all, like, doctor–patient secrets?"

"Confidential," said Chen. He knew now that he would not tell her what her music had meant, the comfort it gave him now that he went alone to listen to her. "I can recommend other clinics, though."

"But you have great reviews online," said Claire. She looked around the room. She sat back down. "Not all of them, of course. But anyone with all five-stars, that's clearly fake. And . . . you seem like a decent doctor. So I think I will . . . okay, what next?" Pulling up her legs, she hugged them to her chest, now looked straight at him, shaking. It seemed not so much like she'd decided to stay; rather, she was too tired to leave.

"I need a bit more info." Chen asked Claire how long it had been since her last shot of down. He had estimated correctly from her signs and symptoms: about twelve hours. He had stopped saying "heroin," since these days it rarely was. The fentanyl came off fast. She was restless but was still able to sit. When she spoke about the recent overdoses, he saw they had frightened her. Visiting the edge of death had not yet become routine—that was something to work with. Did she have a naloxone kit, to reverse overdoses? She did, she said. Did she use with anyone?

She paused, then shook her head, something unsaid, and then, "I just feel I need a rewind, or a reset. If I could just hit a button, start over."

"You've told me about opiates, thank you. Could you tell me your story, how it brought you to this moment? Then we can figure out how to move forward."

He watched her movements, listened for the parts of the story she told with pointed anger to conceal sadness, the proportions of accusation that balanced unspoken guilt. When did she interrupt him, eager to explain and justify, and when did she pause, turning over what words she would reveal? There were the usual plot elements—an initial innocence, necessity, a progressing complexity, a long chain of this-happened-and-then-I-did-this-because-I-had-to-and-then-this-led-to-this-other-situation. In all of it, he listened for the balance in the narrative of how much she felt she had chosen, and how much she believed had been done to her.

5

CLAIRE TOLD DR. CHEN the story of the fall, a stumble and a grab for a railing, while going up a staircase in a university dormitory in Leipzig. Was she tired when she fell, late at night? Jet-lagged? Sure. Nervous? Of course. Not wanting to disappoint. Clumsy? Despite being finely coordinated when playing the violin, she was a klutz, Claire would say with a laugh whenever she explained how she first began to have problems with her shoulder. Laughter put people at ease, even doctors, and then they were more inclined to be helpful.

She had arrived mid-morning, having taken the red-eye from Toronto to Frankfurt, and then a short domestic flight to Leipzig. Too nervous to sleep on the plane, she had put down her bags and violin in the dormitory and decided to push through the day. She asked how to get to the Gewandhaus, got off at the wrong stop, walked the rest of the way. She didn't have tickets to any performances, just sat next to the fountain staring at the glassy, modern bulk of the orchestra hall, the sound of the water lulling her almost to sleep.

There were only three full scholarships for the session at the Hochschule für Musik und Theater. Did everyone know who the winners were? Claire wondered, as she accepted another glass of

Prosecco at the welcome reception. It felt that way, eyes on her as she was introduced to musicians and conductors—some of whom she knew by reputation, some of whom she felt she should know. How could she be one of the three? she thought. If Molly had not been hungover on the day of the competition, she would surely be here instead. Claire slipped an empty glass onto a side table and allowed herself to be served another by a famous violinist who said he had reviewed her audition tapes. She smiled, pretended to know the new concerto he insisted she must play. He had a score, and could show her. Just one more glass to be comfortable, relaxed.

For sure, she had not drunk more Prosecco than the other students at the reception, nor more shots of schnapps at the beer hall afterwards. Claire had allowed a harmless Parisian trumpet player, a fellow student, to walk with her back to the dorms, had somehow ended up in his room sitting next to his unpacked suitcases. She smoked a little hash with him but refused the bump of cocaine, craving sleep, patted him on the knee and called it a night. He insisted on walking her to her own room, and, wondering how to disengage without him entering the room but also without hurting his feelings, she missed the last step, stumbled, and grabbed at the railing.

The hashish was probably why, mid-fall, she was laughing. In this memory, later replayed and recounted as if she were watching her own feet slip on the turn of the staircase, her torso rotating mid-air, Claire panicked for her outstretched fingering hand. Thought of her fragile left fifth finger, stretching up the fingerboard. She'd grabbed for the railing on her right, then felt the wrenching pop in her shoulder like a chicken's leg twisted from the bird. Claire could not move her right arm. She cradled it with her left. Anguish and laughter merged into gasps, while the stoned trumpet player hovered above her. He took Claire's right arm and, before she could protest, yanked on it to help her to her feet. Searing agony produced an audible clunk, and relief. Her arm once again felt attached to her body. It was painful to move, but she could do so.

The next day in ensemble practice, Claire kept playing despite her right shoulder. In her first private lesson, Herr Fischer—an old colleague of Claire's teacher in Toronto—seemed puzzled. *And Josef said such fine things about your tone. But you must be tired from travelling.*

In telling the story to the young German doctor in the university clinic, Claire did not mention that she'd been drunk enough to pass out despite the pain, waking to the throb in full daylight. Claire listened numbly as the physician explained the importance of resting the shoulder following a dislocation, that the delicate muscles of the rotator cuff had been stretched, small fibres torn. They needed time to heal. How long? Complete rest for a week, followed by gradual return to activity. But she was only at the Hochschule for two months. It was an important opportunity. She thought, *I'm a violinist.* Claire moved slightly, and the shoulder stabbed her. She said, *Doctor, it's so painful . . .* and felt her eyes begin to tear. Codeine was prescribed— in careful script, with an exact number of pills indicated—not more than four a day. The prescription was made on a special carbon paper pad. The doctor tore out one copy, gave it to her, and repeated his advice about resting the arm. *I understand, yes, I will rest as much as possible,* Claire replied.

Pizzicato passages, or anything played at the heel of the bow, filled her with dread. The necessary high angle of the arm and the sudden plucking movements sent rapid jabs through Claire's body. She felt like her arm might fall off. As one of the scholarship winners, she had been put in the first desk of a section—the second violins. This made it hard to resort to faking the bowing, but sometimes she did it anyways—fingering perfectly and letting her bow arm take it easy—playing properly again if she sensed a too-long glance from the conductor. In small ensembles it was impossible to hide. Her quartet was to give a recital in a nearby town. She would have to push through. She took an extra pill before the recital, the pain was tolerable, and she also found that it quelled the apprehension that her arm would suddenly betray her. Popped another at intermission. And her inner voice that she wasn't good enough to be at this school, made worse by her injury, went quiet. Half a tablet took the edge off for a reception with the international group of students who she had realized were all far more talented than she was. Swallowed one more in order to sleep.

The same doctor was on duty a week later, and asked if she had been resting. He raised an eyebrow and commented that the pre-scription had been intended for two weeks. *Misplaced them*, she said carelessly, *sometimes I forget to take them.* He explained that they did not normally repeat these prescriptions. *But didn't you say that now I need to gradually mobilize, or the risk is that my shoulder may become frozen?* After that doctor's visit, two pain pills helped her to settle her nerves.

Claire learned that eye contact with the doctor helped when asking if he could give her just a few more days of pills, saying that the Hochschule would demand that she pay her scholarship back if she did not perform, and if that happened she didn't know what . . . The tears felt genuine as they emerged. The earnest young man shifted in his chair, said that he should speak to the school's director, advocate for her. Claire stopped him: *That would just make it worse for me, classical music is cutthroat. And really, I don't want to put you in an awkward position. It's alright . . . if you don't want to increase the number of pills this week. Though I don't know what I'll do.*

Before a master class with Eugenie de Vaal, whom Josef had pointed out to Claire as someone she must not fail to impress, she was shaking from nerves, and sweating. What was wrong with her? She had to run to the bathroom to throw up—had she caught a stomach flu? Her shoulder screamed at her. Her hands trembling, Claire downed the remaining pills in her bottle—the lot for the week. And then she was herself again, her sweating stopped, her bowels settled, her shoulder felt as solid as if she had never fallen.

Claire was calm and alert stepping out amongst her fellow students and the tall, grey-blond de Vaal, whose own violin sat nearby in case she needed to stop a student and demonstrate for them. Already, Claire knew that she would not fail, wondered why she had been so worried about her shoulder. As she opened Bruch's G minor concerto, she felt her tone swelling in both the strength and delicacy required of the opening bars, which Josef had told her many times, *must show ease in order for the audience to be won over by your confidence.* Afterwards, Claire having played the first movement right through, de Vaal nodded appreciatively. With satisfaction, Claire noted that the famous violinist had not touched her own instrument.

The stairs had been wet, and she slipped and injured her shoulder once again, she told the young doctor, who hesitantly reached for his pad.

At the end of the summer, the student orchestra was to play at the Gewandhaus, the major event of their stay. Music agents would be in the crowd. But when Claire showed up at the student clinic the day of the concert, she learned that the young doctor had gone on holidays. The older one who was at the clinic that day frowned at her, flipped through the carbon copies of the prescriptions, and asked many of the same questions but with a tone that the young doctor had not used. *You seem to run out early? But how could you have lost such pills?* He also asked, *And what happens if you don't have these pills?* She explained to him the stairs, now recounting a spiral staircase with old, worn steps, a leaky drainage pipe, the lights burned out, how she dove to save her precious violin. He closed the prescription pad, and Claire sweated and shivered on the way to the concert hall. At the intermission, the school director had a word with her, concerned that she was ill. *Maybe I'm coming down with something,* Claire agreed. A Korean violinist from the middle of the section came up to the first chair for the second half of the performance, replacing Claire. At the end of the concert, from her unfamiliar vantage, she could barely hear the audience's applause, which seemed so far away. *What have I done?* Claire wondered. When Josef later saw a photo from the performance and asked who was sitting in Claire's chair, Claire explained what good friends they had become and that she had suggested Si Woo take the front chair for part of the concert.

Back in Toronto, Claire's whole body ached for a sleepless week, and then finally she slept. Woke with clear eyes and only the sore shoulder, then a bright thought of what would make the day better. And told herself, *No*. She found a physician who specialized in the care of performing artists. Claire explained the stumble, the fall, the grab, how it had happened when she first went to the Gewandhaus, dazzled while walking up the floating staircase in the main hall. This doctor examined her, ordered an MRI, recommended taking a break from the violin, careful physio, gradual reintroduction of movements. *Yes, of course, doctor—until it heals.* She restrained herself from asking if there was something for the pain.

On the way out, he handed her a prescription, the word *Percocet* scrawled on it, *In case you need it*. Burn it? Rip it up? She made a colour photocopy before filling it. In case.

The first semester of university was challenging, and initially one pill helped her get through a long day in music history, harmony, theory. A half more, and her energy and concentration improved. It's not that she needed the pills to practise, she told herself, but they made the time more useful, productive. No question, these were better than codeine.

This doctor, she soon learned, casually wrote more prescriptions for quantities that Claire suggested, although he was surprised at how little the physio was helping. The Germans had been so particular. What was their big deal? After all, the pills worked, though the shoulder remained an issue. Claire assured the doctor she was only doing the prescribed exercises and not playing the violin except for the few minutes daily that he recommended. She was referred to a surgeon, to whom she described rushing up the steps to the stage of the Gewandhaus for her own performance debut, the mistake of wearing heels, and the fall, the grab. The surgeon reviewed the MRI and told Claire that although surgery would help it to not dislocate again, she was not certain that any surgery would give Claire a stable enough shoulder to play the violin professionally. *And with surgery, sometimes pain can worsen . . . the referring physician indicates in his notes that pain has been a difficult issue for you. And I reviewed the prescriptions . . .* Claire asked her to please just book the surgery.

The colour photocopy worked a couple of times, until a pharmacist asked about the date. People normally did not wait to fill these. A girl in Claire's dorm, a dancer, had a prescription for Vicodin. If she showed up like clockwork, never early or late, at the student health clinic, they routinely renewed her prescription for the painkillers. Five bucks per tab, a friend price for Claire, money she earned busking in the subway. The dancer was on student loans, not quite enough to cover her costs. Claire met a guy on the varsity baseball team, who had a prescription for oxy twenties, and Claire let him figure out that the pills relaxed her in a certain way.

Molly, a year ahead in music school, lived in a fancy condo with a guy, but sometimes she stayed with Claire if she and the guy were fighting. One day Claire found Molly listening to music, relaxed on the couch with a look of serenity that she recognized. At first she was annoyed that some of her pills were gone, but then, after she took a few herself, she felt that she should be more generous towards her sister, whom she knew sometimes suffered from neck pain.

After the shoulder operation, pills were prescribed by the surgeon to manage post-operative pain. There were follow-up appointments. *I think I just need one more prescription, doctor.* But then one day her surgeon asked if Claire would pee in a cup for her. *Why?* The surgeon handed her the cup, and later came back into the room with her arms crossed.

"Your urine contains hydrocodone and oxycodone."

"What do you mean? You gave them to me—"

"I'm prescribing hydromorphone. The other stuff comes up different in the drug screen, Claire."

So what was the big deal? A few extra. After all, who beyond herself could say how many she really needed?

"It's because you're just not prescribing me enough, so I have to—"

"You're drug-seeking, Claire."

"Pain is the fifth vital sign!" said Claire, surprised at her own voice. Then apologetically, "I read that somewhere."

"That's it, then. Your surgery was successful." The surgeon went to the door, held it open.

"Wait, you can't just—"

"You don't need painkillers anymore—"

"You cut me open. How can you cut me off the painkillers?"

"—you're out there buying them. That's the only explanation for what's in your urine."

"What are you talking about?" said Claire, "I need these medications. If I don't have them. . ."

Claire thought she detected a moment's hesitation in the surgeon's expression, but then the doctor said decisively, "If you're addicted to these, I definitely can't prescribe them."

"You can't give them to me because I need them?"

"I have other patients to see, Claire."

"You can't just cut me off!"

"Here's the name of an addictions clinic. That's where you really belong."

Claire crumpled the handwritten note and tossed it on the surgeon's desk.

Fine, screw the doctors, she would stop. She had done it before. But this time, after a week, Claire was still sick, could barely play. Exams and end-of-semester rehearsals were about to start.

The shoulder was now solid, and no longer threatened to pop out. But it felt tight, and was in constant pain, which needed to be controlled in order for Claire to play. In certain recitals, her professors wrote comments like, " . . . *a maturity that suggests true understanding of the composer's struggle . . . a sense of line that is pure in its intuition,*" but at others, "*. . . somewhat disappointing since I know what you are capable of . . .*" Josef, who expressed all of his care and warmth through the teaching of music, and from whom she still took occasional lessons, despite being at the university, uncharacteristically asked Claire if everything was alright in her personal life. She had begun to teach at The Little Orchestra School to be able to afford pills, so she told Josef honestly that she was tired. She couldn't tell him that everything depended on whether she had enough pills, and that sometimes she would end up short if Molly visited. Then, mid-year, Claire's dancer friend was asked to do a pee test, and what she was prescribed was missing, so she got cut off and had to take a waitressing job to make ends meet.

The baseball guy introduced Claire to heroin. You just got more for your money with the light-brown powder, even if you were snorting it, as she did—telling herself she would never inject. Heroin put Claire's budget back on track, for a few months anyway, until two points a day became five. The baseball player had rich parents, and as he got more and more into the heroin he didn't even want to have sex that much, so that was easy. The down was better for both of them, and Claire kept hers in a brown-sugar jar at her place—her sister never baked. It was baseball guy who learned how to inject from an online video, and when Claire tried it, she experienced the clarity and peace that had first come when she'd downed a handful of pills before de Vaal's master class.

Claire figured out all the back entrances to sneak in late to lectures, or slip out if she was sick. Her attendance record for practices was close to the failing cutoff although her performance grades were high. Josef asked Claire with unusual bluntness why she was always late for their private lessons these days. She was high at the time, so she reassured him with smoothness and ease. *It's all fine, yes of course, Josef, I remember what you said—one percent talent, ninety-nine percent hard work, yes . . . and the right arm must always flow.*

There was an opportunity to teach and perform at the Banff Centre that summer, but it was out of the question. How would she get what she needed in Alberta? Claire told Josef, who was puzzled, that she preferred to practise on her own in Toronto. She began to dream of the brown powder dissolving in the heated spoon, of the needle tip slipping first into liquid, and then into her vein. Near the start of the next school year, baseball guy experienced an intervention by his family. But Claire knew the dealer now, "Coach," a personal trainer who made the rounds of varsity athletes. He murmured to Claire that if she was ever short, she could always *help him out.*

That summer, Claire scouted walk-in clinics in suburban strip malls. She scoped them out, chose clinics that seemed to have lots of patients and different doctors each day. Claire had the pictures of her shoulder on a thumb drive, and the discharge note which indicated the dose of hydromorphone immediately after the surgery. Whatever else the surgeon might have written in the records, it didn't matter as long as no one requisitioned the full file. At the end of a clinic day, the doctors tired and rushed, Claire's cheery smile and the thumb drive made it easy for them to scrawl a prescription. Pretty soon, Claire had four clinics each giving her a month's worth of painkillers. She used a calendar to keep track of which clinic to go to each week. The pills were covered by the student health plan. Claire used some of them herself, and traded some to Coach for heroin. She laughed at his little remarks, but she would never cross the line and "help him out." *Slimeball.*

She was making it work, putting together what she needed— some powder, some pills, had a solo recital invite to a festival in Sonoma. Until one day, some keen new doctor wanted to take Claire's blood pressure, and insisted that she roll up her sleeves. With a straight face Claire said something about bees biting her on the inside of her elbow. There was new software, he said, that detected double doctoring. All the pharmacies were now connected. That was four years ago, a lifetime, an abandoned degree.

Claire had given Dr. Chen a selective account—the initial injury, the doctor who prescribed without her asking, how heroin was the only way to continue her music. "Things got out of control. It's time for me to sort them out." Claire thought of waking up to Julia plunking on her violin, not remembering exactly how she had got there. The doctor had a softness to his eyes and forehead, curiosity. "But never again," Claire said. "I am done." The doctor looked at the papers she had filled out, turned a page over, nodded. This was the way he listened to her at the Dorado, with the attentive calm that few people showed when she played in restaurants or in the subway. Yet it was comfortable to play over people who were enjoying meals, rushing to trains, who took no notice whether the fingering was sloppy. What would it be like if everyone sat with perfect attention as their food grew cold, or stood quietly letting the trains pass, to listen minutely, to observe in the way that the doctor did now?

She had not intended to cry. With most doctors, Claire had the feeling that their sentences had already begun before her own were completed, but Dr. Chen listened slowly, allowing her to control the silence, as if waiting for the violinist to drop her arm before he made any sound.

She scolded her own sentiment. *Claire, he's met a lot of fuck-ups, you're another. And he's getting paid—it's a job.* With this, she felt harder, less vulnerable for a moment. Then, despite the effort to close herself off, she sobbed again, not having anticipated that the doctor would care. Dr. Chen produced a tissue box. She told herself, *Look at him offer the tissue at a particular speed—not too slow but not shoving it across the coffee table, either. And the tissue box is right there, at just the right spot.* She snatched it from him, honked her nose, again and louder. *So he's a good performer. Get yourself together.*

At a point when she seemed to have said all that she wished, Dr. Chen asked, "And the opioids—what problem did they solve for you?"

"I . . . didn't I just explain? I had a grant to study in Europe, and over there I couldn't take care of my shoulder properly. But I had to play. There was no other option, probably made it worse. Then I came back, and I had to go into my first year. My surgeon botched my operation. I could probably sue . . ."

"So the pills helped with . . ."

"You mean the pain?"

"Was there anything else they helped you with, in addition to the pain?"

"I don't understand," she said.

"Sometimes, if a person spends a great deal of time and energy using a substance, and sacrifices a lot for it—it's because it helped with more than one problem. Yes, there was your shoulder pain. Was there something else you needed them to do?"

Her ankle tapped the air in the staccato rhythm of the words, *you needed them to do . . .* A bead of sweat, cold at her temple. She shrugged. It was her story to tell, and Leipzig was where she chose to start the story.

"Music is clearly important to you," he said.

"The most important thing."

"May I suggest a medication? It might help you to have more room for your music."

"Music should be at the centre, and things got off track." Her back and shoulders were now very tight. "But when I'm like this, I can barely play. So . . . will the medication fix me?"

"It can help you to stabilize." He explained his treatment recommendation. It was good that she was sick, he said, because starting buprenorphine required her to be in withdrawal. It was the safer option, and he suggested she try it first. He explained how to take the medication, step by step, and she nodded immediately at everything, huddling now, shivering.

"Okay, so once I'm stable, I want to come off them. Right away."

"I would recommend sticking with the medication and coming off slowly."

"Like how slowly?"

"For most people, it takes a few years, to stabilize and taper."

"What? I don't have years! I need to get on with my life."

"Claire, has this problem been with you for weeks, months, or years?"

"At first, I was able to stop, take breaks. It was manageable for a long time. Until it wasn't. So I think a lot of it is in my head." She stopped, aware that she had not answered his question. Finally, after a silence that he did not fill, she said, "Years. But I have to get this over with for my premiere!"

"You can play the violin while taking this medication. If that's the worry?" said Dr. Chen, leaving a judicious pause. It was her turn to leave a silence unfilled. "Another way of looking at it . . . the situation you're in now, do you think it happened because you needed a quick solution, or because you were willing to take your time?"

"You've seen this help people?"

"I try to help anyone who walks through my door, but things work out differently in different people."

"Do a lot of people want a shoulder to cry on?"

"Some."

"I want to solve my problem, to change how I'm living," said Claire. "So, this pill dissolves under the tongue?"

"Yes, under the tongue."

Claire said, "So it's not methadone? You're really a junkie if you're on methadone, right?"

To a student of medicine,

You came to me one morning, when you sensed something was missing in your assessment of a new patient. I suggested you close your notes, go back, ask the patient what they were thinking about while you were gone. Then allow room for a silence. Pay attention to the patient, and what you feel in the spaces between words.

You returned afterwards and said, He told me about the town where he grew up, being in the woods with his brother at this time of year, hunting deer. I asked, What did you feel? I felt the brother's absence, a loss.

Consider the role of loneliness in bringing this patient to a particular point in his life, and through our doors. He trusted you with part of a memory; it's good that you did not ask him to name the tragedy. Loneliness is one of the deep, invisible forces that drive humanity. These impact everything but are easy to miss: because the patient walks into the office, sits down, perhaps says, "I have a problem with drugs," it is easy to think the molecules are the crux of the problem, and that we can only combat this problem using our prescription of other molecules, as if the enemy is the black chess pieces and we are playing white.

Early in treatment, look for the forces that travel in pairs . . .
loneliness with resentment, distress with the memory of comfort,
hope with anger. Binding these, there are questions, and the
molecules are merely replies that have already been tried.

If you think in this way, then what you see in the patient may
look different. Physical pain, yes, that is something. But what does it
signify when described? Everything has been sacrificed to evade it,
but the molecules have already betrayed their promise. The open
space that remains, its void, more than the pain itself, is the reason
the patient has come to see you, but the pain must be explained—
the story, the genesis. One possible hint: a feeling that the story has
been told before, and has become both forceful and constraining.

You wrote some things in your notebook, slowly, and looked
up without saying anything. I felt there was something you wanted
to tell me, but left it to you. Were you already taking my advice,
occupying the space between words?

Yours as always,
Dr. Chen

6

DURING AN EARLY afternoon lull, Chen received a routine email:

> An ALERT by Toronto's Drug Checking Laboratory: The most commonly found drugs in samples expected to be OPIOIDS were: Fentanyl: (94% of expected opioid samples); Caffeine: (89% of expected opioid samples); Etizolam: (52% of expected opioid samples); Heroin: (24% of expected opioid samples). Note that multiple substances may be found in each sample so percentages add up to more than 100%.

Chen remembered when his patients had first expressed dismay on learning that their powder was actually fentanyl. This was confirmation, they'd said, because it hadn't felt the same. There was sometimes annoyance, anger, perhaps a vow to finally stop, and a few did so. A few liked the new stuff. Most preferred what had once come from a poppy flower's seed pod, but kept on doing the stuff from a lab, the fentanyl, despite complaining that it was cold, it didn't have soul. There was still heroin out there, it was always rumoured, you had to have the connect. He'd once taught students that a heroin addiction was the end point, the worst-case scenario, the cliff-edge. Now, both heroin and those lessons seemed quaint, outdated, as he watched patients cling to the edge of the abyss, dirt and stone crumbling in their hands. These days Chen was more likely to alert patients that their fentanyl had other drugs in it—carfentanil, etizolam, crystal. No one was alarmed at this news, as if their physiological tolerance to opioids had come with a cognitive tolerance to the actual drugs being unknown, a mystery.

At fifteen minutes to five—closing time—six people registered at the front desk of the Swan. This was typical, the rhythm of many days in clinic. As if he were encouraging a tired student, Chen reminded himself that this was part of the pathology—to leave the essential to the last possible moment—but nonetheless he found himself opening with *Is your medication okay? Same dose alright?* rather than *How are you?* Patients asked questions that they had asked many times before, and while in the morning Chen would have patiently teased out the question behind the question, now he provided answers that were correct but brief.

The rule at the Swan was that if a patient registered before the end of clinic hours, they would be seen. A new patient was in full withdrawal, and vomited in the garbage before completing any paperwork. Pamela sat next to him, helped with the forms. Chen sent a text to Charlie at Varitas. He would be at least another hour. Maybe they could manage the meeting without him? There was no immediate reply. Chen became hopeful, but then was disappointed when the little bubble of text on his phone announced: *We'll stick around.* The doctor texted that they should go ahead and start. Cover what they could without him. A few minutes later Charlie messaged—they were ordering pizza, what kind did Chen want? *Duck confit and pear for me,* replied Chen.

When the doctor finished with patients at last, he checked his phone. No new messages saying they had sorted things out without him.

Varitas didn't need a doctor for the problems that Omega, the sponsor, was currently upset about. Even so, Chen wheeled his bicycle out into the night, navigating the streams of fast-moving taxis towards the business district. A streetcar rang its bells, hurtled past a stop where no one waited. Having crossed half of downtown, Chen locked his bicycle outside the office building that housed the Varitas headquarters and lab, grabbed his panniers. The empty lobby of the office building was dark except for a light at the desk. During the day, the lobby was a rush of people, a busy sandwich shop off to one side, fresh flower boutique on the other. At night it echoed. The guard looked up from his paper, recognized Chen, already turning away.

To a student of medicine, he thought, *Do you remember the first time that I suggested a quick lunch here?* Her first publication. A small journal, but still, and flowers from that boutique to celebrate. He had made sure they were on behalf of the lab, asked a few people to sign the card, as if it were simply routine that they bought flowers to mark a trainee's first publication.

Without stopping, the empty elevator whisked Chen up. Half of the hallway lights were off; a boardroom glowed bright.

"You've solved all the problems?" Chen said.

Bella, the project manager from Omega, wore a smile with a quality like origami—sharp angles inflecting a smooth, white surface, beautiful if schematic. "Glad you could join us, Dr. Chen." Chen sympathized with the ennui in her greeting. "Charlie has gone over the update, but I wanted to review things with you directly."

"Recruitment," Charlie said.

"Management is concerned," Bella added.

"Aren't you management?"

"As I said, management is concerned."

"There are three key variables in recruitment," said Chen. "It is possible to control two out of three, but never three. Omega has specified its priorities: speed, low cost—"

"I think I've heard this one before," a tight-lipped smile—"but now we're asking for execution?"

"And narrow eligibility criteria."

Bella ignored this, a subject of previous disagreement. Chen had recommended wider criteria, both to make enrolment easier and because he felt it would result in a more representative cohort. Omega wanted a narrower criteria, hoping that it would improve the chances of a positive trial—but did not say this, instead saying that the motivation was cleaner data. "Which two of three are you presently delivering, Dr. Chen?"

"You mean which are Varitas delivering? As you know, for some time I have been an independent consultant in all trials, and to Varitas."

"And still a significant shareholder."

Grease-stained pizza boxes lay jumbled on the side table. Chen flipped them open. The box labelled "duck confit" was empty. Bella's lipstick was perfect. No doubt Charlie had eaten all the duck confit. There was only broccoli and bocconcini, the cheese waxy and hard. Chen flopped a slice onto a paper plate.

Charlie sighed, as if tasked for the evening with the care of difficult children. He fiddled with his laptop and breezed through the slides on the projector screen—initial budget, original schedule and milestones, recruitment spending, results to date—clicking through with a certain gusto, coaxing his charges to behave. Then, without slackening the pace, he talked through slides that outlined revised targets and schedule, proposed social media strategy and clinician outreach, updated recruitment and budget projections. Charlie's recruitment numbers were optimistic, of course. His budget aspirations yet more so. Chen wondered what Bella would say, predicting that she would neither agree nor balk at the ambitious budget increase, deferring it to *our leadership team,* and instead would focus on the recruiting projections. Chen found some remnants of antipasto in a clear plastic container and settled into a chair.

Of the numbers of recruits Charlie projected, only a proportion of subjects would pass screening. Of those who passed, only a proportion of eligible subjects would show for admission. Of those who showed for admission, a proportion would be dismissed for having drugs in their urine. For this particular trial, although they would be recruited precisely because of their experience with opioids, their urine needed to be clean when they came in. *Tricky to predict that dropoff,* said Chen. This was to be the first of several PowerPoint decks, one for every study that Omega was paying Varitas to conduct.

On the wall, a massive Morrisseau. Fitzgerald had decorated the research lab expensively, winking and saying that original art was the kind of thing that companies paid for, and might later donate to galleries for tax deductions. Fitzgerald had been like a kid with a new toy, with the angles that Charlie, as the new finance director after the sale of a majority stake in Varitas to private equity, had introduced. Since then, Chen had read that the prices of Morrisseau's work had appreciated considerably. Fitz was good at certain kinds of judgments. Chen's student loved the painting of the shaman and bear.

When Charlie was done with his slide deck, Bella said, "I assume no reminder is needed that the investigational products will expire in three months." The compounds, all experimental, had an approved shelf life. Beyond this, they could not be used in the trials and had to be destroyed. The base compounds would need to be resynthesized, the tablets reconstituted, the final products reassayed, quality controlled—all to rebuild the house of cards to precisely the point where it now stood, its construction currently stalled for a lack of experimental subjects. Bella questioned Chen about plans to "get things on track," and he heard her questions as if through sound-cancelling headphones. He channelled responsive facial expressions as if he were lip-reading.

Opposite the office building was a condominium, a glass expanse divided into picture frames by the skeleton of its structure. Chen remembered a late evening in this room, making corrections to source documents with his trainee. They'd enjoyed a sashimi platter. Franck's A major violin sonata played on her phone. As the condo's squares of light turned on, each one a snapshot of a life, they would look up from the rack of binders and invent one-line stories, quandaries for the backlit figures who appeared. He said, *He's getting ready for work—the night shift.* She said, *in a factory where they prepare breakfast sandwiches for coffee shops.* He said, *She's a spy, for sure. Do you see how she walks, her stealth?* She said, *He changed his tie three times, for someone.* Chen teased, *That's each of their stories—what's yours?* She placed her hands on the binders, the data, *It's here, I hope.*

Bella asked what was the circulation of *NOW* magazine, where they had proposed placing recruitment ads. What was the click-rate for the online banners on the Whitelight forum? How to target the social media outreach to local viewers? The answers that Chen gave were all confident, reassuring, and vague. *In my experience . . . What we have seen in the past . . . It's hard to put exact numbers . . .* He threw in a few things that Charlie might have said: *We prioritize strategic execution towards our shared goals . . .*

Chen dipped the edge of his cold pizza in a shallow dish of chili oil, drank from a can of very cold, unsweetened lime soda that he had retrieved from the fridge in the meeting room. Was it giving him an ice-cream headache, or was that something else? He nodded appropriately, offered non-word noises intended to convey collaboration without commitment. He knew that Bella wanted more.

He was saying the right things, but it was about emphasis. Having spent all day giving people what he could, he now felt unable to give her what she wanted—confidence in the trial. His daily quotient of the profession of faith had been exhausted.

In a glass window across from the office, a man changed out of a postal uniform. As he heard his own voice enunciate words such as *targeting high-impact communications* and *organizational commitment*, Chen had a mental image of his patient of many years, Konstantinos, a postman. Konstantinos had always believed his dealer to be reliable, his wife Sonya explained, vowed to never use another. While Chen discussed strategies which imparted *a structural understanding of Varitas's best practices*, he thought of their daughter Zooey's birthday, the Children's Aid Society worker coming to talk to him earlier that day. *Any advice, doctor, on the kind of family that would be best?* He didn't want to ask who had found Sonya's body. The last time he spoke to Sonya, Chen hadn't had the heart to challenge her when she said that the only way to escape the heartache of her loss was a few pills. Whatever pills, anything. Chen echoed the corporate terms Bella seemed concerned about, but repurposed them with different pronouns, verb tenses. It occurred to Chen that he had adopted a similar technique earlier that day with Morgan and Petrov, who had turned up late in the afternoon. Morgan wanted Chen to *Tell Petrov to stop sabotaging my recovery.* Petrov said, *So what am I supposed to do when she's the one who won't stop using?* Chen's answer: *What do you each think you are supposed to do? And is that different depending on what the other person is doing?* He had asked them both: *Why do you want to stop using?* On this they agreed, for their children.

As Charlie emphasized something on a PowerPoint slide, Chen watched Bella twirl a strand of hair in her fingers, saw her glance over to him; she had seen him watching her, and he felt his face flush. She smoothed her hair; was that smile ironic? Could Bella tell, Chen wondered, that as he sat in this expensively decorated meeting room eating now-cold gourmet pizza, he was merely playing the part of being deeply invested in the success of her trial? If she saw that, what part was she playing?

Would the new patient, the violinist, come to the clinic again? Many people came for a first assessment, and never a second one. Many never even picked up their first dose of medication. They changed their minds, or ran into someone on the way to the pharmacy, someone who had something else. First assessments were like watching the patient stand on the other end of a swinging bridge. Chen could beckon, encourage them, but could not tell if they would walk across. How many times had he asked someone, *What is your deepest desire for the direction of your life?* And his follow-up: *What you can control is what you do.* What if someone had asked Chen, *What do you want, right now? What is your desire?*

"Dr. Chen? Your assessment?"

"Excuse me . . ."

Chen had no idea what Bella had asked. Charlie piped up and did his thing. Various words floated out of Charlie's mouth—*marketing and outreach impact . . . understandable budget concerns . . . complexity of your exciting project . . .* Chen knew that his most useful contribution to recruitment was accomplished on his early morning bicycle rides to a friend's house, which did not feature in any of Charlie's slides. *So can I please go home now?* he wanted to say. And finally, somehow, the meeting ended.

Before leaving, Chen went to the mailroom. Two boxes full of clean syringes and needles were waiting for him. He emptied them into his panniers. There were no security cameras in the mailroom, not that he was doing anything wrong. He fastened the panniers shut before going to the elevator. Charlie was downstairs in the lobby, poking at a ride-hailing app on his phone. He glanced at the bulging panniers: "Party favours?"

"Keeps bad from getting worse."

"Hey, whatever works."

"I appreciate it, Charlie," said Chen. A few boxes was insignificant within the lab's purchase orders. If his clinic were to make the purchase, Chen thought it might look strange. They did not prescribe any injectable treatments. It didn't hurt to be careful.

"Listen, though, I got a call. Police. Some junkie they arrested. I guess the brand we buy is distinctive. Who knew? I told him we're a research lab, and we buy a lot of needles and syringes. Maybe expired ones get thrown out." Charlie paused. "I don't even know— do these things have an expiry date?"

"It's not like there's anything wrong with giving out needles," said Chen.

"You told me that before," said Charlie. "Anyways. You're a consultant, not even an employee. So you tell Varitas you need supplies, and Varitas buys them. Why should we ask you why you need so many? That's my story." He winked.

Chen rode home, careful of the dark sewer grates lest they swallow a wheel. He rode past the Dorado, its lights off, the doors locked, the stools upside down on the bar. The only music was the strumming of a talentless busker, banging at an out-of-tune banjo somewhere across the square.

7

FROM THE DOCTOR'S office, Claire hurried to the pharmacy. She sweated near the counter, and a cramp forced her to hunch slightly. With pleading eyes and a pained smile, she caught the pharmacist's attention. She noticed that he approached her with what seemed like a caring dog-owner's expression, presumably because Claire was pretty but unwell. What she hadn't expected was how his expression changed when he read the prescription, how he rolled his lips inwards, glanced over the top of his glasses with the look of a naughty dog's owner. *Just a minute.* He came back and asked: *Young lady, do you know what this medication is for?* She nodded, small. *Just making sure you are aware that it's for—*She interrupted him: *My doctor said I should take it.* The other customers checked phones, drew in sharp breaths of impatience. Hearing it said out loud, she thought, would not help to align her moral compass.

She listened, shivering, to his instructions. Spears of ice pierced her gut. *Dissolve them under your tongue . . . The potential side effects include . . .* He gave her two tiny pills, said they were two milligrams each. *I'll be watching, let them dissolve.* They had a sickly lemon taste. An elderly woman stood to offer Claire a chair, which she accepted, embarrassed. Molten lava seared her skin. Liquid churned inside her—was there a bathroom nearby? As the pills melted, her worst discomfort eased. Claire closed her eyes, retreated into relief.

Then at some point the pharmacist said, *Are you okay?* All the customers who had been waiting were gone, replaced by different ones. *You didn't spit them out, did you? Show me your hands.* Claire opened her eyes, dazed, unsure how much time had passed. *These hands?* She felt a little better. *Don't be smart with me, young lady.* Not perfect, but the medication had helped. Still too tired to tell the pharmacist what she thought of him. She just shook her head, *No, sir.* Had she really said "sir"? That seemed to placate him. The main thing was that it was working, the lemony balm seeping into her bones. Faint, a scent of normalcy at a distance.

Finally, the pharmacist gave her four more pills in a little canister, along with lengthy instructions: *Take one every one to two hours*—pausing to look over his glasses—*not more than that, young lady* . . . there was the "young lady" thing again, but she just nodded . . . *if you feel sedated or drowsy do not take any more and return whatever remains* . . . ha! . . . *and if you feel complete relief from your withdrawal, you must also stop taking them and return whatever is left* . . . double ha! . . . *and whatever you do, do not take more than one an hour* . . . he held the plastic canister in front of her between thumb and finger, hostage. *Yes sir thank you very much sir.* Satisfied with his own authority, he gave her the canister, which was all she really cared about.

Claire went home. Hands shaking, she immediately put the four tablets under her tongue. Did anyone take one an hour, she wondered? Spit collected in the floor of her mouth, and she let it pool there, tried not to swallow. The pharmacist said it absorbed in the mouth but not in the gut, and she was greedy for every last molecule to enter her bloodstream. Until her own mouthful of saliva was too much, and she thought about spitting it into a glass, saving it. But with that thought came repulsion and nausea, and so she swallowed it. Made toast. Drank water. It had been days, Claire realized, since she had slept, and now she might be able to. She went to her bed.

When she woke, it was dark. When she picked up her phone, it glowed with a text.

Hey, how RU?

It was a message from Molly. It was from a few hours ago, had been waiting for her in the night.

OK. U?

Doing AMAZING. Everything is FABULOUS, babe. Why don't you come down here?

Where's here?

An image appeared—a selfie of her sister on a beach in a bikini, sunglasses, drink in the other hand: *Really—send you a ticket! Surf's up!*

Claire sent the thumbs-up emoji. Obviously her sister was high. Or maybe she wasn't; maybe Molly was just in a beautiful place, living a wonderful life.

She sent another text:

Can't go anywhere. I am getting clean. Saw a doctor. Have to take medicine every day.

She tried to sleep again, but could not, looked for a reply on the lonely abyss of the screen. Began to have a chill, muted but recognizable.

About an hour later, *Ding!* came the reply. *Party on!* Molly wrote.

Over the next few days, Claire went to the pharmacy every day for the pills. Taking home part of the dose was unique to the first day. Although this did not make sense to her, she tried only once to argue the point. *Do you want them or not?* was the pharmacist's counter-argument. Now she was expected to put them all under her tongue, and remain until they had all dissolved. Each morning, she resented the time the pharmacy visit required—standing in line, listening to the pharmacist's quips, waiting for the medicine to dissolve—afraid she might end up being late for teaching. The pharmacist checked her mouth and hands before she left. But if she tried to go after teaching, could she even make it through the day? At almost a week, it was hard to believe that she had been so sick. It *was* all in her head, she thought. And then felt her legs begin to ache. At the one-week mark, she went to see Dr. Chen.

"The medication helps a lot," said Claire, grudgingly. "Sometimes I think: How could it make such a difference? But of course these are opiates too, so why should I be surprised?"

"I'm glad it's helping."

"Though I'm not feeling perfect. I still get a little sick, but it's not too bad."

"What do you feel when you're sick?"

She went through her withdrawal symptoms, considering them, as if turning over stones in her palm. "Probably if it were higher . . ."

"We should increase the dose."

"No."

"But you just said—"

"How fast can I get off?" She heard him sigh, but she went on, "Do you ever wake up from a bad dream, and you feel so relieved that it was a dream—that's how I feel when I take this stuff. But then there are those times when you realize you were dreaming about something real?"

"—you just said that it's helping you. But only partially? We're aiming for a dose where you go twenty-four hours from dose to dose without withdrawal."

Just like a good dealer, thought Claire, *he's pushing me to have a little more.* "I want to get off this as quickly as possible. Every day, I feel more . . . normal. Like I said before, I think a lot of it is just in my head." It was as if she had been hypnotized, and the little lemony pill was the hypnotist's snapping of his fingers. Shouldn't this be the moment when he set her free from the illusion, and the audience clapped? "I don't want to just trade one addiction for another."

"If you're not in withdrawal, you can do things. You can live your life."

"Your point?"

"Are you addicted to oxygen?"

"Sorry?"

"If we take away the oxygen in this room, we will both die. But we don't say we're addicted."

"But are we, then?"

"We depend on oxygen. You are now dependent on opioids. Addiction is about needing more and more of something, about it pushing other things out, not being able to do things that matter to you. This medicine is settling the chemical imbalance that's already there. From what you just told me, it needs to be a bit higher to do that properly."

The dose increase was helpful, or at least it did what the doctor said it would. The dissolving lemony pills were like airplane blankets—they made you un-cold. The pills made her un-sick, that was all. The pain in her shoulder was still there. And after a day of teaching, or a night at the Dorado, or sometimes for no reason at all, Claire still found herself hovering over her last text exchange with Scooter. He had messaged a few times since she started treatment, saying that he would be in her neighbourhood. Claire hadn't arranged to meet, but hadn't told him to leave her alone, either.

Soon she felt physically alright, but something else was raw. She said to Dr. Chen, "I thought that getting clean would be better than this."

The doctor replied, "Sometimes, when people stop using, begin to level out, there are things which float to the surface, that drugs had pressed down."

"Is that so!" she said brightly.

One day, it took longer than usual at the pharmacy. Half an hour for the pharmacist to take the prescription, another fifteen minutes while he fiddled on the computer. Her class was about to start. After giving her the pills, he seemed to be paying no attention, and Claire walked quickly to the door. *Young lady . . .* and a hand on her shoulder. *Do as you are told . . .* A long discourse in the potato-chip aisle—*serious treatment . . . at least fifteen minutes of observation,* he said over the top rim of his glasses. Claire did not reply. It was not because she had nothing to say, but because she was afraid that some of the medication beneath her tongue might be lost.

Having shopped at this pharmacy before she was one of *those patients,* in order to purchase toothbrushes, shampoo, overpriced bananas, sour gummies; and also having filled prescriptions (yes, some forged) here for painkillers—plastic canisters cheerily passed across the counter, stapled in a paper bag—Claire felt it unfair that only now was she of interest to the staff. The pharmacist motioned her towards the chair. *Good girl,* he said when she sat.

A text arrived as she sat there, the first from Molly in weeks.

All clean now?

Yup.

U have a sponsor?

It's not like that.

U on the methadone or something?

Pills. Same deal. It sucks.

LOL!

The pharmacist called a trainee over, spoke as if Claire were not there. *Make sure they don't spit it out and put it in their pocket. Check inside their cheeks to see if it's dissolved.* She had become plural, Claire thought. She wanted to tell them this stuff wasn't good enough to steal, but stuck out her tongue, lifted it for inspection. After the educational moment, Claire wandered to the fragrances. The trainee whispered to the woman at the counter. Claire made her way to the hair prod-ucts, and soon the trainee in his short white jacket was halfway down the aisle, tidying the bottles of conditioner. Claire went to cosmetics, waited until she was sure the guy was looking, and pocketed three lipsticks. Several packs of disposable razors went in her purse, an expensive bottle of sunscreen. The trainee tapped a message into his phone. At the quarter-hour mark, Claire asked if the time was up and whether she could leave. The trainee nodded. The cashiers were tense, and the security guard stood at the exit. At the front of the store, Claire dumped all the pocketed but not-yet-stolen items into a red plastic shopping basket, placed it next to the door, and left.

"You know how they treat me?" Claire complained to Dr. Chen, "Like a criminal."

"It shouldn't be that way. But I'm not going to pretend it isn't, in some places. Why don't you change pharmacies?" he suggested. "Some are better than others."

"It'll be the same wherever I go. Because now I'm a junkie. But doctor, I'm a junkie who has little kids waiting for me to teach them scales. So going to the pharmacy every day doesn't work. Frankly, I could just text my dealer—and he delivers."

"And does that occur to you, because we should talk about—"

"I haven't used. If that's what you mean. See my pee test? I'm fine."

"Any cravings? It would be normal."

"Absolutely, totally fine. Really." In truth, every time she heard one of those electric scooters on the street, she looked to see if . . . Then, heart pounding, she was both disappointed and relieved that it was not her guy. She would pull up his contact and look at it, then close the phone.

"Alright."

"And besides, if I use down it won't work, right?" asked Claire. The doctor seemed to be considering something. Before he could speak, she continued, "But Dr. Chen, I can't spend my whole life going to the pharmacy. This cure is worse than the problem."

"Now that you're stabilizing, you could start taking your medications home, gradually. You will need a lockbox to store the medicine you take home."

"You know if I buy an ounce of fentanyl I can just stick that in my sock?"

"I don't recommend either fentanyl or your sock," he said. "How is your music going?"

Claire had been able to make lesson plans for the Little Orchestra School, instead of just winging it. At the practices of the Punk Fugue Trio, she was playing well, at least from a technical standpoint. She had been able to practise more, and had felt that certain tricky passages were becoming quite solid. But Jake had made some comment about *spark, come on, fire, where's the passion? I know it's in you!*

Even when she was small, Josef had often complimented her on her diligence, she just needed to free her expression, her passion. Some people had one, he said, but when the two came together music happened. *Unless, like my sister, you can just wing it on passion, talent,* Claire had thought. Now, for Jake's trio, she loosened the pace of her playing a bit, exaggerated some vibrato, and he praised it, but Claire found herself thinking, *That's just sloppy, Claire, what about real feeling?*

She told the doctor, "I'm playing a little. It's okay. Hey, I was just wondering, since I started coming here"—and unexpectedly, her voice caught—"how come I haven't see you at the Dorado?" His absence felt like the difference in the treatment she received at the pharmacy. For the doctor, she had been a violinist, before, at a restaurant where he liked to eat. And now?

"Oh, I mean, well . . ." Usually, Claire had the impression that most questions she asked of him landed in familiar territory. Not that his answers were formulaic. He seemed to be genuinely trying to explain medical issues. But now, he seemed unsure. "I thought . . . Just busy, mostly. Ordering in."

"Of course," said Claire. "Well, there's some new specials. If you get a night off. Thursdays—tonight, actually."

That evening at the Dorado, the doctor's usual table was empty.

On Friday, Claire went to a hardware store and got a lock, which she attached to the clasps of her violin case. The pharmacist said that a violin case wasn't a proper medication lockbox at any rate, so she would have to purchase one in order for him to dispense the take-home doses. He showed her a plastic box with a flimsy, tiny lock. Claire objected that her doctor had told her any lockable box would do, and explained that she guarded her violin with her life. The pharmacist tried to call Dr. Chen, who wasn't in the office.

"But my doctor authorized the carries," she said.

"Right here on the prescription you need a lockbox for carries to be dispensed. That's a violin case."

"You want me to buy your stupid little plastic box."

"I don't like your tone, young lady."

"Oh, screw you, old man!" said Claire, and she left the pharmacy without any medication.

Saturday evening, Claire felt perfectly fine after having missed two days of her medication. *Maybe I'm cured?*

Sunday, woke restless and early, a little tired, legs ached. *No big deal,* Claire told herself.

Monday, Claire was still able to teach, but was feeling the difference. Okay—so it wasn't purely in her head. The start of dopesick was like clanking towards the top of the roller coaster. *Don't psych yourself out.*

Tuesday, Claire checked on Whitelight. People said coming off buprenorphine was as bad as coming off junk. Worse, according to some. It's not like it had been preplanned, that she would kick. But was she going to stay on this stuff forever? Jake sent a practice schedule—things were getting busy with the trio. Claire decided, *I'm going to tough this out.*

By Wednesday, she couldn't practise, or sleep or sit still. On Thursday, she barely made it to the Dorado, where she delivered limp renditions of "Apres Un Rêve" while sweating through goosebumps, muscle aches, and anxiety. After an evening of terrible playing and corresponding tips, she found herself walking in the wrong direction, towards the GO train tracks, Julia's house, and then she realized what she was doing. Called a car to go to her own home . . . At home, she searched Whitelight for advice. Someone recommended injecting water, with the notion that half of the high was the injection. Claire boiled the water, waited for it to cool—she was always careful with technique—tied off her arm, found a spot. There was a tiny satisfaction, not quite a rush, as the needle pierced. Then worse—her body's expectation of *It's going to happen!* giving way to *What the hell? That was bullshit.*

She stared at Scooter's number. She had a few bucks now. He had stopped messaging recently—probably assumed she was dead. Hands shaking, Claire counted her tips. Told herself she wouldn't spend it all. Just half of that night's. No, not even half. Just enough to get un-sick. Rent was already put aside. Maybe she should see the doctor, but now what would he say, now that she had missed so many? Another person to disappoint. She was determined to show up triumphant, clean, medication free.

If you go see a doctor they're going to tell you to restart your methadone or the bupe again, someone wrote on Whitelight. *Just dealers in white coats, who will say you were stupid for stopping.*

She scrolled through pages, looking for something useful.

. . . The bupes are worse to get off than the junk . . .

. . . Methadone saved my life . . .

. . . now you're a slave—liquid handcuffs, dude.

. . . anyone injecting their bupes? Can you beat the naloxone? The cop-in-a-pill?

. . . Ever think about what would happen if the world were to end? When the people actually rise up against the overlords? Think your meds will be a priority when the shooting starts? You'll be shitting yourself while the shit is hitting the fan. Free yourself now!

A day later? Two? Instead of sleep, she tossed in bed, longing for oxy, heroin, fentanyl, anything. The phone dinged with a schedule reminder. Rehearsal coming up. She could not screw up the trio. It was her chance. But there was no way she could rehearse as she was—jonesing off the drugs that Dr. Chen had prescribed. So what was the difference, really, she thought ruefully, between him and Scooter, whether she was withdrawing off fentanyl or his little pill? One difference was that his pills took a few days to work properly—and even if she went today, she would not be better in time for her rehearsal. Just one little shot, Claire thought, and she could probably get through the rehearsal without her arm feeling—as it did now—like it was being torn from her body. And then, following an episode of cramping and emptying herself on the toilet, it wasn't as if it was a decision. It was more that she stopped resisting, stopped pushing against something. She would buy only what she needed. She began to feel relief as she tapped into her phone, *Hey, you around?* Already thinking she might dip into the rent a little, since Scooter was coming anyways, earn it back later.

To a student of medicine,

You are taught in medicine to give everyone the best possible care, to assess each situation objectively and manage it according to the highest quality evidence. It shouldn't matter whether the patient is tall or short, a man or a woman, or whether the colour of their skin is black, white, or purple. But it turns out that gender and race matter—different tests are ordered, different prescriptions made. These implicit biases have been studied.

What of the patient who shouts that you are taking too long, that you should hurry up and do your job? Or who leers at you. You figure out the correct prescription—yes—and hand it over. Or, the patient whom you enjoy talking to, who has interesting stories that draw you in? And one day they say, doctor, I need a favour . . . not that I would ever ask you to break any rules.

Take note of your reaction when a patient doesn't show up. When certain patients fail to appear on the day you expect them, you are relieved, spared. With others, you don't even notice they are missing until months later when they re-surface. What does that tell you about the doctor-patient relationship? Then there are those whom you anticipate, and when they don't attend, you are worried, or perhaps disappointed? Is all of this more about you, doctor, than your patient? Similarly, when we teach, we also learn.

Yours as always,
Dr. Chen

8

CHARLIE CAUGHT UP with Chen in a long, brown-carpeted hallway at the International Innovations in Psychotropic Pharmacology conference, Charlie reminding him to attend the conference dinner after the last talk: "Not your usual 'Oh, I forgot,'" he said, wagging his finger. "We need to play nice with Omega. They're all in on ayahuagaine," he said.

"Memorex? The psychedelic?"

"Magic mushrooms, baby."

Chen held himself back from correcting Charlie, that it wasn't *actually* mushrooms. A tiny startup had synthesized, then tweaked the ayahuagaine molecule and filed a patent, found a route through the FDA's *compassionate grounds* to run a small trial in a Chicago palliative care unit using their version—Memorex. The dying subjects reported feeling more at peace, described a sense of openness, and following publication of these results the startup promptly cashed out. Omega had been one rumoured suitor.

"Whatever. If we sign Memorex, it's tie-dyed shirts for everyone. Novel molecules in early pipeline! Bingo!" That was Charlie's mantra, the ideal niche for "the Varitas brand". It should be known for small, custom studies—*on weird molecules that no one else will touch. But with enough promise that investors get all frothy. Then we're offering hope, not competing on price.*

"Omega wants to diversify?"

"Spreading their bets," said Charlie, "in case re-packaging the poppy isn't the answer."

"The lawsuits are sending that hint?"

"They have a project manager at this conference—learning about science. Isn't that what you're always saying they should do?"

"For this I have to eat rubber chicken?"

"Chat, mingle, yada yada."

Fitzgerald had once taken the lead on the glad-handing file, when Varitas had been the two of them and a few part-time nurses. Back then, Chen had envied the ease with which Fitzgerald gossiped about the yacht clubs where he'd raced dinghies as a teen, chatted about the features of high-tech sports cars and mechanical watches, what new restaurants and old wines went well together. Fitzgerald sensed the flow of topics that allowed people to be both complimented and comfortable. The form and function of it was clear to Chen, but he could only manage to agree with his friend, and follow along, laugh at a few jokes. After all, what could he contribute—his childhood knowledge of the free days at museums, his family's awareness of which used economy cars ran for a long time?

Fitz would find a shared interest, guide a potential client towards the bar at a conference hotel. It had nothing to do with the science, and yet often seemed to result in a new research contract. Chen cringed slightly at his own attempts at small talk: *So, where did you go to school?* His standard follow-up: *I've heard good things.* Into an awkward pause—*What did you like about that program?*

The science was what interested Chen most about the trials. There was a feeling of order and resolution that came with a solid set of statistics buttressing data, whether for positive trial results presented at an international conference or a negative trial whose results were destined to be forgotten. A disappointed sponsor sometimes trying to dredge the numbers with post-hoc subgroup analysis, which Chen would rebuff. *We've answered the question*, Chen would say with satisfaction, even as the dismayed project manager asked, *So, how could we reframe this . . . ?* As co–principal investigators at conferences, Fitzgerald would go through the slides and Chen would field the questions. He doubted Fitz could have performed a regression analysis, and Fitz never claimed that he could.

When Fitzgerald's medical licence was placed under review by the College of Physicians, Charlie was concerned for the Varitas brand. Chen began to present solo, and took the questions. He could easily do keynotes, panel discussions, unpack the data. But once he was in the hallways between sessions, at the bar, at the dinners, there were no graphs or p-values to reference. Instead, there were people saying, *Chen, what's up?* followed by a false promise: *You're going to find this very interesting . . .* Then, when Fitzgerald's College investigation became public and gossip-worthy, someone would invariably lean over in the middle of a conference lunch and say, *It's a shame, but you must have known?*

Chen had avoided the Dorado since Claire had become his patient. There was the day she asked about it, mentioned the specials. But he would have avoided a bicycle shop if the mechanic had become his patient. Discretion, for their privacy, wasn't it? Now, after Claire's week-long absence from the clinic, he found himself worrying. Was she alive? People could miss a few days of buprenorphine without being too sick, but longer than that and Chen knew that the tension of abstinence became suffering, the entire body stretched tight like a rubber band. The imbalanced physiology that created withdrawal's agonies was evened out by the medications, held in equipoise. But when people went off either black-market drugs or prescribed medicines, the opioid receptors screamed ever louder even as the body became more susceptible to being overwhelmed. If that rubber band was pulled far enough, it could sting when snapped. By now, Claire either was suffering or had found relief. And always, the third possibility.

Chen was sometimes asked to identify a former patient, weeks after their last clinic visit. The needle often in place, in an arm, a foot, a neck. *Evidence*, a morgue technician might say; *sergeant likes everything left as is. Till the coroner signs off.* It was Thursday. He could go past the Dorado. Just to see. He could stand outside the Dorado for a few minutes, hidden by darkness, and listen to her play.

Charlie tilted his head down the hallway towards one of the conference coffee tables. "Come on, let's go do some stimulants." Charlie dispensed some brown fluid from the carafe. Chen did the same, tasted it, and then put the stale coffee aside and found a hot water flask and a teabag. Charlie continued talking, and Chen used his ability to tune his colleague in and out almost like a radio station. Now, as Chen sipped the mediocre green tea, Charlie said, " . . . and these funky mushrooms—right up your alley! I'm not asking you to kiss ass just to make money. Come on, I know you're into all that buzz about opening the mind to new pathways, and being more accepting of the self, whatever. That's the whole psychedelic thing, right?"

"Glad you attended my afternoon session," said Chen. He had given a seminar on therapeutic techniques, and had been asked about psychedelic-assisted therapy. Charlie had been concerned it was *off-brand* for Chen to be giving a session that was so *touchy-feely*, and must have been glad a pharma question came up. "Emerging field. We'll see."

"And we'll see you at dinner. No excuses."

"If I'm not too tired."

"Opening minds, new molecules, and I know you love to work on something ahead of the crowd. And I like Varitas—"

Chen interrupted, "To be early in the pipeline with a compound that no one else will handle for a sponsor who wants to spend money on their new toy."

"Keeps everyone living in the style to which they are accustomed. The founders still have skin in the game, am I right?"

Charlie's statement was crass, and correct. Chen and Fitzgerald remained significant minority shareholders in Varitas after the private equity sale. If Varitas went public, their shares could one day be worth a lot—or nothing, like many pharma gambles. After the deal, Fitzgerald had taken his share of the cash and dumped it into marijuana startups, hedge funds that his private school friends were running, second mortgages, niche cryptocurrencies. Chen put his in bank stocks, telephone companies, and strip bonds. The returns were steady, more than he needed. Fitzgerald's investment returns soon funded a new German SUV and an Italian convertible. He sold the vehicles in a hurry several months later, lamenting a margin call.

Consulting on trials was now over for Fitzgerald, but recruitment had always been one of the former doctor's strengths. The people who visited his house were best found through a personal connection, which is why doctors who recruited particular subjects could be paid almost as much as the subjects themselves. Fitzgerald would say, *When you call Varitas, tell them you're one of Dr. Chen's patients. Yeah yeah, that's my real name. I know, no one ever guesses* . . . Chen kept a separate bank account for these payments, and Fitz had an access card. Charity had never been an option.

"You know it's not mushrooms, don't you?"

"Just testing you!" Charlie said, "Memorex has you written all over it. Lizard glands! From the deep, dark jungle! The resolution and integration of trauma!"

"You've been on the forums. Whitelight? I would stay away from saying that thing about the jungle."

"Face it, this one excites you."

"It might be interesting. In the Chicago trial, subjects reported a feeling of openness, this sense of profound experience, but had difficulty putting their experience into words . . . how do you even code that data? Which then begs the question, what is the right data? The scientific questions are tricky!"

"You're into it! Healing through forgetting!"

"But it's not. Even though people call it a forgetting drug. The clinical notes are all over the place . . . improved ability to allow the past to exist in the past . . . the present internal experience as mental phenomena, from an observer's point of view."

"See? You've already been thinking about this stuff. Go on, I'm loving it. Omega will, too." Charlie nodded, a tiny bit smug.

"Aren't you the one who says that my problem is that I think too much?"

"I take it back. Thinking is why you get paid the big bucks."

Chen had recently renegotiated his consulting contract. He had hoped that the numbers on the cheques would provide some source of satisfaction, but they ended up just looking like numbers.

"Are you sure my rate includes conference galas?"

"Big bucks, doctor."

At the gala, Chen dutifully sat next to a scientist whom Charlie wanted to tap for a trial, tried to seem amused by the jokes of industry people at the table with whom Charlie hoped to land contracts, imitated Fitzgerald by dipping into discussions of holiday destinations, private schools. The trick was to pick up on one word and ask something specific, engage people by being engaged. Everyone loved to feel that what they were saying was interesting. There was academic jousting too—researchers vying to show that their interpretation of a paper was more original than others at the table, one's awareness of the data's limitations more astute than another's. As the bottles of cheap table wine emptied, people relaxed into gossip of the embarrassments *du jour*—a professor who thought she was beyond fertility until her rugby-playing summer student proved otherwise, the charges for a hotel suite that a dean thought he could slip into a research budget unnoticed.

Charlie worked the room, and from time to time came up behind Chen, tapped his shoulder, introduced him to someone or other as Varitas's *founder* or as *Dr. Chen, whom I'm sure you have heard speak* . . . Hands were shaken. Cards and compliments were exchanged.

The conference awards started with the best student posters, and Chen had a pang of recollection, of a year when he had applauded politely, restraining his enthusiasm for one of the winners. Now, Chen hoped to slip away quietly, and was looking for the right moment. A few at the table excused themselves, but before Chen could make his escape, Bella waved from across the table, a half greeting of extended fingers. Charlie pretended not to be keeping tabs out of the corner of his eye.

Bella came over to Chen, sat in the chair the scientist had vacated, saying, "You look like you're in pain over here. Is it seeing me?"

"Not at all—enjoying the conference?"

"I was in your afternoon talk. So helpful for me to get a sense of your patients, what they're like beyond the data."

Chen had noticed Bella in the afternoon seminar. She had been taking notes.

"I have spent so much time researching the molecules," Chen said, "and I started to think the talking might be just as important."

"Might?"

"It's a hypothesis."

Bella laughed, "And we could also hypothesize that what we are saying now might be important?" She had changed for dinner from business grey into a burgundy dress. Like her suit, the dress was of a tone and cut that was considered, careful, though not shy. Another student award winner went up to the stage. "Did Charlie mention Omega's recent patent acquisition—Memorex?"

"A new direction."

"Portfolio diversification," she shrugged.

"You're the project manager? You'll want some proper trials— you can only get so far on compassionate grounds."

"We're talking to Varitas first. You pulled the rabbit out of the hat, with the last one. I was ready to be disappointed." Omega's current trials had met recruitment targets, were about to begin dosing cohorts, rounded out nicely by subjects who thought that Chen was a funny name for a white guy. "Charlie told me not to worry. So. What do you think about ayahuagaine?"

"The great thing about new molecules is that even before anyone swallows them, everyone can project their desires onto them."

Bella seemed amused, and said coolly, "That's the whole business case of the pharmaceutical startup space."

Chen thought of Claire telling him, *I just feel I need a rewind, or a reset. If I could just hit that button, start over . . .* "With every molecule, it all boils down to figuring out who it helps."

"How to ask the right question? You said something about that this afternoon. Isn't that always the tricky bit?"

Chen had always been aware of Bella's beauty, which was obvious at a distance. She had the look of an advertisement model on the inside of a magazine cover, a glossy figure. Seated near him rather than across a boardroom table, she was less two-dimensional but no less beautiful.

"Now you're thinking like a scientist."

"I'm a woman who needs to hire one."

"What a coincidence." Up close, Chen was aware not only of her poise and symmetry, but also of soft shadow and the movement of breathing. "Fancy us meeting like this."

"Have you given any thought to the best pathway for this class? Psychedelics? I've gone back to look at some of your early abuse liability work. That's all standard stuff now, how those trials are done. But someone had to do it first. Show how to show. Ask how to ask." Chen sensed that her compliments were deliberately placed, but the wine made it easy to just go with it, and enjoy them.

"And where do you think our compound, Memorex, fits? Testing it will be tricky, I know, but we could budget in a way that acknowledges that."

Now he laughed, "You must be really desperate for an investigator. Add a zero to that number, please?"

"I didn't say a blank cheque. In your talk today, you said that a major challenge in treating opioid addiction is simply that people remember how good the drugs are?"

"Even if we make the withdrawal go away, we can't take away the memory of the high."

"And if people could forget?"

"That's one theory, that Memorex might be used as a kind of selective amnestic to treat addiction," Chen said.

Bella said, "I've read that in tight-knit hunter-gatherer societies where cooperation was vital, ayahuagaine was used to forget. It might be easier to raise children if you forgot a stillbirth. To fight alongside your neighbour against a murderous rival village, it might be better for both of you to forget his infidelity with your wife."

"I saw that thread too," said Chen. "Whitelight chatter."

"There's excitement, isn't there?"

"Of course. If you're selling the stuff. Or buying, and you want it to work." The Dark Web placed everything a click away, complete with narrative. What was known: Memorex was a synthetic analogue of the secretion of a gecko. The traditional form, ayahuagaine, was used in ancient sacred ceremonies—so declared the Whitelight pundits, with assurance as casual as if they were giving traffic directions. Modern cryptocurrency in exchange for ancient insight—a bargain by any measure. "Have you surveyed the range of compounds discussed on Whitelight? Recipes for frying your brain. There's always a trip *du jour*."

She reddened. "So it's hard to know exactly . . . But is that signal?" she asked.

"What are the odds, you mean?" Might a scientist—with enough investment—demonstrate some underpinning mechanism which transcended the vision in the campfire flicker and the glib assertions of forum posts, to become a statistical relationship? An FDA approval?

"And are they on our side?"

"The thing is, if you throw up and seize, you think the world is different. Bloodletting went on for centuries—because people *felt* it, and so they believed it did something."

Ayahuagaine had notable side effects—violent diarrhea, urticarial rash, reported seizures. That, according to the Dark Web sellers of what was also referred to as "gecko goo" on Whitelight, was part of the cleansing process. Memorex was supposed to be the clean version, made in a lab, the same basic molecule without a nasty little side-chain that was thought to cause the side effects. The modification that rendered synthetic ayahuagaine into Memorex, of course, also made it possible to patent the molecule.

Bella said, "Early data shows that Memorex is much better tolerated."

"And there are posts about how *super clean* Memorex is, no hangover, no brain zaps, just a bright, fresh morning the next day. One guy said it cured him of PTSD, depression, *and* addiction," Chen said. "And he became far more handsome. Funny that people are managing to get their hands on some."

Bella shrugged and said, "There's as many rumours on Whitelight about how people are getting their hands on Memorex as there are about the compound itself. That's what happens with these little start-ups. Everyone needs revenue, right? So part of the role of Omega is to bring legitimacy, consistency, respected science."

"So then, it's not a coincidence that we're talking?"

"And in your population, listening to your talk—I wonder if Memorex fits with some of what you're trying to do? You've read the Peru paper?" One of the few respected papers on ayahuagaine was by Dr. Quinones, a medical ethnographer, and preceded Whitelight by a decade. It described how the introduction of alcohol by loggers to a long-secluded community in Peru had nearly destroyed a village. Then, how elders of the community began to collect the shy lizard whose glands—it was said—only yielded aya-huagaine if the creature was at ease. One had to befriend the animal with certain songs, until it came, docile, for its salivary glands to be massaged. The paper referred to dream exploration but noted this was an imperfect translation from the local language. The elders began to administer the substance to their community's alcoholics, Dr. Quinones wrote, singing over them as they did. After a cere-mony using this substance, the drinkers seemed to have forgotten what alcohol was like or their desire for it.

"That's where this idea of it being a forgetting medicine came in. But like everything on the internet, it's an oversimplification. Quinones qualified his descriptions."

"More research is needed. That's where we were hoping that you would come in. And with your interest in therapeutic techniques? It doesn't seem like this molecule functions in isolation."

"You want subjects from my clinic."

"Your subjects have a higher completion rate than others. We've run the numbers. Informally." Bella laughed. "How do you do that?"

"It's about having people's trust," said Chen.

Bella nodded thoughtfully. "So simple? And how do you get that?"

It's not something you get, he thought of saying. Instead, "It's not always simple."

She asked him about his start in addictions research, and Chen rolled out his usual line, about intellectual exploration, and a desire to bring the best of science to addictions patients. It all sounded so serious that he added a few self-deprecating lines, at which Bella laughed. Chen asked Bella how she had ended up in pharma, and she gave what he recognized to be her own standard précis. Her punch-line was that if it were not for one chance meeting, she would still be selling bonds. They were both Toronto kids, once upon a time. Different neighbourhoods.

Bella said, teasing, "You know, whenever I meet really smart people, I notice that small talk is an awkward thing for them. But sitting over here . . . when you weren't trying to make nice—very convincing, for the record, I almost thought you cared about golf—it looked like you got lost on the way to the clinic."

She had been watching him carefully, he realized. It was not necessary to observe someone from afar in order to sign a contract. No one was on stage. At some point the presentation of student research awards had ended. Closing remarks had been made, and the lights were coming up. Around them, the remaining few clumps of people were dissolving into business-card swaps and handshakes. Charlie had vanished. Chen was about to say good night and wish her well.

Bella said, "Isn't this the point in the evening when we both wonder if someone is going to suggest a drink?"

Her hand lightly on his arm.

"I know a place. It's a bit of a walk."

"Sure—some fresh air."

It was a clear, cold night. They were downtown, walking towards Chen's neighbourhood. Perhaps they would just walk past the Dorado, and he would just glance in. Bella laughed about small things that had happened to her in the city, gossiped about people they both knew in pharma research. *The game*, she called it. There was a feeling that although they were both within that world, just for this moment they had stepped out and could look inside, poke fun. Chen remembered another walk, with his student, after she'd won her award at this same conference. Had their route through the city been the same, though deliberately at arm's length? Her ideas about research were challenging, poignant. Chen had found ways to explore them, teased at the weak points of her arguments, drew them out with exaggerations. His student flushed but did not concede, mounted a passionate defence as they walked a sidewalk-square apart from one another. When they got to the Dorado, his student had been pleased that Claire was playing, as if this had been arranged especially for her, as a celebration. They had a meal, a glass of champagne, and Chen made sure his student got safely in a car to go home.

Tonight, Bella's hand found its way easily enough into the crook of Chen's arm. Whether something in his body language or in shared laughter had served as an invitation, she drew closer, no big deal.

"Let's go here," he said, and tilted his head towards the Dorado.

Entering the warm restaurant, Chen scanned the room for Claire. *Special guest*, it said on the chalkboard—a saxophonist. The maître d' greeted Chen and asked if he would like his usual table. *A booth, please*, Bella replied. They ordered a bottle of Chardonnay. As they spoke, she touched the back of his hand, as if the conclusion of the evening had already been decided. Their conversation floated on the surface, and Chen realized that she did not speak much of herself, instead shared anecdotes and confidences with him in matters that did not involve her. At some point, Bella murmured, "Did you say your place is nearby?" Her cool fingertips met his.

Afterwards, as their breathing slowed, she pulled his body against hers as one would a pillow. Her body curved around his back, and he relaxed into her embrace. Only then did the edge of tension go out of her, and she settled into the night. She inhaled deeply, her forearm draped over him. She breathed out on the back of his neck— already asleep. He could have been someone else, Chen thought, and Bella would still have what she wanted. This did not bother him; it freed him from expectation, obligation. That night Chen did not wake to check his email, or to scroll through the photos of his patients. He slept far beneath the surface, as if he had successfully gone into hiding.

9

CLAIRE STOOD ACROSS the street from the dirty, white-painted brick front of the Swan Clinic, shivering against the damp, along with a few others waiting for it to open. Its neighbours were a butcher, and a place that sold candles, incense, and glass bongs. It was the first snow, as if from a fairy tale—heavy with beauty, thick with certainty. White cold settled, one flake upon another on a mailbox, a hydrant, a car window. *Bad date?* a girl asked Claire. She shook her head. A cough. *Got a smoke?* Claire responded again with the same gesture. *Bitch,* the girl declared. The doctor arrived on his bicycle, the doors opened, the patients went inside, but Claire was undecided. She watched the clinic patients come and go, simultaneously feeling that she hated them, found them pathetic, and that they were the only people in the world who understood what she was going through. A hot flash, and she began to sweat despite the cold. Then shivered, was the chill her sickness or the winter?

Claire had missed the Dorado gig because she was sick. Perfectly true. It's what she told the maître d'; though she also wished it were as simple as being sick—with a cold, a pneumonia, or cancer. She had tried to get there, to fix herself.

The mistake, she told herself, was waiting too long to address her withdrawal. Scooter had looked terrible when he finally arrived, sores on his face and trembling hands—he shouted, *What are you looking at? There's shit in the crystal.* Promised herself she was just going to grab one point of down, maybe two, enough to get to the Dorado. Then back to getting clean. But then he had the stuff. In his backpack—the beautiful baggies—and Scooter eyed her cookie jar of cash, saying, *How much you got? Let's do a deal . . .* Claire bought an eight-ball. He was upfront about it being fentanyl. No heroin this week, he shrugged, next week for sure. Did she want it or not? Scooter suddenly dancing up and down, cackling, *So strong, I was wrecked. Off a point of this shit! I had to do tina just to get out of bed! You're lucky I got here! Don't let me down girl!* It was a great price. Never mind rent. He bounced away with the money still in his hand.

But with the shot, there was a rush as her heart jumped, but none of the comfort. Claire's hands trembled—she needed to at least settle her hands in order to play. Tried a few bars of Mozart—a mess. Was the second bag a different batch? she wondered. It looked the same. She just wanted something, anything, and did a shot from the second bag, did fentanyl even look like this? Her skin began to tingle and buzz, and her hands shook even more. Claire had the presence of mind to text a melancholy saxophonist, asked him to sub for her at the Dorado, emphasized that it was her regular night—tried to be proprietorial but chill.

Claire decided to rearrange her rosin box, and began moving the amber pieces around: Folded the violin cleaning cloth into a small square. Took the rosin out. Folded the cloth in a triangle. Put the rosin back in. Took it out. Wrapped it in the cleaning cloth. And soon, Claire realized that Scooter had set her up, that if she stepped out of her apartment the police would nab her, that the maître d' and the saxophonist were plotting to steal the Thursday, and were obviously lovers, that if she could just get the rosin box arranged properly . . . And then she organized her sock drawer, and her fridge.

Scooter thought it was very funny, when Claire texted that she was getting paranoid instead of chilled out, that he had given her crystal meth and not fentanyl. He sent the weepy laughing emoji. By the time he came to swap it out Claire could barely prep her shot, but did a big one to come down off the jib.

Scooter said, *Now it's just fenny. You'll learn to love it.* But it was hard to measure, impossible to gauge. Claire tried to get to a level place in order to be able to teach, to play. With heroin, she had been able to figure it out. The previous batch of down must have been a mix of the two. It had been different, but manageable. With this batch, she did not even think of the Dorado for several days. One shot became the next, days vanished, Jake's number showed on her phone—she let it go to voice mail. Same for the music school. One night, angry texts from the maître d', *Where are you?* Had it been a week?

A car passed on the street between Claire and the Swan, snow swirling in its wake. Rent money gone, stash gone, so what was there to decide about? She walked into the clinic.

In Dr. Chen's office, Claire was sweaty, shaking.

"I guess I screwed up."

"You're back. I'm glad."

"I can't believe I'm here again. Like this."

"What brought you back now?"

"Umm . . . because I screwed up? Because I'm sick as hell? I want to get back on your pills—the stuff that doesn't cure me and just keeps me hooked. If that's the best you've got."

"It worked for you. Let it help."

"Unless you have something better—something that can just fix me. Zap me out of myself? Isn't shock therapy a thing?"

"For depression, psychosis."

"I've just been through both."

"And why did you walk through the door today? Tell me about this particular moment."

He looked like he actually wanted to know what was happening with her, and this surprised her. Josef, her old teacher, would have that look when she came in with new repertoire, and she raised her bow. Now Claire had the feeling, again, of someone actually listening. Curiosity was a particular kindness. Except that now she was horribly sick and wanted to vanish into the floor.

"I wish there was something special about today, this morning," she said. She did not say that she had screwed up her steady gigs, spent her rent, or that Scooter didn't front anything otherwise she would have called him, or that if the clinic hadn't been open this morning her next move would have been to find Julia's house, and she didn't say that the two things that she wanted most desperately right now—equally—were to get high, and to never see the stuff again. Claire said, truthfully, "It was just more of the same . . . getting worse. So I'm here."

"If you learned something by going through what you went through, you're not in the same place anymore. And you're here, you're alive. I got a message from the pharmacy—that you didn't have a lockbox, then you didn't take your prescription."

She had expected anger, annoyance, not patience. "Dr. Chen, people treat you really badly when they know you're a drug addict. That pharmacy—never mind, it doesn't even matter."

"I have some lockboxes. You can take one."

"It wasn't just that. I want to be off everything. The drugs, the medicine. So I stopped. And then . . . well . . . *cold turkey* sounds so simple. Cue shitshow. But I was okay, for a bit . . . and I remember thinking, *I am fine. It's all in my head.* And then it *did* get worse."

"Your head is full of billions of neurons and a soup of

neurotransmitters, and their physiology has been altered by the use of opioids. So yes, you're right. It's all in your head."

Claire nodded thoughtfully, and then said, "That's a good line."

"The medicine works slowly, that's why it can help you to stabilize. It leaves slowly, so if you miss a day it's not so bad. If you miss multiple days, same as coming off the down."

"So you just prescribe me this stuff, and I'm hooked on something that's slow, instead of fast?"

"That's one way of looking at it. Whether you're cold-turkeying street opiates or buprenorphine, the risks are the same." Now, he seemed intent on impressing this upon her. "Tolerance decreases as you go through withdrawal. Then people use and overdose. A lot of people die."

"When I say I want to be off everything, it's true. But then something happens . . ."

"The science is about molecules and neurons. Beyond that, you have to figure out why treatment matters to you."

Claire thought of Josef, how she once tried to copy his phrasing of the *Thaïs* meditation, only for him to say kindly, *Yes, good reproduction, now play it your own way.* She looked at the ceiling for a while, waited for her eyes to swallow her tears, and then turned to Dr. Chen. She said quietly, "If I just hadn't been weak."

"I'm not sure it's about weakness or strength."

"Then what does it take? To get better?"

After a moment, "Maybe flexibility," he said. "You'll find out."

Now the tears fell down her cheeks, she wiped them away . . .

"So—my wiring is all screwed up, and the bupe keeps it that way?"

"Holds you steady. Takes away withdrawal."

"A little pill holding me steady. I've spent years relying on little pills to do that."

"But the difference is that short-acting opioids are like a remote control for your feelings. You can change the channel, turn the volume up or down, but gradually you have to push the buttons twice, three times for them to work, until eventually the buttons don't do anything. That's why it's important and different that the buprenorphine holds steady. It does what it does—when it's stable, it shouldn't feel like anything."

"The channel doesn't change. It's still playing my shitty life."

"Should we start you back on your medication?"

"I guess we should."

"Get a naloxone kit? In case things go off the rails again?"

"You don't think I can do it, do you? Why else would you say that?"

"You have to survive, in order for me to help you again. You found something that meant a lot to you. There are reasons people use. The goodbye is hard." He looked pained.

The doctor went over the starting procedure with Claire—the initial small dose on the first day, followed by adjustments. She would have to attend the pharmacy every day again until she was stable, he said apologetically.

To a student of medicine,

How much of addiction is about memory? Searching, over and
over, for what can no longer be found. The pain of once having
grasped it—the moment of wholeness. Everyone says that it's never
as good as the first time. How much is driven by recollection?
That first time did not announce how singular it was, that it
would never again be the same. And now, with absence, the ache
of the inverse. How different is it, we can speculate, if the empty
impression is left behind by a molecule, or a place, or a person?
One could design a functional imaging study of these neuronal
patterns, examine how absences of different types reveal their
imprint upon the diffuse physiology of the opioid system, or the
brain's navigation centres, or the patterning of facial recognition.
Cellular activity would paint the multicoloured images of PET
scanning . . . portraits of loss. One would then wish to define
both similarities and differences, comparing these phenomena
that are all in one's head.

    Of course, for the materialist, it is all about neurons and
receptors. And at some level we doctors must be materialists,
otherwise we would throw away our prescription pads. I still use

that line, the one you teased me for using too often, when patients say "it's all in my head" and I invoke the tangle of neurons. When I say that, am I trying to console or to convince? Or to shift a perspective, a way of seeing? Just the other day, a new patient recognized that it was a line—someone whom you once admired. She noticed that these few words were less than perfectly spontaneous. Clearly, she has an ear for the flourish of performance.

To think that somehow longing, loss, regret, is a sequence of action potentials . . . I do find that consoling. To picture it . . . a complex array of changes in the electrical state of membrane surfaces, charged impulses whizzing down axons oblivious to the suffering they embody, the cellular walls depolarizing, repolarizing, ions rushing through channels. Although it still hurts.

Yours as always,
Dr. Chen

10

THURSDAY EVENING, HAVING waited until dark, Chen slipped down the lane near his building towards the Dorado. He watched Claire from outside the restaurant. She appeared to be struggling with her instrument. But when the door opened, a strand of music escaped and the melody was strong, the tone clear. She sounded better than she looked. He had the urge to go in, to sit down and order some food and a drink. But he told himself it was merely a longing for another time, when he was a teacher with a student, binders of data splayed before them as a kind of justification. Chen stayed carefully in shadow, listening. In between pieces, he saw Claire go to her violin case, take something from the rosin box, put it in her mouth. He knew her prescription continued to be witnessed at the pharmacy. She was taking something else. She returned to the instrument and within a few minutes seemed more at ease, still forceful but with more grace, a greater fluidity in the notes. At one point Claire could have been looking straight at him, but Chen knew that from inside the lit restaurant she would only see the dark laneway outside, that her look of focus was directed towards the music.

———

In clinic, it was clear to both of them that the medication was beginning to help again, but the dose that had previously worked for
Claire was no longer sufficient. This was a disappointment to Claire.

"To be expected," said Dr. Chen. "Often after a relapse, a higher
dose is needed to stabilize the opioid receptors."

"I dug my hole deeper."

"Your tolerance will increase, as long as you're still using."

"You see that on the urine test? I have excuses ready."

"You don't owe me any. People tell me it's like saying goodbye
to the most wonderful partner, to love."

"Maybe it has been a little tricky." Claire recognized what he
said, although if she had to choose between a past lover and some
really good heroin, it would not be the dilemma that she wished
it were.

He said, "Can I confirm that the urine test is correct?" He asked
her the details of her use, the quantities, the route. He asked if the
needles were clean and new, and whether she had picked up the
naloxone kit—she had. Had she used with someone else who could
rescue her?—no. The doctor asked as if he were cataloguing the
aches and pains of an arthritis patient. With the buprenorphine now
lasting only part of the day, he recommended a dose increase. Claire
said that she didn't want it, then mused that perhaps she should, and
reversed course once more and told him firmly to leave the dose
unchanged.

Dr. Chen said gently, "At a constant dose, the level in your blood
may still rise a bit—because of the long half-life. We can reassess in a
little while." He made the prescription. "And . . . how are you doing?"
he asked.

"I just told you. You saw the pee test."

"No, I don't mean what drugs are you using. How are *you* doing?"

She had the prescription in her hand, and it occurred to her that
she could just walk away. Maybe that was the point of doing all the

prescription stuff first. So that she could choose whether to stay. "I feel like I've thrown a lot away," said Claire. "Wasted time, my talent. Maybe my whole life."

"It's only your whole life if that's what you let it be."

"Okay. My whole life until now. The rest of my life starts today? Tomorrow is a new dawn? Turn over a new leaf? What's the slogan on the T-shirt? Whatever. Unless I overdose and die."

"Good point." The doctor nodded. "Imagine you have a magic wand."

"I want to wave it and go back. To before I ever took a pill."

"Although imaginary, it only works on the future. If you could wave the wand so that it made your life what you want it to be in five years, what would that look like?"

"Five years? Magic wand: in five years, please make it so I'm not selling my body. I'm not living on the street. I'd like to not be dead." It was both annoying and reassuring that these possibilities seemed normal to Dr. Chen.

"Hmm . . ." He nodded as if she were outlining the disadvantages of a career in plumbing. "Those are all the 'nots.'"

"And?"

"But if you're not dead, homeless, or doing sex work in five years, you are what?"

"Alive?"

"And what are you doing in five years that makes life worth living?"

Claire had the impulse to stand up, thank him for the prescription, and leave. She also had the impulse to cry. Then, the impulse to ask him, What would *he* be doing in five years? Would he be here, if she needed him? Because if not, why should she tell him anything? She hadn't known any doctor for five months let alone five years. In fact, she hadn't known a doctor any longer than it took for them to tell her what they thought she should do, or not do.

Should she say what anyone would say? That in five years she wanted to be paying her rent, to have food in the fridge, someone in her life.

Claire said, "In five years, I want to be playing music. Performing pieces that I love—new work—modern compositions for the violin. I want to show people what the instrument can do, what I can do." She was aware of sounding ardent, and felt exposed, but went on. "It's not about being famous or anything, but I want to be heard. When I am playing well, it's all there is, all that matters." Now she became aware of the doctor's focus, that it seemed to matter to him that this was so important for her." It's the only thing I'm good at."

"And what does that mean to you? To be good at it?"

"There's a lot to it."

She thought of Josef, his approach that was already old-fashioned years ago. But even now, she turned to what he had taught her. "Well . . . first of all there's technique. You can't do anything else unless your technique is solid. That may be boring, but it's the start of everything. Body position, fingering, bowing, everything should be precise and controlled. And yet, the violinist must be so proficient that it is absolutely relaxed and natural, the way you move your hands, control the instrument. And then there is expression, that if you seek to convey an emotion, you should both feel it in yourself and through your playing; a lot of that is in the bow. Balance—between firmness and suppleness."

"Knowing when, and how much of each?"

"Yes, and I want to play what I cannot say. To express . . . feelings that do not have words through my instrument. That is music—a thing which breathes, which resonates even after the last note has faded." She paused, a little frightened of being so open. But that, too, was music, a vulnerability.

Sometimes, when she played well, Claire transported herself into her playing, and then returned to the room with the people in it, to the reverberation that remained. Dr. Chen now regarded her as if he were amongst such an audience. She remembered that on more than a few occasions, he had listened to her in this way at the Dorado. And then, the other night, as she played the second part of the Janacek sonata, high on just half a point of smoked fentanyl—this time it's what she asked Scooter to bring—there had been some of that feeling, but no one in the restaurant seemed to be paying much attention. Outside the window, there was a familiarity to a silhouette. Now, she wanted to ask her doctor if he had come past her restaurant that night, paused in the shadow to hear her. Before she could do so, he said, "And what is the next step? Towards the next five years?"

To think of the near future was more jarring than her distant hopes, and she trotted out a student's answer. "I have to practise. Every day. Consistently. I have to keep on improving, otherwise I get sloppy. And I have to stop the fentanyl," she added. It felt so nice and simple to say it. She had the prescription in her hand, was on the edge of her chair—"Isn't it amazing that music always vanishes? Whatever I do in the next five years, it will disappear. Unlike a painting or a sculpture which is there for people to look at, or to gather dust in the basement of a museum. They're objects. But music is the motion of molecules, vibration through the air, and once it exists it is already gone. Somehow that makes me feel better. Is that strange, doctor?"

"I don't think so," he said, "we all care about things that vanish. A conversation is the same, in that way, as music."

At the next visit, there was still junk in her urine. Claire was not surprised, admitted that early in the week, she had found a tiny bit around the house and used it.

"Is it heroin?" she couldn't help asking.

"Amongst other things."

"I had a little bit—for emergencies. I wasn't going to throw it away."

Her prescription was helping, but she confirmed what the doctor thought, that it wasn't enough. More than half of the span between doses of her daily medication she was free of the physical symptoms of withdrawal, but she still woke too early in the morning, achy and sweating, with not enough sleep, with chills and a runny nose.

"But leave it where it is. I don't want the dose to go up," she said curtly when Dr. Chen again recommended an increase. The buprenorphine settled her to the point that she could do most things—make food, teach tone-deaf children (after spinning an elaborate tale of excuses and apologies to Frances for the week during which she had simply vanished), and exist. But she did not want to tell him that on her current dose of buprenorphine alone, she could barely practise, and her shoulder ached. Unless she did something about it.

Claire had used the emergency flap of the real brown stuff on the day after her previous doctor visit. It was the only thing she could think about—the baggie of heroin's relief, tucked in her sock drawer. Best to get rid of it, she told herself. She savoured the edges of the paper packet, the pleasure she knew would come as soon as she unfolded it. And after a few hours, that was it. Gone. Done. Over forever. Because the fentanyl was just not the same, so that was a line she could draw.

And that evening, while the half dose of buprenorphine was softening the let-down, Scooter had texted, *Brown sugar. Really. Give you a good price—sorry for the last batch?* The shrugging-hands-and-smile emoji. It was like when you fought with a guy, and he gathered up all his stuff from the apartment as you cried, and left—duffle bursting, door slammed—but then later his phone call, *I miss you so much . . .*

Scooter also had some pills, said there were more around recently. *Package price?* The hydromorphone was mild compared to the down, but it smoothed things out. Two tabs, swallowed, bought her an hour of almost pain-free practice. For evenings at the Dorado, she crushed four in advance and excused herself to the bathroom a few times during the evening.

"Tell me why you don't want to go up."

"It'll be harder to get off. If the dose is higher, I'm worse, right? More screwed up. Like if you have a lung problem and you need more puffers, it must be that you're worse. I'm already a fuck-up," she said. "Having to increase my dose would be more proof. So just leave it."

But the point of it was to preserve something inside her. How could her doctor understand that? That Claire was willing to be sick, in order to preserve the painful space within her receptors to still be able to get high when she needed to. Whitelight had explained what to do. A partial dose of bupe, and you could chip. Use on top. A full dose, maybe not. She felt the difference already, that the day-to-day stability of buprenorphine came at the cost of what the hydromorphone and heroin could do.

Claire initially promised herself that the heroin was only for practices with the trio, and hopefully at some point performances—because she had not explained everything that she knew about music to her doctor. Yes, it started with practice, but it was rare to have the gift of taking it to the next level, that of beauty, and that was worth any price. Out of hydromorph one night, she used a point of heroin at the Dorado, and pulled almost twice the usual in tips. The extra gave her what she needed for rent, which the super had agreed to let her pay late. *Just as a favour,* he had said.

"Think back to when the pills first came into your life," he said. "What was the thing they helped you with?"

"Helped? They've messed up my whole life."

"Yes . . ." said Dr. Chen. "But at some point they solved a problem."

"They've made a lot of problems."

"You said that you feel like you are not good enough. How has that feeling affected you?"

"I've always had to work harder, try harder than everyone else. And then I still didn't quite belong. You wouldn't know."

"I might have some idea."

"And then, it was never quite enough. No matter how hard I practised. There was always someone better."

"And did pills affect that feeling?"

She did not want to tell him that for all her talk of technique, and phrasing, and expression of emotion, the thing that allowed each to grow into the next was feeling free. If she wanted the notes to dance, she couldn't think about fingering. In order for the bow to sing, she had to be beyond the conscious exercise of the balance of pressure across the shaft and into the horsehair. And that had always been elusive.

Dr. Chen asked, "Did opiates allow you to feel the way you needed to feel? That you were good enough? At first?"

Another week, another visit, and Claire asked, as she came into the consultation room, "Well? Am I clean?"

The doctor went to the computer, pulled up a screen with the urine test results, saying with a nod, "Wonderful! I'm so pleased for you! We can start doing take-home doses. Tell me what worked." Claire wished that her own satisfaction was as clear and simple as his appeared to be.

"When I decide to make a change, that's it." She had forced herself to pay the rent, and to try being clean for a week. So now it was a week. She had wanted to get this far, to pee in a cup, to show him and herself that she could do it, and without going up on the medicine. It had been a miserable week. Claire had been in agony at the Dorado, nursed her arm by playing only slow, schmaltzy pieces. She made it through her lessons by picking up her own violin as little as possible, asking the least awful-sounding students to demonstrate. She had not bothered to practise at all, and had skipped the trio practice—saying she had hurt her shoulder. The best lies contained some truth.

"Super," he said. "And did you miss it?"

With the few bucks left over after rent, Claire had bought food so that she would not have any cash on hand. She had blocked Scooter's number and she had downloaded an app that disabled her phone for hours at a time in order to keep from calling him herself. It had been a week-long high-wire act, balanced on a tightrope of buprenorphine, tilting to one side and then the other, and just barely managing to stay upright. "Never felt better. Can't believe I let it screw with me for so long."

"Here's what I want you to do: don't think of a pink giraffe."

"What are you talking about?"

The doctor appeared very serious. "Whatever you do, do not think of a pink giraffe."

"Okay, yes, got it."

"Do not think of its long pink legs, and that it's eating leaves from a pink tree. How's that going?"

"Fine, fine, I guess this isn't your first pink giraffe rodeo. Pink giraffes. Brown heroin. Purple fentanyl. I can't think of anything else."

"But you didn't use."

"Big deal. A whole week without sticking poison into my body. La-di-da."

"And what can help you get through the next week? It can help if there's something that you're working towards. Apart from abstinence."

"It's coming together," Claire said. She explained to the doctor that the date for the Punk Fugue Trio premiere was being finalized, that there was buzz. Jake hoped that a music streaming service would pick up the live show. "It's my chance. So much of my life has gone off track." And then, "When I'm telling you about this, it sounds so small. Compared to where I should be."

"Doing what matters to you is what matters."

"There may be a tour in the spring," she said, although as far as she knew, that just meant that Jake had a calendar and had written down some dates of existing music festivals, from whom he was hoping to wrangle invitations. "A tour means travel. I can't go to a pharmacy every day. So for sure, your drugs are really good—I will admit that—but by spring, I have to get off them."

"Haven't we . . . just seen that movie? We should be talking about you having take-home doses of medications," said Dr. Chen. "So that it works in your life."

"Okay . . . so if I needed, say, a month of medications to take with me this spring?"

"We can judge closer to—"

Surprising herself, she raised her voice. "I know what you're thinking. I'm in a rush and I need to slow down. But I can't have you *judge* closer to the time, whether you'll loosen my handcuffs." Claire put her head in her hands, her elbows on her knees. All week, she had been on the verge of tears, but there had been no one to cry with. "I came to you to feel better, and I do but I don't. I wanted to escape a trap, sure, one I made for myself, but this is just another one."

"Claire," he said gently.

"What should I do?" Now, sobbing.

"You're in a place where you can't do without the medication, and yet it's not helping you the way it can. You stayed off the junk this week, but I bet it took all the effort you had. And that's fragile. It could easily slip. Let's increase your dose."

She said, "Will that make me feel better?"

"More stable."

"There's that word again."

"Better comes and goes. I'm just being honest."

"Tighten the handcuffs?" she said, though now with sadness rather than anger. "Isn't there another way? I'm willing to be a guinea pig. I don't care if it's risky and experimental, but something that would set me free from this whole . . . mess?"

She saw him hesitate. He said, "Why don't we make a deal?"

"I'm wary of deals."

"Good policy."

"And?"

"Let's get you to the dose that you need. Where you feel normal without withdrawal. If you stop the street stuff, I will make sure you can take enough medication with you, when you go on tour."

"And . . . why would you do that?" she asked. In her experience with dealers, there was always a trade.

"For your music. I believe in it."

"So why don't you come to listen to me anymore?"

The doctor coughed, smiled uncomfortably. "I've been meaning to. Just busy. You mentioned some specials on the menu?"

"There's something else," she said, emboldened, "I don't have one of the little plastic lockboxes. But I have a violin case. It has a lock. Can you write a note to the pharmacy, that they should dispense the medications to me with my violin case?"

"Of course," said Dr. Chen, turning to his computer.

The following week, her doctor was at his usual spot in the restaurant, listening attentively. He was with a man who polished off three old-fashioneds before their main courses arrived. Claire played Sarasate's "Danza Espanola", and wondered if she should say hello. She didn't want to make him uncomfortable, and she was relieved that apart from listening to her more intently than most diners, Dr. Chen did not signal any connection. She was a bit annoyed, though, when, instead of putting cash in her violin case, he left a gift card for a grocery store.

The dose increase worked, which is to say that it did what it was supposed to do. It took away the withdrawal. In her practices for the trio, Claire knew she sounded a bit wooden, subdued. It's not that her fellow musicians criticized her playing, but the compliments were absent. In her violin case, safely stored, was the medication that she had taken unusual satisfaction in having dispensed.

11

THE RESTAURANT WAS one of Charlie's usual picks. Chen already knew that everything would be infused, sous vide, plated in fussy-small portions, impeccably wine-paired. Charlie had said nonchalantly, as if it were plausible, that there was no particular reason for the meal—couple of people from Omega just wanted to have a chance to connect—and added, *Chen buddy, why are you trying to slow everything down for Memorex?* Chen replied that the premise of the question was inaccurate—he was not trying to slow anything down, he was just trying his best to guide the sponsors. They might not fully appreciate the complexity of assessing the compound they had invested in, he pointed out; and what did they need Varitas for, if not guidance? The *potential* sponsors, Charlie had corrected him.

When Chen arrived at the restaurant, Charlie and a venture capital guy barely stopped laughing, each at the bottom of a cocktail. *Omega isn't taking all the ayahuagaine risk itself,* Charlie had previously explained to Chen. *They've brought in some money people.* The available seat at the table, on the banquette, was next to Bella, who sat with a glass of white wine before her, almost full, a faint lipstick smudge on the rim, politely amused at whatever the men found so hilarious.

When Chen approached, she slipped her phone into her bag, smiled warmly, as if they had kept in touch. Chen had hoped to hear from Bella, and thought he might. Their parting had been warm. But so what, really? It was the age of apps. She had decided, perhaps, to swipe left. Bella had been cc'd on some of the emails about the Memorex trial. She had his work email address. But she had not accepted his wordless invitation to connect on LinkedIn, nor his follow-up in corporate politesse—*good to chat at the conference*—*hope we collaborate soon.*

Despite the absence of contact, Bella was friendly and engaging now, and seeing this made Chen a bit more reserved. He sat stiffly next to her and Charlie leaned over, saying, "I brought your fan club," with a guileless smile that made it hard to tell if he was being complimentary, lascivious, or was simply on his second cocktail. It turned out tonight's restaurant was Bella's choice, Chen understood from the chatter. The other two men teased, how would she make it up to them if the restaurant disappointed? Chen saw how she managed a couple of comments in response, laughing a little more heartily than they did; then, when Charlie was about to step over a line, turned him away adroitly. He thought of her arched back, her pressed fingertips.

Things happened between people at conferences, Fitzgerald had said, during their dinner at the Dorado. A *hookup*—his old friend emphasized the word. *You've heard of it?* Was that the Moeran concerto? Chen tried to focus on the music. *Getting laid. That's just what you need, old buddy.* Of course, Chen had poked around on social media platforms. Bella's pages were not blank, but she was careful about what was publicly available. Her education was listed, but not much else. Her Facebook connections were hidden. Her LinkedIn profile was CV stuff—education, jobs, skills. No celebratory announcements, no virtue-signalling activism to give away her sources of vanity. Private school, Queen's business school, the usual for old-money kids, Fitzgerald had told Chen, the crowd who just had to get the ticket and then *who they knew* would take over. *I should know. Those are my people. Actually, it's who their parents know . . .* Bella was a corporate debt analyst, then broker, then a lateral move to pharma. She must have a good head for numbers, Chen concluded.

He could have sent Bella another email, but Chen had decided to let it go.

The good thing about being ghosted was that it made things clear. Well, sort-of ghosted, since they were both on some shared work email chains. Bella hadn't been obliged to reply to those; so far it was all preliminary, scientific wrangling. Chen certainly had to weigh in, and whatever Charlie's anxieties might be regarding not-yet-signed contracts, Chen wouldn't have been fulfilling his role without asking questions about previous trials—lab work, animal studies, chemical stability assessments, all of which he found skimpy. He was not being difficult, Chen had insisted. If asked—and not that anyone was asking—he would have said it had nothing to do with whether or not Bella was ghosting him.

Charlie spoke sympathetically about how it was always tough to get human trials off the ground, the money guy nodded and parried with how hard it was to keep investors happy. The waiter brought wine glasses, a bottle, and spoke in detail about the organic, bio-dynamic farming practices, the stony terroir from which this Sancerre was hand-picked.

"Bella really cares about this stuff," said the finance guy. "Everything at this restaurant will elevate your soul as well as your palate."

A few years earlier over a beer, when Charlie was a new hire straight out of his MBA, he had asked Chen and Fitzgerald why they had decided to sell the business they had started. Chen explained that it was about objectivity—to be able to reduce potential conflict of interest, *either real or perceived,* when it came to scientific guidance around trials. It freed them to be better at what they really loved doing, said Chen, which was science. *Absolutely, integrity,* Charlie had said. Fitzgerald had nodded seriously, murmuring his agreement. Afterwards, Fitzgerald laughed and said Chen's answer was perfect, and it sounded so much better than saying they wanted to cash out for serious coin.

Bella sat across from him as comfortably as if they had never met, or as if they were lovers and this was well known. Wherever they were in-between, it did not bother her. Chen had come across the money guy, who wore a well-tailored jacket and no tie, a few times. He had not retained his name. The money guy was not on the email chains, although his assistant was. Whenever he popped up at meetings he was casually unconcerned about issues that were vexing to everyone else, and when a discussion arrived at some technical impasse that Chen suspected the money guy did not understand, he would straighten up, take a big breath, pause, and then say something about *the big picture*, and *trajectory*. It was the effect this had on quelling the room without actually solving the problem, that Chen would not have admitted he envied. Now, Chen had met him too many times to ask for his name again. Slight tan, very even. Excellent posture, and taller than Bella. Her kind of guy? The waiter appeared wordlessly, extending the wine bottle to refill glasses with an outstretched arm. Bella gracefully shielded her glass, still only a few sips down.

"Of course, you're the go-to shop in a tight spot, the pinch hitters," said no-tie, turning to Chen. He mentioned a difficult trial for which Varitas was well known, one that had taken a novel seizure medication to Phase 3 trials at the FDA when everyone thought the compound was dead. "Dr. Chen, you were the principal investigator on that one, right?"

"It worked out okay."

"Modest. Some inspired thinking, I understand, to get it through."

"Isolating the problem. A bit of luck and creativity. It's the work we most enjoy."

"Approval review is under way for that molecule," Bella said.

"And the sponsor is happy," said Charlie. Another venture capital fund had seed-funded the molecule, and already sold their stake based on the go-ahead for Phase 3 trials. He added, "And hopefully it will become a new treatment option . . . Can you imagine how that could change someone's life? So amazing if we can help."

"Which is why our partners assure us that you are the right people to be taking this on," money guy said, glancing to Bella. "Memorex is something we care a great deal about. Because of what it could mean."

Chen made a point of not looking over, though he was aware of the slim tailoring of Bella's charcoal skirt, matching jacket, ivory blouse, her pearls. Did beautiful people assume their desirability? he wondered. He realized that he was now being complimented on something to do with his management of another trial, which as far as he was concerned was old news.

"That's what we do," said Chen. One could always say that.

Bella said, "Didn't Varitas develop a 3-D driving simulation to assess pharmacodynamics in-house?" She turned to Chen, and the way her hand grazed his leg was so light, so brief that it could have been unintentional. "It's the ability to think out of the box that stands out." The waiter came, and Charlie suggested the tasting menu, the everything approach. Bella adjusted the hem of her skirt.

The thing is, you need to get out more, Fitzgerald had advised him.

The money guy laughed. "You guys are an awesome science shop, but you know, I've played your driving simulation . . . You could use a video game developer. My fund happens to have a stake in one." He told a story about preparing to drive a sports car on a racetrack in Europe by using a simulator to learn the braking zones, the apexes—and the gaffes that he made on the actual course as a result.

Chen recognized the chatter from seeing Fitzgerald do it. The story was self-deprecating, funny, but you couldn't be the character in the story unless you were the kind of person who did certain things. Charlie replied with his own anecdote, to do with motorcycles. He and the money guy triangulated the geography of *who do you know, how did you get here, what can we both get out of this* with a liberal sprinkling of mutual praise. Before that two-person conversation became uncomfortably long, the venture-capitalist-amateur-race-driver turned to Chen:

"Dr. Chen. I'm so glad we have this chance to talk—just talk. I've heard you also run an addictions clinic. It's rare—a researcher who also takes care of patients. And really good care of patients, from what I have heard. Bench to bedside. Or the other way around? The main thing I want to ask you is, What do you need? How can we help you to move ahead with Memorex? I know you have questions. They come up in meetings. We can only get so much done in meetings."

Bella shook her head, saying, "The opioid crisis—such terrible loss. Families left behind."

"That's why I can barely get him into meetings, Matt," Charlie said. "He's always at the clinic. Chen is very committed to his patients."

Matt! His name was Matt.

"Let us share in your commitment," said Matt. "That's really what it comes down to with Memorex. We want to move the molecule forward, because it could help the patients you work with every day. I do this because it gives me a chance to make a difference. The thing I want to know from you: could Memorex be the answer for your patients?"

Chen recognized Matt's cadence, that of the well-worn premise, repeated to win the allegiance of the listener or to excuse oneself from something. It was a rhythm he had heard many times in clinic, sometimes in himself. Chen said, "It's complicated. I don't think there's a magic bullet to erase addiction."

"But perhaps an eraser of specific stuff . . . whether it's habits, inner demons, whatever drives someone's addiction. Would that be a helpful tool? Isn't that what Memorex could be?"

Chen sipped his wine. He wanted to ask Matt, who didn't seem like a bad guy really, and who began talking about the role of pharmacology in confronting "systemic bias," "trauma," "colonialism," about the futility of saying these things in fancy restaurants. Tut-tutting oppressive structures—who did that help? As if clicking an angry-face or a crying-face emoji on an outraged post, or adding a name to a petition calling for some kind of change, or popping a pill, was doing something to right the scales. Mostly, Chen thought, it just allowed someone to demonstrate that they *knew* how bad the world really was. Matt waxed poetic about the potential of private industry to provide tools that might alleviate suffering . . .

But yes, maybe for one person at a time, if some thought could be forgotten, lost, life might be easier. Chen tipped his glass up, polished it off. Looking around, Chen caught the eye of the waiter, who approached with the bottle of wine wrapped in a lovely, smooth white cloth, the neck of the green glass sweating onto linen. He shrugged and said, "It might help."

Matt said, "The media thinks it's simple—the opioid crisis is all the fault of pharma and the doctors. But I remember when everyone said that a doctor was a cruel, bad person if they didn't treat a patient's pain. Now, it's the evil doctors that got them hooked. But you doctors were trying to do the best for your patients."

This little bit of Matt's soliloquy, Chen thought, also had the cadence of prior use. Chen thought of Amanda, whose image he had recently added to his folder of photos. She had threatened that if Dr. Chen didn't double her dose of methadone, she would stop taking the medication. She pleaded, *Why bother, if it's not enough to stop the sickness?* He had tried to explain bioaccumulation. A hastily raised dose of methadone could creep up in the blood levels over the course of a few days until it stopped her breathing. *Whatever. You're sticking to the rules. Covering your ass. It won't be enough,* she said. *I'll just do what I have to do, to get what I have to get—you know it.* Chen felt guilty that he knew this was true, and also resented her thrusting it upon him. People walked out of the clinic, and beyond that the world was not his to control, he reminded himself. He had a line, which he used often, *My responsibility is practising good medicine. Your decisions remain your responsibility.* Another patient, looking for a place to turn a trick, found Amanda's half-clothed body in an apartment building's boiler room, bruises encircling the neck. Overdose, the coroner ruled.

Bella said, "Matt, Dr. Chen gave a remarkable presentation at the Innovations conference, a month or so ago. About how to talk to people, working through words, and the therapeutic relationship, to change habits and behaviours—alongside the use of medications." Her glance recalled that evening . . . admiration, and was there something else? That look was unrehearsed, he decided.

"Interesting," said Matt, "can words really change what people do?"

Chen thought of Nick, who had just gone back to his job—steady work, at least in autumn and winter, rustproofing cars with oil spray—*They always rust, don't they, doc? Makes you think,* he had said, offering Chen a coupon though the doctor had declined, since a bicycle can't be rustproofed. Every winter, the chain rusts. It was Nick's wife who called. She had thought everything was good. They were even making progress on the credit cards. Chen had also thought Nick was on solid ground, and maybe he was. Solid ground was subject to tremors. Nick got a bonus, it turned out, an unexpected thank-you for working hard in the busy rustproofing season. After months of clean time. Nick was the kind of guy who came to clinic and bragged about it all being over, a thing of the past. But he cashed the bonus cheque at a payday loan place instead of putting it into the joint account. He made a phone call, a number he had not used in a while.

"Do you think it's beyond just the drugs people use, sometimes?" Bella asked. "We know about physiology, of course, and that drugs change physiology. But beyond that?"

"Often it's beyond a specific drug. Many people get rid of one addiction, and find another. It's a kind of stuck-ness, a need to escape. From pain, from trauma, from feeling . . ."

"From life?" asked Bella.

"When substances are the only way someone has of coping, they can get stuck. So getting better has to be about learning new ways of thinking, doing. How do we help people get unstuck from molecules, even though we prescribe them?"

"I think I understand—you are trying to add that to the medications you prescribe, or maybe despite them," said Bella. "What if there was a medication that made your relationship with the patient, the words you use, more powerful, more effective? In the case reports, the way ayahuagaine was used in the alcoholics was not just that it was given to people and something magic happened. It was administered to those who lost their path by elders whom they knew and trusted, who helped guide them back towards a better path."

"This idea that it helped them to be receptive to—something like therapy . . ." said Chen, "Whitelight speculation."

Matt sat back. "Only one way to find out. Without proper studies . . ."

Bella asked, "Haven't there ever been patients who you really wanted to reach, but something didn't quite get through?" Her eyes, when fixed upon him, were remarkable.

Chen tasted the amuse bouche—a tiny sculpture composed of pickled shellfish with an acidic tinge, a slightly sweet note. He thought of Claire, what she had said of music—*a thing which breathes, which resonates even after the last note has faded . . . vibration through the air, and once it exists it is already gone*—but played in a certain way, he thought, the music changes what it touches. He said, "Sometimes, you see something great in someone. You feel sure that if a door could be opened, you could help. But part of therapy is lock-picking, and with this lock, the tumblers are always right on the verge of turning."

There was *foie léger*, the geese having been allowed to go about their lives until their livers were cut out. A chilled soup was served, garnished with shreds of seared, line-caught Arctic char, delicately sprinkled with finely chopped fresh herbs grown in the chef's own greenhouse, hovering on an artfully laid foam of free range goat's milk. With each course, the server came and discussed not only the ingredients and their preparation, but their provenance—the sustain-ability, the minimal footprint, sprinkling a kind of virtue to garnish and balance the richness of the meal.

A shift in the conversation, questions about recruiting. There had been some back and forth in the emails, a couple of teleconferences, but no final agreement on the inclusion criteria for the first trial that Varitas was being asked to run.

"The feeling at Omega," said Bella, "is that Varitas's general direction on the inclusion criteria makes perfect sense. We are entirely supportive, at least in terms of the thinking process. It's just the details, really, where we wished to clarify. The way it is written gives so little room for . . . investigator discretion."

"Omega just wants the doctor on the trial to be able to exercise some judgment," said Charlie, "which is what you always seem to favour, Chen."

"Judgment, yes, but there is a very specific population that we need in order to be able to perform meaningful assessments."

"But Chen, be reasonable," said Charlie. "Opioid-dependent, stably unstable, both short and long-term recall intact at baseline, and a *perfect* mini-mental score? I read that, and almost fell over.

I couldn't get a perfect mini-mental! Come on, you want addicts on the honour roll?"

"This trial is more complex than most. It's a difficult balance," said Chen. Inclusion criteria was always a delicate discussion. Tighter meant more difficult to recruit, and therefore more slow and expensive. Too loose meant it was harder to predict what would happen—unexpected variables might confound the results, making the trial results more open to critique of their validity. And the validity of Varitas's *brand*, Chen would remind Charlie, which extended beyond quarterly results. Chen raised technical issues with the inclusion criteria, revisiting concerns he had already expressed in emails and meetings. He found, however, his dining companions more receptive than he had assumed they would be. Maybe it was best to meet in person. Perhaps the wine helped. There were nods, suggestions of ways to implement what Chen wanted. Was he the one who had been difficult? Chen wondered. A steak arrived for each of them on a bed of greens, next to plump white asparagus. Bona fides were elaborated by the waiter regarding the unsurpassed treatment of the Wagyu cows, and the carbon offsets which had been purchased to negate all impact of their husbandry and the shipping of the freshly butchered flesh. The size of the portion was enough to be satisfying, and not so much as to overwhelm. A red wine appeared, sultry and deep, and yet did not cling to the palate. Chen swirled it, inhaled, and believed he could indeed appreciate the bouquet of violets that the waiter invited them all to notice. He had another sip, sliced the warm, pink steak, felt that perhaps he had misjudged Omega.

Midway through this course, Bella said, not as if she had been persuaded but as if she were setting the tone, "What we know is that Varitas is strong at recruiting. Dr. Chen, if you think these are the right criteria, we will absolutely use them . . . as the starting point. Details of course, a few . . . we might discuss?" She went on firmly,

"Matt, I had my doubts with the last Omega project, but Varitas's recruiters came through."

That was the multi-site trial, with very specific inclusion criteria that had come to a head over cold broccoli pizza. Vancouver, Chicago, and London only found a handful of eligible subjects. A minimum of six more were needed for the trial to have sufficient statistical power. Chen had put in a call to Fitzgerald—*Do you know anyone like this?* Fitzgerald had rounded them up in his house, fed them gyros and hydromorphone overnight, and then rented a van to bring them all at the same time to Varitas. Fitzgerald parked out back, promised each of the subjects a sixteen-milligram tablet on the spot if they passed screening and a "special grab-bag" to take home. He only shared the details of his recruiting strategy later, when the trial results were published. The understanding between Chen and Fitzgerald was that the former doctor did not do anything for recruitment that was beyond what he normally did anyways. So who could really say there was a confounding variable?

The next course came—morsels of braised guinea fowl in noodles. Did the waiter look at him when he said it was Asian-inspired? Chen wondered. In any case, it had elements that were surprising, and yet the overall effect was composed enough to be satisfying. Chen relaxed into the dish, thinking that if it were a Chinese meal, this would be the final carb-load comfort course, but the two delicate forkfuls of noodles were not up to it.

"Good enough for me," said Matt. "I'm not a science guy. We're coming to you. Trying to get to the starting line. Big picture, Dr. Chen . . . we just want to figure out how to move ahead with Memorex, hopefully it will help your patients."

Charlie had tried to get Omega to sign a memorandum of understanding while they sorted out the details of the efficacy trial, but as he had put it, Omega wanted to make sure the bases were loaded before stepping up to bat. Chen's view, which everyone kept saying they agreed with, was that this was a high-risk trial, and therefore should only include stably unstable patients. This made it about ten times harder to recruit, like catching lightning in a bottle. Everyone knew that. But with both long- and short-term components of memory testing within high–normal ranges? Chen insisted: How else could the results of cognitive and memory testing be meaningful? A hundred times harder to recruit, was Charlie's complaint. *In what universe will you find these people?* Omega's position was that they could accept Chen's inclusion criteria, with liberal room for investigator discretion built into the protocol, if Varitas swallowed cost overruns in recruiting. Charlie balked at that.

The basic development pathway that Chen had outlined, which would require multiple trials—and this opportunity was not lost on Charlie—would be to try to create new short-term, non-drug-using associated memories first, and see how ayahuagaine impacted these. Then, to move on to cognitive associations of drug use, and then finally to behaviours. Omega suggested merging some of these steps. Chen held firm; a methodical, stepwise approach was needed.

Still risky? Yes, hence the use of addicts, who had more to gain and less to lose. For the ethics submission, it went like this: *Facing an ever-increasing public health disaster . . . the need for new therapeutic options . . .*

"Sounds simple, of course, that if memory can be changed, behaviour can be changed. But memory is not like cell counts, or a hormone level," said Chen. He felt the wine saying, "What is the memory of a song? Without the words, does the melody remain? And what happens to the memory of the place where I first heard the song? There's a lot to figure out about how ayahuagaine might work, if it does. But I'm guessing that it's not so much that the memory disappears—it's something about how memories are perceived, and linked."

"It's not like you to guess," Charlie laughed.

"Sometimes it's all you have to start with," said Chen, sipping his wine.

Chen's and Bella's eyes met, briefly, and then the salad was served. The waiter stood by the side of the table relating a touching anecdote regarding the cultivation of the kale by a local youth outreach, and the provenance of the maple sumac vinaigrette. Chen nodded attentively, as if fascinated by the waiter's explanation, and Bella tapped at her phone. Chen wondered how much Omega stood to gain from a few decent publications on ayahuagaine. Maybe they didn't even need a full paper publication. Maybe a "clinical report" would be enough, or a poster presentation at a conference? Getting Memorex to market was years, and an unknown sum of money, away. Did the current investors actually want to carry this molecule all the way through, or did Matt already have a buyer, someone whose private equity fund parameters just required Memorex to be a little further along the pipeline? Bella slipped her phone into her purse.

Charlie sat back in his chair. "Matt, have you told Dr. Chen about your big-picture thinking on the potential market here?"

Claire had told Chen, *I'm stuck, you say, and I need to get unstuck . . . And where will I go once I get unstuck? Sometimes I just want a life transplant. Can you do that, doctor?*

"Big picture—help people forget their drugs, so that you can do what you want to do—with your talk therapy."

"Behavioural work."

"I get it," said Matt, with a ring of finality. "Methadone just takes away the jonesing, right? You want to help your patients live better lives. They are suffering, and if there's any way we can help you alleviate that, we absolutely must do it." There was a slightly unnatural emphasis on the *must*, thought Chen. "That's why we want you to show the world how Memorex can help your patients." Again, there was that leaning in on certain words, *the world*. "And doesn't everyone have something they want to forget? A painful thing they wish had never happened? What about the full range of medical problems that come out of what people remember? A guy who needs to lose weight, but loves baked goods? What if we help him to forget fudge brownies? Or performance issues? Star basketball player, can't make a three pointer, because he keeps thinking of the one he missed. Why not erase the memory? What if a medication could free all of those people of the knowledge that holds them back? And the beauty here—people are taking it already. The lizard juice."

"It might not be erasing, exactly," said Chen.

"Bottom line: this is an ancient practice," said Matt. "You'll find something we can use. To help your patients."

"Eating dirt can be as ancient as the pyramids, and that doesn't mean the FDA will approve it for a trial," said Chen. He noticed that his phone had buzzed—a short reminder buzz, a scold that he had missed an earlier notification.

"And of course," added Charlie, facing Chen, though it felt to the doctor that he was not the intended recipient of the comment, "that is why it's so important that the FDA hears it from someone they respect, a credible voice like yours."

"I have a risky patient population," said Chen to Matt. "You think there's a better chance this trial will get past an ethics review because you're trying the lizard juice on a bunch of addicts?"

"Dr. Chen," said Bella, moving her hand across the linen table-cloth, closer, "You wouldn't be here if you didn't believe this might help your patients. That this could matter."

Claire said that she wanted to get unstuck, but like a leg trap in the mind, something gripped her. So many patients had said the same: *Get rid of this, doctor, I want all of this to be done with, and I want to never use anything again.* Yanking on the limb just caused the trap to clamp down even tighter, he wanted to tell them. But no one wanted to hear him say: *Understand the mechanism of the trap, release it by moving towards it, ease it open, and walk away, but this is key: you must leave the trap sitting there in the woods. You must not cover it with leaves, or shove it into a shadow. Hiding it simply means that you might step in it again, unaware.* What did ayahuagaine do? Did it help by causing traps to vanish? Or by making them easier to see?

As desserts arrived—architectural confections in artful puddles of sauce, accompanied by port and the cheese cart—Charlie prompted Matt to tell him how Omega had come across Memorex. Chen knew this story, and was certain that Charlie did as well. But Chen recognized the conversational technique—encouraging people to talk so that they felt important. People who felt important were more agreeable. He fished out his phone, and saw that it was Bella who had texted him. She had written, from a few feet over to his right, *Sorry, I meant to be in touch. Lovely to see you.*

Everyone laughed, and Chen obliged with a smile as Matt continued to talk: " . . . they have a guy at Omega who just surfs the druggie forums—prospecting—and I guess he's really into this psychedelics thread. On Whitelight. Reads about ayahuagaine. Next thing you know, flew down there, went into the jungle, licked a lizard or whatever, and couldn't remember what colour of underwear he'd put on that morning and said he was reborn. I'm paraphrasing . . . So after getting sick as hell, he reads that a startup has already tweaked the molecule, taken out the seizures and diarrhea and whatever, so now he thinks Omega should buy those guys out . . . takes that to the board! You should have seen . . ."

Chen texted back to Bella, *Same.*

Bella glanced at her phone, smiled, tapped a reply. Chen felt his own device buzz within his pocket. She laughed at something that Matt said, which was intended to be funny, and now Chen felt more on the inside of things, felt that he knew that she was humouring her co-investor rather than pandering. He continued with the disassembly of his dessert, nibbled the aged cheddar, sipped his vintage port, savouring. Eventually, he looked at his phone. Bella's text, *A walk later?*

"Well, I think this is just great," said Charlie. "To have touched base like this. To have a connection. Don't you think, Chen?"

"Here's to a way forward," said Chen, raising his glass. He had not agreed to any changes in the inclusion, although he took their point about investigator discretion. Where that would be applied in the protocol was still important. Overall, Chen would later think, it was not so much that anything had changed over dinner, but it did sit a bit better. Perhaps, after all, he had been a bit rigid.

Leaning on the coat-check desk, one leg crossed over the other knee, Bella changed from heels that matched her dress into fur-lined winter boots that zipped up her calves. Her coat was forest green, long, a down-filled item that was as attractive on her as it was practical for the stark, cold night. Stepping out of the restaurant, her face appeared brighter in the street light, her smile emitting small halo puffs of breath. They passed the glass-fronts on the street. One window was streaked with wet darkness on the inside, condensation, it was a crowded watering hole—fans cheering a sports event on television, huddled up against the bar. Another framed a blaze of lottery tickets and chewing gum, a lonely attendant presiding, staring out. Behind the window of a mom-and-pop Syrian restaurant where Chen would have rather eaten than the place they'd just dined, the blue-orange light of small oil lamps warmed the middle circles of red-checked tablecloths. The snow was mostly plowed away from the concrete sidewalk slabs, but they were now in the part of winter when shining, icy berms abutted the curbs, and clumped upon the bases of trees. There were places where the sidewalk plows had veered around postboxes and hydrants, leaving little ridges to navigate. She slipped her forearm through the crook of his elbow, as if to steady herself, although she was sure-footed in her boots.

Bella stopped in front of a sleek, modern building, one that stood out from its neighbours both for its height and for the polish of the glass-and-steel adornment that thrust itself skyward from the old brick-faced street. She glanced into the lobby, back at Chen. They had arrived at an unannounced destination.

"Coming up?" Bella asked.

12

"EVERYTHING IN MY life has to change," Claire declared, tapping her fingertips on the chair in the doctor's office, jiggling her feet.

"Everything?" Dr. Chen asked.

"Now I'm clean. I have to stick to it. I'll do what you tell me to. *Doctor says . . .*"

"Because you want to? Does it relieve you of something, if you're just doing what I tell you to do?"

"I thought you would be pleased to hear it."

"What I have is a map with route suggestions, sample itineraries," he said. "You still get to choose where you go and how exactly you get there."

"Get to choose . . . You mean have to choose."

"There's no way around that."

"I screwed up, though. With my choices."

He tapped a few keystrokes on the computer. "Your urine sample looks okay?"

"I called my guy, and he didn't have any stuff," Claire shrugged. "But I still phoned. Asked. So I'm counting it as a screw-up." She did not explain that when she had called Scooter the previous evening, annoyed that he wasn't answering her texts after bragging that he had an amazing batch, another man picked up the phone. Said he was Scooter's father. *Can he call me later?* she asked, heart already thumping, but craving hard (and wanting to reward herself for her clean-time). *He's on life support, so he won't be able to call you,* said the man. *Oh. I'm sorry,* said Claire, and then a question that sounded stupid even when asked, *What happened?* The father's level-voiced seething gave way to something else, *Are you one of the low-lifes feeding his habit?* A pause. *I'm just a friend . . .* She wanted to hang up, but was paralyzed, and the father said, *I can see your texts—you're not his friend—you're one of his junkie customers—you paid for his overdose!* Claire heard herself reply, angry and feeble at the same time, *He's selling the stuff to me, mister!* Now, the father shouted, *And if it wasn't for low-lifes like you he wouldn't have money to buy more! He would have to get a job! Clean up! If he survives, he's going straight to rehab! Don't ever call this number again! And know this: if he dies you killed him.*

Dr. Chen said, "Maybe fortunate? But he'll have more soon. You still have to choose."

"My guy might be getting out of the business."

"That will be his choice to make. But now that your stability allows us to give you take-home doses . . . hopefully you have more choices? You've earned them."

"What did I earn?" Claire asked, "The carry doses or the choices? And if I earned something, is that like some kind of special reward? Now I need this medication in order to feel human, and I need the carries to live my life. Why should I have to *earn* something that I need?"

"Would you prefer a different word?"

"I don't know. I wish I knew."

Despite her grand statement that everything would change, her life was the same. Whenever Claire rode up the elevator of her building (if it was working), turned the key in the lock, she saw that the apartment was as it always was. She would kick her shoes into the corner where there was already a jumble of footwear, thinking, *Healthy people eat meals, and I am supposed to be getting healthy.* Within the fridge, naked fluorescent light illuminated a humming mausoleum for a bottle of barbecue sauce, an almost-empty tub of cream cheese, a half-eaten container of limp french fries, and a number of pickle slices slumped within a jar of fluid. An empty spot where the microwave had been before she sold it to score. Harder to sell a fridge.

Dr. Chen asked if Claire was interested in behavioural therapy. "Exercises for your brain. Sounds like gym class, I know. It's about ways of handling thoughts, feelings. Not getting rid of them, but dealing with them. Without drugs. Would you be interested in that?"

"Brainwash me? Fix my junkie ways?" she said, saw him pause. Although she corrected his language, he did not edit hers. Was he aware, she wondered, that she was enjoying this privilege?

The first time Dr. Chen tried to teach her how to be mindful in the moment without judgment, she instinctively closed her eyes, breathed deeply. He suggested keeping her eyes open, engaging her sight, her hearing, to focus her attention on what was around her. On what? *On whatever you find—it is about being present with yourself and your surroundings. When we close the eyes, there may be an attempt to escape. Or not—you may simply be closing your eyes. But right now, would it be okay to keep them open?* He smiled, and she kept her eyes open. It was like someone had left the lights on in the concert hall, and from the stage she could see the audience, could not pretend at invisibility.

Claire discovered that she liked talking with the doctor. It was not that he probed for dark, buried memories, or sifted out the deep structures of her unconsciousness. Things emerged anyways, the way objects that had been encased in crystalline, winter sleep appeared like bright lost treasures in a city park during the spring melt: a scarf, a ring of keys—also a soft clump of dog shit that would stink until dissolved by rain. So this was therapy, but sometimes it just felt like talking. She talked about music. An escape, he asked? No—she wouldn't say "escape." It had always felt like home. At first music had been a way to keep Claire and Molly busy when their parents were working late. Violin lessons were in the roster of after-school activities along with soccer and dance, the nanny driving them to one thing or another. They happened upon the violin in order to check off the music box, and because Josef was an old friend of the family. The friendship was not why he declared them talented—ribbons and prizes also decorated their musicality. Claire discovered that unlike some of the other children, she did not shy away from the depth of darkness that surrounded the stage. To raise the bow, to play, to know that her parents were in the audience and Josef was in the wings at stage left, but that she was both reassuringly alone and yet connected to all who heard her.

By the time Molly was in middle school with Claire about to start the following year, people in Toronto music circles thought Molly had *a shot at it.* Their mother was offered a promotion to the bank's head office in Boston. Molly complained—What about her friends? When this did not elicit sympathy, she changed tack. What about their violin teacher? And their chamber music ensemble? They were supposed to compete at provincials! Their school had a boarding option, and Boston was a short flight away. Without Molly's protest, Claire would have gone along as their father did—and as he did again a few years later, when the bank promoted their mother to a job in Hong Kong.

The violin, an instrument, was there whenever Claire picked it up—a reliable presence whose wood and strings always responded to her emotions. Any time she liked, Claire could pick it up and play, without having to think about time zone differences or whether her parents would be at work if she were to phone. The city youth orchestra was Josef's idea—natural enough for two young musicians, and, as he suggested to their parents, it would keep them busy. Out of trouble, he did not say. An audition was arranged, and Claire got a decent seat, Molly first desk.

Claire told the doctor of the fun parts—a youth orchestra exchange in Bangkok, a summer holiday with their parents skiing in New Zealand. "I mean sure, it's different when your parents are on the other side of the world. But Molly was always with me." Unless Molly snuck out of their room at night. And then Claire would be up, worrying where she was.

How long had it been, since she had really talked with someone? Just talked—without the need to get something from them? A fix, money. Or fend off something they wanted. Of course, she reminded herself, she needed to get prescriptions from the doctor. But somehow she almost forgot that when they talked. The listening felt real. That she was heard.

At least once per visit, exasperated, Claire burst out saying one of the following: that she had ruined her entire life, thrown everything away, fucked it all up for good. *And then, what happens next?* he would ask.

Dr. Chen asked Claire, "What do you dream of doing?" He asked such questions in the present, and leaning towards the future. Never in the past tense, which was where, she gradually saw, she had often protected her ambitions, by relegating them to the safety of loss.

"I dream of the music being more important than myself." Telling Dr. Chen about this desire, realizing that it was still there, made her excited in the telling, then fearful, then embarrassed, then vulnerable, then suspicious. "Why do you ask?"

"Why do you ask why I ask?" said the doctor, his expression curious.

"Is that like some therapy bullshit—where, if I question your question, you don't answer and you just turn it back around at me?" And then, after a moment of pause during which she wondered if a moment of pause was a therapy thing too, she said in a smaller voice, "Because you know, I asked you a question . . ."

"That's fair." He hesitated. "I ask because if you care about your dreams, then I care about them."

Claire nodded.

On the way drugs worked, on the way they became everything, some of what Dr. Chen said sounded like what someone who had never used drugs would say. But then some of what he understood surprised her. Even so, words that had seemed insightful when she sat with her doctor felt less so when she stared at her own apartment, faced her own fridge, where artifacts that should have nourished her had taken root, sprouted appendages.

In front of her open fridge door, Claire practised her mindful awareness, and also saved the moment. She saved up bits like this, moments in which she had been a good student, in order to later recount them to Dr. Chen. Like demonstrating a passage that she had practised.

Her visual sense engaged with the sharp, dark edges of the jar of barbecue sauce rimmed with brown-red crust, focused on the label with the chicken motif. *Notice. And if you judge, notice the judging.* She flipped the lid off the container of cream cheese, inhaled the sharp funk of spoiled dairy, noticed her own slight nausea. She remained present with the cold flicker and buzz of the fluorescent bulb in the fridge. Claire was attentive to the bilious colour of the fluid within which the pickle slices drifted when she lifted the jar, the bits of seed and spice that swirled alongside. This, she thought, was why Buddhists constructed beautiful gardens—so they wouldn't be mindfully contemplating mouldy condiments.

She flopped into the same beanbag chair into which she had melted into eternity via heroin, from which she had woken many mornings or afternoons into the slap of life—late to teach, late for a gig, text messages filling her home screen. It was an okay beanbag, cast off by a former classmate, a violinist who had moved to New York to become famous—and succeeded. Claire put her feet up on the same old curbside-find coffee table, and viciously kicked aside one of the milk crates that served as extra seating for guests since she had sold her Eames knock-offs for twenty bucks apiece. Guests! Ha!

Molly was back in touch. She had been sending images from Colorado—selfies in front of snow-dusted ridges and canyon vistas, and then a text: *a complicated story—I was sure this guy would be different—then I pick up the phone and of course it's the wife. Not quite so divorced. LOL!* All of this was familiar in rhythm, part of Molly's thing. Instagram posts of fluted glasses, meals that looked like cubist paintings, piers leading nowhere except into the sunset shot. Some details changed from one such ending to another. Movie producer guy who promised to get her a speaking role (later she laughed that she had never believed it), Dubai guy (going to London for the weekend, then he ghosted her), senior citizen guy who promised to buy her a condo (Molly didn't say exactly, but Claire guessed from Molly's uncharacteristic lack of ridicule that he had died), professor guy (book smart doesn't mean life smart, Molly explained), finance guy (so boring—could only talk about money, but he spent it and that was fun). Designer name-dropping—designer purses, Michelin-starred restaurants, Relais & Châteaux hotels in the Philippines, which Molly had assured Claire was the *next hot destination. And I'm going to blog about it. And my Instagram is taking off. And I just need to get the right producer for my YouTube channel—and promoter*—the concept was Molly playing her violin in random places—a mountaintop, on an airplane as the stewardess demanded that she sit down and fasten her belt for landing. Claire didn't get the appeal of it, was quietly dismayed by her sister's technique in the videos—knew she could play better, and there were few subscribers. *It just needs momentum*, Molly declared.

Claire remembered Josef murmuring from side-stage, after a recital when Claire was still a child in awe of her just-that-much-older sister:

What a talent. Molly had played Prokofiev's First Violin Concerto in D with such lucid vibrato and control of the swaggering, double-stop trilled sections of the Andantino that the audience could not help but forgive a few clumsy moments in the Scherzo and reward her with a standing ovation. Josef said, If only she would work like you do, Claire.

Now, instead of attending master classes, it was therapy. *Imagine your best future. Imagine the tiniest step that could take you in that direction. Now find an even smaller step.* The doctor somehow made this miniaturization of her life sound grounded and inspiring when they were together, but it, too, felt dispiriting when she was on her own. *Everyone around me is so much further ahead. How can I shrink my steps any more?* She could imagine Dr. Chen asking her, *Who do you need to catch up with?* when all she wanted to do was take a run, and a massive flying leap.

Each day, Claire got up, took out her violin, put rosin on her bow, adjusted the tension of the horsehair, slowly began to play her scales. She tried not to pull the bow. To let it flow. She tried to ignore the mess of her apartment. When she moved into this not-so-great but cheap apartment a couple of years ago, she told herself that with a coat of paint, and maybe if that orange carpet were pulled off . . . It had potential then, and the same potential now. At least she had cleaned up the used syringes, recycled the empty bottles. So that was progress.

When Claire was using heroin, everything had been divided into four- to six-hour chunks of time. It was like having a built-in stopwatch—she had to get fixed, then hopefully use the time it gave her, and then use again, each time resetting the watch. Efficiency was important. She needed to get something done in those short few hours, and be sure to have a pill or shot waiting. Sometimes, she would practise after doing a point. Or, sometimes the shot would disappoint and she would not feel well enough to play. Other times, the down would be amazing and Claire would just luxuriate in it, abandon practice, listen to music. Then there was the organizational issue, being sure to get enough that it would last through the next day at least. A week's supply was ideal. Of course, the hard part was making it last that long if it was sitting right there, beckoning. The medication she was on now, the buprenorphine, did not provide the same rhythm. While the heroin announced its arrival with a calm, joyful energy, and departed with sadness and dread, buprenorphine was just like the air. She had to simply believe that it was circulating in her blood-stream, although she felt nothing. That was the point, the doctor explained. The buprenorphine gave her all the time back, but the momentum to do something with each minute and hour was missing.

Without the countdown towards withdrawal following every shot of timelessness, stillness, peace in a needle, Claire was left with sec-onds, minutes, hours without urgency, an entire day of *blah* in which to properly examine the mess. Claire swung her bow away from the violin. It hung from her fingertips and curled thumb. Josef had always stressed that the heel of the bow must rest in the hand naturally, softly, the fingers draped. Claire wanted to seize it in her fist and smash it to splinters. Instead, she took a deep breath, and tried to notice.

13

ONE EVENING, CLAIRE ignored the doorbell that kept on ringing, probably a scam or an ex . . . then thought the neighbours would eventually complain. She heaved up out of the beanbag, peered through the peephole. There was Molly in the hallway, standing there as implacably as an assumption: that there was no need to ask if she was welcome or to announce her arrival, that water passed under the bridge, that sisters were always sisters, that time healed—and so there she was, ringing the doorbell again as if it were a musical instrument.

"I'm so happy to see you!" said Molly, her red hair in a bob-cut, slamming the door as she came in, dropping her suitcase and wrapping her arms around her sister. "No need to apologize, I wouldn't expect you to come to the airport for such a late flight."

"Oh, I didn't know . . ." said Claire. She said, "But anyways, I don't have a car or—"

"But we can't go out like this, can we?" Molly looked Claire up and down—not unkindly, but with an older-sister twinge of amusement. Claire wore an old T-shirt from a music workshop, the sleeves cut off for practising with free movement. Molly said, "My stuff will fit you. Now that you've lost some weight! Tell me how you did it!"

"Oh you know, just keeping busy." Actually, when she started on the medication, Claire filled out a bit, bounced back from skin and bones. She checked her phone. There was no text that Molly was coming, or that they were going out anywhere.

"I am just so glad to be here. I wish it wasn't going to be such a short visit. I brought you something, gorgeous! Homey touch here, as always," she said, glancing around the apartment.

"Where are you staying?"

Like all of her stories, this ended the same way. The specifics varied, this time with Rimowa luggage, a new Musafia violin case, a Louis Vuitton handbag, some dresses that still had the tags on them, a smattering of fancy cosmetics, and a half bottle of Moët, no doubt from a hotel fridge, all stuffed into the luggage, the detritus of a glamorous lifestyle, and from it, Molly extracted an incredibly soft, maroon V-necked sweater.

"Just for you!"

"Umm . . . that's nice."

"Alpaca," said Molly, "softest wool on earth. This is woven by monks. Or nuns. Yes, I'm sure it's nuns. Certified virgin nuns!" she laughed. "Either that or the ones fleeing their scandalous lovers."

"Thanks for the sweater. Where are you staying?"

"Oh, Claire," she said, "no need to be self-conscious. Your place is so cute. It'll be fun roughing it. I'm just on a flight stopover, anyways. Try this on." She reached into the suitcase again. She draped a chartreuse frock over Claire's front, admiring both the dress and her sister. She radiated the same guileless optimism as when she had once pressed a stolen ice-cream bar on her sister, whispering *Get rid of the wrapper when you're done*, the same impending hilarity as a few years later, when she persuaded Claire to cause a distraction while she poured vodka into the punch at a post-concert reception—just for kicks, *the adults at these things? all boozers, they'll thank us*, and the same kind irony with which she'd convinced Claire to come on double dates because she had promised some guy she'd bring someone for his friend—*just flirt, you don't have to do anything else; possibility is catnip for men—makes them crazy—they show off like little boys.* It was the candour of this grin that caused Claire to feel, more than think, *it's really not a big deal.* Whatever it was. Molly was never demanding—rather, she telegraphed to the object of her attention that she would go out of her way to win them over and, because she found them worthy of this effort, they should be grateful. Who could resist?

"It's just a tricky time," said Claire.

"Oh," said Molly, looking around, "you didn't tell me. Is he awesome? Is he hot? Don't worry at all, I won't cramp your style. I have some meetings booked anyways. I'll hardly be here."

"No, there's no guy."

"Not for long! Now that I'm here!" Molly glowed. "Speaking of which, we're late, let's see how this looks on you!" She selected a party dress for Claire.

"I've stopped the dope," said Claire, taking the cool fabric in her hand.

"So great!" Molly beamed, without missing a beat. "You mean heroin?" she said glibly, as if her sister had sworn off cauliflower. "Is cocaine alright? Not that I have any. You know, flying."

"Anyhow, all the down is fentanyl now."

"Oh sure, unless—" and then a lips-pressed smile, "so *great* that you stopped!"

"Didn't I tell you?"

"You're so right too, about stopping," she nodded rapidly, "if you can't keep it under control, then—"

"And it's been a lot of work."

"You do look like . . . you know, as if you've been working. So we should have some fun and celebrate!"

"How do you want to celebrate?" asked Claire suspiciously, but went to her bedroom to change. The short dress fit well and, she had to admit, complemented her.

When their parents went to Boston, Molly was the one who found a recipe for Lean, and whenever one of them caught a cold mixed up cough syrup and soda for all the boarding students in the dormitory. But Claire was the one who tucked a sports bottle of it between her bed and mattress. A few sips helped her to sleep so soundly. While Claire practised every day, scales then arpeggios, finally the repertoire, Molly would watch soap operas in the student lounge, and then pick up her violin the day before their youth ensemble rehearsal and learn her part in six non-stop hours. After a performance, Claire would revisit difficult passages and work them through until she perfected them, rewarding herself with a sip of the vodka that Molly had shoplifted. Molly never touched the repertoire again, and was already hanging with the percussionists, who smelled like pot when they came back from rehearsal breaks.

When Claire came out of the bedroom, Molly was not there. The bathroom door was closed, a minute of quiet.

"You okay?"

"Just my makeup!"—the reply confident.

Another minute. Molly swooped out of the bathroom. With admiration, she proffered an amber necklace to adorn her sister's neck. "Come on, let's go! We're late!" Molly had changed into a perfect black long-sleeve dress.

"But before we go—" said Claire.

"I'm not going to screw up your sobriety."

"Are you still? I mean—where are you at with . . ."

"Drugs? Take it or leave it. Like always."

"I can't have anything throw me off. You know, trigger me."

"Okay! Glad you said so. No triggers. Not even a BB gun." Molly made a little gun with her index finger and thumb, let the hammer fall. Her phone dinged—"Great! The car's here!"—and she was out the door.

By the time they reached the party, Claire was giggling from Molly's stories. At the party Molly's enthusiasm simply projected itself forward into the home of a professional basketball player to which she had somehow been invited; into a crowd of very tall men and very thin women, steaks on a charcoal grill being cross-cut and served on tiny plates with chimichurri, deep-fried morsels of lobster tails dripping garlic butter, tiny lamb chops with mint sauce. The house drink was a paper plane delicately assembled by a bald, muscular bartender; Molly knew a few of the girls there and within minutes was sharing whispers with them. Seated in the centre of a couch, sipping delicately from a champagne flute, was a woman who was older than most of those at the party, and she beckoned to Molly. Claire saw Molly's level of enthusiasm temper to careful friendliness as she leaned over and greeted the woman with two pecks.

"Beatrice," she said, "but everyone calls me Beauty."

Claire almost laughed, for up close the effort in Beauty's make-up was more obvious.

"I'm Molly's sister."

"The resemblance is obvious." She took Claire's hand between both of hers and murmured, "If you ever need anything." Claire thought she felt a tiny plastic bag that Beauty had flattened against her hand, and she quickly withdrew.

When they were out of earshot, Molly hissed, "I saw her do that. Total witch—avoid." Then she whispered, "But it means she thinks you're hot—wants you to work for her."

Some girls who knew Molly swept the sisters into the den, which was packed with dancers. Claire moved to a Daft Punk remix, and felt herself let go for the first time in months. She had another shot of sambuca, and realized that one of Jake's beats had come out of "Get Lucky." Middle-aged men with elegant watches and clumsy dance moves openly eyed what they wanted, and Claire avoided contact while Molly toyed with their hopes. Molly's energy flagged ever so slightly, and she downed a glass of champagne. She maintained her high spirits through more dancing, teasing, and the delicate task of departure, disentangling a guy's hand from Claire's waist, another's lips from her own neck.

Back at Claire's place, Molly asked hopefully, "Did you have fun?"

"I did," said Claire. "I needed to get out."

"I could tell."

"It's been . . . a bit of a time."

"That's why I came!"

There was still the mattress from the last time Molly had crashed with Claire, and they rigged up the old bedsheets again as a little sleeping tent in the living room.

Every day—sometimes for lunch, sometimes for dinner—Molly went out dressed like a fashion model, said she was networking, which Claire took to be Molly-speak for "finding a new sugar daddy." Molly never really said anything about extending her "flight stopover" as days became a week. She brought home bouquets of flowers, boxes of delicious French truffles, a pair of earrings from Birks, which she said she had chosen for Claire although the box was unwrapped. Her violin sat untouched in the corner.

One afternoon, Molly did Pilates while Claire practised.

"What's that weird music?" she asked, from a side plank position.

"My trio? Punk Fugue? The premiere? I told you the date . . ."

"Yes, I remember. Of course. It's the main reason I came back—to hear you!"

"If you want to practise, I'll be going out soon," Claire rolled her eyes, "to see my doctor." Claire spoke as if it were a chore, although she had begun to look forward to talking to him. She said nothing of the medication she was taking.

"For sure. While you're out."

Claire told Dr. Chen casually that Molly sometimes did a line of cocaine, but never in front of Claire, both of them pretending that Claire didn't know. The doctor was concerned. Claire assured him that she was not triggered. Coke wasn't her thing, anyways. And relapsing? *It's not even a possibility*, she told him. *Except it always is, Claire*, he said, which annoyed her, mostly because it was true.

Claire helped Molly to take some new photos, Molly explaining that the arm-extended selfie was the ubiquitous cheap-call-girl pose. Not a good look. Some of the photos were glamour shots—perfect makeup, filtered on the phone. Others were straight-up innocent girl-next-door. Two profiles, Molly said, for two different sites. Claire offered to help Molly get a waitressing job at the Dorado, which was shrugged off.

When party invites came, Claire went with her sister if she felt like a change of scenery, perfected her technique for escaping men at the end of the evening. Molly went to a trio practice and sat quietly in the corner, afterwards expressing genuine admiration. And upon a fresh snowfall, she appeared with toboggans and cajoled Claire out to a nearby hill. She made hot chocolate with brandy to go out and see a planet at midnight—they had no idea what they were looking at, pointing and guessing, but it was a beautiful, dark night punctured by the light of stars.

Looking for a tampon one day, Claire came across it in Molly's toiletry case. The white cocaine powder in a little plastic bag did not surprise her. Next to it, a dainty glass tube, tucked into a box that had previously contained sanitary products. But there were also pills familiar to Claire, and a crusher, swabs, filters, syringes, needles, nice and tidy—the works. She reached for them reflexively, and stopped. Was Molly truly able to pace herself carefully enough that she didn't become dependent and get the withdraws? She had tried to be discreet. And in her own defense, Claire told herself, she had only been looking for a tampon. Beneath the works, another plastic bag, some crumbly brown powder. Claire's heart thumped and her vision tunnelled. Could it be? Did her sister have a heroin connect? Claire had assumed that no one had heroin anymore. She could hear Molly saying that everything depended on who you knew. *Put it back. Close the box. Don't even taste it*, Claire commanded herself. *Just a tiny crumb . . . just to know if it is?* She was liquid inside. Wiped the sweat from her brow. Her back tightened. Didn't open the bag, but knew anyways. Knowing, just knowing was enough to bring a brief flash of sickness.

Claire did not bring up the stash, but one day, over a kale, clementine, and roasted almond salad that the sisters had made for lunch, she drifted the conversation in that direction. The distinction between recreational and dependent users, Molly claimed, with a casual authority that Claire found both annoying and enticing—like YouTubers with their "three easy secrets" on how to lose fat without cardio—was between want and need. You just had to recognize the difference in yourself. Want was okay, Molly expounded. She said yes to whatever she wanted. If what she felt was need, she said no. That way, she was still in charge. Claire had a faint memory of the way it had once been for herself, tried to map this to her recollection.

Once a week, was what some of the Whitelighters advised, if you wanted to be a recreational user. *Once a week, and then if you feel yourself getting sick, back off for a while. Once you get dependent, the withdraws come harder and faster, so don't go down that wormhole.* That sounded easy enough. And a later post: *The recreational user is like the sasquatch, everyone knows he's out there . . .*

The point of "recreational" was not needing to use, but being able to use. Of course, Claire had tried that, made all those tiny promises, *Just one pill, just one point, once a week, once a day, once an hour.* But maybe now with the buprenorphine on board, it would be different? And honestly, she had been pretty stale recently at the Dorado. Not that she really cared about the Dorado but still . . . Her playing had been both stale and pain-ridden, and she had a real performance coming up with the trio.

Stop it, Claire told herself, *you've fallen down that little trap door so many times. Why are you even reading that old Whitelight thread?* But she kept going back, poking around the site, clicking here and there, until she saw a five-page thread with the title: "Tips and tricks—chipping on top of bupe?"

She clicked to the first page, and began to read.

To a student of medicine,

The domain, my dear friend, where you will discover that your
training has been most inadequate is that of holding yourself to
the middle ground. It is assumed that your work as a physician must
stand upon some kind of stable centre: science, professionalism,
humanism. This is the subtext of your physiology textbooks, with
their tidy line drawings of organs (which are in real life bloody
squirms of flesh), your professional codes with bullet points in neat,
shaded boxes, your ethics textbooks written in third person. Your
training, your foundational texts, assume that it is sufficient to
point out this supposed middle ground, which you shall naturally
occupy. Simple. But humans are instinctive rather than scientific,
act from impulse rather than professionalism, are ruled by the
ultimate expressions of subjectivity—anger, longing. Try to
suppress these completely, and you will be imitating an algorithm,
a robot, an app. People still wish to explain their problems to
a person, a mortal like themselves. Doesn't everyone crave the
human touch? That can be complicated.

    Consider anger, a patient's flames igniting your combustible
material. Your de-escalation training emphasizes calmness of voice,

and that you should reflect a patient's concerns. "What I hear you telling me is . . ." Your safety training directs your eye to the nearest exit from the room. Your medico-legal seminars emphasize the required documentation after the fact, to protect yourself from the fallout of unconstrained emotions. So, fine, you know the procedures with which to handle anger. But are you taught about diagnostic usefulness, how the observation of anger can help you to formulate the case? Try this: use anger as a filter, a coloured glass. You may be peering through both yours and the patient's, both of these layers distorting the image and yet important in determining meaning. Gaze through the red pane of indignation, to see what burns hot. Add the sickly blue of blame, and you find an enticing purple. Slide a piece of yellow glass—a threat—behind it, and a quizzical brown begins to emerge. Take green glass, the bottle-green glow of injustice churning like the sea, and line it up. It's getting dark, isn't it, looking through this kaleidoscope? All of these panes can be added until you get to black, the most solid colour. Technically, not a colour but a shade. Fury crowds out consideration of other nuance. What is the function of this? With all anger, ask if it permits escape, evasion, the blacking-out of some feeling that is yet more painful.

Anger is simple, in comparison to longing. Within the mist-like uncertainty of longing, we fold hope, desire, wishing, wondering what has happened to the person who has disappeared. This range of feelings fluctuates like the weather, comprising high- and low-pressure zones, seasonal variations, and daily temperature changes. As the backdrop to longing, you may remember the mild wind of shared goals between doctor and patient, blown by success and mutual appreciation, which promised that all would unfold easily. Perhaps you recall the sticky humidity when too much was expected, which happened on both sides and the still air was hard to breathe. With a damp shiver, there was the unexpected cold snap of a tiny slip, the low rolling thunder of sustained relapse, the funnel cloud of overdose, which made you want urgently to pull the patient in from the storm. Except they were dancing in the rain; shook you off, insisted they were just fine. Was there any way to disagree, and remain standing upon your middle ground?

What about frustration, the child of anger and longing? In your attempt to hold the patient somewhere near the centre (in case you have not intuited the subtext of the subtext of the textbooks, which is that you should guide the patient with you to this imagined middle), it will comfort you to remember that your frustration exists only with reference to an unrealized dream, this vision that you try to fly, kite-like, with the patient. The wind gusts, or dies, and the kite tumbles into the dirt, rips. Sometimes you patch it up and launch your paper-and-chopsticks contraption to the breeze. At other times, you learn the patient has already flown their own kite, which flies so high that the patient can barely see it—and your contribution is to help hold on to the string. You can be forgiven the mistake of thinking that your patient's dreams are yours, or that yours are what your patient wants. Although both suppositions are gambles, follies, you should commit them from time to time, if you wish to do more than prescribe. Which fancies? Which hopes? That is hard to find in a textbook.

You are—on the surface of it—paid to assess patients, diagnose conditions, and prescribe treatments, but your actual work is to peer through anger and frustration in order to nurture dreams. If you care, you risk yourself, and every patient wants their doctor to care.

Is that also the work of the teacher, dear friend? "Friend" is the best term, so versatile. Was any of what I taught you true? Or if not true, at least useful? A place to start?

There is another thing for you to learn—I am not sure if I mentioned this. When you don't know if someone is doing well, whether their life is unfolding as they had hoped, it can be disorienting. Perhaps everything is as good as it can be, but without knowing you feel a sense of loss.

Are you well? That's what I want to know. Mostly.

Why have I used so much metaphor in this letter—is it to illustrate or to conceal? And what does it say about me—that equal to my desire to know if your kite is held aloft in a steady and kind wind, I want you to know that I have asked?

Yours as always,
Dr. Chen

14

IT WAS A STEADY mid-winter morning in the clinic. Long-time stable patients of Chen's rushed in from the cold, the doctor visit a morning errand on their way to jobs on construction sites, in offices, bakeries. He asked about their work, partners, pets, alert to life's shaky guardrails. The unstable patients flitted in and out, appeared on his digital queue, but were often absent when he looked for them in the waiting room. They had told Pamela they were going out for a walk—which might mean they had gone to score drugs instead of waiting for medication, or there was a nearby free meal, or they were avoiding someone to whom they owed money, or that they had simply gone for a walk. Winter was old and settled, and it seeped into the clinic via the grey porridge of slush tracked by boots onto floors, in the white salt spiderwebs on pant cuffs, in the holes in mittens, and in the complexions that were both faded from long nights and reddened by weeks of cold.

"Taking your sweet time, huh, doc?" shouted Walter as Chen called another patient, Alison, from the waiting room. She walked briskly into the office ahead of the doctor, tossing her hair as if to shake off all the world's scumbags. Walter's legs were spread wide, and he leaned forward, hands gripped over a cane with a silver lion for a handle—"Haven't got all day!" He turned to Brandon, who sat next to him, and said, "Problem is all the fuckin people who shouldn't be here, right? Who are fuckin stealing everything that's rightfully ours." The young man, whom Walter must have assumed would share his perspective as he did his pale skin, appeared uncomfortable, but nodded at Walter's loud *sotto voce*.

Walter grunted. "Hurry up, doc," without looking over. "Fuckin Chink."

As Chen passed her locked Plexiglass cubicle, Pamela said, "You should discharge him." She sipped her tea. "Don't we have a policy?"

Chen scanned the waiting room. "If there were Asian people in the waiting room . . ."

"Oh, like . . . you?"

"Probably off his meds. Or intoxicated. Maybe both," said Chen. "Or in withdrawal," he added, trying to sound like a medical diagnostician rather than a target of offhand racism.

She shrugged. "You have any drug trials for jerks, with a high risk of them becoming mute?"

"Call the pharmacy, see if he's getting his antipsychotic. Maybe they can send it over."

"Take your sweet fucking time!" yelled Walter. "I got all the time in the world for my favourite Chink!"

Pamela shrugged. "If he called me a cunt, he'd be out on his sorry ass."

Chen felt himself redden, and he stopped. "Of course."

"And?"

"If any women come in, and Walter is still here, tell them they can wait in the kitchen." Claire usually came in the morning. Her script was up.

"So that's the solution? The women need to hide?" said Pamela, crossing her arms. Then she grinned. "Just making it harder for you!"

Alison perched on the edge of the patient's chair as Chen walked in. "So, how's it look?" She glanced towards the computer screen.

"Sorry. I know that guy in the waiting room can be—"

"Whatever, doc, I'm a big girl. How's it look?"

"How should it look?" said Chen, turning to the screen, clicking to the urine results.

"Pretty good, I'm hoping." She peered over.

"Umm . . . I'm seeing cocaine, and some hydromorph?"

Alison looked deflated but not surprised. "So little. The tiniest bump. Can't you see on that test, how little?"

"It only shows whether a substance is present or absent."

"And the dilly—shouldn't it be a plus? Better than the fentanyl?"

"Some say."

"No carry, I guess? I really need one this week."

"I should see the clear sample, but what do you need the carry for?"

"A night at my parents' cabin—snowshoeing and a bonfire."

"Sounds good. I'll write for an exceptional carry."

Chen pulled up Walter's chart, confirmed that he should have had remaining doses of methadone. Two reasons that Walter boiled up above his usual simmer were a lack of antipsychotics and a lack of methadone. The oblong brown bottles of orange-flavored narcotic were somehow lost, stolen, spilled, far more often than his thyroid pills, insulin vials, and blood pressure medications.

Chen called out to Pamela to send Walter in.

"So you had something stolen . . . are you talking about your carries by any chance?"

"Whadya going to do for me?"

"They could kill someone, Walter, a person who doesn't have tolerance."

"Yeah yeah, I know, loaded gun blah blah. You gave 'em to me, so you're on the hook too. Only reason you care. Why are you looking at me like that, doc?" An upsweep in the phrase.

"Like what?"

"Your little Buddha look, floating on some fuckin cloud. Like that." Menace in the low drop of the second word. "They're gone. Stolen. So I need more."

"Once they're dispensed to you—"

"Sto—len! How's that my fault?"

"—they're your responsibility."

"So if I put my bag down for one second on the subway, then turn around, and then my bag is gone, that's somehow my fault? And you think it's just my methadone that's gone? Least of my concerns. I had other things in there. Valuable things. My stuff, doc. So I'm not in the mood! Write me a new script!"

Chen sighed. "We could replace your doses—as witnessed doses. But no more carries."

"You gonna do me like that?"

"As you know, missing carries are—"

"That's how you gonna do me?"

"—a serious matter, a safety matter—"

"Do your job."

"—we're going to make sure you get your medications—"

"Do. Your. Job."

"—but carries would no longer be considered appropriate, I'm afraid." Chen was aware of this tendency in himself. The more annoyed he was with someone, and the harder he worked to mask that, the more formal his language became.

"I'll make you afraid! If you don't do your job!"

"Walter," said Chen, "this is my job. To take care of you while considering safety. I'll replace the doses. Witnessed."

"What? Fuck that, go to the pharmacy every day? I earned those carries, Doc, I want those carries! In! My! Hand!" His voice rose. "How's it my fault? I got jumped for them!"

"I thought you put them down."

"What?"

"The carries in your bag? The subway?"

"Well, yeah, I put them down to fight off these guys. Black guys. But they don't know what I know—" Walter stood, demonstrated his fighting stance, his dexterity with fists and cane— "Taught them a lesson. But they got the bag."

"Walter, has anything else been bothering you?"

"Oh, don't start."

"I'm just wondering, you know, if anything else has changed. You seem . . . upset."

"Okay Doc, okay, here you go now, you're doing that thing you do . . . you think you're Svengali or something. Isn't this when you ask me if I'm hearing voices, and all that bullshit?"

Chen fixed Walter's eyes with his. "Did you stop taking your antipsychotics?"

"You're not my psychiatrist!"

"Because I could bridge a prescription while we get in touch with your psychiatrist."

"Oh right, you don't want to give me my methadone but you want me to take my shrink pills! I see now. Did he call you? I asked him. What shrinks in a shrink? He didn't like that."

"Walter, I'm trying to help. You need your medications. All of them. You seem upset."

"Why do you keep on saying that?"

"What?"

"About me seeming upset." His position on the chair was like a man on a motorcycle, heels up, balls of the feet light, gripping his cane horizontally in front of himself instead of handlebars.

"Or are you getting into the crystal meth again?"

"Who fuckin cares?" Walter stood. "You're keeping me hooked, and it's time I got off. I'm getting off the fuckin junkie juice." He stalked to the door. "I'm glad they got stolen! That ain't nothing when I got my country stolen! Whose? Mine! Stolen from us white people! That's the way it is! No! Doc! I'm gonna say what's what." One hand rested atop his cane, tap-tapping the end of it on the laminate wood floor, whose veneer had begun to peel. "You know that story everyone tells, about how the Nazis invented methadone? Garbage! The Jews invented it! What better way to control the world?"

"You know, it's a treatment for your condition, just like the antipsy—"

"The kikes. But now they make it in India. That's right, the Pakis make my loony pills and my meth! Do you know who India shares a border with? That's right, China. You think that's a coincidence?"

"Walter, *Paki* is an inappropriate slur, but I believe it refers to—"

"China's where you're from, all comes together doesn't it?"

"Walter, we actually have an anti-racism policy in this clinic," said Chen, feeling more at ease now that he was defending Blacks and Jews and Indians and Pakistanis alongside Chinks.

"And they probably courier it direct. From China to you."

"Your methadone helps keep you safe. But it needs to be kept safe. I'll make your prescription. All doses at the pharmacy."

"Wanna know why I'm not safe? Because I'm being fucked over every day by you people! Right here! My country! You think I'm crazy? I'll tell you what's crazy—we bring refugees! Afghanistan! Syria! We give 'em housing! Let's give some towel-head from Fuckmeistan a big new condo. What the fuck? This is supposed to be a white country!" He took a breath, seemed to catch himself, continued with a tone of forbearance, "I think you're a great doctor. Don't get me wrong—I like you. As a person. But don't say I'm racist. I'm not against any race. Just certain cultures."

The prescription emerged from the printer, and Chen signed it. "Here you go. No carries."

"No carries! Fuck you! That's my freedom we're talking! You're always telling me to be open with my thoughts and feelings. Right, just like mister Buddha sitting right there, la-di-da. Tappity-tap on his little keyboard. Well, fuck you! I've had enough of your handcuffs!" He slammed the door behind him, without taking a prescription.

After Chen sat to complete the clinical note, Pamela poked her head into the room.

"Having fun yet?" she asked. "That felt long even to me. And I wasn't in here. The day is young!"

"You're telling me."

Chen glanced at his screen. Claire had not checked in.

A few patients later, Chen called Valerie, who crumpled after sitting down, her shoulders heaving, and only after accepting a tissue managed to say that her beloved Shih Tzu Tommy had died.

"I'm so deeply sorry," said Chen.

"It's somehow painful today—that the weather is so nice. He loved to walk when it was sunny—I could see the spring in his step," she said.

"I can only imagine the loss."

"I do have one small favour to ask."

"What is that?"

"You see, doctor, in the last few days, Tommy was suffering so much, and I couldn't afford to put him down. So you see, I naturally thought of my methadone carry . . . and I knew you would understand if I helped him . . . He was in so much pain. Which leaves me one day short."

Next up, Brandon, who shrugged when Chen apologized for him having to listen to Walter. Chen recalled his look of sheepishness, from another time. After crossing paths at Fitzgerald's house, and Chen asking him about it when he was not high, Brandon had the same expression. He admitted that he had figured out how to time his use and his testing so that he appeared clean. Chen had tightened up the urine-testing schedule, dialed down the carries, asked Brandon what he wanted to write in the story of his life, and he stopped using. All of it—oxycodone, hydromorphone as well as fentanyl. For once, as far as the doctor could tell, things had turned out as they should. Brandon was now determined to finish his college diploma—"Not that they teach you anything useful, Doc." He wanted to get his driving licence reinstated, and lease a car—at least a Civic, or maybe even a Camaro—his parents had promised to co-sign—and then he'd be cruising and going out with girls, "like *normal* girls, doc, *nice* girls, *clean* girls, from my church, not like these *druggie* girls. Because you *know* doc, I'm not like the other people here." All of this he rattled off like a catechism. "So have I been clean long enough? Can you fill in this form?" Chen filled in his Ministry of Transportation attestation, that he had been free of illicit substances for six months, although it had been slightly less than that. Was that the right message of solidarity, that they were on the same team, that the doctor was flexible? Or the wrong message, that rules could be bent?

Chen called Ashley, who did her friends' hair and took their Backpage photos in Airbnbs that they rented by the week for in-calls. She was proud of her photography. "See doc, they're ironic. Because irony is sexy." She told him about a gallery show that was about to happen, had been about to happen for a while now.

"When are we going to work on carries?" Chen asked. "Still cocaine, huh?"

"It's just, you know, if a guy wants to do a line you can't say no . . . because it will like damage his fragile male ego or something—but I explained to you how I pretend, right?" Ashley had previously demonstrated how she put her hand on the line of powdered drugs while pretending to snort it and then brushed it off. "I don't even want to be fucked up when I'm working. Dangerous. You would think I could get some carries."

Did he believe that she brushed the drugs off her hand? Did it matter? "Rules," said Chen.

He had given Ashley an old Nikon a few months previous, far better for photography than her iPhone, and it was true that these days they weren't worth much even a couple of generations old. It would be a trade, he said, for a print. Shortly afterwards, another patient had tried to sell Chen the Nikon for twenty bucks, the price of a point of down, or a decent-sized rock of crack. Although Chen wanted the camera back, he made it a rule to not buy stuff from patients. Neither Chen nor Ashley mentioned the print or the camera again. That day, as always, he made her another prescription with no carries, and promised, when she insisted, that he would attend her gallery show when it opened. She said, "Because for sure it's happening soon."

As the afternoon drew to a close, Claire had not appeared. It was not the first appointment she had missed. The previous week she had called and said that her Punk Fugue Trio had scheduled an extra practice. Last-minute, super-important to be ready for their premiere. Could the doctor just extend the prescription? Now, again, the end of the day, a phone call into the clinic, *I'm so sorry to ask you again* . . . A pause during which he felt certain that if he asked her to tell him the truth, she would. But was that what he wanted? He agreed to the prescription extension, knowing that there were at least two possible meanings: that she had relapsed and did not want to reveal the drugs in her urine, or that what she said was true—her ensemble had a last-minute practice. He knew which possibility he wished to be true, and buprenorphine was less dangerous than methadone. He extended the prescription for a week, without reducing the carries.

15

SOMETIMES, MOLLY OFFERED to do things around the apartment. She could be a thoughtful house guest, and when she did things like cleaning up, cooking, it was always with a special touch. Cut flowers in a jam jar. New soaps in the bathroom. She made spaghetti one night, with fresh pasta from a place that made it daily. The red wine was a bottle that a "friend" had given her. His vineyard, supposedly, and Molly laughed that the sausages in the sauce were his pigs. After dinner, a heritage strain of marijuana, fragrant and earthy, which was much better than what Claire usually picked up. Molly had her own "guy," Danny, whom Claire saw at a distance a couple of times when Molly connected with him in a parking lot. Why did Molly want Claire to wait for her on the other side of the street? Probably because then she was too far to see what, exactly, Danny handed over, as if it were still a big secret. Danny had a not-quite-new Lexus—tan with scuffed bumpers, discreetly forgettable, and Molly described him as *a gardener for a few friends of mine. Knows his bud.* The sisters passed the fat joint back and forth.

Molly giggled, "Oops, I'm going to get you in trouble. With your pee test."

"Dr. Chen doesn't care about marijuana."

"Oh really? You said he was such a careful doctor."

Claire remembered saying that he was caring, but he also did seem careful. Had that come through? "He said that to bother his patients about pot would be like giving speeding tickets while murders were being committed."

"He's prevented lots of murders recently?"

Slowly releasing her burned-flower cloud, Claire said, "He's not a bad guy. He's helping me."

"Well, that *is* his job," said Molly offhandedly. "I mean, you do understand he gets paid to write prescriptions. So he's like a dealer. Basically."

Claire took another puff, held it in, passed it to her sister. Though she had once said similar things, she had stopped thinking of her doctor as a dealer. One of the differences was that he was there, consistently, during his clinic hours. No need to text, set up a meet. It was also a consistency of seeming both curious and as if he had seen all of this before. His advice was rarely stated, usually pulled from her whether she was vexed about a development with the trio, or frustrated with the pain in her shoulder and wishing she could just get high. She wanted to say to Molly, *And I get paid to play music. But it doesn't mean the music doesn't matter to me.* Instead, she just shrugged. "He acts like he actually cares."

"So how long do you have to do them?"

"What?"

"The pills he has you on—this caring doctor."

"As long as I want to. As long as it's helping me."

"I see—as long as *you* want? Is that what he says?"

"I don't know, exactly, but I'm trying to sort stuff out. The trio is taking off. Did I tell you the premiere is going to be broadcast on CBC? I can't believe Jake scored that. And I have to get my life back. I'm just afraid of . . . So the medication is like a platform I'm standing on, something stable while I try to work on myself." Claire realized she was using Dr. Chen's metaphor—and she took the joint back. Had a drag.

"So the trio is sounding good?"

"I'm trying my hardest. Jake's a nice guy, but he's a composer. You know what they're like. Wants every bar to sound . . . the way he imagines it. But better."

"I've heard you practising. It sounds . . . just fine."

That was the word Molly used most often when they were kids, in appraising her little sister's playing. *Fine* bounced around in Claire's head. "There are very technical passages."

"But they don't quite come across unless they can be loose, and free," said Molly, as if this were not only obvious but easily achieved.

"Really, so that's what you think?"

"It sounds fine."

Claire rubbed her shoulder, the muscles in her back which always ached. The deeper joint pain—there was only one way of getting to it. When she had started the buprenorphine, it had helped diminish the shoulder pain, but did not take it away. Dr. Chen had warned that the pain relief would probably fade—and it had. Beyond the physical pain, there was something else. A caution, a hesitation, especially when it mattered. Claire often thought, when Jake made a suggestion during rehearsals, or even as she practised alone, that she could not be the musician that she had the potential to be, unless she was free. Unless she was good, meaning *good*, she would always be *just fine*.

"And how about you?"

"Me?" asked Molly.

"I would love to hear your interpretation." This gave Claire a little satisfaction, evening out the *fine*. "If you wanted to play through my part—show me how you would handle some of the passages?"

"Oh, Claire, how long has it been for me? I'm over that phase. But I was always just fooling around with the fiddle, you know?"

"You were the gifted one." *Phase* now took the place of *fine*, Claire thought. She said, "According to Josef."

"Josef?" Molly laughed. "What did Josef know about anything?"

What did Josef know? was something that Claire had often wondered. Though he wasn't their guardian, their parents *had* asked him to keep an eye on the girls. This was informal; the boarding school made sure they had everything they needed and kept an eye on them, as they did with all boarders, with roll calls and curfews. Josef and his wife sometimes had the sisters over for dinner after their lessons, and he would ask them with a mock-scolding look—sipping a glass of sherry—*Anything I need to tell your parents, for the weekly report? Boys giving you any trouble?* There was never anything, at least nothing that Claire or Molly told Josef about. They imagined he told their parents they were practising, were studying, or sometimes that they had won a prize, or missed a prize.

"I could probably get you a night here and there—playing at the Dorado. To raise the—"

"Dinner music? Like I said, I'm over that phase."

Claire said, "Rent is coming up."

"Oh, right."

"And you said . . ."

"Yes, of course, I haven't forgotten," said Molly, beginning to clear the dishes. "I'll chip in for sure."

A few days later, late one afternoon, Claire found there was no coffee on the shelf where she expected it to be. She banged around in the cabinet to try to find some. From inside the bedsheet tent, where she had been asleep, Molly asked Claire in a cranky sleep-mumble to be quiet. Molly had been out late every night since their spaghetti dinner, sleeping through most of the day. Nothing more had been said of her promise to contribute to rent. Claire said in an icy hiss that when people used up the coffee, it was polite to buy more coffee, because this wasn't a hotel.

Claire went into her room with her violin, hammered away at some challenging sections of Jake's score—through which no one could sleep. She heard the front door when her sister left, and was surprised that she returned after about a quarter hour. Shortly after, there was the delicious fragrance of hot coffee, freshly roasted, ground, and percolated. Claire succumbed to the cheery call that breakfast was served. Molly's foul mood had been completely wiped away, and instead she was relaxed and happy. There was a box of pastries, and an envelope of crisp banknotes.

"Rent this month," Molly said. "Sorry it took a while. It's the whole thing."

Claire had only asked for half of the month's rent, and thought of Molly's recent nights out. "Your consulting work."

"Yes." Molly smiled. "I found a regular contract."

Claire recognized the undertone in the air, a vinegary odour that the aroma of strong brewed coffee could not conceal. She had not expected a whole month of rent, just wanted some recognition. Standing there with the envelope of cash, she could not bring herself to mention the unmistakable scent, or how much it affected her.

After paying the rent, Molly began to brew a pot of coffee at least once a day. Claire had always preferred smoking heroin, although it was a luxurious waste—smoking didn't go as far as a needle. Now, Claire envied her sister's excess—not the lingerie strewn here and there, not the new bag and shoes, not the creeping in with dawn— just the heroin.

When confronted, Molly at first denied that she was using in the apartment, casually dismissed Claire's suggestion as ridiculous. When Claire opened the bedsheets a little, and the works were sitting there on a tea tray, the pipe blackened, Molly expressed outrage that Claire was snooping, violating her privacy. Next, she declared that she was leaving right away—had been on the cusp of doing so anyways, had a place lined up.

Claire did not show her sister the door, and Molly did not pack to go. They both sat down. Finally, with a similar distance from her own words, Molly apologized but pointed out that she had been doing what a good sister should do—knowing that Claire wanted to be clean. Kept it away. True, she hadn't hidden it well enough. But she had tried in order to protect her little sister. Claire knew where her sister's current equanimity came from, how it made everything sweet and simple.

Claire asked, "Your guy—Danny the gardener?"

"All organic. Not just heritage strains of pot."

"And that's . . . the real deal—heroin? I thought no one had it anymore."

"Connections." Molly twirled her hair, smiled innocently, and said, "Need or want?"

"My shoulder's really bad today."

Some things were automatic, like tying shoes, putting rosin on a bow, smoking a little heroin and then having some coffee, nibbling a corner of pastry. Claire was pleased that it only took the tiniest bit, and she was already completely satisfied.

That evening at the rehearsal, Jake complimented Claire on her playing. Something had finally clicked for her, he enthused; there was a flair he hadn't heard since the Dorado. Her fellow musicians praised her as well. She went home clear-headed—no longer in the soft, warm place, but drifting in the last wisps of what she had smoked a few hours before. Amongst a riot of magazines on the floor, fancy clothes here and there, Molly was blissed out on the beanbag pouf. It was pretty obvious how she had spent the evening. The next morning, Claire was fine. Almost no withdraws—just the slightest chill. She took her buprenorphine, and everything settled. So there it was, something she had learned herself—the doctor hadn't told her about chipping. But why would he? To be fair, his job was to get her to stop. But it was possible, just like they said on Whitelight, to use on top of the bupe, and come out fine. Another couple of days passed, during which Claire looked forward to the trio practices more than ever because this was her deal with herself—she was only going to use for the practices. And of course, the performance.

Freed of the need for discretion, Molly smoked a few times a day, the time between shots growing ever shorter. She was in and out of the apartment at all hours, would hurriedly do her makeup and a shot, and then another when she came back. In the mornings, she stumbled out from behind her bedsheet, vomited in the toilet, cramped up over it, sweat pouring. One morning, Claire found her curled up on the living room floor in a small black dress, shaking to hold the syringe. Claire had to help fix her, find the thready, depressed line of a collapsed vein. Felt a little rush herself, as she hit her sister's vein. Then came Claire's own sweat. She reminded herself of the deal. Only for practices with others, and performances.

Claire called the doctor, asked him to extend her prescription for a week. *Yes, everything's fine, just under the weather.* The next days were effortless; one thing slipped into the next. It felt so easy—a reminder of how much work it had been to stay away. It was an exception, she told herself, that she was using every day for her own practice. Just until the premiere. After that she would take a break. But Claire noticed that each shot did not last as long as the previous. Still, the buprenorphine was like a floor, it kept her from falling into Molly's place of misery. When they were out, unable to meet the connect because Molly was doubled over, she gave Claire Danny's number, saying, *Make sure it's the right stuff.*

He was on time, in his scuffed-up Lexus. Claire knocked on the window, and he paused. Perhaps remembered that he had once seen her at a distance, when Molly was picking up. There was the resemblance, too.

"I thought it would be your sister."

"She's busy."

He laughed, "I bet."

"Is it good?" said Claire, hoping to sound like a discerning customer.

"Is the sky blue?"

Several days later, when that batch—which was meant to last a week—ran out, Danny didn't answer the phone. Claire called the clinic to ask the doctor to give her another script. She blushed hot when she lied to him. If he just asked her to tell the truth, she realized, she would instantly do so, it would have been a relief. She was surprised, disappointed, and triumphant when, after an uncomfortable pause on the phone, Dr. Chen agreed to extend the prescription a second time without questioning her. Claire picked up the medication at the pharmacy, told herself that these were her carries and she had earned them, but also thinking, *I'm using again, so I don't really deserve them.* And then, *This is what I need! Isn't that enough?* When Claire got home with her buprenorphine, Molly was shaking, sweating, barely able to get off the toilet. Claire told Molly to lift up her tongue, and she put half of her day's dose of medication under Molly's tongue. Told her to let it dissolve—that this was how it worked best, and embraced her, helped her to bed. Claire put the other half under her own tongue. After about an hour, Molly was much better. Not perfect, but comfortable.

When Danny picked up the phone again, Claire arranged to meet him. She emptied the cookie jar, the tips from the violin case, every last coin. Over the next few days, there was the discovery that on a half dose of buprenorphine, the heroin worked better. The safety net was also shaky—on half her prescribed dose she felt uneasy rather than solid.

Claire asked the doctor for a third prescription, spoke to him and said she was just so busy with preparations for her premiere. She had been planning to go to clinic, she said, had been looking forward to it. An extra practice had been called today, last minute. There was a little part of her that hoped he would call her bluff, insist she come to clinic, and the truth would be in her urine sample. That part remained quiet— besides, it was his job to sniff things out, wasn't it? What did he expect from an addict? Claire told the doctor how demanding Jake was, said, *You've helped me so much—I'm starting to feel like the musician I could be . . . but everyone in the ensemble is so good. I'm catching up. They don't want to say this extra practice is just to get me up to speed, but I know . . . Of course if you really need me to I could go to clinic. If you insist.*

The doctor extended the prescription, asked her if everything was okay.

Definitely, she said. She knew that he was trying to do the right thing. But that was the space within which to manoeuvre. The doctor was trying to do what he thought was right, in a world where people did what they had to do.

So now, most mornings the two sisters each dissolved a half dose of Claire's medication under their tongues. Some days they didn't take any, in order to feel the heroin more. Now, between shots, Claire was withdrawing for sure. But the low dose of buprenorphine kept things within a certain bandwidth, even with a day missed here and there. Instead of paying rent, with the premiere coming up, they got a half ball from Danny. Claire put on a tight-but-not-slutty blouse and went to the apartment office. She told the superintendent the school was late paying her—that rent was on the way. The only thing that mattered was that there was a good shot of down for the premiere. Claire put an emergency flap aside, two points, hid that shot away from Molly. But Claire couldn't begrudge Molly half her buprenorphine. After all, Molly was the one putting on lipstick, heading out for dates while Claire practiced. The stash was gone in a few days—Molly having used more than her share. As long as she had her flap for the performance, Claire thought.

16

The premiere of the Punk Fugue Trio was held in an inner court-
yard at the Art Gallery of Ontario. The room was several storeys
tall, through which a kinked, floating staircase of blond wood
seemed to both rise and fall. A spring downpour thrummed on the
skylight panels. Chen stood to one side of the space with Fitzgerald,
both of them holding little plastic cups of Prosecco for which they
had each redeemed the single drink ticket that was included with
admission. They heard the musicians before seeing them. A raucous
and muscular beat was set by the tabla and santouri, over which an
initially shy, then swaggering melody of the violin emerged. It
sounded like Claire, Chen thought. Gradually they could glimpse
the players—the tip of the violin bow, then the heads of the musicians as they descended the staircase.

When Claire came into view, in a long-sleeved green velvet
gown and matching leather pumps, it seemed to Chen that she was
in her element, within the music. He heard, as she launched into
a section of strange glissandos, that in this moment this was all that
mattered to her. Perhaps everything she had said was true, and she
simply hadn't been to the clinic because she needed to prepare for

this glowing performance. She had said on the phone, *My dream is freedom, remember? Come on, doctor, just one more week of the medicine.*

"It's wonderful music," whispered Fitzgerald. "Which one is your patient?"

"The violinist. I promised her I would attend," Chen lied. Would she notice him? Did he want her to, or did he prefer to be invisible?

Once, sitting at the Dorado, Chen's student had said she wished she could hear Claire play in a proper venue, a performance, not just as background music. They hadn't found any upcoming shows online. Chen suggested they ask the violinist, but his student did not want to bother her. Now, the atrium was packed with people Chen thought looked like musicians or artists. Their clothing was more funky than expensive, and they wore expressions of amusement, or evaluation. His student had once listened with an expression of something more vulnerable, a look of captivation—was that what every artist sought?

The trio built a set of intertwining voices to a crescendo, accelerating in pace, until suddenly the other two players dropped away, left only the violinist's simple melody in a minor key. Was this section improvised? Its purity was both sad and free. Chen felt himself drawn into the music as Claire explored the instrument, as the cadence slowed, and then after a few minutes the top line retreated into a meditative repetition of a key motif. As if entering on tiptoes, the other musicians rejoined. Even as they did so, the room applauded for the violinist.

The final movement of the fugue sounded conversational, a voice passed back and forth between the instruments. It was now, in watching the action and interplay between the players, that Chen's clinical eye began to probe. Was the slight delay that the violinist occupied an expression of suspense, or were her reflexes slowed for some reason? Her feet were slightly apart. There was an appearance of strength, but was it also that she was a bit off-balance? The vibrato and tone were lush, but did the fingering lack a little of the precision of which Chen knew Claire was capable? The three voices came to their peak in a relentless build, and then a flourish which seemed to drop off a cliff to booming silence.

The room burst into applause and cries of *bravo!* A woman whose family resemblance to Claire was obvious approached her with flowers, moving with a fluid ease. The sister was definitely intoxicated. Maybe just too much Prosecco, Chen thought, trying to make himself believe it.

"Should we say hello?" asked Fitzgerald.

"I don't know," said Chen, tilting his head at the congratulatory scrum, "they're having a moment."

"No rush," said Fitzgerald, "our dinner reservation is nearby." He sidled over to the bar.

Claire spotted her doctor, and rushed over. "What a surprise!" she beamed, her cheeks flushed. "Thank you, I can't tell you how much it means." In her unfiltered enthusiasm, her unguarded pleasure at seeing him, in her comfortable embrace of both of his forearms—as if this was always how they greeted one another—in her assured nod and open laughter, in the warmth of her gratitude, in her ease with placing a moist peck on each of his cheeks, and in her tiny pinpoint pupils despite the soft indoor lighting, Chen knew.

He wanted to ask, *What did you take before you went on stage?* And he didn't want to know. In the way she had played, something had been exposed, soulful and messy, brilliant. Was this the music his student had always hoped to hear in Claire, always choosing the Dorado over other restaurants? Had she glimpsed it, sensed it just needed to be uncovered? In clinic, he would have told his patient, "You could play like this without using whatever you took," wanting to believe it, and to persuade his patient to believe it as well.

But tonight, he reminded himself, they were both here for music, not medicine. He said, "So beautiful."

"Oh, please," said Claire, as if they were in on a little joke together.

"Truly special," he said in a low voice.

"Thank you," she grinned, "so much, doctor—you've really helped me."

"We'll see you in clinic . . ."

"Oh for sure," she said, and slipped away.

Outside, the heavy rain had eased, leaving the slow tears that wept from tree branches and the eaves of houses. Chen and Fitzgerald went to a dive in Chinatown, a noisy place that had excellent seafood chow mein and potent boilermakers. Tsing Tao beer with a shot of Baijin. Chen was quiet, and halfway through the meal Fitzgerald said, "Your patient can really play that fiddle."

"I extended her prescription three times, three weeks—all carries—she told me everything was going well."

"The music sounded great."

"I trusted her. She told me she was staying clean."

Fitzgerald rolled his eyes. "How long have you been doing this?" He squirted some rooster-brand hot sauce onto his noodles. "You wanted her to be clean. So you believed her."

"Now she thinks I'm great just because I did what she wanted."

"And that's so bad? You wanted her to be at her best. Tonight, she was. Way better than when I heard her at that cheesy bistro." Fitzgerald took a big gulp of his drink. "How's everything with . . . you know, your drug rep?"

"Project manager."

"That's the one."

"I don't know," said Chen, "whether she's using me, or I'm using her."

"Rule of thumb: if you don't know, then . . ."

———

The next day, there was a call from the pharmacist. Would the doctor be renewing Claire's prescription on the phone again? She was already at the pharmacy, asking the pharmacist to call. This time, Chen told Pamela that he needed to see the patient in clinic. An hour later, Claire called the clinic from the pharmacy, and Chen asked Pamela to put the call through. Once she transferred it, Claire wasn't on the line anymore. Then a call from the pharmacy: Claire had told the pharmacist that a week of carries was being prescribed, that the fax would come. Was that correct? Chen told his receptionist to tell the pharmacist that the patient needed to come to clinic. A standoff through intermediaries. The pharmacist informed the clinic that the patient had left. At the end of the day, a few minutes before closing, Claire called, asked to speak to the doctor.

"I'm not feeling well. I can't make it in."

"Claire, yesterday, I got the distinct impression you were . . . under the influence."

"Yesterday?"

"Your premiere?"

"Thank you for coming, it was so good to see you! Do you think you could send the script?"

"I need to see you in clinic."

"It's just that today . . ."

"I've been extending it so that you could prepare for your premiere. Which was great. But that was three prescriptions. And now the premiere is done. Let's get you back on track. Come into clinic. I can't just renew this again."

"And I thought you were on my side."

"Claire, it's not about sides," he said, his sentence ending against the dial tone.

17

THE REVIEWS—CLAIRE'S FIRST in years—were not just good. Although they were for the trio, critics singled out the violinist, writing with the exuberance of having discovered a brilliant talent otherwise unknown; between the lines was the self-congratulation of their own acumen and originality. *The passionate flares of hidden mastery . . . a cadence seemingly unhinged . . . the audience is entranced by this fine violinist, not always perfectly controlled but the listener finds themselves forgiving minor missteps . . . matured beyond the years during which we did not hear her voice . . .* Since then, the YouTube recording of the performance was gaining steady views, the classical music equivalent of going viral. She had received Facebook friend requests from musicians she admired, messages hinting at collaboration.

An email from Jake—there were actual festival invites, and he was really putting together a tour for the summer—could she keep her schedule open? It was just as well that she was going off the buprenorphine. How could she reply to Jake that she had to check with her doctor, ask for enough medications to travel? That was like checking with your parents for permission to go out. If only she wasn't gradually feeling more sick each day, she would have been able to better enjoy the afterglow of the premiere. It wasn't a complete cold-turkey, because they had some leftover buprenorphine, from the days they had skipped. Now, the sisters split the few remaining tabs of medication into halves and quarters, so that it was a reduction over about a week. Whitelight said that a proper taper took months at least. Each day, the need for something more.

"You know what you need," Molly assured her, crushing some hydromorphone tablets in a brass mortar and pestle, for them to inject. Someone at a Rosedale party had eight-milligram hydros, that they got from the neighbourhood doctor. A recording of the premiere played on a Bluetooth speaker that Molly had "found" one day when she was out for a walk.

"I told Dr. Chen that the whole point of getting his help was that I wanted freedom. So why would he insist I go see him in clinic? Just to get that stupid buprenorphine pill?"

"Totally hypocritical."

"And it's a pill you can't even feel."

"Pointless."

"For sure," said Claire, wishing it were so simple. It wasn't that Claire did not recognize the value of things she and the doctor worked on—daily routines, consistency, communication skills. Yes, she wanted to be on time for her rehearsals, and to have food in the fridge, and to have a kind doctor who listened to her, and to be the sort of person who always said please and thank you. And she also wanted to be in a ring of light on stage throwing music into the abyss, to be flown to appearances with nothing more than a beautiful dress in a backpack and her violin. The buprenorphine worked pretty well, and she needed what it offered—to be able to sleep through the night, and to wake rested instead of shivering. But it didn't give her what she desired most deeply, which was to take flight with the bow and rage across the strings and declare her otherwise unexplainable soul as she played. In fact, did it get in the way of that? At least a little. Everything had a price.

Most of all, Claire wanted to experience her own music as she had when she played her part of the trio into that MP3, because each time she now tapped the little sideways triangle on her phone—heard the santouri set her up and lead her in—the melody's introduction, the attack, sounded more distant from her. She knew she had been there. That was the real Claire—but day by day, to hear her own recording of the premiere was to feel as if she had been shut out of the pure version of herself that was crystallized on that digital file. She was more aware of the mistakes, too—heard the pressure come off the tip of the bow a fraction too early, the little errors in intonation. She relived the moment of descending the staircase, instrument aloft, the first notes, wanted to do it again, to do it better, to once again feel the freedom she wanted to feel. No, needed to feel.

Molly still got dressed up, but more often than usual she came back soon, too soon. Sometimes guys arranged to meet in a café or hotel lobby and then just flaked out, made an excuse. Molly looked on edge, bedraggled, and Claire supposed that if they were paying for the cool, fun vibe in her profile photos—that was not how she showed up. Were they at least kind? Or sheepish? Claire was too ashamed to ask. Soon, Claire was barely functional but Molly lay all day on the beanbag, ignoring the text responses to her online ads. It wasn't as if Claire was going to tell her to slide into her little black dress, but they still had to sort out rent. The building super slipped an ominous and official notice under the door.

One morning, buoyed by a smash, Molly looked up from her phone and said, "I have a plan! We're going to help Danny out!"

"I don't think I'm comfortable with . . ."

"No, not like that kind of help. Come on, like when we were kids. We'll end up with rent and a half-gram."

It was mostly for the thrill when they were teenagers—a Club Monaco, a Levi's outlet—not that their parents didn't pay for clothing. There was a time in a Reebok store when they both tried on sneakers, were about to bolt, and right then a sketchy-looking guy did a grab-and-run, enabling the sisters to saunter out while the shoe sellers were distracted. "There's just something Danny needs. A little trade—and he's got a good batch!"

Claire slouched her way into Sephora, trying to worsen her posture with the kind of effort that she imagined non-performers must make to improve theirs. She wore floppy overalls with large pockets and carried a tattered no-name shoulder bag, as if she were a caricature of a shoplifter. It was a simple plan. *What do you choose to leave behind?* she started to hear Dr. Chen asking from one of their sessions, but she focused on getting herself into the role. It was kind of like being a mime, and there was a little thrill in performing. Claire lingered at displays, picked up jars of skin product, glanced around furtively, and put them down again. She hovered over whatever was expensive. She held a jar of cream for a moment and then, as if just noticing the security camera, placed it back on the display. She went to the makeup counter, asked to try a bright, slightly orangey lipstick. The sales associate stood a little distance away with a strained smile. The ridiculous lipstick made Claire appear like a demented clown in the little round mirror, and she suppressed a laugh. She imagined someone recognizing her as the brilliant violinist in the recent premiere of the Punk Fugue Trio, how pleased and how embarrassed she would be.

As Claire finished the edges of her lips, she glimpsed her older sister reflected in the mirror—trim suede jacket, white blouse, like someone on lunch from the bank. As Claire wiped off that first lipstick to paint her mouth in an even more ridiculous shade of purple, asking the salesperson very seriously for an opinion, she saw Molly flirting with the guy behind the fragrance counter. Claire thanked the makeup person, walked towards the eye rejuvenators, picked up the smallest box of the most expensive stuff, which she checked to be sure that it had a security tag, ambled towards the register, and then right between the security sensors, she collapsed. She got it just right: she was still in the store, and the alarm system blared.

Prone, Claire moaned (was that a bit too dramatic?) as Sephora employees appeared around her. The guy from fragrance fussed over her. She asked plaintively, "Where am I?" He directed someone to get a handkerchief, to soak it in water, and when it came Claire accepted it gratefully, made a show of wiping her face, her neck. And there went Molly slipping out right through the security sensors, the alarm still going *beep-beep-beep*, no one paying attention to her and her now-straining Prada bag.

Two large bottles of Tom Ford's Costa Azzurra—gold fluted stopper— and two large bottles of Fucking Fabulous fragrance, squat in black pedestals, were lined up on the kitchen table. Altogether, about three grand in fragrance. Danny made sure the seals were intact, the bottles fresh and unmarked.

"What, no gift bag?" he complained.

"Go and buy a lipstick," said Molly. "They'll give you a gift bag. Get the orange. It's your shade."

"That's okay—I've got lots of gift bags." He began to put the bottles in his knapsack.

"And? The deal is a half-gram and a thousand bucks for the fragrance. You know this isn't a pickup for Goodwill donations."

"I'll meet my customer, and be right back with the cash."

"Hold on hold on hold on," said Molly, hand on the knapsack. "Danny, this is more of a cash-and-carry type of arrangement. That's my understanding of the wholesale transaction of stolen goods."

"Like I said, I'm meeting my customer. She's paying me in cash. I'll be back in an hour. Two—tops."

"What, and she's probably giving you two and a half grand for that?"

Danny shrugged. "Wholesale pricing versus retail."

Claire spoke up. "But you've got the down?"

From his jacket pocket, Danny retrieved a baggie. Just seeing the flaky brown, Claire felt a little rush. He tossed it on the kitchen table. "I have to move the perfume to get the cash. So you just have to wait." He seemed untroubled. He opened the knapsack, invited Molly to extract the perfume. "Or you can keep this and soak yourselves in it. Unless . . . ?" From an inside pocket of his jacket, Danny produced a pill bottle. The pharmacy label had been peeled off, and the bottle itself was grimy and worn.

Green monsters—eighties. An eighty milligram tab of oxycodone was like a fifty-dollar bill, a known value. The eighties could be crushed, snorted, even injected in a pinch. Claire had once had a prescription for three eighties a day, and swore dutifully to the walk-in clinic doctor that she used them exactly as prescribed. On time, swallowed. *Crush them? Why would anyone do that, doctor?* batting her eyelashes. Because the eighties were predictably worth something, she knew how much she could get in order to upgrade to heroin. The perfect classical musician patient—of course she was a good girl. Until the doctor realized that she wasn't, and cut her off. Claire stared at the bottle. "They hardly prescribe those anymore."

"I have a customer. Her mother died—cancer. You know, some chit-chat when I dropped off some Obsession. Turns out there were forty of these bad boys sitting in the medicine cabinet. I told her how dangerous they are, and offered to get rid of them for her. What if I give you ten? You know, instead of cash."

Molly began to remove the fragrance bottles from his knapsack.

"A dozen?" Danny put his hand on the baggie of heroin.

"Wholesale versus retail." Molly smiled sweetly at him. "All of it." Claire admired her sister's calm, but felt nervous at seeing the baggie disappear under his hand. The plan had been to get the heroin, pay the rent. The math of the green monsters was appealing, though. They should end up with something extra.

"Here you go," Danny laughed, sliding the heroin over, and rattling the pill bottle gently before setting it on the table. "This, and I don't need to make a return trip. Because I like you."

Molly snatched them. "Forty?"

"Or so."

She counted them, in a piece of tissue paper.

"Thirty-nine."

He smirked. "Okay, a friend of mine needed one. It's still a bargain."

Molly poured the pills back into their bottle, pocketed it, and Danny took the fragrance. Despite her fond memories of oxycodone, Claire's heart sank a little to see him go out the door. Just knowing that each oxycodone eighty was worth at least fifty bucks wasn't the same as having rent money. Not that it was rocket science to move them.

"We'll play it just like we did when you had your own prescription!" Molly enthused. "Like old times!" Molly got ready to go— pulled on floppy grease-stained jeans, a crappy blue windbreaker that didn't fit, and a fisherman's knit cap into which she had stuffed all of her beautiful red hair. "It's my scumbag loser dealer ensemble, like it?" She did a twirl. She grabbed some scuffed-up Doc Martens out of Claire's footwear heap.

Even if you believed that users recognized users, a little advertising didn't hurt. Molly would do the slouching in doorways, waiting for the right people in the wrong neighbourhood. Claire would dress . . . like Claire: *like a super-hot librarian!* according to Molly, and sit in a streetcar shelter, watching for cops and the regular dealers whose stretches of sidewalk they would be temporarily usurping. If there was a problem she would alert Molly, just like old times. It had always been a thrill, Claire had to admit.

Molly said, "Let's go! But first! A taste test! Come on!"

It would all work out with the pills. If they each took just one, there were still thirty-seven greenies. Rent, and then some. Molly was shaky despite her bravado. They needed to settle themselves. Claire's hand was steady enough to boil the water. It was a tiny pot, intended for Greek coffee, and Claire poured in just enough water to fill a syringe. The green monster dissolved beautifully. Claire went to draw it up, but Molly stopped her—"Let it cool"—which of course Claire knew to do, but had been caught up in the moment of anticipation. "You want to go first?" she asked her sister, who huddled as a chill passed through her. But Molly smiled, shook her head, gestured for Claire to go ahead. She had always been a good big sister, when it really came down to it.

Claire cooled the shot by gently swirling the tiny pot in a larger saucepan of cold water, lifted the small container out a few times, felt the bottom with her hand until it was just slightly warm. Some residue lodged in the filter as she sucked it through, pulled on the plunger. Claire put the filter carefully aside, already thinking that she would later dilute it out for a wash. As she tied off, slapped up a vein, caressed it with an alcohol swab, she felt that mix of desire and hope, and she cheered herself—*Hey, I'm still in control, doing everything right—nice and clean, an oxy eighty! The good stuff. Want not need . . .* The slight pang and give of her own skin as the sharp steel penetrated. The high began even as she pulled back—the red wisp in the barrel.

As the plunger fell, there was the brief moment when the roller coaster paused at the top of the track—that beginning part when the sickness vanished, the roiling water calmed. Then, a silent descent, the world sped towards Claire and she wondered if she was going to go on the nod. She didn't want to miss the soft rush, the best part of the ride. The comfort. The knowledge that everything was okay. She imagined suggesting to Dr. Chen that he try, *just once so that you understand,* because even he would agree, *yes, you're right, it is amazing.*

Then, she stopped imagining, as everything erased itself to give way to oblivion.

Opening her eyes—how had she gotten onto the beanbag? Everything now felt as if it would go on forever, and yet was only the immediate warmth—the most wonderful embrace. There was only the right now, the presence in her high. Everything was good. She was good.

Then she closed her eyes.

And then she opened them.

Had missed something—seconds, minutes?

Strange—she had never nodded out like that on an oxy eighty.

Molly was drawing up her shot, steadying herself, but Claire hadn't noticed her prepping it.

They smiled at one another. Everything was good. She was good, and soon Molly would be too. There was the placid thought that she was now too tired to go out and sell drugs. Or help her sister sell drugs. They didn't have money for rent—but it was no big deal. It would come. Why was she tired? Normally, with an oxy eighty there was the soft warm part, yes, and an energy to it.

Again, Claire closed her eyes. For just a second.

When she opened them, she was surprised that she had nodded out again. She thought she knew her own tolerance pretty well. And there was Molly, a rag doll almost off the chair. Claire stumbled over, eased her sister down, cradled her head so that it didn't bang against the floor. Claire still felt serene, whole, wonderful; she loved Molly dearly and it was just fine to be rolling her on one side, a limp bag— one knee up.

She watched as if she were a spectator, waiting for Molly to take a breath. Molly did not move, did not breathe. She was completely still, and the colour seeped out of her face. Molly needed help. Claire formulated this thought, clearly and with a sense that everything was still just fine. She sealed her mouth over her sister's, held her nose—and blew a breath in. Again, she watched.

Everything was good.

She was good.

Somewhere deep inside, Claire pictured Dr. Chen yelling, *She's not breathing! Do something!*

Claire determined not to close her own eyes, and it occurred to her to open Molly's. Gently, she slid open the lids to reveal the vacant, pinpoint pupils.

Molly's lips were blue tinged.

Naloxone! The imaginary Dr. Chen was now yelling, but to Claire it was still as if his yelling were only part of a performance that encompassed Molly dying on the floor. Claire managed to stand, looked down at Molly's face drained of colour, her lips definitely purple-blue. She got the naloxone kit from the kitchen—the doctor had insisted she have one. Claire felt Molly's neck—there was still a pulse, but her chest did not pull air into her body. Claire understood so calmly that her sister was moving towards death, and rolled up Molly's sleeve. Squirt, into her arm muscle just below the shoulder, no fiddling for a vein.

Everything was good.

She was good.

"Molly, sweetie . . ." she said, stroking her sister's forehead, hoping, praying that she would be okay.

Then the eruption. A one-person zombie apocalypse. A very angry sister, jumping to her feet, flailing out.

"WHADJA DO THAT FOR! WHAT THE FUCK! I was on my nod!" Molly began to shake, and then lunged for the vial of pills.

Claire was still sitting in the balcony seats, watching, but she plucked away the bottle of pills. "That almost killed you."

Everything was good.

She was good.

"OHMIGOD! You NALOXONED me?"

"Or let you die? Molly, you were blue . . . how many shots did you do?"

"Maybe two, I don't know. FUCK! NALOXONE!" Molly jumped up and down, stamped the floor. The drug was fading fast. It had hit too hard and was coming off too ragged. A real green monster was good for at least a few hours. Even if injected, it was an unfurling wave, the warm sea washed over you and then out towards the horizon, dissipating with a slow, melancholy, sunset goodbye. But this stuff—whatever it was—a rogue wave smashing a cliff, then a vicious undertow. Molly was curled in a ball on the floor, screaming from the dopesick that accompanied the naloxone rescue antidote. Claire felt a chill. Already? She split one of the tablets in half. It crumbled wrong. How had she not noticed when cooking it?

But it was something. And now Molly pleaded with Claire to give her something, anything. Claire knew her agony, and even as she felt her own high vanish she cooked half a tab, and then helped her sister do half of the half in a shot. That tiny bit didn't touch her sister, who ran to the toilet and moaned there for a few minutes before she stumbled out. The rest of the syringe still did nothing. There were hot spots in the pills, parts that had nothing, parts that were probably deadly junk—fentanyl or worse. Claire cooked the other half of the tab. This, when injected, put Molly almost on the nod while Claire stood there with another naloxone syringe. Claire popped one in her mouth and swallowed it.

Soon Molly was relaxed, definitely high. She put on her windbreaker and fussed with it, saying, *one for sixty, two for a hundred.* Rehearsing.

Molly said, "Total bullshit, that thing Danny told us—a mom with cancer. How much for three?"

"We should throw them out," said Claire, not even convincing herself as she said it, because now she was getting sick again. She wanted to cook another green tab, take her chances with the hot spots. Her phone dinged, a text from Scooter: *I'm out! Ready to celebrate! Gardener tells me u got greenies?*

"Who's that?"

"Small world. Someone who knows Danny."

Molly peered over, read the message. "First customer?"

"My old dealer. Parents did an intervention or something. Guess it didn't work."

"I can still get the rent out of the greenies." Molly reached for the phone, which Claire pocketed.

"They're too dangerous."

Molly laughed, "I'm gonna say it's a variety pack! Come on, we'll deal to your dealer!" She pulled the knit cap down to her eyebrows, and snatched the bottle away from Claire.

"What? You can't sell them. They're unpredictable. What if— you know . . ."

"Other ideas?"

Claire watched as Molly fiddled with the men's belt on her too-big jeans, selected one hole, then another, back to the original one. Claire could see it all unfold—Scooter unconscious, her sister, sketched out on some corner, shaking a bottle of pills. Kids buying them from her. Until the cops pulled up in a cruiser or she managed to unload the bottle, the fake green pills out in the world. Molly did up her jacket, adjusted her cap, and then, when she leaned down to lace up her boots, Claire grabbed the bottle, outran both her own craving and her sister to the bathroom, dumped the pills into the toilet, and flushed.

18

THE HALF GRAM of heroin was weak, and gone by morning. Claire's back throbbed and she wanted to tear her bones from her legs.

"I can't believe you screwed us over like this. And why?" Molly moaned from her mattress.

"Danny screwed us over. There's always the clinic. We could both go."

"But it didn't cure you last time. And do you want to go like this?"

What would be in her urine now? Not just heroin. Fentanyl for sure, probably carfentanil, the toxic soup Dr. Chen had warned her about—he would never give her a carry again. He had been so proud. Better to not see him at all. Claire texted the school, that she would be absent. Which of her last chances was she on?

As evening fell, Claire and Molly took turns using the bathroom to vomit, and then sitting on the toilet with everything running out. Danny ignored Molly's texts.

"I made the mistake of asking him if he needed help grabbing something else. So he must figure we don't have cash."

"New plan," Claire said, "to get clean. Just push through."

"That's a new plan?" said Molly. "Good thing it worked so well before." Molly stumbled to the bathroom, was soon moaning from the toilet.

A sleepless night, and another day passed. Scooter texted a few times, still looking for stuff. His own connections must have disappeared, if he was looking to score from former customers. Claire only replied once: *Sorry.*

Claire lay shivering under her bedcovers, shoulder throbbing, throat sour and sore from throwing up, asshole raw from wiping after having shit everything out, stinking in sweat that smelled a bit like cheap dope, throwing the sheets off and feeling frozen, pulling them back on again.

Molly called in from where she was lying on her mattress in the living room, "You okay?"

"Amazing."

"It says right here on Whitelight: *Feeling suicidal is to be expected.* Some loser on this thread says you have to think of how much you screwed up and keep on focusing on that, because it reminds you why you're stopping."

Claire found another thread on *Abstinence—Getting Clean.* "This one says: *Surrender to a higher power. Find a sponsor.*"

"If there was a higher power, would she have let me get here?" Molly said. "And half of the sponsors are just trying to pick up, right? That 'surrender' bullshit is just meant to catch girls who like that whole *surrender to the master* dynamic."

That evening, Jake called. The trio had been invited to give a CBC broadcast performance the next day at the Glenn Gould Studio, a last-minute invite—a substitution for a group whose violinist had slipped and fractured his wrist.

Ten minutes, and a phone call later, Molly had someone who was willing to advance a gram of heroin.

"Real heroin?" said Claire incredulously. "And he'll advance?"

"She will. You met her. Beatrice, goes by Beauty."

"You said to stay away."

"Because she's a pimp. Whenever she's out, she has at least two things to sell. It's no big deal. As long as I pay her back, I won't owe her anything. You said you're getting some money for this performance tomorrow, right?"

Molly brought the gram to the dressing room at the Glenn Gould, just a few minutes before the trio was set to go on. No time for a test hit. But it was the real thing, Claire knew, as soon as the middle of her bow began to roll over the chords of the opening passage, and she felt the supple control of her wrist. Even in the most technically challenging passages, her music poured through the instrument, full-throated. Backstage afterwards, Molly floated towards her and Claire hugged her, grateful, and glad they were in this good warm place together.

At the reception, an introduction to Afshin, a music director she had only heard of previously, from La Danse de Minuit. Was Claire up for playing a show? he asked. It was sometimes good money, he explained—there was no session fee, but they passed a hat and split it evenly between dancers, crew, and musicians. The big thing, Claire knew, was not the money—it was that La Danse de Minuit was more a legendary apparition than a performance. There was no fixed venue. Every performance was in a public space, "borrowed" at midnight. The email blast went out a week before, with the venue only announced on the morning of the show so that city officials and property owners had little time to shut them down. The actual shows materialized and vanished, and then clips and reviews later appeared on social media, so that everyone who wasn't there knew the spectacular awesomeness of the event that they had missed.

"I'll think about it," Claire said, though she had already decided. Of course she would. "If I'm free."

"It would be an honour," said Afshin, giving her a card.

Back at the apartment, they each did another little celebratory shot, saving over half the gram, and Claire once again knew that everything would be fine. She had another gig. She had a beautiful sister. There was the relief of knowing that everything would work out, that everything good was also simple and true.

The fee from the Glenn Gould show was enough to pay back Beauty. And buy another gram of heroin. After the radio broadcast, the Punk Fugue Trio was lauded in a national newspaper review, and the sisters each did a point to celebrate. (Coming off that point, there were a half-dozen urgent emails that Claire ignored.) Her shoulder felt perfect, bionic! (Between shots, her shoulder was in agony and she could barely grip the bow.) While high, she did an interview, answered with poise—but still enthusiasm and praise for the composer's brilliance! (She ignored Jake's texts, and when he wrote that he was worried about her, she suggested he mind his own business.) The composer wanted to take the trio on a national tour! Music festivals across the country were asking for them! Here it was—her big break! (Whatever.) Later, she texted Jake with the blowing-kisses emoji and the hands-praying-in-thanks emoji! (When the stash was gone, Claire wanted to be dead.)

Now Beauty was playing hard ball trying to pressure Molly into working at her 'spa.' Danny was not going to make good, insisted that the oxy eighties had been real, denying the heroin had been stepped-on. Scooter was in jail. Claire could practically hear Dr. Chen: *Opioids work. They do—they solve your problems for a little while, but then . . . What do we keep with us? What do we leave behind?—knowing that it is a choice. We all have to choose how to live . . .* "Choice." What choice? she thought. I'm an addict.

The fridge was empty, and the super had slipped a "Rent in Arrears" notice under the door. Claire asked to be on the occasional teaching roster at the Little Orchestra School, citing the demands of her performance career. The one time she got called that week, she was too sick to go in. Molly used the last point in order to meet a guy. When she came back she said to Claire, "Look, I can hook you up."

"Hook me up?"

"We'll do a double date. It's not so bad. You'll clean up okay. Just play dumb."

"Are you crazy? I mean, the trio is getting press. My photo is on the CBC site."

"Please. So famous." Molly rolled her eyes. "I promise you they won't know that you're about to be an almost-big-time-slightly-famous classical music star. And they won't care."

19

CLAIRE SHOOK, SWEATED, rifled a purse; Chen held out a bouquet of flowers but she did not even glance over. The flowers were bundled tightly at the stems, intended for throwing upon a spotlit stage. Her back was turned to him, and he tapped her shoulder but she did not react, not even to shrug him off. Objects tumbled from the purse—a syringe, a cooker, empty plastic baggies, and then she turned the purse upside down, shook it. But now the purse had become a violin, and Claire gripped it by the neck. When she turned, however, it was not Claire but another person whom Chen often thought about, worried about. Missed. He was happy to see her—how long had it been? Was she well? He held out his hand with the red flowers, knowing they were what she needed, the treatment. She looked beyond him. Had he become invisible? Had he always been?—with this, both disappointment and relief. In the way of dreams, Chen knew there was a problem he could solve, but found himself unable to speak.

Chen sat bolt upright in bed, gasped into the echoing night, the dream still vivid. He took his phone and opened his gallery of losses. He swiped through, not rushing. That was how it had to be done—each image given its due. With some patients, he remembered their gratitude when they first felt withdrawal subside. When he first began this work and the medication took away some patients' withdrawal, he naively thought *This is so simple. You just give them what they need.* With others, he recalled struggling to remain above their curses and insults. Some had gone from gratitude to cursing him, and others the opposite. All had ended up here. There were faces of people who he had thought were doing very well—who had clean urine tests at each visit, a smile and an upbeat word—and then one day, when he expected them in clinic, they did not appear. What had he missed? There were the prescriptions he had refused to extend, and the next time he heard the patient's name was from the coroner. There were the ones he had extended, aware that there were things not being told to him on the phone, and that was also the last time he spoke to those patients. It had taken a while for Chen to articulate a difficult truth, and then yet longer to accept it, that the degree to which he worried about a patient did not protect them at all.

This was not helping Chen to sleep. He put the phone aside, closed his eyes, laid his head on the pillow. But there was none of the calm resolution which this remembrance—reviewing his gallery, putting to bed memories of people—sometimes provided. Why not? What, he would have asked a patient who had such a ritual, was the function of this behaviour? Few behaviours were inherently good or bad, positive or negative—it was always a question of function, intent. *Are you avoiding something?* Chen might have asked. Other flashes of the dream: she searched her purse at the entrance of an alley, a leg jutted out from a dumpster behind her—the foot in an elegant green leather pump; it was pouring rain, water ran from a drainspout. Light in a window above, an apartment. He got out of bed, went to his computer, searched for his former student's name in the obituaries, as he had done many times before. Relief—he did not find it.

A browser search of Claire's name brought up reviews of the trio's premiere. He found himself agreeing with the praise and feeling defensive on her behalf towards the mild critiques. In the search results, a link to a recording at the CBC's Glenn Gould Studio—a broadcast. Another hit was the cryptic, minimalist website of La Danse de Minuit, which advertised that Claire would be joining them for the upcoming season; the next hit, a brief profile of the violinist in *NOW* magazine, accompanied by a photo in silhouette on the staircase at the Art Gallery of Ontario. Sitting at his desk, Chen clicked the broadcast recording, listened to it from beginning to end, transfixed. An unexpected shift in the cadence, a flourish of daring where only solidity was expected. Chen thought, with pain, of something his former student had once said about music, that from one listening to the next, there could be so much new to be heard.

To a student of medicine,

The math vexed you one day, as you diligently tried to reconcile what the patient told you with the implacable nature of numbers. You had assessed a patient in clinic who had been absent from clinic for months. He was comfortable, not in withdrawal, casually asked to continue his medication. He said that he had stretched out his own dose of medication, to half doses, although he concluded that the full dose was better—and he wanted to continue it. You did the math, and the numbers didn't add up. With the number of carries he had, you told me, even at half doses he should have run out weeks ago, but the medication is in his urine. So he bought some carries from someone, I said, the obvious explanation. He said he didn't, you replied. And? I asked. You said, I don't want to accuse him of lying—there's nothing else in his urine, no heroin or fentanyl—and he seems like a nice guy. You want him to be telling the truth, I observed. A hesitation, Yes. Sometimes, I said, there's a gap between what someone says and what actually happened, and it doesn't change what you are going to do.

So, sometimes the truth doesn't matter?

That's more succinct, I conceded.

Later that day, you reviewed a stable patient with me—someone with a long history of abstinence, accompanied by clear urine. But that day, cocaine. They said they didn't use, you explained to me, but they were at a party where people were doing lines—and speculated that it was in their system from just being in the room, perhaps from touching a doorknob. Is that possible? Always a quick learner, you asked the follow-up question before I said anything: And will knowing the answer to that change what I should do?

One evening, we were at the Dorado, with the requisite binders of trial results, but we hadn't opened them. You yawned a few times, had a runny nose. Noticing that I noticed, you said you were coming down with something. I offered to take you home—said the data could wait. No, you said, I'll be fine. And excused yourself. When you returned from the washroom, you were better. You were comfortable, and alert, your nose had stopped dripping. You grabbed a binder and began to work through it with more enthusiasm than usual, flagging questions—pointing out some documentation errors.

Was it only later that I remembered that evening's sequence of events—how perfect you suddenly seemed, no longer under the weather? One quick trip to the bathroom. Did I truly not think anything of it at the time? If I had asked, what would you have said? Now it seems obvious, perhaps trite, to write that I wish you had told me that night. But the crux of it—would I have done something differently?

Yours as always,
Dr. Chen

20

IN THE MORNING, half-rested, Chen made a coffee, logged into the electronic medical record from home, and called Claire. Often patients' numbers were not in service, or the calls went to voicemail boxes that were full, but Claire picked up:

"Who?"

"Your doctor, just thought I would check in," he said casually, instead of *I'm glad you're alive.* "Did I wake you?"

"I wish—can't sleep. Oh, it's light out. I'm losing track of time. Do you often phone your patients?"

"When I'm worried, I sometimes follow up." The doctor was relieved to have reached her but only said, "I'm glad you picked up."

"Isn't this what schools do?"

"They call and see if a kid is sick at home?" he asked.

"Or dead?"

"Hopefully that doesn't happen too often. In schools."

"But all the time with junkies, right? Thanks for checking in on me," she laughed. "I guess you're paid to care."

"I get paid to diagnose and treat," said Chen, "I don't actually get paid for caring."

Chen wondered if she would hang up, whether she was again on her own trajectory. Sometimes, that's what happened, mid-conversation, someone was already flying away.

After a silence, "I'm being a jerk. I'm sorry, because you do care. I know. Look, I'm surrounded by assholes. So you get into a certain . . . way . . . of dealing with people. But thank you for calling. For caring."

"I'm in clinic today. Come if I can help you."

Late in the afternoon, Chen was relieved to see Claire's name appear on his waiting room list. Chen had called patients before, and then next heard from the hospital, the police, or the coroner. Only if they were talking on the phone *at this time*, or sitting in his waiting room *right now*, or were in front of him *at this moment*, was he reassured that they were still breathing. Chen worked through the patients who were in line ahead of Claire, hoping to get to her before she walked out. Sometimes, people showed up after a long absence, waited a few minutes, and then their name disappeared from the list on his screen. Too sick, had to score. Pamela would comment, *Went out for a walk— never came back.* The sometime finality of "never" was unintended.

Claire was sick—sweating, slumped, drawn. Leading her into his office, Chen said, "It's good to see you."

"I don't know why you would say that—I'm just another screwup. But I guess a plumber is glad to see a burst pipe, right?"

"Had a slip?" he said. "Exposed to short-acting opioids?"

"You make it sound like radiation. 'I was just minding my own business when . . .'"

His language was chosen to be non-judgmental, but he knew it sounded strange, awkward, as if invoking the power of an alien hand. Chen tried again. "I guess you've been partying?"

"Something like that," she said. "And trying too, to do what matters. With the music. Whatever that's worth?"

"How's that going?"

"So-so." Claire looked down. "It's just I was wrong, and I hate being wrong. Again. Does that sound like a little kid sulking? I shouldn't have stopped the medication."

"Some other substances are in the picture?" he said. The urine sample result was on his computer. As he taught his trainees, questions revealed more than statements, even with the answers at hand.

"My old dealer died. Parents sent him to rehab. Got out, I think he was bored. Screwed up. Went to jail. Got out of jail. And that was it. His dad called me. Crying, and pissed. He was going through all of Scooter's contacts to figure out who . . . and thank God I could honestly tell him that I didn't give him the stuff. He used to get around on this little electric scooter, and now every time I hear one . . ."

"I'm sorry."

"On one hand, I was glad I hadn't sold Scooter what I had when he asked. They were fake pills. Crazy strong. But when I heard what happened I also thought, if he had come to me, I could have watched him while he did it. And then maybe . . ."

"Let go of all the things you didn't do." When he said it, it sounded so simple. *Try to let go* would have been more realistic advice.

"My plan was to use just a little. When I really needed it," she said. "That's always the plan."

"Are you in withdrawal now?"

"If I had something, I would do it right now. But I'm totally out of junk. And everything. Out of money, food, pretty soon I'll lose the apartment. My sister's . . . doing what she can. And I'm sick as hell."

"And so . . ."

"You would be a terrible dealer, you know? Not offering, just waiting for the customer to ask. Yes, I need your help."

Chen thought of Claire at the Gallery, both the lightness and strength of the performance. "Your premiere was incredible. Really, the performance was magical. Imagine if you weren't . . ."

"What? Imagine if I weren't high? That I would have played better?" She laughed. "But why does it always end up like this?"

"You get to choose if it does."

"Easy for you to say."

"When you were off the junk last time, you were able to do things that mattered. You told me you had food in the fridge. That your apartment was clean. That you were sleeping through the night. Wasn't all of that progress?"

"Gold stars. You should give them out."

"Didn't you tell me you were showing up on time for the children you teach? You told me you were practising consistently again. And I heard you at your premiere. The medication is a platform to stand on. It's to support you, so that you can do what matters."

"I'm going to be evicted. I've never been homeless, you know? I don't even know how to do it. Some people know where to go, shelters, food banks, how to survive, and all that." Claire's pace of speech accelerated, a staccato. "But I don't know anything about it. My god, I don't even know where I'll be in a week."

The details were particular, specific, but the texture, the jagged edge of it, was just as always—a ripped-up mess. People's lives became like the explanations that Claire now rambled through—sentences dangling, half thoughts—complaints of betrayals, broken promises. Molly had promised to pay the rent and Claire thought she had done it, but then Claire saw the super and Molly in the hallway, her saying, *Forget it you slimeball, you got it this month*, and meanwhile Molly found some new guy who was going to be "totally different than the others." Vegan for one thing, and rich, from a super-addictive phone game he had programmed. The rich vegan was paying for fentanyl patches. Molly was not smoking them or injecting them, just wearing them and feeling great, getting them from one of the vegan's Rosedale neighbours, a doctor supposedly, so they were real. Sharing was impossible. The vegan checked to see if Molly tampered with them, having promised the doctor, and the used ones were returned to get a new one. So now Molly was always out with the vegan and wasn't sick anymore but the super kept on coming up to the apartment, saying that he and Molly had a deal, foot in the door, better remind her. Looked Claire up and down like a menu while she thought about slamming the door, and he said, *Really, she paid? Where's the receipt?* Claire couldn't pawn her violin, because then how would she make any money, but there was just no other way to get that much fast cash, and then the super saying he would change the locks unless she sent Molly to *have a chat or unless Claire wanted to let him in . . .* What was Claire going to say? *My sister did—whatever—for one month rent, now buzz off.* She didn't have the money so instead of saying what she wanted to say, *You couldn't really manage more than once a month, could you?* she smiled, laughed, blocked the door, waited him out until he removed the foot. "So, that's where I am. And it's not fair—this super is trying to screw me over. Literally. So don't go thinking that you've got some amazing solution. I'm here seeing you, doctor, because you're the drug dealer who doesn't charge me."

Claire stopped, ran out of words as if she had expelled some pent-up energy. Chen taught his students that anger was an escape, that it felt better than whatever had preceded it. At least for a while. The words that Claire had dispersed into the room were like a volatile gas, waiting for a response, a spark, and could explode. Anger expects a force in return, he taught, needs it to be sustained. *Try to find something unexpected; subvert the pattern of escalation.* "Right now, if you could give yourself something, one thing that you need, what would it be?" he asked.

"Rent. But I don't have it."

"Anything else?"

She asked, "Do people often come in here like this?"

"Like what?"

"Just taking their problems out on you?"

Another thing Chen taught his students was that the range of choices—for patients, for doctors—was almost always broader than they initially imagined. In all directions, as Fitzgerald had shown him. And, Chen reminded himself, he always had choices as well.

"What if I were to pay your rent?"

"Excuse me?"

"It sounds like you're in a tight spot. What if I pay a month of your rent? While things settle."

"You're kidding."

"It might be hard for you to work, while stabilizing on your medication."

"Listen, that is . . . generous . . . I'm not sure what to say."

"A loan from our clinic emergency fund"—the fiction he told when this came up, in order to make it sound like it was not his own wallet.

"Really?"

"It's a small fund. We would prefer it not be publicized."

Claire reddened and blurted out, "I'll cut to the chase—what do I have to do? What do you get?"

"Once you get stable, you'll pay it back. I wouldn't offer it to you if I had any doubt about that," he said, by way of saying, *You don't have to sleep with me.* "We'll go see your super, and we'll get a receipt."

Chen kept no account of these loans. He extended them when it seemed like one such kindness might get someone through a tight spot—one tuition payment, one bus ticket back home, one month's rent. If the camel's back was breaking anyways, then there was no point in lifting the last straw. But if a set of tools for a carpenter meant that he wouldn't lose the job, if a new car radiator meant that someone could still get their kids to daycare and finish a last semester in college, if one month's rent meant that a patient didn't have to sleep with a building super . . . Of course, he had only answered half her first question. But what *did* he get? *Don't think you can save people,* he taught his students. Warning trainees of hazards did not mean he was not susceptible to them. Knowledge allowed teaching. Sometimes it just made sense to go a bit further than usual. *Making sense?* A euphemism for the neglect of doubt? Of course, there was also the lesson that he taught, the simple-sounding one, *Let go of all the things you didn't do; the only way to live with this is to continue trying, doing.*

After going to the pharmacy, Claire returned, as Chen had asked her to. With one dose of buprenorphine circulating in her bloodstream, soothing her opioid receptors, she already looked more comfortable. Chen's phone rang. It was Charlie, asking where Chen was. Chen had forgotten a dinner event that he was supposed to attend. He told Charlie, "I'm just finishing at the clinic, go ahead."

"You won't be too long?"

"Go ahead without me."

"But you're actually coming, right?" said Charlie, his voice distant, as Chen put the phone down.

"Thank you for doing this," said Claire. "I'll pay you back for sure. I can't believe it. I'm not sure what else to say . . ."

There was always this awkwardness, both parties careful to pretend that no shift in the balance had occurred between them. "Let's go," said Chen. He hailed a car on his phone, entered Claire's address and the destination of his dinner meeting—two stops. It was towards the end of rush hour, and traffic was heavy but fluid, red tail lights hovering in front of them, people rushing on the sidewalks. Through the windshield wipers, other cars shone like brightly coloured stones, the late afternoon drizzle washing away the winter's lace veils of salt. At Claire's apartment, Chen asked the car to wait, and they went to the office. The super smirked when Chen said he was going to pay a month's rent and gave the apartment number, taking out his wallet.

"That good, huh?"

"A receipt, please."

At the elevator, Chen gave Claire the receipt. She leaned forward, a little too close, and he held out his hand to shake hers, but already she embraced him in thanks, her arms tight around his neck, her forehead on his shoulder. He could smell her hair, the undertone of anxious sweat now dried with the help of buprenorphine, the residue that emanated withdrawal, dopesick. Drawing away slowly, she saw his hand that was still suspended in extension, and shook it. There was a warmth to the fingers that recalled her grasp of his forearms on the night of her premiere. She mouthed *thank you* and was into the elevator, the door sliding shut behind her.

As the car made its way to the restaurant, Chen sank into the seat. This patient would survive the night, at least.

To a student of medicine,

In the clinic I taught you to enter into relationship with each patient, one human being meeting another with curiosity and compassion. I cautioned you that if you engaged your patients with the presence that medical practice deserves, you would feel deep hope for their recovery and often an equal disappointment to follow. Do you remember the metaphor I described to help you with balance, with boundaries? Your patient holds the torch in a dark room, but does not know how to light it. You are an expert in sparks, in how to strike flint on steel, and you are blind. Whether the torch is lit, and what the room looks like, you will only know from your patient's words. But it is no easy thing to light a torch using flint on steel, in a room where neither can see. Most times, you will be told that your spark has vanished into darkness, and you may be disappointed when your patient says—again—doctor, it's just as dark as before. You must offer to try again.

After a month in the clinic with me you asked me one after-noon, Why do you keep on trying? With so many restarts, and relapses, and patients . . . I'm sorry to say . . . who don't even want what you offer them. And then all those who never come back. And all those coroner's calls?

The question was natural and yet surprised me. I answered you, Most of my patients—they are trying to fix something from the past. They once found something that made them feel whole, until it didn't anymore. They are stuck with those old solutions.

But why do *you* keep trying?

I replied, I am doing a similar thing. For all the patients I've lost, for all the patients I will never see again. Each patient in front of me is a chance to get it right. But I try to find a different approach, or at least the right approach for the patient in front of me. I try not to get stuck.

You seemed deep in thought. You asked, All these molecules, which destroy lives, they all started in a lab.

It's not only the science—it's how it is used. You need perspective, context, and flexibility.

So you're willing to be flexible? you asked me.

Yours as always,
Dr. Chen

21

ON A WARM AFTERNOON, Chen came out of his building with his bicycle. The sidewalks bustled with people who had been enticed out of hibernation by the radiance of sun through glass, to go for strolls or walks with their dogs. Chen saw that some were dressed for winter in coats and hats, and some in T-shirts, and it occurred to him that one could do a study—to determine whether such choices indicated that people were more past or future oriented. The thought amused him, as he swung his leg over the saddle, and rolled past cafés where chairs had been hastily arrayed on patios and now people sipped lattes, or hoisted beers to the hazy blue sky.

Chen had suggested a bicycle ride to Fitzgerald, and now rode across the bridge, into the ravine, and then north towards Fitz's house. As medical students, they had explored the city when their bicycles had been both the way to get to the hospital—sprinting through yellow lights when late for morning rounds—and their means of escape from it. Upon graduation, Fitzgerald's parents had bought him a new Audi, while Chen stuck to his two wheels. A couple of years into his career, Chen bought a Mercedes for the price of the lease buyout when a Saudi resident was returning home. He did not drive it much—simultaneously embarrassed by it and protective. He did not want to park it in places where it might be dinged, which was alright because he didn't want to be seen in it—except occasionally when he did. The second time, in one year, that he went to the garage and found the battery dead from the car's lack of use, he sold the vehicle.

Around the time that Chen became carless once more, Fitzgerald declared that he would start riding with him again. Not to the hospital, of course, where Fitzgerald was neither embarrassed nor nervous about parking his latest car, a carmine red Porsche. But for exercise. Fitzgerald outfitted himself with a carbon-fibre race bike, and the complete range of form-fitting garments and accessories to accompany it—bib shorts, arm-warmers, little caps, a tiny computer. They began to ride together a little, but Chen's early morning routine was too early for Fitzgerald, and often Chen would pull his kit together for a planned ride at six and see that Fitz had sent a text at four, saying he was still up and would be lucky if he got to bed for six. This would be accompanied by a little dancing GIF.

Fitzgerald lost interest in cycling around the time of the College inquiry. He said he didn't want to be photographed in a tight, ridiculous outfit. Chen doubted that Fitzgerald's notoriety had quite risen to the level of paparazzi taking an interest in his cycling. After everything was settled, Fitz had lost his medical licence and Chen suspected that Fitzgerald had somehow lost his driver's licence as well, because the cars that had previously adorned his driveway were gone. His errands were now done on a slow, upright bike, and from time to time, like today, he was up for a spin on his race bike. Chen climbed up from the ravine to his friend's house, where he was already kitted out and ready to go.

Fitz shouldered his super-light bicycle and they went down the bank of the ravine, dug in their heels for purchase until they reached the path. Chen unlocked his steel bike from the tree—a frame made to measure with the slim tubes and classic geometry of an older bike, though equipped with the latest electronic shifting. It was nondescript, painted in an olive green. To someone who didn't know bikes, who wouldn't notice the brazed lugwork, it was nothing special. He swung it out of the forest into the clearing, onto the pathway.

Fitzgerald set off at a fast pace. Chen clicked his cleats into the pedals with one smooth motion, and soon caught his friend. They rode side by side, made their way south past clearings where green shoots poked through matted grey leaves. Here and there, thin dirt paths threaded away from the pavement, either mountain bike trails or footpaths to the spots where people lived rough in the ravine. Now and then, a glimpse of a tent, a flapping tarp.

The path rose almost level with the expressway, then swept down under the viaduct. Fitzgerald did not have fenders, nor did he slow or swerve for the puddles, so a mud-stripe painted itself up his back. Chen rode in front of him where the path narrowed, or beside him where it opened up, to avoid the spray that kicked up unchecked from Fitzgerald's rear tire.

"So," Chen shouted over the wind, "you're selling fentanyl now?"

"I wouldn't say it's a regular catalogue item."

They went into a tunnel single file, and emerged to narrowly miss two roller skiers who were alongside one another.

"There's no snow anymore, guys!" Fitz yelled, and surged forward.

Chen spun his pedals in a steady, fluid motion rather than pumping up and down. Fitz rode with bursts of speed, dashing ahead until he was winded, and then he coasted. It was easy for Chen to catch up to his friend, steadily pulling up on him at his unchanged pace.

"More of a special order? The fenny?"

"Sometimes I get a few patches," said Fitz. He coasted for a while before adding, "Word travels fast. Can't keep anything quiet in this town."

"You were trying?"

"I wouldn't say that. Though I've never needed to advertise."

Closer to downtown, there were more riders and runners who came from the other direction, and the pair slipped into single file. They crossed Lakeshore Boulevard, a multi-lane thoroughfare that followed the trajectory of the shore, at a spot where it was hard to tell what was being torn down and what was being constructed. The two cyclists gave a wide berth to the tractor-trailers and dump trucks, hopping curbs and splashing through puddled potholes to enter the docklands.

"I think you're over the line."

Fitz rode the centre of the lane—"No oncoming traffic, coach."

"Not that line. And not that you asked me."

"What line?"

"The fentanyl, Fitzgerald."

"Oh, you're still on about the fentanyl."

"The stuff that's killing everyone? Remember? Fentanyl? Wasn't your big idea that you were going to give people *less* dangerous stuff?"

"Patches. The real deal. Predictable dosing. The street stuff is contaminated with benzos—you know that's half of the reason people are dying."

"And the other half is the opioids. You once said that with the hydromorphone and the oxycodone, it's knives instead of guns. So what now? You're handing out revolvers instead of machine guns? Remember when we used to call fentanyl the contaminant? Fitz, what's happened to your judgment?"

"That's the judgment part. That a nice glass of wine is okay, but heroin and cocaine—oh dear me, no! Who's drawing these lines, anyways?"

Chen rode faster, forced Fitz to struggle a bit to keep up. Chen said, "I know that's how the argument goes, it's not that opioids suppress respiratory centres in the brainstem causing hypoxia and death—it's marginalisation and systemic discrimination that's deadly—let's talk about inclusive ways to give the oppressed more of what's killing them."

"An actual fentanyl patch is safer than the purple garbage. You see the drug-checking reports."

"And if someone is extracting the gel from your patches? To inject? Mix? Sell? But at least it was provided with kindness and good intentions."

The Leslie Street Spit was a jut of land like a crooked finger that extended from the hand of the mainland into the water. Expanded by the gradual dumping of construction waste over years and shaped into a park, it had a road running down its centre, wide enough for riders and runners to travel side by side in both directions. There was no protection from the wind, which at this time of year was brisk off the water. It gusted, strongly enough to catch the steering of their bikes, forced them to correct.

"Man, someone woke up on the wrong side," said Fitzgerald.

Fitzgerald's chain clunked into place as he shifted up two gears and sprinted away. He was out of the saddle, bobbing side-to-side. Chen clicked up one gear and remained seated, pushed the pedals faster. Fitz darted through the puddles and holes in a rough section of road, and Chen followed a different line, a swooping single motion that touched the edge of the road and arced back. He continued a steady but faster pace as Fitzgerald tired, and sat. Chen spun past Fitzgerald and ahead by a couple of bike lengths. He glanced back, and saw Fitzgerald was out of the saddle again, trying to catch him and get into his slipstream. Chen knew that he had enough power to pull away, but he eased off until Fitzgerald was on his wheel, and then kept it steady until they got to the lighthouse at the end of the spit.

Before the gravel loop that circled the lighthouse, Chen touched the brakes, rolled to a stop.

"Nice pull," Fitzgerald gasped, reaching for his water bottle.

"You know the physiology. Your customers have maxed out the hydromorphone, and now they need something stronger. Is that why you're selling fentanyl patches?"

"They're still alive."

"Some of them."

"More of them. Because I'm providing what they need."

"Show me the data."

Fitzgerald looked across the water, to where the city's skyscrapers were arrayed like children's toys. Then he turned, clapped Chen on the shoulder, made an effort to smile. "Haven't we beaten this horse too many times already?"

When fentanyl had first appeared in the heroin, Chen would alert his patients, show them the urine dipstick test. He would explain how much more dangerous this synthetic opioid was compared to heroin, its increased tendency to stop people's breathing. *And when you stop breathing, you die,* he would say, stating the obvious but hoping to add an element of fear to the calculus of decision-making, tipping someone towards change. *I knew something was different,* patients said at first—*I don't like this new junk anyways. Okay, doc. It's time, I just have to stop. For real, this is no joke—thank you for telling me.* Then, they would come back the next week, the fentanyl in their sample: *I know doc, definitely, it's going to change.*

But now, heroin was something that some people recalled wistfully, and others had never tried, because they had gone from pills to fentanyl. Down was fentanyl, and the complaint was contamination. With each month's report on the crumbs from baggies, and scrapings off cookers that doctors and users submitted to fancy university gas chromatography labs—mixed with fentanyl were etizolam, caffeine, xylazine. If there was carfentanil, Chen would impress upon patients, *That's a veterinary tranquilizer. They use it to sedate large animals.* He would add, for emphasis, *Like elephants.* Patients who had not quit but who had survived would say numbly,

Wow, that's totally crazy, but Chen got the impression that they were playing along, long since bored by their doctor's warnings. *Where did those samples come from*, some asked, *so that I can stay away from it?* Chen would say that he did not know, even when he did, because some people wanted to know which dealer had the most potent batch.

"There's a patient I'm trying to stabilize, and your patches aren't helping."

Fitz tipped up the water bottle, took a long drink. "I'll ask you this," he said. "Is water a good thing?"

"It's a simple molecule."

"Essential for life?"

"I sense a rhetorical trap. You're setting up some ridiculous metaphor."

Fitz was undeterred. "There is no life without water. And yet, people drown. Are you going to stop letting people drink water in order to prevent drowning? People get thirsty."

Brandon had come to restart his medications after another relapse, *What did you expect, Dr. Chen? I'm an addict.* Chen had replied, *Someday, I expect that you will do what is most true to yourself—the self that was there before you found drugs.* The young man cried out, *I never liked that person, doctor.* He was no longer welcome at home, was in a shelter, had lost his phone, arm red with abscesses. There was no point asking about the school semester.

"My patient *is* trying to change her life. The violinist. Her sister has been getting your fentanyl patches. She has a rich guy, your neighbour, who's paying. I don't know his name—he's vegan."

"My neighbour's girl of the month. He keeps on thinking he's going to save them. Then it all falls apart. Reminds me of someone else I know."

"What's that supposed to mean?"

"You've got that look of yours, Chen. Your saviour complex."

Fitz jumped back on his bike, and pointed it down a dirt path, a meandering back and forth of S-curves through brush that followed the line of the shore. Park workers had dumped soil atop the construction waste, like icing on a cake. The intent was for nature to reclaim the place, and it was slowly doing so, low ground cover concealing the detritus of a city. A rabbit darted across their path. Within a small bay, ducks and swans paddled with their feet, gave the appearance of gliding without effort across the water. Fitzgerald stood up out of the saddle and burst ahead of his friend, with a flash of speed they both knew would soon come to an end. They came to a grassy flat near the shore, and Fitzgerald slammed his rear brake, sliding to a stop as if he were atop a BMX bike and not a carbon race bike.

Chen pulled out Vietnamese subs from his panniers—baguettes stuffed with spicy hams, mayonnaise, and fresh herbs. He had picked them up for lunch, knowing that Fitz would have given no thought to any such practicality. He tossed one to Fitzgerald.

"Thanks. I see you didn't count on me for lunch."

"You are dependably undependable. Let's go through the current protocols," said Chen. It was easier to go through studies outside Fitzgerald's house, away from potential subjects. Today, the ground was wet and mulchy, so they stood and ate. Chen zipped up his windbreaker and pulled out his Thermos of tea. Fitzgerald drank from his water bottle, and took out a flask—had a swig.

"The view here is way better than the boardroom at Varitas," said Fitzgerald, admiring the corporate headquarters of downtown, the spire of the CN tower. Chen took out the protocols that he had brought with him, for a few studies that were a little slow to recruit. These briefings were always with paper documents. Chen did not want to leave an email trail. As they ate, Chen went through the background of the trials that needed a recruitment boost—the eligibility criteria, the number of subjects they needed. Fitzgerald ate his sandwich and asked good questions. It always surprised Chen that Fitzgerald could make sense even while drinking. Of course, these days he was usually drinking.

"The subjects I've been sending, they've been working out?"

"Not worse than usual," said Chen. Of course there were still dropouts and no-shows. They always booked a few extra to account for it. But Fitzgerald's recruits were less unreliable, on average, than the cold-call subjects. "And you have what you need?"

"Sure. I picked up the mail recently," said Fitzgerald, meaning the funds in the account that they both had access to. "You're really into the Memorex one," he said, flipping through the protocol.

"I'm interested in seeing how it works out," Chen admitted. He thought he had simply described it as he had the other trials, but Fitzgerald had known him for a long time. "It could be something important—we'll see."

"I will find you absolutely the most reliable junkies for the forgetting experiment. Does your little office romance have anything to do with your commitment to this project?" Fitzgerald teased.

"It's not really about forgetting," Chen peered over at the document. "Does it still say *forgetting*? They were supposed to fix the language in the background summary."

"What was the name of the compound again?"

"Very funny. We have medications that address withdrawal, but behaviour is still the issue. We take away the dopesickness but people keep on using. Shouldn't be a surprise. All of us keep on doing what we have already learned. What if ayahuagaine can help open the mind to patterning new behaviour?"

"What? Instead of you dealing methadone and me dealing hydromorphone?"

"We need fresh approaches."

Fitzgerald seemed deep in thought. After a moment he said, "She must be hot?"

"Her job is to get her compound approved, so she wants to make sure the trials move ahead." Chen smiled, "She's definitely persuasive. But that's not the main appeal of the molecule . . ."

"Normally you're so neat and tidy—but this has delicious potential for messiness. Good for you! Does Charlie know you're sleeping with a sponsor?"

"As if Charlie would care. Anyways . . . Bella and I keep work and personal separate. And even the personal . . ." Chen paused. "Anyways, this really *is* a novel compound. Not some little tweak for the sake of a patent. Actual new science. Remember that?" He took a bite of his sandwich, chewed. "Scientifically and therapeutically, ayahuagaine has potentially huge implications."

"People forget stuff all the time—half of what I learned in medical school I forgot."

"Maybe you just crammed it into short-term memory to pass an exam. The stuff that really matters gets stuck in our heads."

"Good luck forgetting that," said Fitzgerald. "That's human nature. Whether we're chasing a buzz or sex or money—we spend our lives wanting something, getting it, then going back for more."

"Right. Same with the stuff that really hurts us, it traps us, gets played on repeat. So instead of forgetting, maybe the question is: Can people do something new, instead of more of the same? Can this compound facilitate that change?"

Nearby, naked dogwood branches were thick with the black commas of cormorants. A few were in the air, but most of them sat in the trees as if waiting for a signal.

"You sound more infatuated with ayahuagaine than you are with the project manager. And if it works, then what? Chen, so many of your patients have already thrown it all away for their drug. Betrayed everything for its sake. If they have already lost family, work, dignity, for their substance of choice and they let go of that? What do they have left?"

Chen finished his sandwich, and neatly folded the empty paper bag. He drank some water. "My violinist still has her music. Listen, about the fentanyl patches, I want you to stop."

"I'm not selling them to your violinist."

"But to her sister."

"Who is not your patient." He dipped a rice paper roll in spicy peanut sauce and ate it slowly.

"Sooner or later she'll give them to my patient. You heard her play. Beyond music, she has a chance at life. And she told me she wants to quit the junk."

"You've been doing this for how long? And you believe that what people say in your office is what they really want? They say what you want to hear, *doc-tor*."

"While you're giving them what they really want?"

"What they need. That's what they tell me. But their actions line up with their words in my case. It can be slippery to climb up that ravine. Must be worth something."

Chen felt his heart pounding, but made an effort to keep his voice steady. "It's a simple request—to not sell opiates to someone."

"Is it? Tell me something—have you already bailed your violinist out of some jam?"

"What do you mean?" said Chen, knowing perfectly well.

"You're always falling in love with your patients."

"Never."

"I don't mean the obvious way. You see more in your patients than they do."

"If it's sometimes hard for them to see, isn't that part of their condition?"

"Always thinking that if you try a little bit harder, just climb a little bit further out on some tree branch . . . that it will make all the difference. You fall in love with what your patients could be. Then, you get disappointed. Remember your electrician?" When they were practising together at the Swan, one of Chen's patients, an electrician, showed up looking for someone to help him get his tools out of the pawnshop, had heard of the "emergency fund." Chen helped him. And then, another relapse, another slip down the muddy hole, and everything was gone again: phone lost, truck towed, tools hocked. This time Dr. Fitzgerald was in clinic when he asked, *If I could just get my tools, doctor, I can work out the rest.* Fitz got the electrician's tools out of hock, but held on to them until the guy installed a few lighting fixtures in his garage as payment. Straightened out for a few more months, and then disappeared. "And your history major who was too embarrassed to see you again?" Chen had paid her tuition just before she was expelled for dealing crystal meth. "She knew what I'm telling you," Fitz said, "that you would be disappointed."

"And what about the taco guy?" said Chen.

This was one insurance payment for a food truck that Chen had renewed, necessary for the vendor's licence. Once in a while the taco guy dropped off cactus and chorizo tacos at the Swan Clinic for Chen, pulled pork and pineapple for Fitzgerald, knowing these were the doctors' favourites.

"Does he still come by?"

"Yup, clean for years now. Pamela and I get the usual order."

"People need their tools, their tuition, but when you try to help them with these problems yourself, it's personal. Deep down, you think that taking it personally is what matters. I have a new theory."

"Here we go. A theory."

"We all choose exactly the wrong specialty in medicine. We play to our own weakness, pretending it's strength. If you don't like talking to people, you go into surgery, and cut up sleeping patients. Imagine if someone forced all the surgery keeners to train in psychiatry, and apply their concrete thinking to a vague, wishy-washy specialty. Hone it into something more precise! Make a decision!

And psychiatrists—they always want to formulate the case a bit more, hedge their bets with a five page assessment note—if they were surgeons, there would be more thoughtfulness before the decision to operate. That's the theory—give people the opposite of what they want, give the psychiatrists and surgeons each other's jobs, and the world is a better place."

"Every doctor would be miserable."

"And you, my friend, want to save people and you don't know where it stops. So if someone forced you to apply your conscientiousness, say, to radiology, and your embrace of humanity were possible only through images and not actual people—imagine the detail of the reports you would dictate? Imagine the care and subtle insight with which you would lavish your interpretations? None of these CT scan reports that just say *Normal study*. And if they made the radiologists practise addictions, sit there with your patients and filter through all the lies your patients tell you—not unlike the way a radiologist has to filter through a fuzzy ultrasound? Come on, you and I both know that half of what people tell you in clinic is utter bullshit. Well, that doctor would zero in on the clear picture of every patient. No sentiment. Just the true image."

"Cute, but ridiculous. Our best chance of being good at something, and finding satisfaction, is if it's our natural interest," said Chen.

"You think so?"

"Yes. I would be a terrible radiologist."

"Then why are you trying to change your patients? They're addicts. Let them be addicts."

Chen swigged some water. "How long did you spend concocting this little rhetorical trap? Addictions medicine is actually where all the patients want to change."

"Or say they want to change," said Fitzgerald, "meanwhile you fall for the idea that your patients could be better than they are, dreaming of their potential, and then you get mixed up in it—come on, I know you—the idea that if you just solve one situation, one problem, if you can help them past that one hurdle . . ."

"Can you just stop giving the fentanyl to my patient's sister?" said Chen, exasperated. "She has music, it means something to her. I paid a month of her rent, so she can get back on her feet. I'm fixing that one thing. And better for her not to have a sister with fentanyl patches."

"And sometimes the one problem that you try to solve, that you think is so important, is just one more moment like the ones that came before and the ones that come next."

"Or it's a turning point."

"You can't tell that when you fall for it."

After an uncomfortable silence, Chen said, "Maybe that's the chance you have to take. Because what is it to fall in love? Isn't it having hope?"

They finished their lunch, discovered that Fitzgerald had a flat tire from bashing his under-inflated bike through the dirt trails. Chen had all the repair stuff with him—a fresh tube, tire levers, a pump. Fitzgerald insisted on fixing it himself, and Chen sat looking out over the strange beach of construction waste, upon whose edge the water curled and lapped.

"Is it worth it?" asked Fitzgerald. "To have hope? And what if two people choose a different branch to climb out onto?" He pumped furiously with the tiny contraption connected to the valve stem.

"We each do what we think is best," Chen said softly. He tried to think of how many patients had pleaded with him—just one week of their pill of choice, one day, one pill. He could not remember them all, or his refusals—only one such request was clear, each word.

Fitzgerald tested the pressure of the tire with his thumb, and said, "No more fentanyl patches for the sister." Chen nodded with gratitude, and Fitzgerald handed back the bicycle tools.

"It's hard to believe this is the city." Chen looked out at the skyline. "Strange to see it, without the noise."

They rode off the spit, the wind helping them now, and then up the valley to the house. At the bottom of the hill, Chen left Fitzgerald with the protocols, which Fitz stuffed into his cycling jacket—the handwritten recruitment shortfalls on each of their face sheets—and rode back to his condominium. He put his bike away wet, in the bike locker, and went upstairs. He sat and wrote a letter to the student he had once known.

To a student of medicine,

Modern chemistry has gifted medicine with molecules that are both wonderful and seductive. Part of our job as physicians is to employ the cleverness of medicines, but we easily become infatuated with them. Then, we risk forgetting another part of our work, which is to restrain the mischief of these potions. Some drugs heal infections, but risk causing organ failure. Some can unstop the clogging of blood vessels, but may set off catastrophic bleeding. Morphine relieves pain, until it ravages the user with suffering. We have a sanguine expression: the risk–benefit balance, as it applies to our patients. Perhaps we should also point out our own trade-off: the cleverness–wisdom tension.

Some patients accuse doctors of using molecules recklessly. Others are angry that we guard them too carefully. We receive praise for the work that drugs do, and answer for their misdeeds. In scientific research, the golden ring to grasp is always more powerful treatments with fewer side effects. All the magic! None of the tricks!

And a further complication—the patient is not healed by the molecule's actions upon receptors and neurotransmitters alone.

The patient wants the doctor to care. The words we say, the desire we have for the patient to do well, these must be felt if they are to matter. If we are uncertain, if we are torn, if we are frustrated—the inverse principle applies, and this feeling may spoil the pills. It is as if we doctors have been squeezed into the pill bottle, and the patient hopes that we will emerge along with the medicine.

In addition to these considerations that make medicine a humanistic science and an art, we are expected to be stewards of the supply: to tally the pills, dole them out appropriately, inventory the potential benefits and mischiefs. When a potential discrepancy was first pointed out to me by the Varitas pharmacist, I thought it was probably an accounting problem, and nothing more. But I asked for it to be investigated, since if there was anything to it . . . it involved a large quantity of missing opioids.

The computer support department proposed allowing the system to appear unchanged on the user end. Keystroke logging would record anyone trying to alter the receiving ledger. Would one of the pharmacy assistants or technicians reveal themselves, I wondered?

When you first arrived to train with me, I had been impressed by your desire to learn about the whole lab—to tour the pharmacy, understand dispensing, inventory management, things a doctor takes for granted that someone else is doing for them. I, too, take an interest in such details. That is why, when the pharmacist mentioned the inventory problem to me, I did not brush it off although, when I learned the truth, I almost wished I had.

When I was told what the surveillance found, I refused to believe it at first. Until I was shown the matching time-stamps on the keystroke logs, and the security footage of the computer terminal. Just the simplest thing, really—anyone with access to the ledgers needed only delete a zero, for hundreds of pills at a time to disappear. The pharmacy implemented a tighter system—counter-signatures, a verification loop, and it was my job to address the rest of it.

Yours as always,
Dr. Chen

22

LATE ONE MORNING, on one of the first properly warm days of the year, the sisters smoked almost all that was left of their heroin stash. Danny had a connect for the good brown stuff again. He was supposed to meet them early in the afternoon. When Molly's vegan had said the dealing doctor no longer had fentanyl patches, she asked the vegan sweetly if he would be willing to support a gardener. It was all organic, she assured him, and he received the suggestion enthusiastically. It saved him the emasculation of being unable to provide. Buying Molly a few eight-balls at a time was more convenient than fussing with the dealing doctor, the vegan said. He liked to show that he had lots of money and not much spare time.

With eight-balls of heroin laying around the apartment, it was easy for Molly to share and impossible for Claire to resist. The thing about having quantities of stuff around was that it just made sense to help others out. Not for free—but that didn't make it any less helpful. Molly's friends knew what they needed, and pretty soon friends of friends called as well. She bought a digital scale accurate to point-one grams. Claire sometimes assisted, spotting her or carrying the stuff. With cash coming through their hands, the sisters picked up from Danny directly, although Molly asked him not to tell the vegan that she was also buying on her own. The vegan liked being a provider. Molly didn't want to spoil that for him, she told the gardener. Also, even though on some days a full month of rent might come into her hands, it flowed out just as quickly. The vegan understood the situation well enough to give her cash as well as drugs when they "connected."

Still on a beautiful high, the sisters went out to the market to meet Danny. While waiting, Molly took photos of Claire in a tank top and a light skirt—choosing mangos at a fruit stand, leaning forward at a café table with an espresso, sitting on a bench in the park reading a *New Yorker*, an engaged expression and mouth slightly open as if in conversation with someone behind the camera. *You have to look like someone in a story*, Molly said. *It's a story they're already making up.* Claire hammed it up. It was an early summer day of dappled light through translucent leaves, children exclaiming joyfully from the high bars of play structures, and the forgiveness of all minor sins. The sisters went out for a fancy lunch and then picked up some groceries. Each of them bought a brocade silk scarf at a small shop that sold fair-trade items from Tibet. The best feeling with money came from being casual with it, buying what they wanted, never mind need—new scarves, charcuterie, and three-point-five grams of heroin.

Back at the apartment, Molly pulled out her phone and showed Claire the photos.

"You look great!"

Even in the tiny telephone screen, Claire could see that being high opened up her smile, made her poses relaxed and inviting, erased worry lines and tension. She laughed looking at the photos, and put on a Thelonious Monk album. Molly got some pipes, and they smoked the rest of their previous batch. What abundance! An old batch to finish off! A fresh, new one in a baggie. Molly lounged on the couch, swiped and tapped at messages on her phone, mentioned distractedly that someone had ordered a few points for tonight, fiddled some more, and then held out the device, on which one of Claire's photos now had a tagline: "Vivacious renegade artist desires soulful encounters . . ."

"Oh come on, I'm not doing it. I can't be an escort."

"Sugar dating. Not escorting. An escort just shows up, like a pizza. The box opens. She spreads her legs. Here, you can be picky. With who, what you're doing. What you get out of it. Have some fun!"

"I want to offer private violin performances," Claire giggled.

"I'll add that to the profile, some of them like to be teased. Let's get a video."

Molly took clips of Claire playing, riffing to Monk, her live improvisation darting in and out of the recording. Molly uploaded Claire, the instrument floating as if she were holding on to prevent its escape.

"What's your favourite thing in the world?" Molly asked.

Claire felt that she should say music, but at that moment she knew what was true and answered, "Heroin."

"Done!" she said, putting aside the phone. "That's your account password."

"What?" laughed Claire. "You did it?"

"I used your regular email address. Your username is 'fiddling-hands.' There's a thing where you can say how much you want—I put 'substantial' for you. You'll probably get messages right away. You look amazing. But show me the messages first. You have to figure out quick who's for real and who's just wasting your time, weed out the Splenda daddies."

"Forget it. Delete the account. It's not the relationship I want."

"Is there any relationship, Claire, romantic or otherwise, where both parties don't want to get something out of it?" Molly was back on her messages. "Anyways, you free tonight? A little delivery.

Someone I've never met. Friend of a friend. I would prefer some company."

"Sure." Claire examined the baggie they had bought from Danny, rubbing the stuff between her fingers through the bag. "Does it look different to you?" she asked.

"It looks beautiful," said Molly, still floating on their earlier smoke.

Lately, Molly got invited to parties even more than when she first returned to Toronto—sports teams, club promoters, sometimes real estate guys. Whoever put together the parties kept lists, had angles— gestures of gratitude from the bars, the restaurants, the racetrack up at Woodbine, the limos that took them there. *You never pay for anything, and you don't have to do anything except look hot,* was how Molly had explained it to Claire—*unless you want to.* But ever since Molly had been getting eight-balls from Danny, she had her own angle. It was safer for one person to do the deal, and another to carry the stuff.

That night, as Molly finished her makeup, she said, "The vegan is going to be there tonight, and he's bringing a friend. Super-nice guy. Loves your profile."

"Molly, no. I said to delete the account."

"This is even better. My guy knows this guy. I met him once. He doesn't want to message on platforms—either shy or married."

They went into parties separately. Claire carried tiny packages, containing what Molly had promised. Molly went and had a chat, and got paid. If something looked or felt wrong, she would touch her left ear, signalling to Claire to leave. If things were okay, Molly drifted away and Claire wandered over, made the delivery.

That night, Claire walked into the club a few minutes after Molly, who had her hand on the shoulder of a guy who sat straight up and wore a forced smile. Something seemed off to Claire, and Molly looked over right away and touched her left ear. Claire turned on her heel and fled to the elevator, her heart pounding. She collided with a boisterous group that was getting off as she pushed her way in, and she stood to one side and pounded on the elevator buttons to take her down. She rushed through the lobby, to the taxi stand. She considered tossing the stuff into the nearby bin, but could not bear to throw it away. They hadn't even had a chance to taste this batch. Claire was craning to see if a taxi was coming when she saw Molly hurrying towards her.

"What's up? Why did you leave?"

"You touched your ear!"

"What?"

"The signal!"

"Ohmigod, I forgot about that," Molly began to laugh, "my ear was just itchy!"

"So it wasn't the police? We're not busted?" Claire gasped.

"What? No, everything's fine."

"And I was about to throw it away. I thought we were getting busted."

"Claire, you have to stop streaming all those shows, come on! Let's go have fun!"

Knocking on the metal door, and the rattle of the flip latch on the stall.

"I saw her go in there," a female voice.

"You okay?"—another woman's voice. "Let's make some room! Come on! Nothing to see here!" Then, towards the bathroom stall, "Are you okay? Are you in there?"

Aching back. She had twisted down into a strange clump, one of her heels—ridiculously high—was off. Where was Molly? The white and black checkerboard tiles ached upon her retina.

Claire's nose and the side of her face were pressed into the inside of the toilet stall, and jolted when someone pounded the door. She had slumped over, must have slipped off the toilet.

"Paramedics here! Someone in there?"

Claire managed to grunt, wanted to stand, but the bathroom stall just spun around her, the smell of urine. Somewhere, there were sirens.

Now she remembered—wandering into the club, watching Molly return to the stiff-backed guy. When Molly left, Claire approached him, slipped the baggie into the pocket of his suit jacket, and that was it. Then sitting down with Molly's vegan, and meeting the guy Molly assured her was not a Splenda daddy. She had said before they left the apartment, *He's the kind of guy who feels left out at a party—so smile nice to him and he'll give you whatever you want. You don't have to do anything you don't want to do,* Molly had assured her, *but just in case, and if we get separated . . .* and slipped her a cosmetics case that contained some condoms, works, and down. Molly put together a kit for herself as well.

Cars, it turned out, were the guy's thing. As an investor, he was quick to point out, saying that he had an interest in several dealerships. *Yes, you look like a car dealer,* shouted Claire above the noise. The car dealer shifted in his chair like he was determined to be comfortable. Claire felt a little bead of sweat. That feeling, like she wanted to squirm and scream—was it that the heroin was wearing off, or was it the way the car dealership guy was looking at her, like an auction item he was considering? There was no way anything was going to happen between her and this guy, but she still had to get through the evening, didn't want to ruin anything for Molly. The last thing Claire remembered was grabbing the clutch purse and making for the bathroom.

Getting into the stall, locking the door, prepping the shot, finding the vein, all of that she inferred, filled in the blanks, but did not remember.

She heard, "Fire department! Hello! Fire here!" A male voice.

"You okay?" called a syrupy but tired female voice. "Paramedics here." A radio crackled, and Claire heard the woman's bored voice:

"We got an unresponsive here. Bathroom stall. Called fire to break in the door. Yeah, I can't—modified duties. Bad knee."

Further commotion, "Hey! Hey! Open up!"

Claire struggled to get up, and found that her legs were tangled and cramped. She reached up for the latch, fiddled it uselessly. Claire remembered the voices of children from the beginner violin class—*Where is Miss Claire? Is she alright? I saw her go in there, Miss Frances.* Then a light, then she was back in the bathroom of the club. Had been slapped in the face by the door as someone kicked it open.

"I'm here!" she said, reaching out to the firefighter. "Give me a minute . . ."

"Sharps! Sharps!" he yelled, seeing the needle in her arm.

"Oh gosh, I'm so sorry," she said. From somewhere, a yellow sharps container appeared and Claire dutifully went to extract the needle but saw that half the shot was still in the barrel, and could not resist sinking the plunger home before she pulled it out and put it in the sharps.

"Saw that," said the female paramedic, chewing her gum. "Waste not, huh?"

How much had she done, she wondered? They had gotten good at dosing the heroin—the good stuff. Maybe a little groggy sometimes, but . . .

Blackness again.

A child's voice in her memory: *She looked like she was going to barf, she was showing us "Twinkle, Twinkle, Little Star," is this how you do it, Miss?* Her itchy nose, tried to scratch but couldn't move. Arms tied down, she realized. Points of light in front of her—delicate and soft. It was the ceiling, and as she raised her head she saw that she was in a stretcher, being rolled across the club. Claire put her head back, closed her eyes, and wished for another shot.

"Yeah, she's out again, better Narcan her," said one paramedic.

"I guess better now than in the truck," said the other.

Before Claire could protest she felt the wasp-sting of a needle in her thigh, and the world exploded. The volume was suddenly turned up—the club an erupting percussion section of guffaws and mocking laughter. Like stage lights snapped on, the overhead halogens blazed, and Claire barely managed to twist to the side of the stretcher to vomit. She caught a glimpse of car-dealership guy, who looked as if someone had brought soured food to his table. Molly running alongside the paramedics as they wheeled Claire away, and clambering into the ambulance, yelling at them to untie her sister. Claire thrashed against the restraints, agony as if her bones were already out of her body and she wanted to throw them away, anything to make it stop.

"I want to drive," said the male paramedic.

"Nice. *Me* in the back with them?"

"You drove the last time we did a Narcan."

"Modified duties, remember? Bad knee?"

"What does that have to do with . . . forget it, she'll be fine. We'll both ride up front."

As they drove off, Claire pleaded with the medics in front to give her something, and Molly did as well.

"We gave you Narcan, we saved your life," the male medic replied.

"Yeah, but now I want to die!" Claire moaned.

Every bump in the road felt like her body had been tossed down a mine shaft, every turn a violent roller coaster. The ambulance stopped at an intersection. Claire fumbled, grabbed, pushed at anything, but she was strapped in tight. She felt a buckle give, Molly was freeing her—and with the strength of agony she hurled herself up, towards the doors of the ambulance, seized the handle, and tumbled out. The sirens were not on.

"Get back in here!" a medic shouted. Then, "OK, see you soon!" But already she was running down the street, Molly trailing her. Claire stopped at a bench to one side of a squat stone church. Molly shushed her sister as a cop car passed. Claire pleaded for Molly's cosmetics case, and they pulled it out, shared it, but the shot was weak—barely did anything. This batch was not the good stuff—it was unpredictable, hot and cold spots. Molly's purse was otherwise empty—she had somehow lost the cash from the sale.

There was the clatter and whoosh of a nearby GO train. Claire recognized where they were. Not far away. They could walk. The door was opened by the girl with the torn earlobe; now her head was shaved on each side, the hair from the top like a wiper blade that she tossed from one side of her head to the other.

"Hey! It's fiddle girl!" said Julia.

The room stank of cigarettes and the acrid tang of crack. The same two guys watched hockey on television, and drank from large cans of Rockstar. Claire collapsed into the fetid couch that she now remembered, holding herself. Julia settled herself next to Claire, petting her head as if she were a cat. Molly stood in front of the two guys, negotiating the price. Then Molly tried to mention, as if it were an afterthought, that they would return later with the money, at which the guys laughed. Claire saw Molly shift, appealing to the camaraderie of junkies, pointing out how sick her sister was, and how badly she needed just a little. The two Rockstar drinkers were unmoved. One went to the bathroom and stood there with the door open and the lights on, savouring a long, bowl-gurgling piss before sidling up next to Julia on the couch, putting his arm around her.

"I'm tired," said Julia, and shoved his arm off.

"So what am I supposed to do?" asked the guy.

Julia changed the channel, stone-faced.

"So now what?" the guy on the couch mused. The other one laughed, adjusted himself. He opened the door, a bed visible within.

"Fuck you," Molly said.

"I was just gonna say!" said the one on the couch, impressed with his own wit.

Next to the bed, Molly stood with one hand on a hip, and her cosmetics case in the other. She instructed the men to close the door to the bedroom, as if they were children who had failed to learn basic manners.

"Don't worry," said Julia to Claire, "those assholes don't last long."

Claire could hear the guys inside the room, a soundtrack of aggression and mockery, ritualistic and banal in its obscenity. Claire knew she should feel worse about it, that she should want to crawl further into some hole of agony and self-hatred, but she had already dug so deep before they got to the house that there was nowhere further to go. The men grew louder, as if to invite a response, but there was no sound from Molly, until after a lull of silence, she insisted on the number of points that she had negotiated, and no, the point she did before they satisfied themselves did not count. The bedroom door opened, and Molly came out first, went into the bathroom, closed the door. The water ran for a long time. The stuff they had was white—they said it was pure, without further detail. Claire was shaking too much to do it, and Molly came out of the bathroom, unnaturally calm, and fixed her sister. Slipped in the needle, injected her with kindness. It was an opioid, yes, without the warmth. But still, a wand had been waved—fluorescent glare rather than incandescent glow. Claire was able to stand, felt the ache in her body vanish, her stomach untangle. It was once she felt better, once she felt physically well, that she looked around her. Julia held a lighter made of purple transparent plastic under a crack pipe, blue flame licking the bowl. One of the guys was on his phone, sniggering, scrolling through the photos they'd taken of the girl who'd shown up with a sister in withdrawal. The other guy was shooting himself up using a vein in the top of his left foot, and then his head drooped. The sweat was no longer running, but cooled on Claire's body, though now her anger transcended relief.

Claire thought of a youth orchestra trip, when half of the musicians were chosen to visit the Kunitachi College of Music in Japan, and Claire was not on the preliminary list, had fumbled in some concerts. After practice, Molly had said that she would talk to the conductor, told Claire to go back to the school dormitory. But Claire had waited for her sister; finally, after what seemed like a long time, she had gone up to the conductor's office—but did not knock when she heard noises from behind the closed door. Claire was on the final list for the trip to Japan. Josef had been red-faced when Claire told him what she thought had happened. Who else would she tell? *I will have a word with the conductor,* he had said. *You must not tell your parents.* Not that she would have. Their parents did fly to Tokyo for the concert, a half-Japanese and half-Canadian joint orchestra, and praised *their girls,* as they still referred to their daughters, for their performance.

Claire launched herself from the couch, grabbed the phone, and started beating its owner with both of her fists. She boxed him around the ears and struck him in the head. The guy fought back until Claire snapped his head back with her elbow. She pummelled him from above, both fists striking his face. She saw the old youth orchestra conductor, the way he had sometimes smirked at Molly. She stood up and kicked the guy over and over in the gut. Then he was quiet. Next to him, his friend was out—the needle still in his foot. Claire grabbed the works, stuck it through his pants, plunged the needle somewhere into his groin. He barely flinched, the syringe protruding, the drug stronger.

Julia lit another rock, giggling. "Good for you. Serves those assholes right."

Claire scrolled the phone, erased the images that had just been taken of her sister, each one searing itself into her memory as she hit delete.

23

AS THE HEAT of a summer day softened into evening, Bella and Chen walked down Queen West, saying little. She had a small overnight shoulder bag, and he had a backpack with a change of clothes and toiletries. The morning after she had invited him into the glass-and-steel condo, he'd noticed an instruction sheet in a picture frame on the wall: how to use the coffee maker, the steam shower, where to put the trash and the key after self-checkout. Bella saw him reading the instructions, and explained that her place was being redecorated. Since then, Chen had seen Bella only as far as the door to her own mid-century brick building in Yorkville, whose uniformed concierge knew without being told to call up to Bella, and then to invite Chen to wait on one of the soft leather club chairs in the lobby, rather than buzzing him up.

Sometimes they went to his place in the Distillery District, but mostly she liked spaces that neither of them had seen before, and would never visit again: the suite over a former coach house, a houseboat that swayed with their movements, a waterfront condominium furnished all in glossy red, flat-pack furniture. Once, when he had asked her why, she said that she was worried about forgetting her socks at his place, or some underwear, and that she would show up and find it neatly folded and waiting for her. *And then what would that mean?* she had asked, with a mock expression of horror.

As they walked together now, with just what was needed for a night they would spend in an apartment she had rented online, her phone rang. She checked the number, then silenced the phone and put it into her pocket, where it buzzed for a few more seconds. He walked a little more quickly, and she caught his hand, squeezed it. They passed from the brightly lit main streets into a pocket of what had once been immigrant homes and backyard businesses— skinny two-and-a-half-storey piles of brick crowned by shingled gables, canopied by maples. With her hand in his, Chen had just begun to relax into the after-warmth from a shared bottle of red wine, an excellent meal, an evening under way, when her phone dinged with the sound of a text. She let go of his hand, pulled out her phone.

Trinity Bellwoods had once been the banks of a stream, but the water had been piped somewhere beneath the city, and now flowed under the feet of those who arrived for a show. A dance performance, Bella had said during dinner, to take place in the sunken portion of the park. Bella pointed out a good place to watch the performance, halfway up the hill. She had seen this group before, and thought Chen would like them.

Bella was the one who knew what to see, where to go. She suggested performance art, meals at pop-up restaurants, obscure musicians who sometimes became big. She heard about these things from friends whom she mentioned to Chen as if he knew them. Another ding, and she pulled out the phone long enough to glimpse the text and put it back. Dance was something Chen knew nothing about, and for that reason, on the infrequent occasions that he saw it, he was relieved of the habit of thinking, and enjoyed it fully.

They sat on the grass, and her phone buzzed again.

"Answer the phone if you like. Someone really wants you."

Her phone made the noise indicating a voicemail. "So sorry." She stood, adding quickly, "It might be a work thing."

The in vitro and animal trials with Memorex had gone smoothly. Chen had been particular about how the work should be done, and Omega conceded, although they grumbled about having to expand the budget. Charlie was happy with that, and Matt stopped protesting once the price was set. That was the way it was with venture capital. The price was said to be outrageous, unreasonable, ludicrous, until they handed it over, and then all they cared about was the data. Chen supposed that this was because the money was never theirs to start with—it was just the hassle of getting it. Later, if the data was positive, Matt would get his piece of the pie.

The first-in-human trials for Memorex had been relatively uneventful—small initial test doses to assess for indications of unexpected toxicity, or, as Fitzgerald used to tell sponsors, *to light a match and see if they explode into a ball of flames.* This had been followed by dose-escalation, gradual increases of the doses, looking for further adverse effects—liver, kidney, and heart issues.

After she listened to the voicemail, Bella said, "Something I have to deal with."

She walked away slowly, texting. Around them, couples and small groups found places to sit. Chen saw Bella walk back towards him, look down at her phone, stop, put it to her ear, and move away again. Then she seemed to stiffen. He heard her saying with concern, *of course, of course,* before putting the phone in her pocket and returning to him.

"Work call?" Chen asked, fantasizing that she would say it was her real lover, and that he would laugh it off.

"Everyone is thrilled by what you've done. To hit the recruitment target so quickly for the next trial really helps our momentum."

"The stars aligned," he said. The abuse liability study came next—to show how much "recreational potential" Memorex might have at the doses they intended to use therapeutically. Going forward, finding the right subjects for the upcoming sequence of trials was a bit like determining the proper temperature of porridge, or at least that was the analogy Chen used to explain the concept to sponsors—*not too hot, and not too cold.* The subjects had to be using illicit drugs, and were therefore unstable by definition, and yet be reliable enough to show up at the lab at a specified time and date, and to follow rules. To be able to consent, they couldn't be high at screening, but if they didn't like drugs, what was the point of having them in the trial?

"So great that we've got the subjects now. So I'm surprised . . . to hear about your response to the institutional review board."

"They made some valid points," said Chen. Maybe that really had been a work call.

"Which you simply agreed with."

"They made some good safety suggestions." Some of the subjects in the dose escalation trials had reported fluttering in their chests, a sensation of their hearts jumping. All the electrocardiograms were almost normal, except for some premature ventricular contractions—a scattering of electrical impulses. The board had pointed out that because the adverse effects were brief and transient, the full implications might not have been captured with "moment in time" electrocardiograms. One of their suggestions was twenty-four hour telemetry to watch subjects' hearts around the clock. And expense was only the first issue it created.

"Well, of course," said Bella. "Safety is the most important thing. But there is also timing to consider. Since the dosing for abuse liability is scheduled to begin next week."

He'd sent his reply back to the review board, accepting all their recommendations, earlier that day. He hadn't thought the news would loop back to Omega so soon. He had intended to give Bella a heads-up over breakfast.

"Starting next week might be pushing it," Chen said, as if he had not worked this through, as if he didn't know the changes would make their current schedule impossible. Around-the-clock cardiac monitoring was a different trial set-up, requiring different equipment, rooms, staff, and a change in the informed consent form for subjects. "Who was that on the phone?"

"I've had your back," said Bella. "I told Matt the best advocate for a new molecule is an impartial but critical investigator."

"Isn't that what you—Omega—is paying me for? To treat this critically?"

"Maybe that's why Matt is surprised you didn't push back at *any* of the board's requests. You just signed off. And without consulting with the client?"

"It will delay things a week. It's hard to use *advocate* and *impartial* in the same sentence."

"Easily two weeks."

"You could always get a different doctor," said Chen, and then, "or I should say, Omega could source an alternate vendor and principal investigator, if the sentiment is that Varitas is not performing to your expectations."

"I'm not questioning your judgment—it's just there are other considerations I have to . . ." Her phone dinged, she glanced at it, seemed to have lost her train of thought.

"That's what the principal investigator does," said Chen. "He makes judgments."

They sat in silence, watched the crew setting up for the performance, testing lights, directing people where to sit. Darkness closed in on the space. Chen knew, of course, the ways he could have quietly mollified the board's requests. He could have emphasized the mild nature of all the reported adverse events, noted their infrequent occurrence. He could have suggested that given the lack of other safety queries, and the impending dosing for the abuse liability trial, it made the most sense to report interim results after the first cohort, and pause dosing if there was any further arrhythmia. To have done so would have been entirely reasonable—and so why didn't he?

Premature ventricular contractions were like hiccups. Monitor someone long enough, and they would probably throw a few beats here and there. Like tiny clouds on the very edge of the horizon over water, they might not signify a storm. You could stand there looking at them, wondering if the slight wind you felt had travelled all the way across Lake Ontario. Chen had looked carefully at the few errant beats on the tracings, matched their timing with the subjects' reports of a fluttering sensation, stared at them as if the jagged squiggles on paper would reveal more than the existence of a tiny, uncoordinated electrical discharge within the heart. Sometimes it came down to feel, a shift in the breeze. Chen wondered if he would be going home alone after the performance; maybe that would be best. Bella reached for his hand.

"Of course," she said, pulling him close, "you're good at what you do, so you get to be particular, right? With whom you do studies, how you do it, what you get out of it." Her usual smile had returned, frustration seemingly vanished. She shared a little anecdote about other people speaking admiringly of Chen, referring to an incident when he had stood his ground. Chen pretended that he hadn't heard it before, said modestly that he was just doing his job. "Let's enjoy the show," he said. "Work is work, right?" The performers quietly took positions around an empty space, and the audience settled.

"I think it's about to start," Bella whispered, and drew close.

One might say they were seeing each other regularly. Bella called when she wanted to—*Are you busy tonight?* Or—*Do you want to see something cool?* Other times—*Feel like hanging out? I am just so restless . . .* He was usually available when she called. If Chen proposed something spontaneous, Bella always sounded surprised to hear from him—was often sweetly, apologetically busy, but always suggested plans for a later date. They'd had a frank conversation early on: work was work. *I wouldn't want you to think that us spending time together has anything to do with business*, Bella had said.

Looking down the hill into the performance space, Chen saw a woman stand up from the crowd wearing a long grey coat draped over her shoulders like a cape. She seemed to be alone, and for a moment appeared lost. Then, with a single motion, she lifted her arms, let the coat fall to reveal her slender outline in a simple, dark dress, and raised a violin and bow. Now, a spotlight found her and Chen saw it was Claire. Her outstretched arms released a lilting, rising melody from the violin.

Had it been a month since he'd paid her rent? After that, one urine sample had been clear, and Chen allowed Claire to take the medications as carries. The visit after, heroin showed up. Chen explained that he was expected to make the doses observed again. *In that case, I'll just stop,* she said, *I can't go to the pharmacy every day again.* He hesitated, and wrote the prescription as carries, for another week, citing exceptional circumstances in the chart. He asked, *Claire, what's happening?* Claire had replied, *There's too much shit going on.* Was it her sister? Chen asked. To get well, he said, she might have to take a break from certain people. *She's my sister . . .* He tried to use a metaphor of two people drowning, that they pull each other down, but she was not listening. At the following visit, fentanyl appeared in the urine test. Claire had brushed off his questions, taken the prescription. On that prescription, the doctor specified observed doses. A message came later from the pharmacy, she had not filled any of it. That night Chen slept fitfully.

Now, Claire walked towards the central performance space, her instrument raised, the crowd parting for her as she played. She was a conjurer, each dancer coming forward according to a phrase, a motif, a chord progression that was intended for them alone.

Billowy streaks of coloured fabric unfurled from high oak limbs, released from above, and the dancers climbed them, rotating their bodies. A man in yellow soared from one tree trunk out into space and back. A woman in white tumbled towards earth, and then arrested her own fall with trust in the silks, held in tension by her ankles and feet. The music elevated the dancers, spurred them to flight, and then they plunged and swung towards the violinist, and the audience. Claire remained on the ground; her bow danced and attacked in careless abandon.

"She *is* gorgeous," Bella said.

"Have you ever heard music like that?"

"You can look at other girls," she laughed, "I don't care."

"She's a patient of mine," he said.

When the aerialists had returned to the ground, Chen clapped along with the approving crowd. People wearing the black T-shirts of La Danse de Minuit, with *00:00* in white lettering, circulated with collection hats, and Chen saw Claire's sister amongst them. Her smile projected a canny charm as she worked the crowd. When she reached Chen with her hat, he stuffed too much money into it. A wink, and she was already on to the couple next to Chen.

"I should go speak to my patient," he said.

"Of course," said Bella, engrossed with her phone.

Chen navigated the clusters of brightly clad dancers, knots of young, beautiful people who laughed and greeted the performers. Other musicians—a percussionist with hand instruments, a keyboard player at a synthesizer—chatted with Claire. He was happy to see her with her friends, fellow musicians. He was relieved just to see her. But as he came near he wondered, what was he going to say? *I'm so glad you're still alive?*

As he stepped back, about to fade into the crowd, Claire saw him and waved, "Dr. Chen! What did you think?"

"Magical."

Claire said excitedly, "Did I tell you I'm about to go on tour? The trio! Five provinces, starting next week! I should have told you. About the medication. I couldn't continue anyways. On the road. And I get it. You could only go so far."

"The pharmacy called. They were worried."

"Oh I'm sure," she rolled her eyes, "but it means a lot to me that you tried. Don't worry. I've got it figured out. And I haven't forgotten the loan. I'll make good by the end of the summer," she said.

"That's not what I'm worried about—" he said, but she was no longer listening to him. Claire crouched down to the violin case to put away her instrument. She opened the rosin box, and Chen glimpsed a syringe.

Bella appeared and took Chen's arm.

"We had better go," said Chen, turning to his date. As they walked along the pathway, he heard Claire behind them, already in animated conversation with someone else. A few blocks from the park, they walked past small, squat warehouses and factories in laneways.

"Your patient seemed quite happy," said Bella.

"She played beautifully," said Chen, "she must have been pleased."

"Almost too happy?"

"What do you mean?"

Bella raised her eyebrows, amused.

The place they had booked, described online as a renovated industrial space, was not far. Sirens echoed after them as he read the lock code from the email, then unlocked the doors. According to the listing, it had once been the warehouse of a metal fabrication shop. Did Claire still have her apartment? Chen wondered. Had he seen pills with the syringe? Or powder? Did it matter?

As they stood in the entryway, he tasted the salt of Bella's neck, touched her back, knew the areas of softness, the shadows and cliffs. She undid his shirt buttons, he felt her breath on his skin, but the movements felt methodical rather than passionate.

Moving to the couch in the living room, they sat beneath a pair of paintings—two life-sized figures in pastel and crayons whose heads were from some avant-garde fantasy, proportioned relative to their naked, eroticized bodies like the heads of toddlers. Bella had chosen this rental after she'd spotted these paintings in the online photo gallery. A phone rang from the entryway where they'd hung their jackets. Chen felt some annoyance, but Bella ignored the ringing, silenced him with her mouth, and he relaxed. The phone stopped. It started again, persisted, stopped. After a little while, the phone buzzed with a text message.

"That's yours," she said.

Chen went into the hallway, fished out his phone, and saw a text from Fitzgerald. *Sorry to bug you, can you give me a call?* As he spoke with Fitz, he heard Bella in the galley kitchen, opening cupboards, the louder hum of an open fridge. In the background at Fitzgerald's, crashing and yelling. Fitzgerald seemed unconcerned by the commotion, asked if Chen had access to some intravenous antibiotics. *No, that's a hospital stock item,* Chen said. *I might ask you to swing by, tomorrow,* said Fitzgerald.

When he returned, Bella had poured herself a drink; there was one for Chen too. He kissed her.

"Everything okay?" Bella asked.

"Just a work thing—scheduling a meeting."

He sipped the drink—light, and potent. That was the kind of thing Chen had come to expect from Bella—she knew how to talk to anyone, what to do on a summer evening, how to mix cocktails in unfamiliar apartments.

"Anything I need to know about?"

"No."

"Then let's forget about work." She relaxed, leaned into him.

24

CHEN SET OUT after his clinic, bicycle panniers bulging, into the hazy oppression of the afternoon. He rode down into the valley, his jersey clinging with sweat, stopped at a familiar spot, locked the bike to a tree. He swatted mosquitoes as he went up the hill to Fitzgerald's house. Fitzgerald had told Chen many times that he could use the front entrance, that climbing up into the backyard from the ravine was really for "the public," but they both knew that while "the public" had to keep out of sight so that the neighbours would not complain, Chen was sensitive about who might see him.

It was on a similarly hot afternoon a few years previous, when Chen saw a man in their clinic who had a prescription for large doses of hydromorphone. It had been written by Fitz. That much was clear in the brief chart note, though the rationale for the prescription was not. Chen clicked through the chart, saw that the man's journey had started with back pain, and that the patient had been injecting his hydromorphone before turning to heroin and then fentanyl and then the Swan Clinic. The patient had already had an epidural abscess drained—an infection in his spine from shooting drugs, narrowly escaping paralysis. He came to the clinic and didn't stabilize with buprenorphine, then was on and off methadone for a few months, fentanyl in every sample. Now he had a prescription from Fitzgerald for hydromorphone. The patient said to Chen, *You're going to give me more, right?* Chen asked the pharmacy to bridge it for a few days until Fitzgerald would next be in clinic—prescriptions for opioids couldn't just be stopped. He assured the pharmacy he would get Fitzgerald to sign for it later.

Chen brought it up with Fitzgerald. "Hey, I saw a patient of yours. Curious about your management. Hydromorphone?"

"Three overdoses in three days. Bad batch of fentanyl, naloxone barely saved him."

"He's had an epidural drained already."

"That's it, exactly."

"And you're treating his addiction with the drug that got him hooked?"

"But which is safer than what he found next. Is it so different? Methadone and buprenorphine are both opioids."

"But with decades of scientific literature behind them," said Chen. "And he's just walking away with the tablets, right? You *know* they're ending up in a syringe."

"Why give people clean needles if we're not going to give them clean stuff to put in the needles? Why tell people we're helping them to make choices in their lives, without letting them choose what they want?"

"It's a reasonable argument." Chen mulled it over. He said cautiously, "Why don't we plan a study? We can randomize people—"

"Chen, how many patients have we lost in the past month? And how many more while you do a study?"

The two doctors' practices diverged, and Chen could see in the electronic medical record that Fitzgerald began writing prescriptions for oxycodone, hydromorphone, immediate release morphine, for more and more patients. Chen stuck to the rules, though some of his patients switched to Fitzgerald. Some Varitas trials required a subject to be a current user of oxycodone but not hydromorphone. Or hydromorphone but not oxycodone. Or fentanyl patches but nothing else. Or all three. Varitas became known as the shop that could fill a study cohort with any profile of subject.

It was a mother dying that set things off. The lawyer for the husband had been emphatic in referring to his client's deceased wife in this way, *a mother who died.* She had been found with an empty bottle of hydromorphone prescribed by Dr. Fitzgerald. As Fitzgerald's malpractice lawyer immediately pointed out, she also had alcohol, benzodiazepines, crystal meth, and fentanyl in her. The impossibility of demonstrating which molecule actually killed her, the judge ruled, did not justify the hydromorphone prescription. When being questioned by the press, Fitzgerald began to tear up, *It's not like I set out to become a dealing doctor.* Fitzgerald did not intend to give the press their tagline for him, but it was catchy. The Dealing Doctor.

Now, Chen joined Fitzgerald in the kitchen where the stovetop coffee percolator bubbled. Chen emptied the pannier bags of injection supplies into the drawers, Fitzgerald poured them each a coffee, and rummaged in the cupboard.

"Black is fine," Chen said.

"Are you sure?" Fitzgerald located a bottle of Hennessy, and poured generously into his own mug.

Chen took the coffee off the counter before Fitzgerald could add alcohol to it. "You said there was someone you wanted me to see?" He pulled his stethoscope, his blood pressure cuff, his thermometer from the bag.

"Jon and Janet are here. Jon is crashed out in the living room—since last night." They had been Chen's patients for a few months, stumbling into the clinic once in a while, usually after an overdose, saying, *This time, we're going to take it seriously.* Chen kept giving them overdose kits and restarting them on methadone, never got it up to a useful dose.

They were in-your-face pleasant when high, equally miserable in withdrawal, stank of marijuana, woodsmoke, and unwashed clothing. Sometimes Janet fell off the chair if she had just done a shot. And then one day, Chen said, *Why don't you come with me after clinic?* He took them for a walk in the ravine, wheeling his bike along, pointed out the tennis shoes tied in the tree, and led them up the hill.

"I thought you made people leave after they did their shots."

"I'm getting a bit soft."

Jon was sprawled on a recliner, his feet on an ottoman.

Now, Chen saw the couple at Richmond and Jarvis, their regular intersection, when he rode past. Janet brandished a paper cup at drivers with her gap-toothed smile, and Jon wielded the squeegee. At first they were happy with the pills, but after a while they seemed ragged, rundown again. *Fucking hydros aren't doing it anymore. Back to the purple, doc!* Chen heard from other patients that they were selling hydromorphone to buy fentanyl.

"What's going on, Jon?" the doctor asked.

"Just a flu," said Jon.

"No, he's not right," said Janet, "he's burning up. Telling me to put out the fire, and we don't have a fire in the summer—brings the cops." When Jon and Janet were at the Swan Clinic, Chen had asked them about housing, told them about couples' shelters. *Fuck that! We got a spot no one could ever find. Bend in the river, ducks sometimes. Waterfront!*

"We gotta go, gotta work, honey—we owe Fitzy here," said Jon. He was drenched in sweat, although the house was cooler than outside. Chen noticed that Jon's shoulder had been cleaned, a fentanyl patch applied. If he had simply been sweating from withdrawal, that should have settled it.

"Take your time with it," said Fitz. He usually insisted on payment up front, emphasized that he didn't do credit, until he did. To Chen: "Fever, borderline blood pressure, new murmur, new back pain."

"Sepsis."

"Multiple possible sources of infection."

"Why don't you let me take a look at you?" Chen placed the stethoscope in the V of Jon's shirt. Jon's pupils were tiny. There was a mushroomy white paste in his mouth. His heart rate was well over a hundred. Stiff neck, too. "There's some kind of infection. Could be in your heart, your spine, almost anywhere." With sepsis, the question was always, What is the source?

"Yeah, Fitzy told me."

Jon's legs were swollen, and Chen's prodding fingers made impressions that remained after he had removed his hands. "Your fluid's backed up. Heart failure." To Fitzgerald, "I don't know what you think you can do, here. He needs an ambulance."

"I told him that," replied Fitz.

"I'm not going to any fuckin hospital. Those assholes treat us like shit."

Janet said, "He's also an asshole, but you can fix him, right doc?"

Chen's training had equipped him with lists. There were the lists of questions to ask, lists of signs to check for, lists of tests to order. These allowed sorting through the lists of possible diagnoses; a network of possibilities, a package of uncertainty. But then, in the end, he was crouched beside one single person who did not want to go to the hospital, in one crumbling house on the edge of the ravine.

Jon tried to stand. "Come on, Janet, let's go." Jon seemed to have found a sudden strength, and managed to get his boot on and tie it.

"Tell me where your camp is," said Chen. "So I can come and check in on you."

"More like so you can get the police to bulldoze it!"

"Jon," Chen asked, "is it okay if I take your photo?"

Jon grinned and raised his middle finger—"One two three, fuck you!"

Chen tapped the screen softly to take the photo, gave Jon a thumbs-up. The man lumbered out of the house, Janet following him.

Chen sat in a ruined art deco chair in front of the fireplace. The arm was scarred by people using razors to cut lines on the wooden arm.

"How is your fiddler patient?" asked Fitzgerald.

"She played in the park last night—as part of a dance show. The performance was beautiful. I went to say hello. She was high."

"I'm sorry, Chen." A lazy overhead fan turned; it occurred to Chen that Fitzgerald had electricity. Through a window somewhere, whether broken or open, there was a breath of air.

Fitzgerald said carefully, "I know you used to go to the Dorado with your student. She mentioned something to me once, about a violinist. The same one . . . ?"

"Claire's music meant a lot to my student," said Chen. He thought of his trainee, lost in a phrase of Claire's playing, completely immersed. She had once told Chen that she wished she could exist within a moment of beauty as Claire did—that that would be enough for her.

25

CHEN CALLED CLAIRE, but her phone was out of service, and so he followed her digital shadow. The trio's first gig in Ottawa was a success, and there was a profile article which included shots taken at the Dorado, entitled "Discovered in a Bistro." There were photos of Claire with her trio partners at the gallery, images of dancers at the summer performance of La Danse de Minuit in Trinity Bellwoods. Claire was often caught as if midway through forming a facial expression. As if she were on her way to a grin, or a laugh, or a ridiculous grimace. Chen did not find what he was looking for—a contact link. Chen found Punk Fugue Trio's social media pages, featuring a campy headshot of Molly, who was identified as the "publicity manager."

Then, a *Gazette* review—of a two-night engagement at a *New Music* festival in Montreal. There were photos from the event, and audio clips. There was a message from Jake, thanking the wonderful fans in Montreal for being both welcoming and understanding of the "unexpected challenges." The *Gazette* reviewer wrote that he was so captivated by the violinist when he heard Punk Fugue Trio on the first night that he went back a second time to indulge in the *transcendence, a new voice.* But on the second night, he wrote, it was as if a different violinist were playing—making sloppy mistakes, playing the wrong movement at one point, shaking and sweating, and during the second half of the performance had to be given a chair. She tried to get through the show but ultimately gave up, fled the stage while her collaborators muddled through as a duo. *At first I thought it was part of the show, a deliberate element of chaos,* wrote the reviewer. *I soon worried that she was sick.* The next two dates, in Quebec City and La Malbaie, had been cancelled. Halifax was postponed.

Without announcement, a couple of days after the Montreal review, Claire appeared in Chen's office, sat down in front of him. The clinic was sweltering, the air conditioning on the fritz.

"I thought you were on tour? What's happening, Claire?" he asked.

"It was for the music, that's all that matters to me. Can you help me?" The rest of it came out in a staccato. "Molly had a heroin connection for a while, Danny. Mostly reliable. Except when he wasn't. But he swore he knew people everywhere on our tour. We should just call him. Then after Ottawa, he stopped answering his phone. Molly said don't worry, and she made some calls. Someone else—said she would take care of it. Some biker in Montreal shows up, with just enough for us to get through one day. Next day, he said Molly would have to go for a ride with him to pick up the stuff. I was the one who said, no way. But we need another solution! This is my breakout opportunity! I told Jake I couldn't play because I'm sick and that I had to fly back to Toronto to get my treatment. So he bought me a ticket. Molly's still in Montreal. Says she'll figure this out, but I'm scared for her. I flew back to find Danny. I can't find him. I heard he's dead." Claire paused for a moment, but seemed to have already shaken this off. "But here's the thing—I need something strong. Molly told me this dealing doctor has got what we need—so I went to his house, this trashed place in Rosedale." She looked at Chen angrily. "She was doing okay with those patches, you know? That was working. I assumed she had just pissed someone off. But this guy, Fitzgerald, I recognized him. You brought him to the Dorado. So then he tells me he cut Molly off and won't sell to me because you don't *want* him to? So now I'm here . . . begging. They're looking for another violinist. I have to get back to the tour."

Chen scrolled through the urine test results on the computer—heroin, fentanyl, crack, crystal meth. "The crystal meth will start to make you jumpy. Spasms, and movements you can't control. How could you play?" He wanted to say, *The medicine worked for you when you took it . . .*

"I already felt terrible. I tried some crystal—hoping it would get me through the show, but it was a disaster. I know what I need—unless you have something else, something fast that can fix me? Has one of your experiments finally worked?"

"The fastest way is always to take things as slowly as possible."

She threw up her hands. "I was hoping you would just take a chance, and let me have what I need right now. And the whole 'slow-is-fast' thing that you're always on about? Right now I have to be fast! You know, Dr. Chen, I play the best when I'm high. My best music is the sound of opiates."

"It may be that you feel that way—"

"No. Really. That's the way it is."

"But drugs can't hold a violin."

"Yes, it's me that plays, not the drugs, but how do you think I get to the real me?"

Chen wanted to argue, but what was there to say? When you are at a loss, he taught his students, focus on practicalities, the essentials. "Claire, do you still have your apartment?"

"The tour is supposed to be the rest of the summer, so I gave it up. To this girl, Julia, she's dealing out of it and she'll ruin it. It was kind of a fuck-you to the building super."

"Do you have a safe place to stay?"

Claire began to cry. "Last night, I played all night in the subway. Kept me going on crystal. That's what I could get. Tonight, I don't know." She said through tears, "What was I thinking? That I would get an ounce of heroin and fly back to Montreal? I don't even have a return ticket. But I could manage on pills . . . if I had enough . . . couldn't you just . . ."

Chen's heart ached, as he pictured the flourish of his pen signing the prescription. It was a gesture that had been performed so many times that the action was no longer deliberate—his hand's tiny muscles produced the signature of their own accord. He imagined her gratitude, a moment of thanks. And if he denied this to both of them, then what?

"We should try methadone," said Chen. Claire had upped the molecular stakes. Her opioid receptors would have upped their tolerance, too. Methadone, the full squeeze of the receptor, might be necessary to hold them still, instead of buprenorphine's gentle grasp. "We'll try to stabilize you. Maybe you can get back to your trio in a few weeks. We can find pharmacies at your tour cities and . . ."

"A few weeks?"

"Meanwhile, you need a plan for tonight."

She said bitterly, "So you really don't have a magic pill, do you?"

26

THE PLACE THEY had rented for the night was on the fortieth floor, one of the earliest condominium towers that had been constructed along the shore. It stood directly on the water's edge, like a tentative foot testing the lake's temperature, glass walls abutting wind and storms. Chen woke in the middle of the night. Sometimes the tidal regularity of Bella's breathing calmed him back to sleep. Tonight, he was fully alert. Closing his eyes was no help—faces, words, appeared.

After work, they had arrived at the rental with a bottle of straw-coloured Sancerre, drank it while the slow sun sank into the expanse of placid water. They ordered Thai food, to dine with this view of Lake Ontario. Before sleeping, they had made love with the blinds open, clear sightlines of the water, toyed with the frisson of exposure though their lights were off. Indifferently, airplanes flew level with the bed, beacons flashing at wingtips, drifting down towards the island airport. Now Chen eased himself out from the covers, shifted his weight gradually to avoid disturbing Bella, went to the living room. Stood before the large window. Across the great body of water, where it met the sky, a fragile chain of lights traced a different city, a different country. It was only at night, and only at such an elevation, that one could see that demarcation.

On his phone, Chen opened his photos. Faces glowed in the small rectangular talisman of glass. With each face there was something different that he could have done. *Should have done?* There was no way to prevent this thought from beginning, but he must not allow it to become lodged, for this could impair decisions he had to make in the present, for patients whose future was unknown. As he swiped the images, faces shimmered together with his own unsettled feelings—sadness, relief, guilt, and hubris. Sadness at the losses. Relief for some—whose suffering was most of what he knew. Guilt at this sentiment. Enough hubris to continue.

He hadn't set out to create whatever this was—an archive? Not a shrine. At first, after speaking with a coroner, he had thought, *I don't want to forget this person.* Here was Jon, finger raised, whose image Chen had added to the folder after hearing from the intensivist. Jon had ended up going to the hospital after all—heart valves shredded from injecting. Pills or powder: the heart didn't know. Chen went with his bike into the valley to try to talk to Janet, but could not locate their spot in the river bend.

"You're checking in with them again?" said Bella.

He looked over. Her silhouette in the door, sexy without trying.

"Like old friends . . ." he said.

She came to him, put her hand on his back, rubbed it. "Who live their own lives, but show up in yours."

"I want to learn from the past. When I should have pushed a little harder. Or pulled back, just let someone go their own way. Did I nudge someone off balance, thinking they would learn something? But what if I had stood still, simply given them something to hold on to?"

"What about letting go of the ones you've lost? Or having a gallery of some of your patients who are doing well? You have patients like that."

"I see them when they come into clinic. If I had images of people who are alive, I would probably worry more."

"But what if understanding patients doesn't keep them from dying? If they keep doing what they're doing." Bella massaged his shoulders. "Maybe you'll have a new treatment to offer. At some point. If it ever gets through the red tape."

"Slow is fast," said Chen. "You think I wouldn't like to just give a big dose of ayahuagaine to people? See what happens?"

"Shh . . ." she said, teasing, "I'm just poking fun." She yawned. In the office, Bella had lined up with Chen, smoothed over those of her colleagues who grumbled when Chen added yet a few more safeguards. "I'm going back to bed."

Even if everything went smoothly and quickly, emergency-use authorization for Memorex's ayahuagaine was still at least a year away. The Adverse Event reports had just been submitted for the abuse liability trials, and Chen's recommendations had again delayed the first treatment efficacy trial by a few weeks.

He had gone through all the Adverse Event reports himself. He had hovered over hundreds of pages of source documents, reading through the descriptions of the events, the hasty lines written by nurses, research assistants, other doctors—*subject describes things looking funny.* Chen's pen hovered—*confusion,* or *hallucination? Confusion*— it could be left at that. Almost every trial that Varitas undertook resulted in transient confusion. If it were coded as *hallucination,* that would be a sentinel event within the Memorex trial, and a sentinel event meant a sentinel report. But had something been perceived which was not there? He hesitated—

There had been further alarm events in the telemetry—the machine's lines scrawled as if by a toddler—was that artifact, or was there danger lurking beneath the jagged, jumping lines? The risk of more monitoring was to discover risk, some said—look and you shall find. Two wide beats were premature ventricular contractions—no big deal. Three beats defined ventricular tachycardia, classifiable as a *serious adverse event*. His pen had to land on one check box or another after hovering over the pages. Charlie had been attentive to Chen's work, knowing that the principal investigator was making a judgment call on squiggly lines—*not that it should affect your judgment, Chen, but we're already pushing the budget here. I mean the patience budget, as well as the financial one.* And later: *fine, fine, safety first, okay, I'll talk to Omega about your protocol amendment, don't tell me about anything else.*

Chen had satisfied himself on the issue of cardiac risk, but insisted on adding EEG—brain activity monitoring.

What did a few more weeks matter in the grand scheme of things? Omega grumbled that those weeks meant longer until the Phase 3 trials, and longer until emergency use authorization. Of course, the principal investigator's job was to ensure the trial was done properly. It was worthless if sloppy.

Chen sat at the glass dining room table, and opened his phone, found one of Claire's publicity photos. It was the exception—a photo of a living patient. He opened his laptop, went to the portal of his own apartment's security system, and logged in.

In clinic, Chen had told Claire that he had a vacant place— between tenants—and that he could use a house-sitter. She asked, *Is this a deal? Like, I take your medications and . . .* There was no deal, Chen said. She could house-sit until there was somewhere else for her to go, or she found a way to rejoin the tour. If she wished, he would prescribe her medications to help her. Claire accepted a prescription for methadone, and drank the first dose of medicine mixed with an artificial orange beverage at a pharmacy en route to his apartment. When they got there, Claire held the violin close to herself, cautiously. I'm staying with my girlfriend right now, said Chen, and he saw Claire relax. Then he left. Bella would have probably laughed at being called his girlfriend. He extended the stay on the waterfront apartment.

Logging into his condo security system, Chen saw that the door had not opened since he had left Claire at his place. That was a relief. It meant two things: that she was still there, letting the medication begin to work; and that no one had yet delivered drugs.

27

THE FIRST THIRTY milligrams of methadone, dispensed at a pharmacy that Dr. Chen took her to a few blocks north of the Distillery District, took off the edge. Enough to allow Claire's exhaustion to win over the raw nerves of withdrawal, so that she fell asleep in the car during the short ride to the apartment. Stumbled through the lobby, sat in the elevator hugging the violin case; Dr. Chen helped her to her feet and into the apartment, barely registering him showing her the stash of naloxone kits, and curled into the bed as soon as she saw it, drifted into sleep as the doctor packed a suitcase. When she woke, early the next morning, she felt sick. She was still tired, but had just enough energy to get to the toilet, and back to bed. Was it possible to be a connoisseur of the varieties of withdrawal? She had been going for a few days on the artificial energy of crystal meth, and crack. The comedown was this exhaustion—mingled with dopesick. Claire woke again—an hour later? A few hours? Light out. And looked around the place—its view of the expressway and the lake beyond, nice art on the walls, books on shelves. If this were a rental, he wouldn't have needed to pack a suitcase. The fridge wouldn't contain fresh fruit, eggs, soft cheeses. It was strange to be staying in her doctor's apartment, and she wondered how she was going to get her methadone. At first, she was too dazed to think any further. A note on the kitchen counter provided the address of the pharmacy a few blocks away where the doctor was sending her methadone; also the fob for the lobby door, and a door key.

So, her doctor did live close to the Dorado, in one of the towers whose offset balconies traced fanciful geometries in gleaming white above brick lanes. From the doctor's balcony, the laneway to the restaurant appeared narrow and scruffy. There was no pharmacy in the Distillery District, and if there had been, it probably would have been too fancy to dispense methadone—for that she went down the elevator, took a circuitous route to avoid the Dorado, and walked a few blocks to a pharmacy on King Street that was not so gentrified. Thirty milligrams, the bitterness of the medicine alloyed with the cloying sweetness of Tang—not enough that she felt human again, but she did remember what it was like to feel that way, could spy it in the distance. She set up a corner of the living room to practise, and began playing a few simple pieces to keep her fingers moving. She texted Jake that her doctor needed her to stay in Toronto for a few days, to do some tests. Jake replied with a thumbs-up emoji.

In the middle of the night Claire lay shivering under the covers. She willed herself to ignore the phone on the bedside table. Who had Molly reached out to when the gardener vanished? It was someone in Toronto. Should Claire just get a number? What if she couldn't get what she needed—when she really needed it? Although she preferred this apartment to a shelter, Claire felt as if she had been on a train platform and somehow, in a hurry and a panic, she had jumped on the first train that appeared, heedless of the destination. She appreciated the clean hot shower, the tidy, well-chosen furniture, the unnatural calm in the middle of the city—and resented them.

For the first few days, there were only a few decent hours after the methadone, when Claire forced herself to run through the trio repertoire. She forced herself to eat some of the doctor's food, and then lay in bed moderately, achingly sick. Claire went to the clinic on the third day, and was relieved that the dose could be increased to forty-five milligrams. While the buprenorphine just took away discomfort, the methadone had a soft touch to it.

"I'm not trashing your apartment," she said.

"I didn't think you would."

"When do you need it back?"

"No rush, eat what's in the fridge—wouldn't want it to go bad."

It was obviously not a place he had been renting out. Dr. Chen's fridge was like the snack bar in airport business-class lounges—bottles of Perrier, crackers and cheeses, some fancy-looking items in take-out containers, a box of pomegranate seeds, a flat container of figs, each nestled into crinkly plastic pockets. He didn't cook much, but snacked well. After she saw him at the clinic, a cardboard box appeared at her door—his door; it contained meal kits. Did he receive these regularly? Had he ordered them for her? Little plastic packages with portions of ingredients, instructions on assembling them into meals. The tiny bags of condiments were just the right size for heroin, she observed. Why should she chase little baggies when these were delivered to her?

When's the next show? Claire texted Jake. *Where?* She would be sure to make it, she texted, wanting to believe it. He would have to front her airfare once more, but he could take it out of her performance fees. He replied with the thumbs-up emoji. Easiest for her to book—she found herself texting, her hands shaking—could he just e-transfer her a few hundred bucks? She felt her heart beating quickly, already imagining—just a little treat, which she deserved for sticking to the methadone. It's not like she didn't want to fly out to the show, and she could sort that out later, but right now if she could just get a little boost . . . Jake went silent at the request for money. A text from Molly, who had ditched the trio, sold her violin, and gone to New York City "with a new friend."

Then, at the clinic again, following the sacrosanct three days that were needed for a dose adjustment, the dose was increased to sixty milligrams. Claire desperately needed the dose increases, and as they went up she resented them. That part was the same as with the other medicine. At least at this pharmacy they were friendly and helpful, as if their patients were stopping by for a daily coffee. *A week away from the tour!* she fumed, *were they auditioning replacements?*

Claire received a text from a guy named Pinkie, who claimed to be taking over Danny's accounts. Molly told Claire that word was that after Danny died, Pinkie had hacked Danny's phone, and was making the most of the contact list. Molly owed a lot of money to that account, Pinkie claimed. Molly said Claire should ignore him, although he now offered a running tally of the amount that the sisters owed, claiming daily compounding interest. She told herself she was not scared when his texts gave up on mathematics and settled into a steady stream of . . . *kick your ass . . . teach you a lesson, bitch . . .* He sent a GIF clip from some movie, a woman being punched in the mouth. Claire sent one back, a fat man in leather, bent over, being violated in a rhythmic manner.

At sixty milligrams of methadone, most of Claire's day was usable, though the early hours of the morning were still unbearable until she had her drink. But overall, she was not feeling too bad. Her usual Dorado gigs were spoken for because she was supposed to be on tour, but Claire sent word she was in town briefly, and was asked if she could sub in for a dinner? The flamenco guitar player had a busted finger. That day, she took the methadone as late as she could, so it would carry her through the dinner service. Her playing was mediocre, but no one seemed to care. She turned down a guy who asked her if she'd like a drink after closing, but when he added that he would make it worth her while, she thought about it. How bad would it be? To have what was *worth her while* in cash—sending a text to Pinkie. Not paying some fictional debt, but a new order. *Not tonight*, she told him, but playfully, kept that door open. So that's how she looked on sixty milligrams, she thought, attractive enough to ask, hungry-looking enough to offer to make it *worth her while*.

"This will be my last increase," she told Dr. Chen in the office. "I don't want to go up any higher."

"Don't go up. If that's the right dose. I tell my patients not to—"

"I know, I know, not to get fixated on the numbers."

"Let's adjust. Then we can reassess," he said in a thoughtful way that Claire found infuriating, because when people spoke that way, they had the luxury of kind deliberation.

Then a text from Beauty.

How did Beauty get her number?

Pinkie said you're in town. Molly owes me—cash or shifts.

Beauty sent a link to "Best Health Asian Massage." *They miss your sister.*

When Claire asked, Molly said to just ignore Beauty. Molly ignored Claire's question about the debt.

One day, Claire picked up a "private caller" thinking it might be the doctor. It was Beauty, who tried to be sweet at first, as if she were presenting a really good deal. Claire could keep half of the money from *extras*. Afterwards, Beauty sent concise texts: *I'm short a girl—tonight or else.* Claire ignored them. It was Molly's tab, even if Claire had used much of what had come from that tab. Claire texted Jake that her doctors had figured out the problem, gotten her on the correct medication, that she was well enough to travel again, where should she rejoin the tour? There was no reply, though the text was marked as "read."

In clinic, the doctor asked, "Are we almost there with the dose?"

"I don't want to be on too much. As soon as I'm better, I want to get off."

"The right dose is when it covers you for the full—"

"I have to get out of town. For the tour. You have to give me carries."

"We go more slowly with methadone carries. We would normally . . ."

"I need a few weeks. And I know you usually go a day at a time, work them up, so I need to start. Today. Every day Jake is after me, texting. They need me. He wants to send me money, for an airfare. So I can't just sit in your little birdcage, drinking methadone." Part of her was hoping he would refuse—she played it forward, stalking out of the office, grabbing her stuff, texting Julia, Pinkie, Beauty, anyone, going on a bender, and she could say it was the doctor's fault. It would be a relief, to prove to herself once more her destiny of failure.

"We'll start carries. One at a time."

She was surprised, began to say, "I need to . . ."—then his agreement registered. Her voice more subdued: "Isn't that the point of doing this, to follow my dreams? And yes," she admitted, "the dose needs to be up a little more. As for safe storage, I guess it doesn't get safer than your place?"

At eighty-five milligrams, the methadone allowed Claire to imagine that there might be a world in which she wanted to live, but did not give her the feel of that world. It was possible for her to play without making mistakes, but playing without mistakes was not music. One day, she got a call to sub for a class at the Little Orchestra School, and discovered that when she was not high the kids sounded even more terrible. Frances came to the door, stood there with arms crossed. On a clear blue afternoon, Claire went to busk in the streets, smiled madly at passersby, let broken horsehairs fling loose from the tip and heel of her bow, tried to appear dramatic, pretending to feel the music's energy.

"How is it?" asked the doctor.

"There's no more withdrawal. It's good for twenty-four hours— as advertised. And I don't know how to thank you. I mean, well, I did some cleaning. Your baseboards, for instance, better than new."

"You didn't have to."

"And I might scrub the grout in your shower, it's getting those black spots. It's the kind of thing you can do on methadone, right?"

"And the music?"

"Oh, great," she said, thinking of her lacklustre attempts to produce music, instead of a sequence of notes. "It's great—just amazing."

"Soon you'll be back to your group, your trio?"

"You want your place back, right? Is that it?"

"No rush. Take the time you need."

"Well, I am in a rush. My whole life is waiting! How many carries can you give me? Give me a week at a time, I can fly out to the trio and back."

"I'll do a week of carries," he said. "Exceptional circumstances."

That night, sipping a cup of herbal tea, Claire texted Jake, *I'm really better now—ready to come out.*

Long minutes without reply.

No big deal.

You should really take care of yourself, rest, recover, came the answer.

Tell me where to fly—I'll get the cash for the tickets, she texted, feeling the emptiness of the flashing three dots between texts. Whatever it took, she would make it work. There was that guy at the Dorado, balding and heavyset, lonely, but it could be worse. A shift with Beauty, and she could fly to Vancouver.

I'm sorry, Claire, came Jake's reply. He sent a link to the trio's website, updated earlier that day. There was an announcement—the tour was on again, they had found a new violinist, *and we send all our love to the amazing Claire—who had to step away for personal reasons.*

When were you going to tell me? she texted Jake.

There was a long pause, the three dots indicating that he was composing something, and then the three dots went away. No reply.

Claire met Julia at a bar. Julia looked fed, rather than cachectic. Her hair was clean. She was obviously high, Claire noted with envy, and despite her ripped earlobe she looked so much better with colour in her skin, comfortable in a breezy summer dress. It wasn't drugs that made you sick, Claire thought, seeing how much better the girl looked. It was being poor, and now Julia had some money.

"How are things at my place?" she asked.

"You said to trash it. Trying hard. Thought you were supposed to be on some kind of tour? With your band?"

"Trio. It's going amazing. Just taking a little break. So, I texted you about . . ."

Julia slid a bar napkin across the table, the plastic baggie folded within. "First one's free."

Claire did a shot of Julia's purple stuff in the bathroom of the bar—a little tester—and then later in the condo before going out to play at the Dorado. The restaurant patrons stopped talking—all eyes were on her, which she took as proof. She played better when high. A tinge of sickness the next morning, but saved by the methadone carry. Called Julia, and met her at the bar again. Handed over all the tips from the Dorado. Woke up in the bathroom of the bar this time, not having been as cautious. No one had noticed she had gone under. A day later, Claire texted Julia for an advance, and received no answer. She texted Pinkie, straight up told him she had no money. *I could use a little help,* he replied. She wasn't a working girl, she texted, but if there was anything else she could do. Puglia's Gourmet Butcher, an easy boost, so she agreed. A junkie who worked there and owed Pinkie "forgot" a cart of tenderloins in the alleyway behind the butcher's after emptying a truck. The minute after the truck pulled away, Claire just strolled past in her black hoodie, kept her side and back to the loading-dock camera, and rolled the small bin away, around the corner, to Pinkie's car, which was Danny's old Lexus. For that, a measly flap of purple.

He held up a pill bottle, saying, "You want this too? Hydromorph eights."

"Real?" she said. Life sometimes felt like it was on replay.

"From the dealing doctor," he murmured, far more seductively than if he was just straight-out asking for a blow job. "If you want to help me out."

"I'm busy today." Claire grabbed one of the tenderloins before Pinkie slammed the trunk of the car.

"Don't overcook it, it's better juicy."

She ate tenderloin and fixed herself, made it stretch until both the meat and the fentanyl were gone. She tapped out a text to Pinkie, *Do you need help with anything?* but did not send it. It had felt like the thrill and dread of peering over a cliff edge to tap that text, almost like preparing a shot. But she was still in charge, she told herself, she could choose. Delete. Her legs started to cramp, then her back, and now that familiar ache throbbed deep inside, more to her right shoulder and back, the place in her shoulder where the knife twisted. This despite the methadone. Had they made a dosing error? No, she knew better, the fentanyl was jacking up her tolerance, and the dose that had kept her even was no longer enough. She looked around at the doctor's nice couches, his jazz prints, and wanted to slash open the cushions with his fancy kitchen knives, torch the art, which had lulled her when she should have been doing something, anything, to get back to the trio.

So quickly, in just a couple of days, a rhythm could feel familiar—stealing for Pinkie, busking, buying off Julia, who of all people was telling her to take it easy. The condo was a good place to use; sometimes she got into a groove watching the car lights fling across the elevated expressway. Like them, Claire sometimes floated high above the lake. She sometimes slipped beneath the surface of the water, resurfaced hours later, waking shivering and wet, checking if she had anything left. Maybe the rhythm felt familiar because it had never gone away, thought Claire; it had been right there beneath the surface.

Now the phone rang again, so loud her face vibrated.

Awake. Claire was twisted into a couch. Where was she? She recognized the fine woven fabric of the cushion—the doctor's couch. How long had she been out? She remembered doing the shot in the living room. The phone continued to ring, until it didn't anymore. Began to ring again—

"Hello?"

"Are you okay?"

"Who is this?"

"Dr. Chen here."

"Oh, hi . . ."

"I was expecting you in clinic today . . . I was a little worried."

"What? That I was dead?" A laugh, but not a laugh.

"Yes."

"Well, I'm not. Yet."

"How's it going?"

"Terrible. What's new?"

"I know I'm calling late. Hope I didn't wake you."

"Well past my junkie bedtime. But I'm up."

"Are you okay now?"

"I just have to do what I have to do. I know you're trying to help. But I don't know what to say . . ."

28

CHEN WAS ALONE that night at the lakefront place. He had told Bella that he was having some work done on his condo, and was keeping the rental for a while. The concierge called him a car. The Lucky Dinette was open twenty-four hours, and was busiest after midnight. The sign in the door read, "No Outside Food, No Outside Business, NO Outside BULLSHIT!" At four in the morning, Chen entered the diner's haze of tobacco smoke and stale grease. A couple of cops sat at the counter, facing a mirror behind the bar. Chen found Claire in the third booth from the back, and sat across from her.

"It's good to see you—"

"Alive? At least someone cares."

One glance confirmed how she was doing. He said, "You know where the overdose kits are? You should keep one with you."

"To save myself?"

"There needs to be someone there. To use it on you."

"You *really* shouldn't care this much."

"Slips happen. It's a chronic illness."

"I have a confession—I didn't go on tour this week with the carries—they found another violinist."

"I'm sorry."

The waitress came, and Claire ordered the Hungry Hangover breakfast, with the pan-fried steak add-on. Chen asked for an espresso, and the waitress snorted, *Sure. And?* He would have the same breakfast, he added. With the anticipation of food, and the relief of Claire being alive, Chen suddenly felt tired, wondered how he had come to be seated on this bench in the Lucky Dinette. Sometimes, in the office, people slumped over in the chair in front of him. The shot kicking in. So he couldn't have just hung up the phone, left her to the night. Chen had known all week that Claire was not on tour. The trio's website, which he looked at after writing the prescription for carries, explained the situation. But he had hoped the carries would work out, and then she didn't show on her clinic day.

"What's the difference between nodding off and overdosing?" Claire asked.

"Waking up."

"So I woke up. A few times. On your couch. And I've been meaning to tell you . . . I think I should leave your place."

"You have somewhere to go?" he asked.

"I have to get on with my career." She drew herself up. "Make music. Not sit in your condo."

"Is that holding you back?" said Chen.

"Maybe," she said. "I'm sorry. You're trying to help." She leaned her head back against the partition between booths.

"I know the tour is a disappointment. There's always another chance."

"Do you believe that?"

"I do."

"Must be nice."

The food came, together with Chen's espresso—a tiny cup of something that looked as if it had been scooped from the bottom of a coffee pot. Claire asked for one of those, too. They ate in silence while addressing three eggs and extra bacon, whole wheat toast with lots of butter, pan-fried steak.

"Is it your job to be here right now?" She squinted her eyes a bit, so slightly that it was surely unconscious, but Chen knew it well— the face of curious appraisal. "Before dawn in some shithole diner with your patient?"

Looking around the restaurant, Chen could pick out at least three people who could probably *hook them up.* He was sure that Claire could read the room as well as he could, probably better.

People who were high had a lucid honesty. Chen responded in kind, "I carry my patients around with me, and that compels me to do things."

"That sounds like an addiction," she said.

"Maybe, when I feel like I don't have a choice."

"Your experiments, your trials. That's how you got into all this stuff, right? I looked you up on the internet. You and the *dealing doctor* cashed out big. So where does this fit?" She speared a piece of bacon, folded it into her mouth, crunched it. "Well, you ask me personal questions all the time."

"Fair point."

"Is it that you try so hard, and your patients are still dying?" She nodded obligingly, like a judge acknowledging technical points in a music competition. "So trying harder is your way of coping? That's why I'm living in your place? Why you called me? Why we're here?"

"One of the classic questions about generosity—who gets the most out of it?"

"I wish you had figured out a magic pill, instead."

Chen signalled for another espresso. Neither said anything as they finished their meals. Chen said, "I had a friend. We used to eat together at the Dorado. On your nights. It was mostly to hear you. She admired you, loved to hear you play."

"The binders," said Claire. "Yes? Always with binders."

"Listening to you took her to some true place." Chen suspended a sugar cube at the surface of his coffee, watched the brown seep up into the white cube, until the bottom of it crumbled into the fluid and he let it drop.

"A few years ago . . . right?"

"She was a friend," said Chen. "She was also my student—"

The seeping edge of dawn peeked into the restaurant. People who had slept a full night, and who were now grabbing a quick breakfast before an early shift, appeared. Their cheerful, morning alertness made Chen even more tired. With the morning rush, the waitress plunked the bill onto the table. She was cashing out, she said, tapping her foot. Chen paid and the waitress went away for change.

In the cool damp outside the restaurant, Chen asked, "Should I call in your prescription?"

"Sure."

"I need to cancel the carries. It's for your safety."

"But then it's harder for me to get the methadone. What's the point of you going out of your way to help me, if you don't give me what I really need?"

"There's a structure to these treatments, there's science, there are professional standards and—"

"Always being the doctor," she said.

"That's what I can do."

29

CLAIRE TOOK HER methadone after breakfast with the doctor, but missed the next day because she got to the pharmacy too late. Missed another because she was high and days vanished, and another because she was too sick and knew that methadone wouldn't cut it. Dr. Chen explained to Claire on the phone that after three days without methadone, he had to cut her dose in half, but could increase it again quickly. With less methadone in her, the fentanyl hit harder. She picked up more down than she could pay for, then owed too much to Julia to beg another advance. Drank a couple more days of medication, busked on the street to buy fentanyl from Pinkie, and then missed five doses of methadone. With this long gap, Dr. Chen told Claire on the phone, she had to restart. But a full restart required him to see her—she should come to clinic. Claire said she would be right down, but then lay on the bed staring at the sky, too sick to go.

That evening, Claire was woken on the doctor's couch by someone buzzing up from the lobby of the fancy condo. She was disappointed that it was not her doctor. Beauty was in the lobby, but said nothing of Molly's debt. She was in the area, said she got the address from Julia, had brought a little something. *Bitches,* thought Claire. Julia had sworn not to share the address, when she had dropped off a flap. But Claire was sick, so she buzzed Beauty up. Sitting across from her in Chen's living room, Beauty placed a bag of purple powder and a naloxone kit on the coffee table. She launched into a complicated story about the guy who usually tested her batches, who had been arrested and held briefly, was released, *and then like an idiot* went on a binge, got his hands on some crystal, tried to climb into a sewer yelling *they're after me!* He was under arrest again, for punching the city sewer worker who pulled him from the entry of the manhole, and so couldn't be Beauty's tester right now.

As Beauty explained all of this, Claire shivered. When she saw Beauty sizing her up, she looked away from the plump bag of drugs, pretended to be gazing out the window, thinking, *I don't give a fuck about your idiot tester—*

"So, on the house. Julia said you would appreciate the gesture. It's supposed to be strong. And I'm right here." Beauty nudged the bag of drugs, toyed with the rescue kit.

Reaching for the gorgeous bag of purple, she thought of Molly's warning. Claire paused, and asked, "About that money you say Molly owes you?"

"Never mind that. Look, I have to see . . . what this batch is like. You'll be doing me a favour. And it looks like you could use a little something right now."

Claire went to the kitchen, to get her own works. She didn't like using in front of anyone except Molly. It was a private thing—but she was sick. The fentanyl was strong. It went straight into the rush, the release of claws, the clarity, but then already it was coming off, and instead of afterglow an ache, the want. Claire shuddered, looked up. Beauty was on her phone, tapping with her thumbs.

"So?"

"It's okay."

A smirk—"Looked like more than okay."

"Yeah, it's fine," said Claire, already craving more. "Fades fast."

"How good is it?" Beauty twirled her hair.

"I don't have any money."

"We could use some help at the spa."

Of course. "Why don't you try some?" said Claire. "It's really good, actually."

"Comes on hard?" asked Beauty, whose eyes appraised both Claire and the bag of purple. Claire envied people who could calmly weigh up whether or not they wanted to do a shot when it was sitting right in front of them. She wanted to lunge and grab it, lock herself in the bathroom with it. "Because I just dabble."

"I think you'd be fine," said Claire. "And I'll be right here with the kit." The naloxone was on the table between them. "It comes off quick. Since I'm testing for you, do you think—" She wanted more, but didn't want to ask.

"Well, you had the tester. There's more for sale," Beauty winked.

Claire watched as Beauty drew up the tiniest little shot and tied off. She was dainty, precise. She had a little zip-lock of alcohol swabs, and she swabbed twice. Claire watched as Beauty found a vein in the crook of her arm—she had so many nice plump ones, so maybe she really was that rare being, an occasional user—and then watched as Beauty sank into the chair, limp and blissful.

What she did next was automatic. Claire needed to do the shot quickly, before Beauty woke up. If she didn't know, then Claire didn't owe her anything. The fat bag of fentanyl contained at least two ounces. Beauty would never notice a little missing. She fumbled with the cooker, the filter, the syringe, slapped her own arm furiously to bring up a vein, slowed her hand to steady it—watching Beauty, who was as limp as the pillows upon which she slumped. The steel pinch flowed straight through to warmth, the vanishing of every aching gap, the collapse of past and future into now. She sank into the soft, feather-stuffed couch, embracing disappearance. When Claire opened her eyes, Beauty was still exactly as she had been, not having moved one bit. In the lingering high, Claire knew that she had gotten away with it.

30

AFTER THEIR BREAKFAST, Chen hoped things would turn. The week of carries hadn't helped, but maybe a return to structure would help Claire to stabilize. Instead, she'd missed doses and blamed the misses on not having carries. Then, she missed so many that once she phoned, his only option was to insist on an in-person assessment for a restart. Claire said she would come to clinic that day, but did not show. For days after, Chen found himself watching for her name, hoping that Claire would appear in the queue.

One morning, Pamela called from the front, "Putting this call on hold, doc, the cops. Something about your condo?"

When he logged on to his condo security system, Chen saw that the door to his condo had last been opened five days ago, so either Claire had moved out, or she had been in the condo for the past five days without leaving. He tried her cellphone—no answer. Chen took the line off hold. The officer confirmed that Chen was the owner of the condominium unit in question, and explained that there had been a complaint from a neighbour—a smell. The concierge had knocked, called, and then opened the unit. Would Chen be willing to come to the morgue? *What kind of doctor did you say you are? So you're not staying there now . . . for a change of scenery? Huh. The address where you're staying, doctor? And you'll be straight over after your clinic? Wouldn't want to have to send a cruiser. Kidding, doc. See you soon. We left the windows open—to air the place out.*

He wanted to ask if the officer had ever heard of the Punk Fugue Trio, or eaten at the Dorado on a Thursday? Was there a note? Instead, he said, *Yes officer—right after clinic.* What could he have done differently, he wondered, what should he have done? He wanted to go over right away, but the waiting room was busy—there was shouting, arguing from outside his door. For the rest of the day he blundered through prescriptions, smiled blankly and artificially through a video call with a potential new Varitas client, ignored Bella's text and then her phone call.

At the morgue, the officer copied Chen's ID, put his bag through the metal detector, led Chen to a room full of desks, and offered him stale, hot coffee from a tall metal canister with a red plastic lever that released it through a spout. They sat at the officer's desk.

"So, you haven't been at the place in a little while?" The officer's hand hovered over his papers.

"A few weeks."

"Short-term rental? Income property?"

"Sort of—" Chen wondered if he should have come with a lawyer.

"But you weren't there?"

"I was staying somewhere else. I have receipts on my phone." He could count on Bella for corroboration, couldn't he?

"Relax, doc," said the officer. "This was a totally obvious overdose. Needle stuck in the arm and everything. Just doing procedure, paperwork—sergeant likes it tidy."

"Of course."

"And you weren't anywhere near," said the officer. "We reviewed all the condo security cameras this afternoon. So we know you didn't have anything to do with this."

Chen wanted to yell that he had everything to do with it, that he may not have killed her but it was his fault. While he was in clinic telling people to use with others, he had given Claire an apartment in which to use and die alone. If she had been in a shooting gallery, or Fitzgerald's house, there would have been someone with an antidote. Would it have really been so bad if he had just kept on giving her carries? Or restarted her without an in-person assessment? Claire had been right. What was the point of going out of his way to help her, if he wasn't willing to bend the rules when she needed him to? Chen wanted to shout that he was not a murderer, but he had killed her anyways. Instead, he said calmly, "In that case, what can I do for you, officer?"

"Hoping you could help. With an ID. Maybe we can track down some next of kin . . ."

They went down through a service elevator, and there was a family in the identification room already, so they waited in the hallway. Inside the room, a woman wailed, pleading, *my baby my baby my baby . . .* Other voices, murmurs, and then a man's shout, a slam of fist on metal. A father? The keening again, *my baby my baby my baby.*

When it was their turn and the body was rolled out, the odour came first. Then the sound of the trundling wheels of the tray, the heavy zipper pulled. Then the face, bloated from several days of neglect. Chen stared at her for a while, and was more relieved and happy than he had ever been seeing a corpse. It was an older woman, heavily made-up, who looked, despite the start of decay, as if she had once been beautiful.

"I don't know who that is," said Chen, relieved. "Online rental, you know how it is."

"Okay . . ." said the officer. "Come back to my desk. There's another woman we'd like to show you. In the elevator security footage. We're not sure if she was in your apartment, but she had been in and out of the building for a few weeks. And then not anymore."

"Sure, I'll take a look." He already knew whose image it would be, and that he would not be able to identify her, either.

31

LATE ONE NIGHT, Chen went to the Factory Pit. He brought clean
needles and naloxone kits. He wore rubber boots, and tramped in the
brush, finding people in tents and squats, warning them about the latest
batch of stuff that was dropping people. The matter with Beauty had
been quickly signed off by the police: a known dealer who overdosed,
just a paperwork thing, the officer said. *Fifty-third body this month and
counting.* Soon after viewing the surveillance tape and failing to identify Claire, Chen was free to go. He had requested the toxicology, and
the officer had printed it up for him. It was a more frightening cocktail than he had ever seen before. He called Claire over and over. She
did not pick up the phone. He kept the rental, and a few times a day
checked the security system at the condo to see if she had returned.
After a week without the door opening, Chen scheduled a professional
deep cleaning company. And Claire's number went out of service.

At the parkette, Chen found a gaggle of kids each trying to sound
tougher than the others. He gave them injection and overdose kits.
They asked for cigarettes, hydromorphone, cash. He offered condoms, which they took, and stuffed them absentmindedly along with
the naloxone into the side pockets of backpacks. At first Chen didn't

recognize Brandon, who was with the group but stood at a deliberate distance, looking away as if at something interesting. Chen had not seen him in clinic for months now. His mother had called, and Chen didn't have any information for her. Brandon's appearance told the story, and as the banter with his friends continued a little longer, Brandon wandered away.

"The batch right now is really deadly," Chen said. "Be careful."

"No kidding," a young man said. "Do you know where to get that stuff?"

"Stay away from it. Hey, have you seen a guy, Rick, around here?" Chen indicated a bench. "Used to sleep here?"

"Old guy? He's gone," said a girl, nonchalant at first. "Right here last week, some assholes grabbed me, wanted to—and I didn't want to—and Rick jumped out of his tarp with his knife, ran them off. And then the other morning, I found him. Right here, his spot. Thought he was just asleep." She wiped her eyes.

Sodden earth squelched under his boots, as Chen used his phone flashlight to navigate long, sharp grass, abandoned buildings, looking for plywood shelters and tents tucked into brush. But it was news to no one that the current stuff in circulation was strong. Almost everyone had woken up next to a dead friend, mourned them, and then needed to ease the pain. Chen spotted handwritten signs advertising a performance of La Danse de Minuit. He followed the arrows to a wide rectangular opening cut out of chain-link fencing, which led to an open space, surrounded on three sides by brick walls. A building to the right had loading docks, its doors a few feet off the ground. Powerful utility floodlights sat on scraps of plywood that kept them out of the mud, shining up at the brick walls. Somewhere out of sight, a generator thrummed. The space was filled with people, marijuana and cigarette smoke, booze breath, the tangy whiff of crystal meth and crack, and bodies packed close. In front, against the largest building, there was a cordoned off area.

Now, all the lights were extinguished and a string melody began, lonely and slow. The loading dock doors clanked open; within, bright lights behind a figure projected a shadow, a violinist, on the opposite wall, animating the music. Dancers suspended by lengths of fabric moved through angled beams of light, appeared from above and disappeared below. On their way down, they twisted and spun, walked as if the wall were the ground.

The dancers descended faster and faster, gave the appearance of running down the wall as the music became a frenetic flurry of double stops and harmonics. Was it her? The passion was heard, but the instrument seemed to be handled sloppily, fingers imprecise, bow scraping. The violinist's shadow swayed. Then, as one dancer appeared to climb the wall, slipping, clawing, the music became more focused, and followed her. Did the music lead the one who climbed? Or did the dance lead the music?

Both stopped abruptly.

Was the musician Claire? The player was framed by backlight, held up her bow as if about to strike. Although Chen's patients had been using the deadly batch at an apartment in Kensington, he had not asked whether they had seen a violin lying around. What was worse—to know or not to know? Then, on the wall facing the fence, red and blue strobe light. A couple of siren blasts, followed by a police megaphone, *break this up . . . trespassing . . .* The bodysuited performers slid down one by one and scattered. The violinist's shadow was no longer projected on the wall—only the blank rectangle of light.

People streamed through the gap in the fence, and Chen pushed sideways through the crowd, towards the building with the loading docks. He found Claire next to her violin case, unconscious. Chen removed the needle from her arm, shook her, and she did not respond. Knowing was better. He rubbed her clammy brow with his knuckles, but she remained limp. He fumbled in his bag, took out a naloxone kit, and squirted it up her nose.

"What the—" she mumbled, loose-limbed, swatted at him, her eyes half-opened, and then she went limp once more. He found another naloxone kit, this time intramuscular—and jabbed it into her arm. Then she saw him. "What are you doing here?"

"I came to hear you." He stepped back, gave her room as she punched and kicked without aiming, and asked her, "Are you trying to kill yourself?"

She began to shake. "I just saw the cops and . . ."

"You overdosed," said Chen. Going to jail sober was every user's worst fear, he knew. Not just being locked up, but getting sick with no way to get relief. At least high, a few hours disappeared. "How much did you just do? We need to get you to the hospital."

"No way." Claire hurriedly packed her violin, scrambled to her feet, and ran into the building away from the loading door, darted into a staircase. The second dose of naloxone was kicking in.

Chen ran after Claire, down the stairs, out the door, and into the street. She was half a block away by the time he spotted her in the thinning crowd. Chen knew that Claire's physiology was, like her, gyrating and reeling from the shock of what he had given her to save her life. It was not the effect of the naloxone itself; that simply pushed the opioids off the receptors, unmasked the neurophysiology and laid it bare without the drugs on board, revealing an underlying state, a physiological truth. She ran desperately through the crowd, stopped to strip off her jacket and threw it on the ground, wrapped the violin case in it, picked it up, and kept on going.

Chen continued after her, "Please, wait."

She hugged the bundle, trotted away, insisted without looking back, "I'm okay now. Really, I'm okay."

Chen got close enough to shout, "Like your dead friend in my place? The naloxone is short-acting, you might go down again." It had taken two shots, meaning she would go down hard if she did.

Claire stopped and ran her hands through her hair. "I'm sorry.

I thought she was just on the nod." She crouched, squatted, her arms around her violin. "That's what I thought when I left her there. And—and—she tried to trick me into something—so I stole her stash but I just thought she was . . . Later I heard. Are you going to take me to the police?" She jumped to her feet, began to run again, even faster.

"The police don't care. But are you selling that bad batch? People are dropping!"

She was crying now. "I told people to be careful!" She ran desperately for half a block, and Chen yelled when she almost ran in front of a car, fast-walking after her up the sidewalk. Her steps began to slow.

"Please sit down for a second? Tell me, how much is left?"

A few steps faltered, staggered. "That was it—I used the last right now."

"Really?"

Now she weaved, and when he came near, she flopped her arm over his shoulder, speech slurred, "I was afraid the police were coming . . ."

"The fentanyl is catching up to you." He guided her into a bus shelter, eased her onto the bench as her eyes closed. Chen took out another kit. This time, he only squirted part of a dose into her nose, enough that she started breathing on her own but not enough to wake her up completely.

Chen took out his phone. Call 911: that was all he needed to do.

It would be out of his hands. The paramedics would come, restrain her in the stretcher, then give naloxone. She would resist. Depending on how long that purple lasted, she might need a few rounds of naloxone at the hospital to keep her breathing. She would be discharged from the hospital feeling horribly sick. She would need to do something about that feeling.

In his gallery of losses, there were a few recent faces. Had their last smashes come from Claire? He couldn't let that thought take root.

Should he take a photo of Claire now? With her head slumped on his shoulder, she looked like she was at peace, breathing softly, the molecules of purple competing with the molecules of naloxone—one trying to stop her breathing, and the other trying to block the first. She looked like she was where she wanted to be. He did not take the photo.

Instead of calling 911, Chen called a car. A few minutes later, as a small silver sedan pulled into view, Chen gave Claire another little squirt of naloxone, enough that she could stand with his support. He eased her through the car door so she didn't bang her head, and once they were both in the car he called Fitzgerald. Chen said he was bringing someone to the house, and needed to use the front door. Fitzgerald answered the door with a beer in one hand, behind him the house was noisy and the living room full. The couches were overflowing and people sprawled on the floor, pipes dangling from fingers, lighters fallen to the side, sharps containers scattered here and there.

Claire stood on her own now, but her eyes drifted closed and when she swayed, and stumbled, Chen caught her.

"I'm sorry," said Fitz.

"I tried my best. Already gave her almost three shots of naloxone. Is there somewhere to take her?"

When Fitz gestured towards the living room, the shooting gallery, Chen said, "Somewhere else? You know, safe."

"That's the safest room." Fitz pointed at a scrawny girl who sat on a bar stool, red naloxone pouch in hand. She looked as bored as a department store security guard, surveying Fitz's living room—now a sea of bodies, sharps containers, bottles.

"Listen . . . I know. Now I'm asking you for something different."

"Things change," he said graciously.

"She had some stuff—a really bad batch."

"Isn't that all there is?" said Fitz, and helped Chen to gently lay her down.

32

CLAIRE WOKE IN an expensive chair that had been beat to hell, surrounded by people who were on the nod or just asleep. The dealing doctor sat there with a velvet pouch slung around his neck, sipping from a wine glass.

"How did I get here?" she asked.

"Your doctor brought you here."

"He changed his mind?" She looked around. "I'm gonna be sick."

He got up, and returned with a glass of water and a porcelain bowl, the rim of it chipped in a few places. Then, Claire felt it come up—what little was in her stomach. She retched into the bowl. She tried to drink some water, and that came up. She wiped the drool with the sleeve of her bodysuit. She remembered the performance and the arrival of the cops. Just before the show started, she had injected a tiny bit, a very careful smash that got her to the right place to really make music. She loved seeing her shadow projected to the size of a giantess. The floodlight was hot on one side of her body, and then the other, on her back, depending on how she turned. The dancers climbed and fell along the wall in a performance that the director had called *deconstructed longing*.

Claire sipped some of the water. "So I guess Dr. Chen has given his—whatever it is, permission?"

He held out a foil blister pack. She reached for it and began to push the pill out of the package. "It's ondansetron, by the way. It's like Gravol, but without the drowsiness."

"You think that's what I need?" She regarded the pill, and swallowed it. "Obviously top of your class in medical school."

She remembered thinking, as she played blissfully in the door of the warehouse, that she had gotten the dose just right. It made her music better, and she was better. The great gift of the high was that everything else fell away except for her unity with the soaring vibration of horsehair on catgut, so that *now,* she longed for nothing.

Until the cops, and *deconstructed longing* gave way to a terror of being caught, of being put into a cell to shake, shit, and scream and bang on the cell door. She thought, *Maybe if I do enough, it'll last until I see the judge in the morning, and if I smile nicely I'll get out in time to score before I* . . . She had pre-prepped a syringe to last for the whole performance, and now it was thumb on the plunger then she was gone.

A flash, of Dr. Chen, on the loading dock.

The doctor chasing her.

A bench on the street, her head in the crook of Dr. Chen's arm.

And so the rumours must be true? That Beauty was dead, found in a condo. Some of the people who bought down from Claire were dead too. But it could have been anything, they could have gotten stuff from anyone. Beauty would have sold it anyways.

Now this house.

"Do you want this?" asked Fitzgerald, holding out a thirty-milligram hydromorphone tablet in a gleaming foil package.

"I don't have any money," she said.

"Not a unique problem."

"What do I have to do for it?" she asked, warily.

"Not 'do'. Swap," said Fitzgerald. "There's an especially bad batch. And I heard you might have had some of it? Chen said you used the last."

"All gone." A sweat broke on her brow, and a shiver ran through her. She cramped over, and knew that she was probably too sick to even get out of the house and walk home until she did something. "I'm pretty sure."

"Really? You know, Chen has this weakness—for just believing what people say." The pill package glistened, like a wrapped candy. "I don't do freebies—but I do trade. Come on, this for whatever deadly garbage you have? Which I'm going to get rid of. Pretty fair?"

Claire reached into her bodysuit, retrieved a flap from her sports bra, and gave it to Fitzgerald, who handed her the pill. She pushed it out of the package, swallowed it, and washed it down with the glass of water.

Immediately, she started feeling better. She heard Dr. Chen's observation: *It can't be in your bloodstream yet. So . . . maybe half of this is in your head.*

Claire heard Fitzgerald futzing in some other room. Then he appeared with a martini glass.

"Wow, you look better already," he said. "That must be pretty valuable, the way you're glued to it." He gestured at the violin case on Claire's lap. They sat quietly. She felt better enough to wonder what predictable thing would happen next. Would he suggest that she come closer? Maybe ask her to follow him to a room in the house? "What if we make a deal? The rest of your street fent, and tonight's on me. Until the sun comes up. Hydromorphone, oxycodone, full buffet, but I want your whole stash."

"That was the last of it."

"Okay." He played with the olive in his glass. Claire recognized the look, as if Fitzgerald were running a children's music school, and one more clingy child had been dropped off when he was short-staffed. A woman who was splayed out on a couch started to moan, to mumble. Fitzgerald surveyed the people in the room. Checking if they were alive.

As if remembering that she was there, he said, "Are you still sick? Do you need another?"

"Trade for whatever I want tonight, right?"

"Your whole stash. From me: only proper pharmaceutical-grade opioids. No down, no purple, no shit. Here's the fine print: no dying. Deal?"

Claire reached into the violin case, took out the instrument, peeled back the velvet lining, and took out a gram of purple powder. "Here you go," she said.

"Give me your boots," said Fitzgerald.

"Fine," she said, tossing him the gram and her walking boots.

Fitzgerald felt inside the footwear, pulled out the soles, retrieved a gram from each, and said, "That's it?"

"All of it."

"The buffet is served."

"Do you have any oxys? Like an oxy eighty."

"She wants the good stuff. It's expensive to make the world a safer place." Fitzgerald got up from his chair. "Green monster?"

"Yes, please."

"Before I forget, and before you get too high—your ever-devoted doctor is hoping you will go to clinic to see him when you feel better. He wanted me to pass a message—there's something different he may have for you."

There was no question about it—she got greedy.

Claire swallowed eighty milligrams of oxycodone. Soon after, she felt fresh and well rested. The smell of the people in the living room had nauseated her when she had woken up in withdrawal, but now, with the fairy dust of hydromorphone and oxycodone circulating in her blood, they looked like good people, *real* people. Claire tuned her violin and played for them. She played Brahms' "Hungarian Dances", passages from the trio, parts from La Danse de Minuit. The people didn't know anything about music, heard her with fresh ears. She asked Fitzgerald for another greenie, but he told her to slow down—and gave her a smaller oxy instead. She played Vivaldi and Paganini, as if she were exorcizing them. They watched, listened, crushed and injected hydromorphone, and Claire already knew how her audience felt. They loved her music, and told her so. Claire explored the house, the kitchen, the sunroom in the back, pushed doors open with her hip, playing her violin the whole time. Kreisler's "Leibesleid" was a hit. Now and then she asked Fitzgerald for a hydro, or an oxy, and he reached into the bag dangling from his neck and gave her what she wanted.

A rough, handsome, French-Canadian guy proclaimed his love, told her he had a camp in the valley, a dry spot under a bridge. He offered to take her. Claire snorted some oxycodone, and said she would consider it. He still had most of his teeth. Maybe she should go with him, she thought. Pack up the violin and go live with this guy under his bridge. She kept on playing.

Claire injected some crushed hydromorphone, went into the backyard, walked and played while the dew bathed her feet, the leaves and grass caressed her toes. Her hands were light, precise, strong. As dawn cast a soft glow over the valley, a melody that was original and entirely her own rose from her instrument. The stream along the ravine path was a rare crystalline serpent. The air was starkly pure. People drifted from the house out into the backyard, listening. Others appeared from the woods at the end of the yard, having climbed up the hill to the house. Claire felt as if she were talking, breathing through the movement of her hands, and the music came to life as perfectly as she had always believed it could. She stood at the edge, on the ravine.

When the sun rose brightly enough for her to squint, Claire went into the house and lay on a large stuffed chair. It must have been a few hours later when she awoke, the house empty except for her and Fitzgerald, who was asleep on a couch. When he got up, she asked if he had a clean crusher, and if she could have a greenie. He gave her both. When she had done the pill, Fitzgerald told her it was time to go, and showed her out into the backyard, pointed out the path below the house, explained how to walk back downtown.

To a student of medicine,

When I told you about the time-stamps, the keystroke logging,
your eyes burned with both shame and determination. I could not
tell which was in greater measure. You told me you were fearful
of not graduating, could not jeopardize the medical licence for
which you had worked so hard. No one can know, you said.
Because they don't understand. You do. I'm counting on you.

I was desperate to help you but taken aback by what you
asked. Did you really believe that all you needed was my help
in keeping it quiet, and some prescriptions? Your plan was not
one that would be recommended by any addictions doctor. It
was the kind of fraught and fanciful plan many patients suggest;
and it ignored what you had learned with me. A rapid taper
off everything, with a mix of sustained release and short-acting
opioid pills—and a few benzodiazepines. Instead, I offered a list
of excellent and discreet addiction clinics. You cried. You
pointed out correctly—whatever the clinic, if prescribed methadone or buprenorphine, if treated for an addiction, you would
be required to disclose this to the College in applying for
your licence.

I told you, I believe in what you can be. I will defend you no matter what. The hardest lesson is that we are not so different from our patients.

But there was another vision that I'd had of you. And now, that was gone. Soon, you were well. Although we stopped going to the Dorado, I was quietly relieved and happy whenever I saw you—that you must have sought treatment, and the methadone or buprenorphine must be well-titrated because you were diligent, inquisitive, yourself. It never occurred to me that you would have found another way.

At Fitzgerald's college disciplinary inquiry, how quickly the roles were cast, the lines drawn. Unlike Fitzgerald, blustering that his actions were justified, that he had only been prescribing you and many others what was needed, for you chose a wiser course—accepted responsibility for your portion of errors. Professional colleges squash defiance. Medical schools protect their students, help them to the finish line. Your issue was one of health, not professional conduct. With proper treatment and monitoring, you were offered a way forward. I was waiting for the Varitas pharmacy to come up, but the investigators already had enough in their spotlights without looking for more, and neither you nor Fitzgerald said a thing about Varitas. Were you repaying my silence? Did you know that I felt more guilty because my hands stayed clean? When you graduated and matched to a residency in Calgary, you called me before leaving, made me promise to write. You also promised to send your address once you settled.

Last week, I took your favourite violinist to the house on the ravine. She found what she wanted, and what she says she needs. I usually take people to Fitzgerald when I give up. But I did not lose hope for you, or for her.

Dr. Chen

33

IN THE SHADY corner of a park, they walked together along a curving pathway. Specks of honey-tinged light fell through the canopy of
leaves onto chipped stones, the grass thick on either side. With a flip
of her hair, she laughed about painful childhood events, described
episodes and harsh phrases that had once hurt her. In the way that
a proud schoolboy understands a lesson and is anxious to demonstrate
his knowledge, he wanted to explain to her that her childhood affected
her present. *Don't you see? When you feel this way, it's an echo of . . .*
Except that when he was about to speak, he discovered that he had
forgotten the details of the story. Who said what? Why did it hurt her?
The names and words had vanished. Losing the details did not diminish his conviction that he understood. It was the dynamic. But without the particulars, what could he say? She began to repeat herself, to
tell him once more. With the retelling he felt afraid that she would
not understand how well he understood her.

They came to an old man offering baskets of speckled red mushrooms in open paper bags, arrayed on a folding wooden table. They
pleased her, so Chen took off his watch, in order to exchange it for
the mushrooms. The old man laughed that he had no need for time,

and would only trade for what he needed. She looked away, embarrassed. The mushrooms became red eggs, out of which hatched lizards. The man said it was too late to sell them. Time had run out. Chen said he knew a restaurant that traded time for food, could they go there? It was the season for fried zucchini blossoms, she said. He walked slowly along the path, as if trying to prolong something, but she stepped more quickly. He tried to catch her but there was a fixed pace of his own footsteps. He called out, a sense of panic, hoped she would turn to see that he was trying. She turned, flipped her hair again, laughed at him, and he pleaded with the man—didn't he have one more egg? But the old man had vanished, and so had his friend. Chen continued walking, now alone in the park.

The sun crouched beneath the edge of a purple sky, waiting to pounce. Chen admired the back of Bella's neck, one arm over her hip. He lay in stillness where the dream could be preserved. In this place—if he could just retain the dream's delicate wisps, he could make it right. But he was waking, coming up for air, for daylight, despite his desire to submerge again.

The front of his legs were pressed against the back of Bella's. Asleep, her body moulded to his, relaxed and supple. They understood each other best in silence. Chen noticed the things around him—the placid quiet of the morning that was about to start, the temperature difference between the cool room and the warmth beneath the duvet, his aching elbow beneath Bella's head, the earthy smell of the roots of her hair.

Easing out of bed, Chen padded to the kitchen. He stepped out on the balcony and looked down into the valley. At the base of a scrubby rise, a tendril of smoke, the cooking fire of a squat. He listened for music, a violin, which he had heard drifting up from the streets a few times. Once, he thought it was coming from the direction of a bonfire in the valley, but it was hard to be sure with the wind.

Fitzgerald told him that Claire was an evening and nighttime customer—coming when she had money from busking, or from the restaurant, sometimes climbing up from the valley with people she had met at his house. Chen had gone to hear her once at the Dorado. After she noticed the doctor, she played the first movement of the Moeran concerto.

"You're up early," said Bella. "Worried about today?"

"Just wondering if this will work out."

"Aren't you Mister 'my role is to do the science, not generate specific results'?"

"That's what you're paying me for."

"Omega is paying."

It was the first day of the Memorex treatment efficacy trial. Despite what some had complained were overly cautious calls by Dr. Chen, overall the development program had moved ahead quickly. Research studies were like condos—building them was fast. Permits and financing were usually the rate-limiting factors, and both could be accelerated with sufficient energy and cash. The headlines of the opioid death toll had helped, no doubt. *Bolsters the investment case,* as Charlie put it.

Chen had never run a trial at the zoo. *Unusual problems require unusual solutions,* he had said to Charlie when he explained the concept. *If Memorex is going to make people forget something, how can we be sure it's not something very important?*

That night at the Dorado, Chen told Claire about the trial. She had not appeared in his office, so he sought her out. Fitzgerald had the recruiting information, but Chen wanted to explain it. It was a clear night, with a fresh late summer breeze, and they went outside on the patio, during her break between sets. She seemed healthier—had put on some weight. She had a new apartment, a bachelor in an older condo building. She showed Chen photos. There was no need to ask how Claire afforded a better place. Patients had told him that the girl with the violin always had hydromorphone, and she was easy to find—just follow the music. It was easier to talk, now that he wasn't writing prescriptions for her.

After Chen had explained ayahuagaine, Claire asked, "Why at the zoo?"

"Have you ever had a very important experience at the zoo?" asked Chen.

"I don't think so."

"Good. That would exclude you from the trial. If a medicine makes someone forget apples, what if there is some deep and important memory associated with apples? Something irreplaceable and precious? An apple crumble prepared by a grandparent according to a family recipe? An apple given to a teacher, rubbed bright and placed on a desk? Zoo animals are poignant, and whether or not they can be remembered is testable. But the zoo is a discrete experience. It's less ubiquitous than apples."

"So what you're saying—is that the zoo is kind of random."

"Whatever your experience might be of the zoo, it's not likely to be woven into the architecture of your life."

"Is this the magic pill? Is this going to fix me?"

"We don't know, but it's what we're trying to figure out."

"Thank you."

It was a multi-phase design. The first phase was the zoo, where the aim would be to see if Memorex impacted short-term recall and associations around something trivial, inconsequential to the subject's life such as an aardvark. The second phase would be to see whether Memorex could impact associations, and affective reactions to a familiar item related to drug use—like a syringe or a cooker. The third phase, if all went well, would be to administer Memorex in an attempt to repattern the subject's cravings, desires, and behaviours around their drug of choice. Explaining it to Matt, Chen had said, *Forgetting would just leave a gap waiting to be filled—this is about reorienting the direction of need, the belief that the drugs are a crucial piece of wholeness, and fostering plasticity for repatterning—learning.* Memory loss was, of course, a risk. Too risky for otherwise healthy people. Chen was glad that Matt did not ask the obvious question—what were the other crucial pieces of wholeness?—because Chen did not know the answer for most of the study subjects. In one case, he believed that he did.

It had been hard to hit the numbers. As Charlie put it, *Messed up, but not so messed up that they don't show up on the right day.* Fitzgerald had his methods, pulled enough subjects seemingly out of thin air. They made the numbers, Chen was paid a healthy recruitment fee, which he deposited into his shared account with Fitz.

At Varitas, the first dosing day always reminded Chen of an airplane about to take off, the moment between nothing happening and jet engines firing. The whisper-shouts of harried research assistants; subjects either timid or swaggering in fuchsia surgical scrubs. A milling chaos of bag searches, vital signs, wristbands being affixed, and electrodes yanking on chest hair. Chen knew some of the subjects from the Swan, and they greeted him with more enthusiasm than in clinic—*new drug, doc, and cash to take it!* Chen did not see Claire; had she flaked out? The subjects were fitted with wired caps, electro-encephalographic monitors that recorded their brains' electrical activities. Bella circulated through the screening unit, peering over shoulders. In small groups, subjects were taken out to two buses in the parking lot.

Chen and Bella took the seats in the front of one of the buses marked "reserved for staff." He said, "We're like tour guides."

"You can point out the major attractions. Notable shooting galleries. Sites of major busts. Alleyways of ill repute."

"Pharma offices," he said.

The innocent blue sky was spread above the empty parking lot. The zoo was closed on Mondays, though it could be booked for groups. Wired caps in place, tablet computers in hands, the subjects filed off the bus, squinting into the bright morning. Chen scanned faces and then finally saw Claire—one of the last people off the second bus. The research assistants explained to the subjects that it was like a scavenger hunt. Their tablets would tell them where to go, and what to do. The subjects began to stroll through the zoo.

The tablet computers directed each subject on their own randomly generated tour through the zoo. When a subject came to a testing station—an animal display from which the name plaques had been removed—they scanned a QR code and took a photograph of the animal using the camera on the tablet computer. Subjects were asked whether they knew the name of the animal and, if so, were asked to type it in. They were asked whether the animal reminded them of a celebrity, and the name was also entered on the tablet. The electroencephalographic cap recorded brain activities throughout the tour of the lemurs, wombats, tapirs. Subjects ambled from one place to another, laughing and joking. A few subjects took it more seriously, consulted their computer tablets, and stopped the research assistants to ask for clarification.

"You should have seen Matt's face when he saw the invoice for bringing a cow and a dog into the zoo!" said Bella.

Chen had insisted on including these controls. If a subject claimed not to know that a large black-and-white animal that mooed was called a cow, or that a small animal that barked and wagged its tail was called a dog, this would call into question their baseline reporting reliability and the rest of their results. Bella and Chen strolled into the butterfly house.

"Well, it was either that, or bring a sloth, an ostrich, and everything else into the lab."

Asking the subjects about their knowledge of animal names would allow the data analysts to differentiate between old associations and newly formed ones. If they knew the animals already, these were old memories. The associations with celebrities were more likely new. The pictures that the subjects took would be used later as the prompts. Chen periodically examined a tablet that was monitoring data, the completion rate of tasks, the attention span—which was being measured by the subject-facing camera.

"Every detail accounted for," she said. "You're in your element."

Chen imagined how he would explain this treatment to patients if it was proven that it worked. *You won't exactly forget your dealer, or what a syringe is. We want you to choose what they mean. It will be like how dreams seem so intense, but sometimes when you wake up—the intensity, the urgency is gone. And life goes on.*

What else could Memorex treat? Depression? Anxiety? If Memorex loosened the grip of thoughts, people would still have a life to build, but a clean slate. He imagined himself on a stage: *And it was after showing the efficacy of Memorex in opioid-use disorder that we felt it important to explore broader applications . . .* As they walked, Chen and Bella watched the subjects criss-crossing one another in each of their random journeys through the zoo. Hot dogs would be served for lunch, with a side course of study-drug dose administration. It would be Memorex or placebo. Then, the zoo tour would continue in the afternoon. With recognition and recall exercises both before dosing and afterwards, hopefully there would be clues to differentiate mechanism of action—whether Memorex affected long-term knowledge, and new association formation. If Memorex worked, could it even make methadone and buprenorphine pointless? There were junctures in medicine when a new paradigm changed everything, chucked a previous edifice out the window. Antibiotics for ulcers, stents instead of thrombolytics for heart attacks.

"Matt wanted me to tell you—he thinks it's an elegant study design," Bella laughed, "and that's not something he usually thinks about. He even said you're worth the money."

"Did he want you to tell me that?"

"Maybe not that part," said Bella.

Chen knew that while he and Varitas were being well compensated for running this trial, the biggest potential winner would be Omega.

Near lunchtime, the subjects gathered in the food court. Trays had been prepared and numbered. The subjects lined up, and advanced individually to the hot dog concession, repurposed as the dosing station. When the tray was placed before the subject, they were asked to take the medication cup, swallow the pill whole without chewing, and wash it down with water. The research assistant then took a tongue depressor and flashlight, and examined inside the subject's mouth—asked them to lift the tongue and to push it to the left, to the right. Chen imagined how a choreographer or a composer might feel when their work was performed for the first time.

"Look at you," Bella laughed. "It's like you're the watchmaker, and you've just wound it for the first time, marvelling at all the little gears and levers spinning around." That was about right, he thought. He realized he was blushing. "That's okay—be proud of what you do well."

"Hi, Dr. Chen." The voice was familiar, and he turned.

"Hello, Claire." She was in the line of subjects, wore the same brightly coloured scrubs as everyone else. She held a tablet in her hand, and advanced towards her dosing. The brainwave-measuring device suddenly seemed like a ridiculous thing to press upon someone's head. It looked like something between a Halloween costume and a device intended to electrocute someone.

"How was your morning?"

"A day at the zoo, right?" She winked. "Next up—lunch and drugs."

"Well, hello . . ." said Bella. "I heard you play at Trinity Bellwoods," she said.

"Hi," said Claire, and she continued down the line.

Claire was a few metres away from the dosing station, moving forward. She was objectively perfect for this trial. But what was it that made him uncomfortable now that he saw her here?

The meal was being held in the open-air food court, and each subject took the seat that had been labelled with their subject number. As subjects stepped away from the dosing station with their food tray and sat at their allotted places, a few of them began to smile, and to laugh. They looked around themselves with fascination and found everything to their liking. One subject caressed a hard Formica table as if it were a silk cushion. Another pointed to the leaves of trees, and moved his fingers to mimic the light shimmering through the foliage.

"So much for blinded observation," said Bella, amused. "Exactly half of them are having a great time."

Two of the happy subjects were engaged in intense conversation, as if they knew each other very well. A man remarked that he had never before noticed the redness of red. A woman was transfixed by birdsong, comparing each note to a wind instrument.

"It's not fair," said one girl, picking at her hot dog—which was nothing more to her than a hot dog. "I want to try that stuff."

"It's random," said one of the research assistants. Nearby, a young man seemed to have discovered the intense pleasures of a glass of water. In the line waiting to be dosed, subjects began to say that they hoped to get the "good stuff."

Bella said, "We didn't see this in the abuse liability trials, did we?"

"Some gave subjective reports of liking the ayahuagaine, but not like this." Was it the setting? The abuse liability trials had been in the standard, bland, Varitas facility. The food court was taking on the mood of an open-air event, almost a party. The atmosphere reminded Chen of Fitzgerald's house. Had opioids once appeared this way in trials intended to prove their painkilling effect, with an innocuous side observation that people really liked them? Claire was almost at the front of the line. "I'm worried about that one," said Chen. "I'm going to pull her."

"Mind telling me why?"

"See how drawn she is to what's happening? I'm her doctor and I'm worried—that she'll like it too much."

"Today, you're not her doctor," Bella said evenly. "You're the principal investigator of this trial."

"Investigator discretion," said Chen. The prerogative of the principal investigator was to make judgments, in or out. Ultimately, Chen could just yank a subject, if he thought that was the right thing to do. It was right there in the protocol language. A reason would be expected; he would provide one later.

Bella gripped Chen's shoulder. "We have exactly the right number for statistical significance." A few of the subjects who were still waiting for hot dogs tittered and laughed as if they were waiting in line for a roller coaster. They didn't want to be left out. Claire was transfixed by what was happening with the dosed subjects.

Chen thought of the night he had resuscitated Claire with naloxone, how grateful he had been that she did not die. And then, to realize that she qualified squarely for this trial. He had thought, *What if ayahuagaine is exactly what Claire has been looking for all this time?* A patient's doctor might be nervous. An investigator should be curious. He was both, but Bella was right. Today, Chen was not Claire's doctor, he was the principal investigator of the trial.

The doser beckoned Claire over. She reached for her cup, and swallowed the pill. In the time it took for the molecule to be absorbed, to circulate from the stomach into the blood and up to the brain, and to cross the blood-brain barrier, Claire found her designated seat. Then, a focused quiet came over her.

Chen wondered what she was paying such attention to—the breeze? Its play on the rippled surface of the adjacent artificial pond? The distant siren? Claire placed both hands on the table in front of her, palms flat as if absorbing some kind of energy through them. Something was happening. She pushed the tray away, and laid her head down in her arms. She breathed deeply, like a child asleep at a school desk. Chen wanted to run over, to shake her, to find out if she was okay. He did not move.

One of the research assistants went to Claire's side, spoke to her, then shook her by the shoulder. This was procedure—subjects who appeared to be drowsy were roused. First it was verbal stimulation, then tactile. Ideally, if she woke up to full alertness, the research assistant was to encourage her to finish her lunch.

Following procedure, the research assistant rubbed her knuckles on Claire's brow. Claire's head lolled slightly from side to side, but she did not flinch, did not squeeze her eyes in pain or try to squirm away. The assistant matter-of-factly took Claire's hand, and squeezed the fingernail beds. Again, no reaction. The arm was totally limp. Chen felt as if he were reading a training manual he had once written, the research assistant precisely following the steps. He wanted to scream.

The next step in the protocol for the unresponsive patient was *Notify physician on duty,* and at a glance from the research assistant Chen rushed over. He placed a hand on Claire's neck. The amplitude of the pulse was strong, but the rate was slow.

She was breathing. Her heart was beating. Chen felt like a medical student again, uncertain, muddling through. He looked at the EEG monitoring on the tablet computer, expecting the slow brainwaves of sleep. Instead of the lazy pulsations of sleep, there were wild epileptiform waves, her entire brain surging with electrical impulses. But why wasn't she seizing? In a paralyzed patient, an undetected seizure could be catastrophic, causing permanent brain damage. Where was the crash cart? And then, as if someone had flipped a switch, the waves assumed some strange pattern that he had never before seen. Chen touched her neck again—there was no pulse. Claire's shoulder, her chest, her entire body was completely limp.

Chen knew that he should be yelling for a nurse to start an intravenous, so that he could give her drugs. But what drugs? His own heart raced, his hands gentle on Claire's carotid artery as if his fingers could beg her. He stared at her face, imagining it in his cellphone gallery. He should be sending someone running for a stretcher, and telling someone else to call an ambulance. Standard operating procedures flashed through his mind.

Chen put one hand on Claire's shoulder, the other on her neck. He bent close, and spoke into her ear, "Claire, be with yourself. That's all there is."

Beneath his fingers, Chen felt the resumption of a faint swell and emptying of Claire's carotid artery. Her brain's electrical waves began to normalize, slow-wave sleep rhythms, seas under a light breeze. Her pulse became regular and strong. She opened her eyes.

The rest of the subjects barely noticed that anything had happened. The research assistant who had called Chen over had gone to accompany a subject who needed to use the bathroom.

Claire looked at Chen and said, "I think it worked."

"What?"

"It's a mind-healing medicine, right? Ayahuagaine. So I looked it up, not Whitelight. I read about what the traditional users did. When I took it, I concentrated really hard on what I wanted to find, my truth. And now, something is different. I feel free, and true. Thank you."

Chen had combed the anthropological accounts of how ayahuagaine was used. But finding truth—it was vague, and hard to formulate into a research question. There was no way to write that into a protocol. He had wondered if there was something lost in translation. For research purposes, it was important to break things down into components—discrete measurable portions—hence the zoo, the tasks, short-term memories, associations. Claire had not followed these instructions. She had skipped ahead.

34

SERIOUS ADVERSE EVENT reports had to be filed within twenty-four hours of the occurrence, and it was about twenty hours and counting when Charlie called Chen into an emergency meeting—*the client is not amused*. Yes, Charlie assured Chen, further dosing on the trial had been suspended as the doctor had ordered, but the report of what happened to Claire at the zoo, the Serious Adverse Event report, had not yet been filed. Yes, said Charlie, he understood that Chen had completed the report the day previous, but could they talk first? Before sending it to the review board and the FDA?

Bella and several of her Omega colleagues were in the boardroom, along with Matt, and some venture capital people whom Chen had never met. All of the direct counterparts from Varitas were present. Charlie was unusually quiet. The door was closed behind Chen, and he gave a narrative of events directly from the chart, referencing the physician notes he had made at the zoo: Claire's heart stopped, with no explanation, but then it started. Claire had revived, after the period of unresponsiveness. Chen had documented everything that she had told him.

The cognitive tests for the afternoon were scheduled to begin, and Chen had staff perform a set of vital signs and an electrocardiogram on Claire, which were normal. She resumed her cognitive assessment, and completed the afternoon with the other subjects. Claire was later transported to hospital for an MRI, a PET scan, and a full cardiac workup. Everything came back normal.

A few questions were asked to clarify events. Each person inquired carefully, specifically, and there were often long pauses after Chen's answers.

Matt, who had not yet spoken, then said, "After the subject was assessed in hospital, and all the tests were normal, you prepared this report." He stabbed a piece of paper on the table with his index finger.

"The EEG waves are an unknown pattern. I showed them to a neurologist, who described them as bizarre—he can't explain them. There could have been permanent brain damage."

"And the subject?"

"Clearly she deviated from the protocol. She focused on the way she feels when she uses."

"What you refer to in your report as the internal experience of opioid-induced euphoria?"

"Feeling high," Bella interjected.

"And why did she do that, doctor?" Matt asked.

"It was specifically the feeling of . . . playing the violin while high." He hesitated. "She said that it was her 'truth.' I'm quoting her debrief account. That is not part of the protocol, which in itself should give us pause. When subject adherence depends upon what they are thinking at any given point, how can we ever be sure that we know what is happening in the study?"

Matt read from the report. "'The next day, subject reports that she is not having withdrawal.'" He looked up. "No shakes, shits, shivers. This is what we're after, Dr. Chen!" Matt said. "We should be popping champagne corks and you're filing an SAE report?"

"Do you know why she's not having withdrawal?" Chen asked.

"I'm counting on you to explain that, doctor."

"But I can't. I don't know. First of all, it's just one subject saying this—so we have no idea if it's real. If it is, there are a variety of possibilities, which have to do with neurological plasticity and the reversal of adaptive changes. We have to slow down and examine, figure it out. And there's an SAE that we have to explain, to keep this research safe."

"We're not paying you to give a lecture, doctor. We're paying you to run these trials, to make this all work."

"Aren't you paying me for judgment?"

"Dr. Chen, with all due respect—"

"Her heart stopped," said Chen. The room was quiet, except the hum of a projector.

"According to?" Matt asked.

"I was right there."

"According to your hand on her neck? But no telemetry, right?" Matt asked, smiling. There had been no cardiac telemetry. It was felt to be too cumbersome to have the brainwave hardware and the telemetry running at the same time. The twenty-four hour telemetry in the abuse liability trials had not revealed any ventricular tachycardia, just occasional extra beats, so he had signed that off. "No tracing. Just your observations—if they're reliable."

"An event is considered to be a Serious Adverse Event if it causes permanent disability, if it results in death or imminent risk of death—'"

"You don't have to read me the definition of an SAE," said Matt. "You're going to kill this compound, is that what you're trying to do?"

Charlie smiled a smile that was a good imitation of his usual one, but tighter. "Chen, maybe there's a little room here. I mean, an Adverse Event report for sure. Maybe an Adverse Event of Special Interest? But with a Serious Adverse Event report everyone just gets a little jumpy. You know?" Bella was looking out the window.

Again, Chen quoted from the regulations. "'An investigator and his delegates are obliged to file an SAE report within twenty-four hours when—'"

"I can't believe this," said Matt.

Chen replied evenly, "I'm not saying there's no pathway for the molecule. But the development program needs to take a step back, be re-evaluated. More animal work. Slower human dose escalation. Larger sample sizes. Steady-state pharmacodynamics, not just single-dose peak levels. Thorough cardiac conduction studies."

Chen glanced towards Bella, who was now watching Matt. The difference between a positive therapeutics trial and an SAE report stating "unknown, unexplainable waveforms on electroencephalography in conjunction with a pulseless episode" was the difference between Omega being bought up by one of the big pharmas and the venture capital guys cancelling the next round of funding. For a few people at the table, it was the difference between cashing out handsomely or looking for a new job.

Matt turned to Charlie and spat out, "So this is your star doctor?"

Chen glanced at his watch. "That report needs to be filed in less than an hour. Otherwise we're out of compliance. I'll send it on my own." He stood and left the boardroom, expecting voices might call after him, but only silence followed him to the elevator.

35

AFTER THE END of the Memorex trial, Claire often spent hours practising, unaware of time. One day, she was at home playing scales. It was raining outside, and as Claire played, she was aware of the hissing sound of car tires rolling on wet pavement, splashing through water-filled potholes, all of this a few floors down from her bachelor apartment. Her hearing seemed more acute since the trial. She practised with an upright but supple posture. She remembered how, as a child, she was taught to stand by Josef: *like a tree— your arms grow out, all of you strong, but moving with the wind.* Claire progressed through the major and minor scales, her fingers deliberate on the strings. Steady eighth notes, two octaves to a bow, and she focused on the constant movement and adjustment of pressure through her index finger, that would produce a consistent tone from heel to tip.

She focused on whole bow tone without her mind dancing ahead into something she was worried about and backwards to something she had already screwed up. She was present, aware of the rain, the temperature of the room, took care to narrow the distance between the bow and the bridge as her left hand came up the fingerboard, was attuned to her own movements, and observed memories of past teachers, performances, when they arose.

Ever since Memorex, nothing was different and yet everything felt different. Claire had been prepared for the zoo trial, had understood the instructions about focusing on animals and associations, which she had decided to ignore. She had also downloaded a paper by Dr. Quinones, read his descriptions of how ayahuagaine was traditionally used, and decided that she didn't want to use it in the finicky, computer-games-and-scores way that Dr. Chen and his experimenters envisioned.

"Traditional users bring a state of truth to the forefront of their attention, to imagine it not only as something in the past or hoped for in the future, but to evoke the sense of it in the present," wrote Dr. Quinones.

What was there for her, but music? Playing the violin. That's what Claire thought of while sitting there with the hot dog untouched; her best performances, the purity of line, tone, energy. And all that came with it, the bite of the needle—like a lover's teeth but sharper, the warmth of her own skin prickling and sighing, the ease of her centre, the curving of otherwise sharp angles within herself.

Yet, Claire had not felt high when she was on Memorex, and its lingering effects were not euphoria. She had felt like she was more "there" for the overnight stay at the research lab, for the blood sampling, for the rounds of computer testing that followed. When she was paid her subject's fee, she did not feel the expected urgent impulse to score, the fuel of wanting. It was just money. She cashed the cheque without buying drugs. For weeks, she did little except practise—very slow scales, deliberate arpeggios. That morning, she had just finished the minor range, climbing up the fingerboard of the E string to where the last joint of her pinky finger ached, when the door of the apartment opened.

"Molly!" Of course she had not bothered to buzz from the lobby, or knock on the door. A couple of days before, Molly had sent a text. She might be in town briefly, could she stay a few nights? Claire sent the new address. Molly had the smell of street—the ripeness of days without a shower. Skin raw—sun and wind. Nails cut short, hands dry. Her red hair was streaked through with blonde highlights, but the roots had begun to grow in. Claire knew that Molly was here for help—and embraced her.

"Hey! Gorgeous! Way too long!" Molly summoned an exclamation.

"I was worried." Claire placed the violin in the case, laid the velvet cloth over it. "You could have told me when you were arriving."

"I'm so sorry. You know, busy, life gets in the way, no excuse."

"Another Mr. Wonderful bites the dust?"

She rolled her eyes. "Also, I'm not feeling so good. Can you help me out?" She scanned the room, hunting for a stash.

"I have some pot. No down."

"For real?" said Molly. "I mean, you look . . . good. Whatever your doctor is prescribing? I'm feeling so bad, I'll even take some of that. Buprenorphine or methadone or whatever."

"No, I'm not on anything. I think I'm better, actually. I think I'm over it." The night after the zoo, when Claire was back at the research lab during the overnight safety stay, she had heard two people in white coats saying in hushed tones that the people "in corporate" were upset about the failure of the experiment . . . *massive waste of money, no useful data whatsoever.* The next morning after the zoo, she still felt fine. No achy back, not a single chill, her nose didn't run. Since the trial was for users, there was a morning menu on offer along with breakfast—morphine, valium, methylphenidate. Claire and a number of the other subjects didn't want anything, which caused a flurry of paperwork with the people in white coats, but of course subjects were always free to decline medications.

Molly asked, "So you're not seeing your doctor anymore?"

"No, I'm still seeing him. But I'm not on any prescriptions anymore."

"Then why are you seeing him?"

"I did an experiment. He says he's taking notes on the effects."

Each time Chen saw her, he asked Claire if she was in with-drawal, going through the laundry list of symptoms: *Sleeping badly? Muscle aches? Runny nose? Goosebumps? Vomiting?* Then he asked some questions related to memory—about the zoo animals, the associa-tions—he was stuck on that for a while. *Have you needed methadone again? Have you craved opiates? Have you used any pills? What about street heroin or fentanyl?*

No, and no, she shrugged. Like it was no big deal. It didn't feel like a big deal—something had been detached inside her, something that had clung to her with such persistence. The doctor was pleased that she was teaching, finding gigs, and making ends meet. The thing that Claire hesitated to tell Dr. Chen was that she was not able to play the violin as she once had. The technical skills were there—and if anything she was more settled and comfortable than she had ever been in going through basic exercises. The shoulder pain was in the background instead of the forefront, and now she was able to play through it. But her favourite pieces lacked something. She could play them well, perhaps even very well, but the feeling, of being made whole, of delicious fusion with the music, was not the same. And she missed it. She did tell him that some of the effects of the ayahuagaine—the vividness of colours, the enhanced hearing, the sense of "thereness" in the moment—were still there but seemed to be fading. A little. Slowly.

36

EARLY ONE EVENING, Chen was in the research office signing off charts for a trial that aimed to show that a drug very similar to an existing anxiety medication behaved very similarly, but with slightly reduced side effects in this slightly modified and freshly patented molecule. It was an easy eligibility—healthy, normal subjects—and Chen flipped through the pages, reviewed methodically, and signed. He planned to go home right after finishing the charts. He would order some take-out, and eat alone. He had only seen Bella a couple of times since their day at the zoo. It could not be concluded, he told himself, that the cancellation of the Memorex development program, and then the souring of the relationship between Omega and Varitas, had caused Bella's cooling. Any scientist understood that correlation was not causation.

Charlie appeared at the doorway. "Working hard, doc? Or hardly working?"

"I thought that was your role," said Chen. "I didn't know you were still in the office."

"You know how it is. Lonely at the top. You almost done? Mussels night at Le Bertrand."

"Give me fifteen."

The neighbourhood spot was supposed to be Belgian, but that night's specials were curry mussels and chorizo fries. Televisions were mounted from the ceiling so that from any seat in the place, you could watch some kind of live sports event. Despite Charlie doing his best to dispel what Omega was saying about Varitas, *Can't deliver, rogue investigators*, it was shaping up to be a light quarter. This seemed to have impacted Charlie's choice of restaurants, but Chen was grateful for the screens as he looked above Charlie's head, smiling in a genial way.

Charlie was going on enthusiastically about his new smartwatch, and asking Chen's opinions on the usefulness of certain features. Chen had worked with Charlie long enough to recognize the pattern. First, ardent engagement about some kind of electronic device, or the work being done on his place in Lawrence Park, or some expensive, adrenaline saturated sport that he had just taken up, to be followed by *There's something I need you to back me up on*. But before that, Chen thought, Charlie would offer, and then insist, that Chen handle his new device. As if on cue, Charlie unstrapped the watch, and said, "See what I mean about the pedometer screen? Tell me what you honestly think."

Chen held the watch by the bezel, not touching the straps that had recently been pressed against Charlie's wrist. He poked at the screen, swiped it, and said, "Yes, it could be more intuitive—but you'll get used to it."

"You think so? Could they make the menus more confusing? But I still think it's the right watch for me. Hey, Chen, I wanted to ask you something about the whole zoo situation."

"But there is no longer any situation." Chen sipped his beer.

After the Serious Adverse Event report had been filed, the regulators sent their form letters, telling Varitas to follow up and monitor the subjects closely. Omega's emails became infrequent, and they always copied their in-house counsel. Now, as a championship ten-pin bowling tournament unfolded on the screen above his head,

Charlie said, "You know that Omega had a monitor go through the trial master file. Right?"

"No one mentioned that."

"Oh really? No big deal."

Monitors were a third set of eyes, hired by the sponsor. Their role was to watch a trial while it was under way, to look over shoulders, ask nitpicky questions and ensure that it was implemented as per protocol. "I've never heard of a monitor being brought in after a trial has been stopped."

"We just wanted another set of eyes, but you know, discreetly."

"We wanted? Or Omega?" Chen asked.

"Chen, just to double-check something: When that subject went down, you went to help her?"

"Of course."

"Bella mentioned that you took her pulse."

"Vital signs are vital."

"But *you* actually did it yourself. Just confirming."

"Yes."

"That's great news."

Charlie explained that in addition to going through the trial master files, the monitor had gone through all the training records. He signalled to the waiter for another round of beers. The monitor had discovered that Chen's own training file was a little out of date. A few routine training certifications had expired, including the one on vital signs—six months out of date, to be precise. Charlie raised his hands in celebration, as if this were just the news Chen had been hoping for. So really, he said, at the moment of the *awkward incident*, Chen was not certified to perform vital signs in a trial. If he was not certified, the vital signs he performed on Claire were not valid. Since they were not valid, they were an error in the record. "It will take a little finesse, but there is a way to get things back on track. We've spoken with the compliance department." The beers arrived, and

Charlie tipped his back, as if it were a shared celebration. Charlie winked. "Don't worry, we'll get you to re-train on vitals."

"You must be kidding," said Chen, putting it together.

"What?"

"You're going to say that I don't know how to take a pulse, and so Claire didn't really die? That's absurd."

"You know what some would say is absurd? She recovered with you talking to her. What did you call that in the report—verbal stimulation? Hey, I know you're a sweet talker, doc, but . . ." Charlie seemed to be waiting for a laugh, which did not come. "That doesn't sound compatible with death, does it? Sounds more like . . . a nap? We gave her drugs."

"Charlie, I know how to take a pulse."

"But we all get a bit rusty, don't we? I mean, you're really a big-concepts guy. How often do you take a pulse? No one's blaming you. If you maybe panicked, overreacted, perhaps? She's fine now, isn't she?"

"She is."

"And even if her pulse stopped briefly, an arrhythmia, couldn't drug use have caused previous cardiac damage?"

"Possible. Or she has a genetic predisposition to arrhythmia with ayahuagaine. Needs to be studied. I thought Omega didn't want anything to do with Varitas anymore."

"Which is why we should value their collaborative spirit—that Omega still wants to find a way forward. Why? Because they believe this compound is important, that it could help patients like yours."

Chen sipped his beer. "Or, it may be that with my SAE on file, no buyer or trial site wants to touch the molecule," he said. "So it's a Catch-22 for them. I'm the only problem to solve."

"You're the one who always says you want to run trials that matter. Doesn't this matter?"

Chen had not discussed Claire's follow-up visits with anyone at

Varitas or Omega. There was no obligation for her to see him, or him to report. In fact, because she was his patient, outside of the trial he would need her consent to reveal anything to those companies. Now he wondered, had they reached out to her? Did they know how well she was doing? If they cared, it was for the usual reasons. Publication, the next quarterly report, the exit strategy for the fund. It wasn't that Chen didn't want the questions that were raised by Claire's experiences to be pursued—it was just that he wanted it to be studied carefully, methodically, and not pushed ahead with martinis and press releases by speculative investment people. He wanted to do it himself, the way it should be done.

Claire talked about Memorex having worked like some kind of "reset." But what did that mean? There was no chapter on "reset" in any medical textbook. Chen had checked in with Fitzgerald. Fitz had not seen Claire, though Molly had turned up again, recently. Was it possible that Claire was cured? As he made notes on what she told him, he generated more questions than answers, but he knew that the requirements of speculative investment were the opposite— more answers and fewer questions.

"I'm not saying there's nothing in the molecule," said Chen. "Ayahuagaine has to be figured out. Slow it down. Do more ground work."

"Omega hasn't got enough runway," said Charlie, which meant money. "So why don't you help them push it down the road a little further—to someone who's got the bandwidth? Come on, Chen. You know where Omega fits into the game. But we've been following up with the subjects—the ones who were dosed reported some very positive outcomes. Even the patient of yours—of course we're following up with her, too. The one you got upset about."

"Whose heart stopped beating."

"You thought. And let's be honest, you seem kind of . . . invested? Not to say you would be non-objective. But you agree she's doing better? How many patients of yours could have their lives transformed? Doc, we're in an opioid crisis. Every day is a body count. Think of your patients who are suffering. Do you want ayahuagaine to be one of those molecules that just never gets developed?" Charlie's tempo increased, and he spoke with evangelical zeal about purpose, compassion, humanity. That made it easy for Chen to dismiss him, because he knew that none of these issues really concerned Charlie. Even so, Chen thought of the gallery in his phone, of all the faces. He thought of Claire living her life without a daily clock ticking down to withdrawal, but also remembered the gut-punch dread of her pulseless neck beneath his fingertips—everything relaxed, the looseness of her body, fearing it would become stiff forever.

"Of course, I want my patients to be helped." There was no point in Chen explaining to Charlie that he had already covered this difficult ground on his own—that Claire had brought her sister, Molly, to the clinic, appealed to Chen to get her some ayahuagaine. Molly was sweating, cramped up, trying to cold-turkey, had tried it a few times already but ended up grabbing. Surely the doctor could obtain some of the medication that had changed everything for Claire? *You almost died*, said Chen to Claire. *Actually, you did die.* Undeterred, she replied, *But I came back. Like a reset button. It cured me. Now my sister needs it.* Chen told the sisters, *For the moment, the research program is paused—I don't even know if or when the trials will start again.*

"If Omega goes bust, maybe someone else eventually buys the molecule," said Chen. "Whoever that is—you can snag some of their business." He had done his job. Questions had come up: the scientist should advise slowing down and answering those questions, and that is what he had done.

A couple of days after the mussels, Chen showed up at Varitas and his magnetic pass didn't work. Chen asked security to buzz him in, and gave his name. The security guard called upstairs, nodded a few times, and asked Chen to wait. Charlie appeared with a box containing the personal belongings that had been on Chen's desk, and said they should go for coffee, off-site. For once, Charlie looked a little sheepish. It was nothing personal, he said, but ayahuagaine was too big for Omega and Varitas to walk away from, and they were going to double down on the bet. Besides, Chen was in the wrong: at the time he took Claire's pulse, he wasn't officially signed off to do it. The Serious Adverse Event was a procedure error, Charlie explained, looking away, and they couldn't keep a doctor around who violated procedure, and then who did not co-operate with error remediation. There was really nothing else to do about it, said Charlie, but he had managed to wrangle a non-disclosure agreement for Chen. *Not that it's about money. I'll sign the cheque if you would just sign the non-disclosure right here . . .*

Chen was surprised at the sum, recognized that it was calibrated for quick agreement. An offer he couldn't refuse. The only condition, really, was that he couldn't say anything about what had happened at the zoo. Chen felt a sense of lightness, in having decision removed from him. Was he rationalizing, as he considered the cheque? It wouldn't really matter what he did, Chen told himself. Omega wanted to develop this molecule, or at least move it along far enough for an exit, and they would get it done. Besides, just because someone took a pill and their heart stopped, it didn't mean the pill stopped their heart. It might have, and it might not have. That's what research was for—to sort that out. Chen signed the non-disclosure agreement, and Charlie signed the cheque.

After his departure from Varitas, Chen had some free afternoons. As the autumn days grew sharp and crisp, he and Fitzgerald went for long, fast-paced rides beyond the suburbs, through farm fields, and then back into the city. Late one afternoon, the first leaves loosened by a windstorm, Chen paused in the valley, declined Fitzgerald's invitation to climb up the hill to the house.

"I should get back up there. See if they've completely wrecked the place yet."

When it became clear that the legal options were exhausted, and that he was actually losing control of the place to his creditors, Fitzgerald had given his "public" permission to completely trash the house. He had held out long enough that even with everyone paid off, the land appreciation was enough that Fitzgerald would pocket something. Now, people were regularly seen walking out with furniture, dragging rugs to their squats in the valley. The rule about not dying remained, but everything else was open season. From up the hill came a tinkling sound like glass being smashed.

"I told them not to touch the bicycle," said Fitzgerald. His next move was a Georgian Bay cottage that he had recently inherited from a disgraced, and for that reason sympathetic, uncle. It had an internet connection, and Fitz intended to trade cryptocurrency.

"I'm just curious . . . your customers, anyone I might know . . . ?"

"Your violinist? When Claire first brought Molly back, it was just her—jonesing like anything. Claire looked fine, like she had kicked it. She said she was just trying to help her sister. But then, more recently . . ."

"She hasn't been in clinic, so I wondered . . ."

"They're both pretty regular now."

"So where will your patients—I mean your public—go, when the sheriff locks the place up?"

"They'll find what they need, Chen, people always do."

37

WHEN THEY WENT for screening, it was a different doctor, as Claire knew it would be. The intense-looking woman who had shadowed Dr. Chen at the zoo, and seemed to watch everything carefully, was nowhere to be seen.

The tech slipped a needle into a vein to take some blood, the cold steel in her arm filling Claire with want. She felt a bead of sweat, although she had swallowed a couple of long-acting hydromorphone tablets in order to be sure to get through the screening. One of the research assistants who went through a questionnaire looked at her as if he was wondering something, a déjà vu, but he was intent on the forms that he had to fill out. Molly was herself—gregarious and flirtatious, having done a massive shot before coming into the clinic—and the staff barely paid attention to Claire. A few days later, Claire and Molly both got a phone call that they were eligible for the Memorex Efficacy Phase 2 study. On the appointed date, they both got high, and then checked into the Varitas research facility.

Claire woke at four o'clock in the overnight unit of Varitas. The windows of Female Dorm Six, on the seventeenth floor, faced a condo, an office building, a swathe of Chinatown. Below, in a court-yard off the street, there was a church that had gradually been swallowed by the striving of the city's developers. From higher up, the presumably once-grand structure looked like a little runt surrounded by taller kids in the playground. Within the dorm, it was possible to hear the low, resonant notes of the church bell, but the sound came through as if under water, such was the cold thickness of the glass. Otherwise, here in the lab, the passage of time was marked only by the red LED digital clocks which were placed in each room, visible from any vantage point.

She had been dreaming. A strange dream, of the zoo? Claire had been trying not to think of the zoo itself, to just focus on how to get another dose of ayahuagaine. The evaporating zoo dream did leave a tantalizing gap, the way dreams sometimes did, the sense of one important thing being just out of reach.

The stiff sheets were like sleeping under paper. Poly-cotton blend, both cool and stifling. The climate control hissed from vents above. There were two sounds, one low and hollow, and the other a tighter whistle. A building could inhale and exhale at the same time. Her scrubs were bunched up. One of the nearby girls snored, a flabby, intermittent snort. Above, in the corner, she saw the camera scan across. Bored staff, watching her.

"Hey," a whisper, and a creaking shift in the mattress. Claire turned to see Molly on the edge of her bed. She was curled over, holding herself. With bare feet on the floor, she tapped her heels against linoleum, rolled back and forth over the balls of her feet, lower legs quivering. "I can't take this."

"You have to—just a few more hours. You'll see, this ayahua-gaine stuff will fix you. It's worth all this trouble."

"And what if I don't get the stuff? It's random, right?"

"Well, fifty-fifty."

"And what if?"

"Well, what if? We still get paid."

Though not as badly off as her sister, Claire was restless, and had a runny nose. She had stayed away from everything, and everyone connected to drugs, until Molly arrived. But it was different with Molly around. She took Molly to Fitzgerald—after all, Claire had the cash to fix her sister. Sometimes Molly didn't feel well enough to go grab for herself, and Claire went for her. Molly's gift of bouncing back seemed to be exhausted. On some occasions it was too far to make the trek up the valley for pills, especially when a little fentanyl would work better, and Claire had met lots of people at Fitzgerald's house who delivered. It was a point of some pride for Claire, to be able to handle the drugs without feeling an imperative to consume them.

Then one evening, scrolling on her phone, Claire saw the news— the Punk Fugue Trio was up for a Juno. The new violinist was gorgeous. So what was the point of abstinence, Claire wondered. Bitterly, she saw that the recording available to stream on the site was from her premiere. While high, she had decided to pick up the violin again. Just to hear. And the way she sounded! That night she had a gig at the Dorado, and she gave herself entirely to the music. Within a week, everything was just like before ayahuagaine. The cycles of high and withdrawal had returned. The equanimity, and the presence of mind that came from her initial dose of ayahuagaine, had vanished, and she was prone again to moodiness and unexpected joy, to believing that everything was perfect or that everything would fall apart.

"Shh . . ." said a raven-haired subject. Then she asked, "Hey, you dopesick?"

"Oh fuuuuuck you," said Molly.

The girl grappled for a pillow, pulled it over her own head. "Was going to try to help you."

"What . . . have you got something?"

Claire said to her sister, "Just lie down, it's just a few hours more."

Molly ignored her, said to the stranger with what sounded like genuine contrition, "I'm really sorry. I'm not usually such a bitch. I'm just sick. Have you got some?"

The raven girl raised a single finger, her head still beneath a pillow.

"Please?"

"Hundred bucks—for a point. Really strong fenny."

"That's ridiculous," said Claire, knowing that where Molly was, no price was unreasonable. "Besides, we don't have any cash."

"Repeat after me: *I'll pay you on cheque day, right away.* Say it, I want to hear you say it," the raven girl said to Molly.

"Yes," Molly hissed, and she repeated the words.

The girl's bed was in the corner of the room, and her smuggler's hole was in the ceiling above her where the window met a wall behind a pillar. One spot the cameras appeared not to reach. Standing on the bed in her sock feet, she pushed up the tile of the drop ceiling in the corner.

"I guess you do a lot of studies," said Claire.

"I like to be prepared."

With the drop ceiling tile slipped into place, she climbed down, and moved very casually and slowly back into the camera's view. As she walked across the bedroom towards the exit, she let something fall from her hand onto Molly's bed. Claire lay back in her bed. She wanted some, but was not as badly off as her sister. Claire stayed awake, but after a little while she recognized her sister's deep breathing, asleep with the other subjects in the dorm. That was surprising, that such a small amount of opiates had knocked her out. She whispered to the stranger, "Are you sure that stuff is okay?" but no reply came. She got up and looked out the window, watched as night became day. Gradually a few kitchen lights in people's condominium boxes came on. Traffic thickened and slowed. A guy sleeping on a grate below the lab woke up and propped up his cardboard sign. The night staff poked their heads in and asked if everything with the subjects was okay, not waiting for an answer, hurrying to the next dorm room. About half an hour later, the day staff made a wake-up call. They began to call them by number, to go to the treatment room. Claire helped Molly up; she was still a bit on the nod.

There was a rushed briefing of the subjects, read by a bored guy in a lab coat who read through as if there was no punctuation in the text. It wasn't like the first time—with all the detailed, complicated instructions about what to do at the zoo. This was more akin to the disclaimers read on TV medication ads. Claire sat in her vinyl-upholstered reclining chair. *Like a good girl*, she thought. Next to the large window, opposite the sliding glass door into the hallway, was a view down the long room.

"Like a beehive," said Molly a little too loudly from the next chair. "I read that in a beehive, all the insects know what they are supposed to do, are in fact functioning as if they are one cohesive organism. Isn't that amazing?" The room did look like a swarm of beings crawling over one another. Subjects laughed and joked as staff hurried to check monitors and write in clipboards. Subjects got in the way while staff rushed to grab things and people, all a humming agitation.

"Can you just chill out, so it's not so obvious that you're high?"

Molly tittered, like a teenager with a secret, and then, in response to Claire's glare, said, "Right. Sorry. This is very-quiet me, like a little mouse. I know I haven't always been a *super*-amazing sister, but I do love you."

Definitely more than a bit high. "Just remember what I told you. Ignore whatever directions they give us—do what I did." This was the second phase of the study, and the assessment would involve interactions with virtual works on computers. Apparently, some authority had nixed the subjects actually handling needles and filters, an attempt to minimize *extraneous stimuli*.

Seen from the wide sixth-floor window that went from waist-height to the ceiling and spanned the breadth of the room, Chinatown was blotches and stripes. On each side of the street was a chaotic patchwork of awnings, mismatched in both colour and size. Sidewalk peeked through, shoppers lugged white plastic bags, pulled wheeled trolleys, navigated displays of produce. Through glass and distance, all of it was silent, odourless, a pantomime of life. Claire wished that Dr. Chen were here, and now realized more clearly the comfort it had given her, that he was there the last time. Another doctor observed carefully. He seemed to be new, and often asked staff how to do certain things on the computers.

The staff were moving along, dosing people. In this study, there were no zoo animals to look at. No mention had been made that in a previous study someone's heart had stopped, but they all wore cardiac monitors for this one. White-coated staff rhymed off words they were required to say, checked vitals, and gave people their pills in efficient five-minute intervals. Peering down the long room, Claire could tell that some people were being affected. She could see the change. They became intensely focused on what was in front of them, on the computers. This was as it had been at the zoo, but the subjects had only one option to focus upon, the laptops. Prodded by the staff, they did their tasks.

Molly was before her. While the staff read questions from the sheet so fast that the words all blended together, Molly smiled and agreed each time the research assistant took a breath.

"Haveyouavoidedallnewoverthecounterandprescriptionmedicationsbeyondwhatisonyourmedicationlist?"

"Yes."

"Haveyouabstainedfromallillicitsubstancessinceyouradmissionto-thisfacility?"

"Yes."

"Doyouunderstandtherisksofthisstudywhichincludeserious-sideeffectsanddeath?"

"Yes."

And with that, the pill was in the cup. Molly looked over and winked at Claire, and swallowed it.

The result of the coin toss was obvious to Claire as she watched her sister. Molly's skin relaxed, she exhaled, and slowly eased back into her chair. Claire pushed her own recliner back and watched her sister, knowing that Molly would soon go to a place where everything around her could be observed, and the two of them could get back on track.

Molly opened her eyes, and turned to Claire. It wasn't exactly a smile. It was an expression of sympathy, recognition, presence, and her breathing deepened.

Now, the dosing preparations began for Claire. There was a pill in a canister with Claire's subject number on it, her own coin toss. Two white-coated research assistants went through the flurry of steps that were required. They checked the ID on Claire's wristband, read out the numbers and repeated them. Claire stared at the pill in the small canister. Why did they do that, she wondered with annoyance, putting it in a canister, then transferring it into a paper cup, then giving it to her to swallow? So fussy. She wanted to just grab it. Next to her, Molly's right hand was curled in her lap, and her left hung over the armrest of the chair, flopped down from the wrist. Claire wondered, *Is she breathing?*

The nurse in the monitoring booth said without alarm, "Hey, can someone check the leads on sequence three? When you have a second."

A short person in a white coat checked where the wires attached to the little box clipped to Molly's waistband, moved Molly's limp arms and legs this way and that, rolled up her pant legs in order to check electrical connections.

Claire heard her own voice: "I don't think she's breathing. Can someone help her?"

The white-coated person fiddled with Molly's wires, half-heartedly poked at the little tabs where sticker-probes attached. It will be okay, Claire told herself. Dr. Chen said that she had "died" at the zoo, but she had figured that was him being a bit dramatic. After all, she was still here. *So it looks scary. This is what happens. Molly will be right back. She'll be fixed like I will be, and then everything will be okay.* The two research assistants in front of Claire were unconcerned with Molly. She was their task of five minutes ago, and now their task—the reading-out-loud of notifications, the checking of numbers, the signing of boxes, and giving a pill to Claire—was in front of them.

The nurse called, without looking over, "Oh, while you're there, can you check the oxygen sat probe too? Reading funny. Probably loose."

Now the little cup with the pill was placed in front of Claire, and she seized it, downed it, gulped at the water provided. Then she waited, wanted, expected, insisted to the universe that she must have won this coin toss. Claire noticed that Molly's colour had changed, that she had gone pale.

"Excuse me," she said, feeling that she herself was being quietly strangled, "I don't think she's breathing."

From the monitoring booth, the nurse now sounded more concerned. "Have you got everything connected? Check the hub." She stared at the monitor.

"Yes. She's hooked up," said the person in the white coat. "Are you sure the wireless connection is okay? How's the signal strength?"

"Signal strength looks fine . . ."

"Hey! She's not breathing!" cried Claire. The obvious became obvious. Molly's lips were blue. Her eyes were neither closed nor open, the lids floated somewhere over her pupils in an unnatural position.

"Doctor!" called the nurse with a sudden urgency, now standing. Instead of peering at the monitor, she gestured at Molly. "That subject! That one!"

The doctor ran to Molly. He touched the fingertips of one hand to Molly's wrist, poked at her neck, and thrust his stethoscope into the hollow of her chest where her collarbones arced towards one another. He flipped the reclining chair down so that Molly's thin body stretched out supine and limp. He locked his hands and began to pump the birdcage of her chest, shouted, "Call a code blue!"

What did Dr. Chen say he had done? Claire tried to remember. How had he revived her? He had said something to her, but what? She did not know, and was terrified of saying the wrong thing.

Under her breath, she said, "Please, please, come back, Molly! I didn't think this would . . ."

Someone pressed a button on a wall, and an electronic voice intoned from the ceiling, *Code blue treatment room, code blue treatment room*. The doctor directed an orderly to take over compressions of the chest. Someone wheeled over a cart laden with plastic and metal equipment, objects in plastic bags zip-tied to its stainless steel rails, and what looked like a fishing tackle box full of drugs. The room got louder, and the doctor seemed competent, quick in his movements, like an efficient mechanic. He took a vial out of one of the slots in the box, drew up a syringe of medication, and injected it into Molly.

"Still flatline," someone said to the doctor.

He ordered more rescue medications, asked for a Laerdal bag. The compressions continued, and Claire heard the wet snap of bones breaking—saw her sister's chest become flaccid. Staff pulled open little boxes and drew up drugs, handed them to the doctor.

"Two hundred joules, non-synchronized, please," he said, and he grabbed what looked like a fancy car battery charger. "Scissors," he said, and cut straight down the centre of Molly's scrubs top to apply the paddles to her skin. There was a high whine. "Charge . . . Clear . . . everyone clear . . ."

The doctor's forehead, his cheeks, the surface of his words were all entirely smooth as he gave his orders. His manner did not change as Molly's whole body spasmed. He seemed at ease, sure of himself, of what he must do despite futility. "Resume compressions," he said, and a fresh orderly stepped into the space next to him. Now that Molly's ribs were broken, it obviously required much less force to compress her exposed chest.

It occurred to Claire that she, herself, felt nothing similar to the first time she had received Memorex. She began to sob. Her own coin toss had delivered placebo. In the corner of the room, Claire saw the elegant woman who had been at Dr. Chen's side at the zoo. She clutched a clipboard to her chest, and wept. Claire had an impulse to run to her, a familiar face, ask her to call Dr. Chen, as if that would help now. When Claire caught the woman's eye, she fled.

38

ON THE NIGHT of the first snow, alone at home, sleeping tranquilly beneath the perfect white blanket of a new winter, Chen's phone rang. Jarred him from the deepest part of sleep. It was Bella.

"Can I come up?"

"What time is it?"

"Does that matter?"

He considered lying, saying he wasn't alone, and retreating to the warmth of his pillow. But would he sleep again?

"Hello?" she said. "You there?"

"Come on up." He entered the door access code on the phone. He got up, went to the kitchen, drank some water to wash away the nighttime sour. She was unsteady on her heels, and slipped her tongue into his mouth immediately, tasting of cigarettes and whisky. Slowly, a little clumsy, she took off her heels, then her stockings, still at the kitchen counter. It was as always—she acknowledged no gap between them that might have been created by time, unexplained silences, innocent lies. There was something about waking in the middle of the night that arrested thought. Motions were enough, and complete. Outside, the distant nasal horn of a transport truck.

Afterwards, lying in bed, she kissed the side of his mouth, and said, "I really am sorry."

"It's OK. You've been busy."

Then, when he did not say anything else, "You don't know what happened?"

"Sounds like I should know."

There had been a death, Bella explained. A young woman. The Memorex trials had been stopped again. As she told it, halting, Chen realized that he had never before seen her carry a genuine weight. Omega's ayahuagaine backers were out, Omega was going to focus on its core business—opioids. Bella had decided it was also time for her to move on. New horizons, a hedge fund on the west coast. They specialized in trading options on pharma companies, and Bella laughed when she explained that she would be a hire with insider knowledge.

"Your patient was there," she said.

"You mean at . . ."

"She was fine. It was someone else who died."

Within a week, Bella had moved to Vancouver. Chen texted a few days later to see how she was settling in, and she replied to a few texts with silly emojis. When he suggested that he could fly out for the weekend, she did not reply at all. Chen was surprised at how little he felt—just a minor unsettled feeling, like closing the door to a hotel room, wondering vaguely if there was an item left behind in the room—but determining that no, it was fine, and pulling a roller bag down a softly carpeted hallway.

Claire had last been in the clinic in the autumn, when Fitzgerald still had the house. After an absence of a few weeks, he thought of calling her. At the end of a clinic day he would pull up her file, look at the number. He told himself that it would be better—for her—if she took the initiative, assumed responsibility for continuing treatment, for *engaging with her supports.* Agency, ownership, all of that stuff. Also, he wanted her to be the one to call this time, to ask him for help. He recognized this impulse, which made him uneasy. So he held off. Then Bella had visited.

The day after Bella's last night with him, Chen had dialed Claire, got voicemail, and left a message. *I heard you were in another trial with ayahuagaine—that there was a tragedy. Are you alright? Tell me if I can help you.* Did he want her to know that he had tried to stop it? But had he? Had he just wanted it to be done his way? Chen wanted to say that he was glad she hadn't died, but one didn't leave that on voicemail.

That winter was cold and flat—one chill, damp week simply rolled into the next. There were a few patients who drifted out of care that winter, and Chen called a few of them out of the blue. Sometimes, he just wanted to know if someone was still alive. Were they still struggling? Trying? Had they given up? Could he help? A few were off medication as well as drugs, and were feeling bleaker than the season. Chen encouraged them to persist, that things would improve. The patients who were still using drugs often spoke to Chen as if no time had passed—with complaints about the world and grand plans for the future, sometimes hopes about a new treatment they had read about on the internet. A new pill, an herb; one patient had heard about Memorex and asked Chen if he knew anything about that. Months went by without any of his patients mentioning they bought drugs from a violinist. There was a cellist who now played regular Thursdays at the Dorado.

Chen left behind the habit of writing letters to his former student. Was it that he had written everything he had wished to write to her? There was a flowerpot on his patio, charred inside, where he had burned the letters. That winter, it collected snow. From time to time, Chen looked at Claire's webpage, to see if a new performance had been announced. Then, in the deep part of winter, black ice on the roads, Claire's webpage went blank. He called again—and her phone was disconnected.

On a warm spring day, Chen heard a melody from below his apartment. He went out to the patio, where the outdoor furniture covers were still weighted by lumps of melting snow. Water trickled down the painted white legs of the chairs, tracing the first vertical stains of rust. From somewhere below, a violinist played as if turning the crank on a music box or scooping ice cream—the music was sweet, brightly coloured, but with nothing hidden or uniquely expressive. He looked down and tried to see the musician, but could not. Then there was one turn of phrase, the darkness of a certain line, that held a style and artistry which Chen thought he recognized. He quickly pulled on a jacket to go down to the lane.

Hurrying down the lane towards the violin melody, Chen saw that the cold season itself was melting; the restaurant patios that fringed the square were busy. The best spots for buskers were those within easy hearing distance of the restaurants, in the sun, with a good flow of foot traffic. A pianist with an amplified keyboard had a trick of layering one melody upon the next by setting each on a recorded repeat. There was a man who played jars filled with varying volumes of water, rubbing a glassy tune from their rims. In between pieces, he rubbed his hands, which were red with cold.

Claire was not in one of the prime spots. Instead, Chen found her in a dark shadow near an old warehouse, where there was lots of room but few people came past. Many of those who stood there had put down their bags, crossed their arms against the cold, seemed to be settled into listening. Chen could feel the temperature change, the chill as he stepped into the shaded passageway where Claire played.

She was playing Bach's sonatas and partitas for solo violin, in some parts running through them mechanically. But in others, she tilted an orderly melody into forward energy. In some places there was that cursory sentimentality that first caught Chen's ear from the balcony, but in many passages one could hear Claire's artistry despite her obvious fatigue. She wore bright-red lipstick, and made an effort to smile with listeners who appeared to be toying with purses or wallets. She was bundled into a frayed but clean sky-blue down jacket, and woollen gloves whose fingertips had been cut away. Claire paused to bow between pieces, which was the moment for a tepid sprinkling of applause, and the cue for those with coins in their pockets to offer them. Chen saw that she spotted him, and he went forward along with others, fishing coins out of his pocket.

He slipped his contribution into the violin case. "You're okay?"

"Getting by," said Claire, looking up from the violin case, where she had watched the money—the random assortment of coins and paper—fall into the velvet. "But things are getting better, slowly."

"I'm glad."

"My sister died." Often people spoke like this when they were high, or sick, or just suffering—straight to the most important thing.

"Oh, I didn't . . ."

"It was that ayahuagaine thing. I never guessed . . . it's so hard to be left behind."

"I'm very sorry." Chen's eyes met hers. Bella had simply said a young woman.

Claire lifted her violin. "And knowing it's my fault. That I led her there . . ."

"But Claire, it's not your—"

She attacked the strings with vigour so that one of the horsehairs ripped loose and flung itself back and forth with her bow. Chen stepped back amongst the audience, to listen.

Whatever had happened, it was not her fault. He could have pulled the plug. Sitting with Charlie, the box of items that had been cleared from his office, the non-disclosure and the unsigned cheque in front of him, he had thought, Well, I guess this is the way it will go.

Claire had only a violin case, no stuffed backpack with bags tied to it—no mark of homelessness. She looked past him and to either side, catching the eye of other people in the square, smiling and winking, working the crowd, imitating a person who was full of joy and life. At the next moment between pieces, Chen reached into his wallet, and pulled out everything that was there, and laid the folded bills in her violin case.

"Thank you," she said. "I'm not using drugs. I haven't since . . . And no medications, either."

"How is that going?"

"All winter, I haven't had a good night's sleep, and yet there's no reason to get up in the morning. I'm empty. But every time I think that I can't hold out any longer, I just don't want—it—to have been for nothing. How long will this last, doctor?" she asked, tears welling up.

"The insomnia, the depression, after quitting, it lasts for months. You're probably through the worst. It's a slow recovery, but spring is here."

"I try to play every day. My old teacher, Josef, used to say that it's one thing to play when you feel like it. A real musician can make music even when they don't. I've realised, that's when you're actually free."

"Come and speak to me if you like—I don't have to prescribe you anything. Do you know where I am? You remember my place? Around the corner?"

"Yes," she said, "I remember where you are."

"Is there anything else I can do?" he said.

She shook her head. "It matters to me, that you tried."

"What will you do, next?"

"I don't know, exactly. But I'll practise. I'll find my way."

"If you need anything . . ."

"I know where to find you," said Claire.

Chen realized he was the one prolonging the conversation, and he stepped back, listened to the music for awhile, and then slipped away.

One summer night, on an evening when daytime had bestowed its life upon the night, and the laneways bustled with feet and laughter, Chen heard Claire playing again. But this time, it was the trio. They sounded as vigorous and joyful as when he had heard them at her premiere. Was she with her group again, busking in the square? It could not be the replacement violinist, whom Chen had heard, and whose playing did not compare to his former patient's. No, the flourishes and jumps were unique to Claire. The melody rose with the same dynamism of that evening, and he was transported to the Gallery, watching Claire descend the stairs. He listened from the patio for a while, savoured the music before he finally went down out of his building to find her. He would do his best for her, whatever that was. He followed a soaring cadenza, the interwoven melodies carried by a warm summer breeze, along a brick path, around shops, to a corner of the square. There, a trio of dancers in black tights and top hats, lithe men with expressive hands, somehow both silly and heartfelt, sometimes pirouetted around the audience members, sometimes invited and then evaded them, an amplified sound system next to their hat for contributions, bringing life to a recording of the trio.

ACKNOWLEDGEMENTS

My editor, Martha Kanya-Forstner, and my agent, Sarah Chalfant, have been my steadfast and joyful companions during the journey of this book. I am thankful to Martha for the questions she asked of the novel's characters and its author, which allowed them to fully inhabit and realize their stories on the page. I am grateful to Sarah for her encouragement to continue to move across those pages, for her faith in this work, and for her commitment to writers. Jessica Bullock, at my agency, has been a great support. I am appreciative of Melanie Little for her superlative copy-edit, John Sweet for his attentive proof-read, Emma Lockhart and Hilary Lo for their careful work on the proofs, and my friend Wendell Block for his feedback. I have the deepest admiration and gratitude for my wife, Margarita Lam Antoniades. She is a wise physician, a sensitive reader, and a soul-mate who has made my life and writing richer and larger than they otherwise would have been. Her generosity of spirit makes our life together a daily gift, and makes it possible for me to write. I appreciate the good humour of our three children, who have heard too often about their father's obsessions, vexations, and passions surrounding his books, and yet love to read. Although this novel is a work of fiction, its spirit is intertwined with that of my work in addictions medicine, without which the book would not be the same. I owe a debt to my colleagues, my trainees, my patients and their families. Each day, they teach me about the human heart.